Our Dear
Daisy

Rosie Goodwin is the four-million-copy bestselling author of more than forty novels. She is the first author in the world to be allowed to follow three of Catherine Cookson's trilogies with her own sequels. Having worked in the social services sector for many years, then fostered a number of children, she is now a full-time novelist. She is one of the top fifty most borrowed authors from UK libraries. Rosie lives in Nuneaton, the setting for many of her books, with her husband and their beloved dogs.

Rosie GOODWIN
Our Dear Daisy

ZAFFRE

First published in the UK in 2024
This paperback edition published in 2024 by
ZAFFRE
An imprint of Zaffre Publishing Group
A Bonnier Books UK company
4th Floor, Victoria House, Bloomsbury Square, London, England, WC1B 4DA
Owned by Bonnier Books
Sveavägen 56, Stockholm, Sweden

A CIP catalogue record for this book is
available from the British Library.

ISBN: 978-1-80418-552-0

Also available as an ebook and an audiobook

1 3 5 7 9 10 8 6 4 2

Typeset by IDSUK (Data Connection) Ltd
Printed and bound in Great Britain by Clays Ltd, Elcograf S.p.A.

Zaffre is an imprint of Zaffre Publishing Group
A Bonnier Books UK Company
www.bonnierbooks.co.uk

This book is for Albie Jack Lee Webb, our little ray of sunshine,
born on 2/1/2024
A very precious addition to our family

Chapter One

As twenty-year-old Daisy Armstrong stood waiting for her father to join her at the lychgate of St Lawrence Church in the village of Ansley, a little ripple of unease stirred in the pit of her stomach. Her father was standing to one side of the oak doors at the entrance to the church, deeply involved in a conversation with the widow Peake. This had recently become a weekly occurrence after the service, and for no reason that she could explain it made her feel uncomfortable. Undoubtedly the widow was a fine-looking woman – tall and slim with thick dark hair and always immaculately dressed – but there was something about her that Daisy couldn't quite take to. Possibly it was her eyes, which never seemed to smile.

But perhaps she was being unreasonable. Since her mother's death five years before after an outbreak of flu, Daisy had become fiercely protective of her father. The family had been devastated by the loss of her mother, but worse was to come. Shortly after she died, her twelve-year-old brother Alfie, who had taken to roaming the surrounding hills and villages, didn't return home one night. Desperate with worry her father and some of the men from the village had gone searching for him and the following day young Alfie had been found halfway down a deep quarry in the nearby village of Hartshill, his neck broken.

He had been laid to rest next to his mother in St Lawrence's churchyard. It had been a tragic day for the whole village, for on the same day that Alfie died, Farmer Bailey's sixteen-year-old daughter

Eunice had also been found strangled in Hartshill Hayes, a large wooded area near the quarry. Like Alfie, she had not returned home the night before so people wondered if the two deaths were connected. But during the investigation that followed nothing was found to link the two deaths and so it had to be assumed that Alfie had simply missed his footing in the darkness and plummeted down the quarry side, and his death was recorded as accidental.

The day they had carried her brother's small body home on a door was engraved on Daisy's heart. When she closed her eyes, she could still see his beloved face as if it was yesterday: the glassy eyes, the look of horror and fear. For a long time after that dreadful day, Daisy had feared that her father would go mad with grief, and ever since then they had been everything to each other.

Daisy had taken on the running of the house and very slowly things had returned to some sort of normality, although her father Edward, or Jed as he was known, had never been quite the same. Lately, though, Daisy had noticed that he seemed happier and wondered if perhaps it was something to do with the widow. She had to admit they made a fine-looking couple, for Jed, now in his early forties, was still a tall, upright man with a shock of dark hair, the exact same colour as Daisy's. His was slightly peppered with grey at the temples but rather than detract from his looks it made him more distinguished, and today, in his Sunday best suit and white, starched shirt, Daisy thought he looked particularly handsome. Only his rough, calloused hands gave away the fact that he was a hard-working man.

Jed owned a thriving blacksmith's business, the forge situated next to his home, and he was also an experienced farrier, so he was never short of work. The widow Peake had lost her own husband a mere six months before so Daisy hoped that she was fretting for nothing. After all, the woman hadn't even completed the expected period of mourning for her late husband, so surely it was unlikely

2

that she would already have someone in mind for his successor? *But then*, a little voice in her head whispered, *this is the third Sunday in a row that Daddy has stopped to speak to her . . .*

The leaves from the yew trees surrounding the churchyard fluttered down like confetti and Daisy shivered as the wind whipped them into a frenzy. Her father and the widow were laughing now and she turned her eyes from them to admire the church. It had been built in medieval times and with its tall bell tower and beautiful stained-glass windows, Daisy had always found solace there following the death of her mother and brother.

'Mornin', Daisy love!'

Daisy looked up. 'Morning, Mrs Pratchett.' She smiled as she watched the plump little woman with her herd of children waddle away, and when she looked up again it was to see her father and the widow walking down the path towards her.

'Good morning, Daisy.'

'Good morning, Mrs Peake.' Once again Daisy noticed that the woman's smile didn't quite reach her eyes, but she was concerned now that perhaps she was being overly possessive. After all, her father was still a relatively young man and entitled to have female friends.

'I was just saying to your father how nice it would be if you'd both care to come to have dinner with me one evening.'

Daisy's mouth opened and shut, giving her the appearance of a goldfish as she wondered how she should answer, but that problem was resolved when her father said quickly, 'I've told Victo— Mrs Peake that that would be very nice, don't you think, Daisy?' Turning his smile back to the widow he asked, 'What night would suit you best?'

'Perhaps Tuesday?' The woman flashed him a charming smile.

Her father nodded eagerly and, as one, they walked through the lychgate, where they went their separate ways. And as they made their way back Church End to their home in Ansley Road, Daisy couldn't help but notice the spring in her father's step.

Outside their home Daisy let out a small sigh of contentment – the house always made her feel better. She and her brother had been born there and she loved every brick of it. Her father often told her how it had been little more than a cottage when he had first taken her mother there as a bride. Over the years he had extended it into a very attractive property that now boasted four bedrooms. He would tell Daisy regretfully how he and her mother had always planned to fill the rooms with children, but sadly after Daisy and her brother, that had never come about. Now the two of them tended to rattle around in it with their old border collie, Rags. Rags had been the runt of a local farmer's litter and had been destined for a bucket of water, so Jed had bought the dog for Daisy when she was just seven years old. Now thirteen, he was an old boy but very much loved and a huge part of their lives.

As they passed the forge where her father spent six days of every week working, he asked unexpectedly, 'So what do you think of Mrs Peake, m'dear?'

Daisy frowned. 'Well, er . . . I don't really know her well enough to say,' she answered truthfully. 'Apart from seeing her in church each week and at the odd party in the village, I've never really spoken to her.'

'No, of course not.'

'Why do you ask, Daddy?' she enquired tentatively.

'Oh, no reason really . . .' When his voice trailed away Daisy got the impression that he wanted to say more but they had reached the gate and so the moment was lost.

The smell of the beef joint Daisy had left braising in the oven met them as soon as they opened the kitchen door, and her father rubbed his stomach with anticipation as Rags wagged over to greet them.

4

'That smells delicious, pet,' he remarked as he made for the stairs to go and get changed out of his Sunday best.

Daisy watched him go with a smile on her face as she took off her bonnet and thick woollen shawl and hung them on a nail on the back of the kitchen door, and by the time he reappeared, the tea was mashing in the large brown teapot, and the potatoes and vegetables she had prepared earlier were cooking on the range.

'Dinner shouldn't be long,' Daisy told him as she poured them both a mug of tea. This was the day she usually loved the best, when she had her father to herself, but today he seemed strangely distracted as he settled down to read his newspaper.

'Have you got much work booked in for next week?' she asked as she refilled his mug.

He nodded. 'Quite a bit as it 'appens. I've got quite a few o' the pit ponies to shoe and old Fred Lakin's brought me a load o' farm machinery to repair which'll take most o' the week.'

Daisy hesitated a moment, then asked, 'I, er . . . heard some people talking about the widow Peake's late husband when I went to the dance at the village hall last night.' She was watching him closely for a reaction. 'They're saying that Mr Peake didn't leave her as well off as she thought he would. In fact, they were saying that he's left her with a load of debt.'

'I'm surprised at you, listenin' to gossip! But then I've heard somethin' along the same lines,' he admitted with a frown. 'But I don't believe a word of it. People allus want somethin' to gossip about. I've no doubt her sons will take over the runnin' o' the shops shortly an' the money will start comin' in again.'

Daisy wasn't so sure. Gilbert, the widow's twenty-two-year-old son, was known to be work-shy and, after being expelled from the private school he had attended, he'd been in constant trouble with his father when he was alive. The elder son, Lewis, who was twenty-three, was still away at university.

Mr Peake had owned a number of shops in the nearby town of Nuneaton and it had been well known that his wife spent his money as fast as he could make it, so Daisy wouldn't have been at all surprised if the rumours were true. The Peakes' home was a grand, rambling place on the outskirts of the village and those who had been inside said it was furnished as well as any palace. The widow's taste in clothes was expensive too. She would often catch the train to London only to come home laden with bags full of gowns and bonnets that the local villagers could never have afforded in a million years. She also employed a cook, a housekeeper and a maid, as well as a gardener, and obviously enjoyed a lavish lifestyle.

It was apparent, though, that Daisy's father wasn't going to hear a word said against the woman, so Daisy dropped the subject and began to dust the large dresser that stood against one wall beside the inglenook fireplace. Her mother had once told Daisy that Jed had carved it for her shortly after they were married. It had been her pride and joy, and over the years it had been polished to a deep shine. Now, all her late mother's treasured china, which was only used for high days and holidays, was displayed on it, and Daisy loved the piece as much as her mother had.

She glanced up to see her father staring at her with tears in his eyes. 'Eeh, yer look so much like yer mammy,' he told her softly with a catch in his voice. Mauve, his wife, had been the love of his life and even now, five years on from her passing, he still missed her sorely. Sometimes, when Daisy lay in bed at night, she would hear him tossing and turning and crying softly. She never tired of hearing the story of how her parents had first met. Her mother had come from a small village near Dublin in Ireland and had come to the nearby town of Nuneaton to look for work, for it was scarce back in their home village of Kilmainham. She had met her father at a village dance and, as he was fond of telling Daisy, it had been love at first sight.

'The minute I clapped eyes on her, wi' her long dark hair and those wonderful blue eyes, I knew right off she were the girl for me,' he would say with a faraway look in his eyes.

He had been working on the railways back then but soon after they were wed, he and Mauve had come to live at the cottage next to the forge with the old blacksmith, who had owned it at the time. Mauve had become his cook–cum–housekeeper while old Mr Benton taught Jed everything he knew about blacksmithing. After some years the old gentleman had been forced to retire due to ill health, and had sold the business and the cottage to the young couple for a knock-down price.

From that day on Jed had worked to improve the cottage and the business and now he was the best blacksmith and farrier in the whole county. He had dreamed of teaching Alfie all he knew when he was old enough, so that one day he would be able to pass the business on to him. That dream had sadly died when the lad passed and now sometimes he looked like a lost soul, and it broke Daisy's heart.

With the dresser polished, she hurried off to get the dinner dished up and they sat at the table together.

'You've yer mam's flair for cookin',' Jed praised her as he bit into the succulent roast beef. It was so tender that it seemed to melt in his mouth, as did the crispy Yorkshire puddings. This was followed by one of his favourite puddings – an apple pie and thick, creamy custard – and by the time they had finished Jed was ready for a nap in front of the fire while Daisy did the washing up.

The rest of the day passed pleasantly and as they sat together later that evening enjoying a cup of cocoa, with Rags snoozing contentedly in front of the fire, Jed suddenly handed her some money.

'What's this for?' Daisy looked surprised.

Her father avoided her eye. 'Well, I were just thinkin' seein' as we're goin' out to dinner on Tuesday, you might like to treat yerself to some material for a new gown.'

She smiled. 'I already have a gown that will be quite suitable, Daddy. But even if I do buy some material there's no way I could have it ready in time. I'm not as good or as fast as Mammy was with a needle.'

'Buy a new bonnet then,' he urged. He adored his daughter and liked to treat her from time to time.

'I might just do that.' Daisy flashed him a smile. 'As a matter of fact, I saw one in the milliner's window last week when I went into town.'

He reached across and gave her hand an affectionate squeeze and not for the first time Daisy realised how lucky she was. It had been heartbreaking for them both to lose her mammy and brother, but at least they still had each other, and they were closer than ever. She could never imagine that changing.

Chapter Two

On Tuesday evening Jed stood in front of the mirror and sighed as he tugged at his tie, which seemed to have developed a life of its own.

Laughing, Daisy went to give him a hand. 'Here, let me do it.' She quickly adjusted the tie and stepping back she nodded. 'There, you look a treat.'

'So do you, pet.' He looked at her admiringly wondering when his little girl had suddenly grown into such an attractive young woman. She was wearing her new bonnet – a pretty affair trimmed with ribbons that matched the blue gown she was wearing. 'What time is it now? We don't want to be late!'

'It's three minutes later than the last time you asked me,' Daisy answered tongue-in-cheek. He had been like a cat on hot bricks ever since finishing work.

'Aye well, we don't want to keep Victoria waiting, do we? Are you ready? I've got the trap all set up and Fancy in her harness. Be sure to put your warm shawl on, it's enough to cut you in two out there; I wouldn't be surprised if it didn't rain soon.'

Daisy turned the wick down low on the oil lamp on the table, and after patting Rags and promising they wouldn't be gone for too long, they went out into the bitterly cold evening. The lamplighter was making his way along the streets of the village and little puddles of yellow light were forming on the cobblestones.

Daisy wasn't sure if she was looking forward to the evening or dreading it. She was very much looking forward to seeing inside the house after all she had heard about it, but if she were to be

9

honest, she wasn't looking forward to seeing the widow – or her son, if it came to that. Gilbert was a very arrogant young man. Good-looking, admittedly, but he didn't appeal to Daisy. He was too big-headed by far and although most of the village girls fell at his feet, she didn't intend to. Even so, she knew that her father was looking forward to the evening, so she promised herself she would do her best to make the most of it.

Once they reached the widow's large house, the gardener-cum-groom led Fancy round to the stables, while they climbed the steps to the impressive front door. It was answered by a little maid in a frilly mob cap and matching apron who had obviously been expecting them.

Daisy was instantly impressed by the decor – it would have been hard not to be. Deep burgundy and gold silk paper lined the walls and a huge gilt-framed mirror hung above a very elaborate matching console table. The black-and-white floor tiles had been polished to a mirror-like shine, and Daisy was almost afraid to step on them.

They handed their outdoor clothes to the maid, who told them, 'The mistress is waitin' for you in the drawin' room.'

They followed her to double doors that opened onto a magnificent room, decorated in shades of green. There were heavily tasselled velvet curtains at the enormous window, expensive Turkish rugs on the highly polished wooden floor and green velvet chairs and sofas to either side of an elaborate marble fireplace.

Victoria Peake came towards them with her hands outstretched and Daisy had to admit she looked stunning. She was dressed in a satin gown in a soft champagne colour that flattered her slim figure, and her hair had been fashioned into a smart chignon. Jewels glittered at her throat and in her ears.

'Oh, I'm so glad you could make it,' she told Jed as she took his hands in hers. Then, with a cursory nod towards Daisy, she said, 'Do come and sit by the fire and get warm.'

She lifted a brandy decanter and poured some of the amber liquid into a cut-glass goblet, which she handed to Jed before asking Daisy, 'What would you like, my dear? I'm not sure if your father allows you to have alcohol?'

'Oh, thank you but I'm fine at the minute.' Daisy felt completely out of her depth and was already wishing she hadn't agreed to come.

Her father took a seat at the side of Victoria as Daisy perched uncomfortably on the sofa opposite them.

'So, have you had a hard day?' the woman enquired with a charming smile.

Jed shook his head. 'No more than usual. And you?'

She sighed and fiddled with the gems about her throat. 'Oh, nothing different to any other day, to be honest.'

The door opened at that moment and Gilbert strode into the room looking very smart in a dapper suit and brightly coloured waistcoat. He nodded towards them before helping himself to a large glass of brandy.

'Good evening. I'm glad you could make it,' he said to them both, although his eyes were fixed firmly on Daisy, which made her feel slightly uncomfortable.

Thankfully she was saved from having to answer when the maid appeared to inform them that dinner was ready.

Daisy and her father followed Mrs Peake along the hallway into a dining room that looked as if the table had been set for visiting royalty. It was covered in a crisp white cloth on which lay shining silver cutlery, cut-glass goblets and china plates so fine that Daisy was sure, had she lifted one up to the light, she could have seen straight through it. A huge bowl of hothouse flowers stood in the centre of the table.

Gilbert gallantly pulled out her chair for her as they approached the table and Daisy took her seat feeling more out of place by the minute. This was a far cry from the way she and her father dined at the kitchen table, but she stayed quiet. The same couldn't be said for her father and Victoria, who were chatting away like long-lost friends.

Gilbert did try to engage Daisy in conversation but she was so ill at ease that she struggled to answer him, so after a time he thankfully gave up.

The maid poured them each a glass of wine and when she had finished, Mrs Peake told her, 'You may start to serve the meal now, Edie. I'm sure our guests must be hungry.' Then with a smile she turned to Jed. 'I do hope you'll like the menu. I forgot to ask if there's anything you don't like. Quite remiss of me!'

Jed chuckled. 'Eeh, you don't 'ave to worry about that, lass. Me an' our Daisy are quite easy goin'. I'm sure we'll enjoy whatever it is.'

'Oh good. We have smoked salmon and beetroot for the starter.'

Daisy gulped. She had never eaten salmon in her life. She and her father were cod and haddock sort of people and she wondered if she would like it. In actual fact, it was quite delicious, although Daisy had to wait for Mrs Peake to start hers before she knew which cutlery she should be using. It appeared that she had to start from the outside and work in for each course.

The main course was braised pheasant cooked with leeks and apples, and although it was beautifully presented, Daisy wasn't so keen on that. And then came the dessert, which Mrs Peake informed them proudly was a cherry meringue roulade. Once again it was a little rich for Daisy's taste – she and her father dined on simple fare – but she didn't dislike it. Finally, they were served with coffee and wafer-thin chocolate biscuits, which Daisy did very much enjoy, although she was so full by then, she was beginning to feel uncomfortable.

At last, they went back to the drawing room where Mrs Peake refilled Jed's glass with brandy as Gilbert glanced at the clock. 'Right, would you all excuse me, please? I've arranged to meet a friend in Nuneaton.' He smiled at Daisy. 'And you are more than welcome to come with me if you want to leave these two oldies to it.'

Daisy couldn't have thought of anything she'd rather do less, but on the other hand she was feeling very much in the way, so she answered politely, 'I won't come with you but I'd be grateful if you could drop me at home on your way. Rags is old and he's been on his own for quite a while now, so I'd like to get back to him if no one objects.'

'Of course we won't object, my dear.' Mrs Peake smiled at her, yet Daisy had the feeling that she couldn't wait to get rid of her.

'Are you sure?' Jed looked uncomfortable but he was enjoying himself more than he had for some time and was reluctant to end the evening so soon. 'Are you sure you'll be all right?'

Daisy grinned, her eyes twinkling. 'Daddy, I'm twenty years old; of course I'll be all right. You stay and enjoy yourself.'

After saying goodbye to Mrs Peake and thanking her for her hospitality she followed Gilbert into the hall and soon after they were on their way.

'Seems like those two are getting on like a house on fire, doesn't it?' He laughed as he urged the horse on. The wind had dropped and a thick fog had settled over the fields. 'I reckon my mother has got your father lined up for husband number three, so be prepared!'

'What?' Daisy was horrified. 'Husband number three?'

'Oh yes, she was married once before to a rich older chap from London. She married my father soon after he died, and I think she's ready to take the plunge again. My mother's never been one for letting the grass grow under her feet.'

Daisy pulled her shawl more tightly about herself and scowled. 'I'm sure you're mistaken,' she told him primly. 'She and my father are just friends.'

He chuckled. 'Hmm, we'll see which of us is right, shall we?'

They made the rest of the journey in silence, but when he drew the horse up outside her house, Gilbert put his hand on Daisy's arm. 'Are you sure I can't persuade you to come with me? It would do you good to let your hair down now and again.'

Daisy was one of the very few girls who hadn't fallen at his feet when he turned on the charm but that only made her more desirable to him.

'I'm quite happy as I am,' Daisy said primly. 'But thank you for the lift.'

After she clambered out, he grinned down her. 'You know where I am when you change your mind. Goodnight.'

Daisy hurried into her home with a sick feeling in the pit of her stomach. Despite her denials, she had seen how well her father and Mrs Peake were getting on and she just prayed that Gilbert wasn't right. The woman was the exact opposite of her mother in every way, and she just couldn't picture them together. Her mother had been a hard-working, home-loving woman with simple tastes, whereas she very much doubted Mrs Peake had ever done a day's work in her life. Still, all she could do was wait and see how, or if, their friendship developed.

Daisy let Rags out for a while and damped down the fire, then once he was back in and settled, she took a candle to light her way to bed, leaving the oil lamp glowing for when her father got in. She lay awake for a long time listening for his return but eventually sleep claimed her and she knew no more until the first grey light crept through the crack in the curtains early the next morning. She could hear her father moving about the kitchen downstairs, so slipping into her robe she pushed her feet into her house shoes and hurried down to him. The fire was burning brightly and the kettle was singing on the hob.

'Ah, here you are, pet. Just in time for a cuppa.' He was clearly in a good mood as he placed two mugs on the table before giving her an affectionate hug. 'How did you enjoy last night?' he asked cheerily. 'The food was lovely, weren't it? I have to say, though, I think I had a drop too much brandy, or so me head's tellin' me this mornin'. Still, it's me own fault.'

'Er, yes . . . it was very nice,' Daisy forced herself to say. She couldn't bring herself to tell him that she had felt completely out of place the whole time they were at Mrs Peake's.

She shot away to get dressed and when she came back down, she began to cook her father's breakfast.

'Not sure I'll be able to eat all this after what I put away last night, pet,' he chuckled when she placed a plate full of bacon, sausages and eggs in front of him. Even so, he soon cleared his plate before pushing it away. He hesitated for a moment, then said tentatively, 'I were thinkin' it might be nice if we returned the favour.' When Daisy raised an eyebrow, he rushed on, 'Invite Victoria – Mrs Peake – to dinner here, I mean. What do you think?'

'Erm . . .' Daisy dithered. 'I'm not so sure about that, Daddy. What I mean is, I couldn't cook anything like the fancy food we were served last night. Mammy only taught me to do plain, simple cooking and I'm not so sure Mrs Peake would enjoy it.'

He laughed. 'O' course she would,' he assured her. 'Why, you're a grand little cook. So what do you say? I thought perhaps we could invite her and Gilbert for lunch after church next Sunday.'

'Well . . . all right, if you think I'm up to it.' Daisy looked about the cosy room trying to see it as Mrs Peake would. It was nowhere near as grand as her house but the last thing she wanted to do was upset her father.

He beamed at her. 'Right, that's settled then. I'll pop along one evenin' after work an' invite her.'

After he'd gone, she looked around her. The house was always clean and tidy, just as it had been when her mother was alive, but if Mrs Peake was to visit, then Daisy determined that everything would gleam like a new pin. With a sigh she went to collect the beeswax polish and set to as Rags lay watching her from his place by the fire.

Chapter Three

On Sunday morning Jed attended church alone, leaving Daisy to put the finishing touches to the meal. The table was covered with her mother's best lace cloth and the best china was laid ready, along with the best cutlery – although it was nowhere near as fine as Mrs Peake's. Still, she had done the best she could and all that remained was to cross her fingers and hope that her father would be pleased with her efforts.

Daisy was no fancy cook and had stuck to doing a traditional Sunday roast of pork. She had made her own stuffing with onions and sage she had grown in the garden, and there were crispy roast potatoes, cabbage and peas – which she had also grown – as well as creamy mashed potatoes. For the pudding she had again stuck to something simple. With apples from the orchard, she had made her father's favourite apple pie with thick cream. She knew he would be happy with it but whether Mrs Peake would be remained to be seen.

After glancing at the clock for at least the tenth time in as many minutes, she ran her hands down her apron and smiled at Rags. 'You be sure to be on your best behaviour when our guests arrive, do you hear? No jumping up at Mrs Peake's beautiful gown now.'

Rags wagged his tail in answer and she bent to stroke him. But time was moving on, so now that she was satisfied that everything was as it should be with the meal, she hurried upstairs to get changed into her best gown. Then she brushed her long dark hair and turned to survey herself in the cheval mirror. A solemn-faced young woman stared back at her and suddenly she giggled.

Anybody would have thought the queen herself was coming to dinner the way she had fretted about it, but at least it would soon be over and then hopefully she and her father would be able to get back to some sort of normality.

Hurrying back downstairs she opened the door to the lounge and peered in. It was a room that was normally only used for special occasions but today she'd decided her father, Gilbert and Mrs Peake could sit in there while she put the dinner out. The fire was burning up the chimney and there was not a cushion out of place on the sofa and chairs, so she shut the door again to keep the warmth in and went back to check on the dinner once more.

Another glance at the clock told her that they should be back at any minute, and sure enough, just then she heard the sound of a trap pulling into the yard.

'Do go in, my dear,' she heard her father urge when the trap had come to a halt. 'Gilbert and I will just put your horse in the stable with Fancy for a few hours. It's too cold for him to stand out here.'

She heard a tap at the door and rushed to open it. Mrs Peake stood on the stoop holding her skirts up around her ankles. With no word of greeting, she strode past Daisy into the kitchen and smiled. 'I'm not used to having to cross yards. I usually leave my home by the front door,' she explained. Rags sidled up to her with his tail wagging nineteen to the dozen and she frowned. 'Oh goodness me! It doesn't bite, does it?'

Daisy sighed. 'No, Mrs Peake. Rags doesn't bite.' She laid her hand gently on the old dog's head. 'He's so old now that I doubt he'd have enough teeth left to bite with even if he wanted to.'

Daisy shooed him to his place by the fire and asked politely, 'May I take your bonnet and coat? Then perhaps you'd like a warm drink while you wait for me to serve the meal. Tea or coffee, perhaps?'

Mrs Peake was staring about the room as if she could hardly believe what she was seeing. If the look on her face was anything to go by, she wasn't particularly impressed. 'Don't you have a formal dining room?' she asked, staring at the table that Daisy had so lovingly dressed for her.

'Er, no . . . we don't. Father and I always eat in here. It's cosy, especially in the winter, but I'll take you through to the lounge and you can wait in there until everything is ready.'

Mrs Peake followed her across the hallway to the parlour. Once again she looked around her. 'Everywhere looks charming, my dear,' she said eventually with an ingratiating smile.

'Tea or coffee?' Daisy asked again.

'I'll have tea and I prefer it in a china cup, *if* you have such a thing, please, dear.'

Colour rose in Daisy's cheeks. 'Of course, Mrs Peake. Do make yourself comfortable.'

'Oh please, call me Victoria. Mrs Peake is so formal, don't you think?'

Once out in the hallway Daisy took a deep breath then entered the kitchen just as her father and Gilbert appeared through the back door bringing an icy blast of air with them.

'Brr, it's bitter out, pet,' her father said, rubbing his hands together. 'I wouldn't be surprised if we didn't 'ave some snow soon. But now, is there owt you want a hand with?' He knew how much time and effort she had put into this meal, and he appreciated it.

'Absolutely not, everything is under control. You two just go through to the lounge and I'll bring a tray of tea through in a jiffy,' Daisy told him with a smile and a nod at Gilbert.

'I could stay and help you if you like,' Gilbert offered.

She shook her head. That was the last thing she wanted, although she wouldn't be rude enough to say so. 'No need,' she assured him. 'Just go and get warm.'

Once she'd taken the tea into the sitting room, Daisy hurried back into the kitchen and began to put the food into the serving dishes she'd had warming in the range. Then she called everyone through, and they took their seats.

'Do you normally allow that animal to stay in the room while you eat?' Mrs Peake said, glaring at Rags asleep on the hearthrug.

Daisy was instantly annoyed. 'He's not just an animal, Mrs Peake, er . . . Victoria. Rags is a member of the family and I assure you he's quite clean. I bathe him regularly. He's far too old to be shut outside.'

'How sweet!'

Her father looked embarrassed and quickly changed the subject. 'Shall we eat then, while it's nice an' hot?'

'Of course. Why this looks delicious, my dear,' Mrs Peake declared with a simpering smile as Jed began to carve the pork.

'She's a fine little cook is my Daisy,' Jed said proudly as he put the pork onto their plates and they all helped themselves to vegetables, potatoes and thick, creamy gravy.

The conversation between Jed and Victoria flowed easily throughout the meal and when everyone had finished the main course Daisy brought the pudding to the table.

'She's a rare good pastry cook an' all,' Jed boasted as he served them all slices of apple pie. He had even bought wine for them to have with their meal and now that it was almost over Daisy began to feel a little easier. She knew that the meal she had cooked was nowhere near as fancy as the food Mrs Peake and her son were used to, but they hadn't complained – in fact, they had been very complimentary, and she was relieved.

'Right, I suggest we all retire back to the sitting room now,' Jed said jovially when they had finished eating.

Daisy shook her head. 'No, you go through with the guests, Daddy. I'll stay here and clear the pots away.'

Victoria frowned. 'You really should get a maid, Edward,' she chided gently, batting her eyelashes at him. 'Poor Daisy's hands will be ruined with all this washing up.'

'I don't mind,' Daisy told her as they rose from the table.

Once the others were gone, she let out a sigh of relief. 'Phew, I'm glad that's over, boy,' she said to Rags.

But her relief was short-lived, because as Daisy was putting the dirty pots to soak in the deep stone sink, Gilbert reappeared.

'I feel a bit like a spare part in there.' He grinned as he came to stand beside her and stared out of the window. 'This is quite some set-up you have here,' he observed. 'Your father must be raking the money in.'

Daisy frowned. 'We do well enough. Daddy is a hard worker, although we obviously don't live in such a posh house as yours.'

'Hmm.' He paused as if about to say something, then went on in a hushed voice, 'Well, now our families are getting so close I don't suppose you could see your way clear to lending me a bob or two, could you?'

Daisy was shocked and it showed in her face as she stared at him. '*Me* lend you money? Why . . . everyone knows that you and your mother are the richest people in the village. Why would you need to borrow money from me?'

'Ah well, it's like this you see . . .' He tugged at the collar of his shirt looking slightly uncomfortable. 'The thing is, I've got myself into a bit of bother in Nuneaton. I went for a game of cards and it all got a little out of hand. I ended up owing far more than my allowance and if I don't pay up . . . Let's just say the person I owe money to has a bit of a reputation as a hard nut, if you know what I mean?'

Daisy shook her head. 'I'm sorry but I think if that's the case you'd be best to tell your mother and let her help you out.'

Gilbert's handsome face darkened and he narrowed his eyes. 'Thanks very much. I know exactly where I stand with you now, don't I?' He snatched up his coat and headed for the door where he paused to spit, 'Tell my mother I had an appointment with friends and I'll see her this evening at home.' And with that he was gone, slamming the door resoundingly behind him.

Daisy sighed as she began to wash the pots, leaving them to drain on the large wooden draining board. It seemed the rumours about Gilbert having a gambling habit were true, but she certainly didn't intend to get involved. Let him sort out his messes himself.

Half an hour later when the kitchen was spick and span again, she made a large pot of tea and carried it across the hallway to the sitting room. Her father and Mrs Peake were sitting side by side on the sofa looking very cosy indeed, and again the little niggle of unease stirred deep in her stomach.

'Gilbert told me to tell you that he's gone to meet friends in Nuneaton, Victoria,' she said as she placed the tray down in front of them. She saw a flash of irritation on the woman's face, but then she was smiling again, and Daisy wondered if she might have imagined it.

'Has he indeed?' The woman sighed. 'Boys will be boys, won't they, Edward?' Suddenly remembering that he had lost a son she stroked his hand. 'Oh, I'm so sorry, my dear. I didn't think. I do hope I haven't upset you?'

'Not at all,' he assured her. 'Now how about this tea, eh? There's nothing like a good brew, especially on a cold day like this. On a working day, Daisy is back and forwards all day long to the forge with tea for me, aren't you, pet?'

Daisy smiled in answer and discreetly left them to it, heading back to the kitchen to sit with Rags and do some darning.

Very soon the light began to fade from the afternoon and eventually Mrs Peake and her father appeared.

'I'm just going to run Victoria home, Daisy. I shouldn't be too long.' Her father was already helping their visitor into her coat and Daisy nodded.

'Thank you for a very pleasant meal, my dear,' Mrs Peake said as Jed escorted her to the door.

'You're very welcome,' Daisy answered, but she hoped it would be a long time before she came again. On their previous meeting Daisy had got a bad feeling about Gilbert and this visit had only reinforced that they had absolutely nothing in common. The same went for Mrs Peake and she silently prayed that her father wouldn't have his head turned by her poise and good looks.

Chapter Four

The snow arrived with a vengeance the first week in December and suddenly the whole village was covered in a crisp, white blanket. Daisy made sure to keep the fires in the house burning brightly, and the forge was always warm thanks to the huge hearth and enormous furnace where Jed heated the metal before hammering it into shape.

'I reckon we'll be snowed in if it keeps comin' down at this rate, pet,' Jed told her one morning as she delivered one of his regular mugs of tea. He sighed and said, 'I were goin' to suggest that it were time you paid a visit to your gran'parents in Ireland. We've only seen 'em once since your mammy's funeral. I know you write to each other all the time, but it ain't quite the same as a visit, is it? I thought it might be a good break for you to slip over for a week or so before Christmas. But now I ain't so sure that the trains an' the ferries will be operatin'. What do you think?'

'It's a lovely idea,' Daisy agreed enthusiastically. 'But as you say, we'll have to see how the weather goes. And who would look after you while I'm gone?'

Jed chuckled. He seemed to laugh a lot lately and Daisy guessed it had something to do with Mrs Peake. 'I reckon at my age I'm more than capable o' lookin' after meself for a few days. After all, you ain't goin' to be around to look after your old daddy forever, are you? You're a bonny young woman now, an' one o' these days a handsome young chap is goin' to catch your eye an' you'll be wed.'

'I wasn't planning on it anytime soon,' Daisy giggled. 'But I must admit I'd love to see Granny and Grampy. Let's just watch what the weather does, eh?'

Luckily it stopped snowing that same afternoon and within days the snow had disappeared, so Daisy decided to go ahead with her plans, although she was a little nervous about travelling on her own. Her mother or father had always gone with her to Ireland before, but she knew that her father was too busy to take time off. And so, a few days later she packed her carpet bag and early the next morning, Jed drove her to the Trent Valley railway station in Nuneaton in the trap.

'Now don't forget,' Jed fretted when they drew up outside. 'You take the train to Liverpool Lime Street station and from there you head to the docks and go straight over to Dublin. You should be there for this evenin', all bein' well, pet. But just you take care o' yourself an' don't get talkin' to no strangers, specially round the docks! I just wish we'd had time to write an' warn 'em you were comin', so they could 'ave met you.'

'I shall be fine, Daddy,' she promised, planting a kiss on his cheek. 'And you take care of yourself while I'm away.'

He'd been dining at Mrs Peake's house quite a few evenings a week lately so at least she knew he would be well fed. She clambered down from the trap, gave Fancy a stroke then, gripping her carpet bag, which contained small gifts for her Irish relatives, she hurried to the ticket office, then went to stand on the platform. When the train drew in in a hiss of steam, Daisy found a carriage with a seat by the window and after heaving her carpet bag onto the overhead rack, she settled back in her seat. Despite her brave words to her father, now the journey was about to begin, she felt a little nervous, yet she was confident that she was more than capable of finding her way there.

The train journey was uneventful. Daisy even managed to doze for part of the way and shortly after lunchtime the train pulled into Liverpool Lime Street station. From there it was a short distance to the docks and once she had safely boarded the ferry, she began to relax a little. The difficult bit was over and she knew she would have no problems at all finding her grandparents' home once she was in Dublin.

The crossing was rough and by the time they finally docked Daisy was feeling queasy and her legs were wobbly. But she soon felt better once she reached firm ground and so, gripping her bag, she set off through the streets of Dublin towards her grandparents' home in the small village of Kilmainham, which was just under a mile and a half away. It was dark by then and a cold wind was blowing making Daisy's fingers turn blue and her nose glow red. She soon left the busy streets behind and once she was on the lanes her footsteps slowed. With no streetlights to guide her, and with the wind whistling through the bare branches of the trees, she began to feel nervous again.

She passed a few isolated cottages along the way but at last she turned a bend in a lane and there were the lights of her grandparents' cottage glowing in the distance. Instantly forgetting how weary she was she quickened her steps and soon reached the gate that led into their yard and to 'The Taigh' – which Daisy had been told meant 'The House' in English.

Connor and Bridie McLoughlin owned a smallholding on the edge of Kilmainham. They were both in their late sixties but thankfully still spritely and able to earn their living. Daisy could barely wait to see them. As their old dog, Padrick, came wagging out of his kennel to greet her, she smiled as she thought about how surprised and happy they would be to see her.

'Hello, boy.' Daisy bent to stroke his ears, pleased that he still remembered her. It had been a long time since her last visit and yet she instantly felt at home. Her grandparents had a way of always making her feel like that and as a young girl she and her brother had spent many a happy holiday there.

Opposite the house was a large barn where her grandfather stored the food for the animals and, on hearing Padrick, he suddenly appeared, clad in his old corduroy trousers, a weatherproof coat and thick rubber boots.

'Now then, Padrick, what's to do?' He stopped talking abruptly as his eyes settled on Daisy and with a delighted whoop he crossed to her and gave her a hug that almost lifted her from her feet. 'Why, me darlin' girl, this is a surprise, to be sure.' He held her at arm's length. 'And aren't you just the spit out of your dear mammy's mouth now that you've grown, to be sure! Why your granny will be tickled pink to see you, so she will. But have you come alone now?' He peered into the darkness behind her.

Daisy giggled. 'I have that, Grampy. I'm a big girl now and I'm dying for a cup of tea. I've been travelling since early this morning.'

'Then let's get you into the warm.' His big arm came around her while his other hand took her bag and he led her towards the kitchen door with Padrick pottering along at the side of them.

'Bridie! Where are you, woman?' he shouted once they were inside. 'Get yourself in here for I've a lovely surprise for you, so I have!'

They heard the patter of feet in the tiled hallway and seconds later the door swung open and there was her granny.

'What's all this ruckus then, Connor,' she retorted but as her eyes came to rest on Daisy she fairly flew across the room and enveloped her in a bear hug. 'Oh, me darlin' girl.' There were tears in her eyes as she stared at her granddaughter, thinking how grown-up she looked. 'And you've grown into a beauty to be sure. Why, you gave me a right gliff back there, so you did. I thought it were me own dear Mauve for a minute. But what are you doing here and how long can you stay? Why didn't you write us you were comin'? Your grampy could have met you at the station, so he could.'

Daisy hardly knew which question to answer first and she laughed. 'Me and Daddy sort of decided it at the last minute,' she told them as her granny hurried away to swing the sooty-bottomed kettle over the fire. 'And once he'd put the idea into my head I could hardly wait to get here.'

'And how is he?'

Daisy looked towards her grandmother and felt a lump rise in her throat. She looked exactly how Daisy imagined her mother would have looked had she not died so young.

'He's fine,' she assured them, but she couldn't stop the smile slipping from her face and her granny instantly picked up on it. She had always been able to read her granddaughter like a book.

'Is he now? Quite sure about that, are you?'

'Oh yes . . . he's very well. In fact, better than he's been since Mammy and Alfie died. You see, he has a new, er . . . friend.'

Granny scowled as she pushed a strand of her still thick, greying hair back into the bun on the back of her head. 'And what sort of a friend might that be?'

'It's a lady friend, actually. She's a widow, and she lives on the outskirts of our village. She lost her husband earlier this year and she's very good-looking.'

'Is she now?' Granny was quiet for a moment but not wishing to spoil Daisy's arrival she smiled again. 'Well, we've all the time in the world to talk o' such things before you go home, so we have, so come an' sit by the fire an' get warm while I make this tea. An' there's a nice pot o' stew an' dumplin's bubblin' on the range an' all, so we'll not go hungry. Now take your coat an' bonnet off an' look like you're home, eh? I'll just pop up an' light the fire in your bedroom to air it, for it's not been slept in since the last time you an' your daddy came. I'll not be more than a minute.'

The kindly woman grabbed a candle and scuttled away upstairs while Daisy sank back into the comfy old chair to one side of the fireplace, feeling glad she had come. Ever since her father's friendship with Mrs Peake had begun, her mind had been all over the place. There were so many thoughts troubling her that it was a relief to have this time away from it all. Not only that, she was glad to get away from Gilbert's advances for a while, because lately he had taken to dropping in unexpectedly, usually when her father was busy in the forge. On a number of occasions, he had asked her out, but Daisy had always refused. He had also pressured her to lend him money again, but she had stood her ground.

Worse still was the fact that her father now visited Mrs Peake regularly when he finished work for the day and Daisy found that she was spending the majority of the evenings alone. After the first night she and Jed had dined at her house, Daisy had never received another invite. This didn't trouble her in the least, but the amount of time Mrs Peake and her father were spending together did, and now Daisy was wondering if their relationship had moved beyond friendship. The woman was always friendly and polite to her, but still Daisy couldn't take to her, and she wondered what would happen should they ever decide to become a couple. Would she no longer be needed then? She sighed. At least here, she would have time to put her thoughts in some sort of order.

Soon after her grandfather came in from feeding the pigs and putting the chickens in their coop for the night, and they all sat down in the cosy kitchen to enjoy their meal.

They were almost halfway through it when her granny asked tentatively, 'So, this widow that your daddy's becoming friendly with . . . do you think anything will come of it?'

Daisy stared down into her stew for a moment. 'To be honest, I'm not sure. Daddy certainly seems to be very at ease in her company.'

'Does he now? And is she at ease with him?'

Daisy nodded. 'Very much so. There's barely a day passes when she doesn't pop in to see him and he spends a lot of evenings at her house.'

'Oh, so she does have her own house?'

'Yes, and very grand it is too,' Daisy admitted. 'Her husband was a fairly wealthy man, and she still owns a number of shops in Nuneaton, although she's closed two of them down and they're standing empty at the minute.'

'And why would that be?'

'Daddy said she'd told him that she's looking around for new managers to run them.'

'I see. Has she no relatives that could do it?'

'She has two sons: Gilbert and Lewis. Lewis is away at university at the moment, although I think he finishes his course early in the New Year, then he'll be coming home. And Gilbert . . . Well, I doubt he'd get his hands dirty.'

'Do I detect you don't much care for him?' Granny raised an eyebrow.

Daisy sighed. 'No, I don't, to be honest. He's work-shy to say the least, and rumour has it that he's heavily into gambling.'

'Then just make sure you give him a wide berth, lass,' Grampy told her with a frown. He had always been protective of Daisy, and her mother before her – although they had been more than happy with Mauve's choice of husband and had always got on well with Jed.

They went on to talk of other things and Daisy realised it was one of the nicest evenings she'd had in ages. It made a nice change from having to sit on her own each evening as she had done lately.

Chapter Five

Daisy had been at her grandparents' cottage for two days when her granny asked one morning over a cup of tea, 'So, lass, when are we goin' to see you get wed, eh?'

Daisy grinned. She'd had more than her fair share of admirers over the last few years but as yet she hadn't met anyone that she wanted to walk out with. She was quite content at home with her father. Most of her school friends were already married and some of them even had children, but until the right man came along Daisy was fine as she was, as she told her granny.

'Hmm, well that's all well an' good,' the old woman told her solemnly. 'But what will you do if anythin' comes of this friendship your daddy has with the widow?'

Daisy had wondered the same thing and she sighed. 'I'll cross that bridge when and if we come to it.'

'Fair enough.' Her granny could sense that it was preying on Daisy's mind so she lightened the mood. 'An' how long will you be stayin'? We do so love havin' you here, to be sure!'

'I'm afraid I shall only be staying for a week.' Daisy smiled at her. 'I'd love to stay longer but it'll be Christmas before we know it and I've got lots to do when I get back. Besides, we could have more snow any time and if I don't get home, I could well be stuck here. It's held off up to now but the sky is full of it.'

Granny thought that Daisy being stuck there sounded like a grand idea and looked slightly disappointed, but she was grateful for any time with her granddaughter and determined to make the most of it.

In the afternoon Daisy set off across the emerald-green fields with Grampy's collie at her heels. She loved the countryside and had gone walking every day during her stay, something she didn't often have time for when she was at home. Two hours later, as the sky was darkening, she set off back and as she passed the barn across the yard from the cottage she glanced through the open door and spotted the wooden sledge Grampy had made many years ago for Alfie. Without thinking, Daisy went into the barn and stroked the smooth wood. In her mind's eye she could see Alfie flying down the slope outside whooping with delight, his scarf streaming behind him and his nose glowing with the cold.

'I could never bring meself to get rid of it.' Grampy's voice made her start and she whirled to look at him, seeing that he had tears in his eyes as he too remembered. 'He were a grand little chap, that he were,' he said in a choked voice. Then with a frown he asked, 'Did they ever get the person that strangled that poor girl the same day Alfie died?'

'No, they didn't.' Daisy was frowning now too. 'It came out that Eunice was having a baby, so they think that whoever had got her in the family way did away with her, but they never found him. There were gypsies camped just outside the village at the time so they think it may have been one of them, but they were never able to prove anything.'

'Poor girl. Life can be cruel, so it can. An' our poor laddie. I still struggle to believe that he died because of a slip. He were so sure-footed. Why, he could skim up a tree faster than any squirrel I ever saw.' He forced a smile to his face. 'But at least we still have you, lass, an' sure it's been grand to have you here. I only wish you could stay a while longer.'

'I'll try to come again in the spring and stay for a little longer next time,' she promised, and after pecking his ruddy cheek, she went to help her granny get their supper ready.

The rest of the week seemed to pass in the blink of an eye and all too soon Daisy was packing her carpet bag ready to go home. She had given her granny and grampy the little presents she had bought for them and now their gifts to her and her father were tucked safely away in the bottom of her bag to be opened on Christmas morning along with a gift for her twenty-first birthday, which would be on Christmas Eve.

Outside, Neddy, Grampy's old horse, was impatiently pawing the ground as Grampy waited to take her in the trap to the ferry, and so she reluctantly gave her granny one last hug.

'To be sure I'm not at all happy about you travellin' all that way on your own,' the dear old woman fretted.

'Like I told Daddy, I'm all grown up now and I shall be perfectly all right.'

Granny followed her outside and as Daisy clambered up onto the bench seat next to her grampy she stared worriedly at the sky. 'Eeh, I just hope the snow holds off until you get home, lass.'

'Stop worrying, will you.' Daisy couldn't help but smile as her grandfather urged the horse forward. 'Bye, Granny. Take good care of yourself and hopefully I'll see you again very soon.'

Her granny waved until they turned a bend in the lane and were lost to sight.

As it had been on the way there, the ferry crossing was choppy but they arrived in Liverpool in good time and soon she was on the train heading for Nuneaton. By the time she arrived Daisy was cold, tired and hungry, and greatly looking forward to seeing her father. Since the death of her mother and brother they had been everything to each other, and although she had loved spending time with her beloved grandparents, she had missed him. Once she had left the station, she hailed a cab – she was far too tired for the long walk to Ansley and she just wanted to get home.

As the horse clip-clopped along, Daisy looked at all the familiar places and was glad to be back, but her happiness was short-lived, because when the cab drew up in front of the house she saw that it was in darkness. Her father must have gone to visit Mrs Peake.

Swallowing her disappointment, she paid the driver and made for the back door. It was open – they rarely locked it – and instantly Rags rose from his place by the low-burning fire and came wagging towards her.

'Hello, boy, have you missed me?' Daisy ruffled his fur affectionately. 'Seems like you're the only one who has.'

Luckily her father had left the oil lamp burning low on the table, so at least she hadn't come home to total darkness, and after turning it up she threw some coal onto the fire and put the kettle on to boil. She'd been hoping to chat to her father about her trip but it seemed that it would have to wait until morning. She made herself a hasty meal of slightly stale bread and cheese, noting that she would need to bake some fresh bread the next day, then with a yawn she went to bed and slept like a log right through until the next morning.

Once she was awake, she wrapped her old robe about her and slipped down to the kitchen, but everything was just as she had left it the night before and she realised with a little jolt that her father had not come home. Normally he would have been downstairs before her, coaxing the fire into life and putting the kettle on. Daisy let Rags out into the yard and bit her lip as she wondered what she should do. Eventually she decided on nothing. Her father was a grown man, and he couldn't be blamed for not being here to greet her. He hadn't even known when to expect her back. When she'd left, she'd just told him she would be gone for about a week.

Once she had the fire burning, she hurried back upstairs and dressed before going back down to toast the rest of the stale bread on a long brass toasting fork in front of the fire. She washed it down with a large mug of tea and set about her jobs. She noted there was a large pile of washing waiting to be done, but she decided to make a start on the bread first. She'd probably have to go shopping as well. Knowing her father, he wouldn't have a clue what to buy. Once she had kneaded the dough, she covered it with a damp cloth and was placing it on the hearth to prove when her father appeared through the kitchen door.

'Daisy! Why, it's lovely to have you back. Me an' Rags 'ere have missed you, ain't we, boy?' He looked guilty as he crossed to kiss her cheek and give her a hug. 'I, er . . . I'm sorry I wasn't 'ere when you got back, pet. I wasn't sure when yer were comin' an' it were so cold last night that after we'd 'ad dinner, Victoria suggested I should stay over . . . In the spare room, o' course,' he ended hurriedly, blushing like a schoolboy.

'Oh? You must be getting on very well,' Daisy teased.

'We are as a matter o' fact. She's a fine woman. But come on, tell me how your grandparents are. Are they well? Were they pleased to see you?'

'Yes and yes, they are very well, thankfully, and they were delighted I decided to surprise them. But how have you managed on your own?'

He blushed an even deeper shade of red, if that were possible, as he blustered, 'Well I, er . . . I dined at Victoria's most evenin's. She didn't like the idea o' me havin' to cook for meself after workin' all day, so she kindly had me there.'

'I see. Would you like some breakfast?'

He shook his head. 'I've already had some, pet, but thanks for the offer. An' now I really should go an' get changed an' get to work. I've got Bill Wright bringin' his mare in to be shod shortly. We'll talk more over dinner, shall we?'

Daisy nodded. It sounded like her father and Victoria were growing closer. With a sigh she got on with her chores.

Later that morning, as Daisy was kneading the dough on the scrubbed table, the back door opened and Gilbert appeared. 'Ah, I just called into the forge and your father told me you were back so I thought I'd pop in and say hello.'

Daisy continued her kneading but said nothing and he went on, 'Did you miss me . . . just a little bit?'

'I didn't actually,' Daisy responded as she sliced the dough and put it into the prepared bread tins. 'And I am rather busy as you can see. I've got a pile of washing to do when I've finished here, so I'd like to get on, if you don't mind.'

Gilbert chuckled and he leant back against the wall. 'If I didn't know you better, I might take offence.'

Daisy's eyes flashed with annoyance as she looked him in the face. 'As I said, I'm rather busy.' She lifted the tins and placed them in the bread oven to the side of the fireplace before crossing to the sink to rinse her hands.

'So not even an offer of a cuppa before I go?'

'No!' Her voice was firm and finally taking the hint he quietly left with a grin on his face. She looked pretty when she was angry and he wasn't about to give up on her just yet. In fact, the more she pushed him away the more he wanted her, and Gilbert usually got what he wanted eventually.

'Will you be home for dinner this evening?' Daisy asked when she took her father his mug of tea later that morning. He had already shod the farmer's horse and now he was shaping a long piece of glowing metal to make a new part for a farm tool that he was repairing. He rose and swiped the back of his arm across his sweating brow. His shirtsleeves were rolled up to his elbows and he wore thick leather gloves and a leather apron to protect him from the heat. It was always like a furnace in there and Daisy wondered how he managed to bear it.

'Yes, I'll be in, pet.' He had actually made arrangements to dine with Victoria yet again but now that Daisy was home, he didn't want to leave her so soon.

Her face lit up. 'Good, in that case I'll make your favourite steak and kidney pie. After the bread comes out of the oven, I'll pop into the village to get the meat from the butcher's and anything else we might need, then I'll be right back.'

He smiled at her as he took a long swig of his tea and Daisy went back to the house with a spring in her step.

An hour and a half later she returned with two large wicker baskets full of shopping from the village store. Once back in the warmth of the kitchen she gratefully dropped them onto the table, smiling as she saw that the two cats her father kept at the forge to kill the mice were curled up fast asleep with Rags on the hearthrug. Her father must have popped home and let them in.

Humming softly to herself, she crossed to the tin on the shelf where she kept the housekeeping money her father gave her, and lifting the lid she was about to drop the change in when she frowned. The tin was empty, but she knew there had been at least two pounds still in there when she had left for the shops. Maybe her father had borrowed it to give one of his customers some change, in which case he would put it back that evening. She resumed her humming as she took off her hat and coat and set about making the pastry for the pie.

She and her father were halfway through their meal that evening before Daisy remembered the missing money. 'Daddy, did you borrow some money out of the housekeeping tin today?'

'An' why would I do that?' Jed frowned.

'That's strange. It was there when I left for the shops but when I got back and went to put my change in, the tin was empty.'

'So, who's been here today?' he asked suspiciously.

'No one!' And then she remembered. 'Only Gilbert, but that was this morning before I went out.'

'I see. Well, don't get worrying about it. I'll make the money up so you'll not go short, pet.'

She nodded but the thought that someone could have stolen from them left a bad taste in both their mouths.

Chapter Six

'I was thinking we ought to be picking a Christmas tree up from the market soon,' Daisy told her father hopefully as he straightened his tie in the mirror above the fireplace in the kitchen. Once again, he was going to dine with Mrs Peake and another lonely night stretched ahead of her.

'You're quite right,' he answered guiltily as it occurred to him that they usually had it up and dressed by now. 'There's only ten days left until Christmas. How about I take the afternoon off on Saturday and we'll go into town and get one?'

Daisy's eyes sparkled as she nodded enthusiastically.

'And while we're in town you could perhaps give me some idea of what you'd like for your birthday. It is a special one after all. You're only twenty-one once. If your mammy was here, she'd no doubt be throwing a big party for you, but I'd have no idea where to start.' His eyes clouded with pain as he thought of his beautiful wife.

'I'm not bothered about a party, Daddy. Really, I'm not. And I don't need a big present either. But I shall enjoy us picking the tree together.' It was a ritual they had followed every year since they had lost Mauve.

Jed turned from the mirror and gently stroked his calloused hand down Daisy's soft cheek. 'Your mammy would be so proud if she could see the lovely young woman you've grown into,' he said softly.

Daisy felt a lump form in her throat. 'Oh, get away with you.' She was slightly embarrassed and gave him a gentle push towards the door. 'Now you'd best be off or you'll be late for dinner and Mrs Peake won't be best pleased.'

He turned to do as he was told before pausing and turning back to ask, 'Are you *sure* you don't mind being left on your own so often? I feel that I've been neglecting you.'

'I'm fine, I've got a big pile of mending to do, so plenty to keep me busy. Now go on.'

Once he'd left, she securely locked and bolted the back door and drew the curtains across the small leaded windows. Shortly before she had gone to visit her grandparents, Gilbert had taken to calling in of an evening when he knew her father was at his mother's, and he made Daisy feel uneasy. Admittedly, he had never tried to touch her, but his lurid comments made her feel uncomfortable so now as soon as her father left, she would shut herself in so that if he knocked, she could pretend she was out, and eventually he would go away. Then when she was ready for bed, she would unlock the door for her father's return, as she knew that by then Gilbert would probably be in town with his friends or involved in some card game somewhere.

Once the mending was done, Daisy let Rags out into the yard and made herself a cup of cocoa. A few moments later, when she heard him barking, she went to let him back in and almost jumped out of her skin as Gilbert appeared out of the darkness and walked in through the door.

'What are you doing here at this time of the night?' she demanded angrily. 'I was just about to go to bed!'

From the way he was swaying it was obvious he had been drinking and a feeling of unease spread through her.

'Now that's hardly the way to greet a chap ish it, my lovely,' he cooed as he wobbled towards her. The door was swinging open behind him letting in blasts of icy air and Daisy shuddered as she backed away from him towards the sink. 'But I like the idea of going to bed. I thought you'd never ask!'

Daisy's fear was replaced by anger as her hand closed around the rolling pin, which thankfully she had left on the draining board.

'I think you had better leave . . . *right* now!' Her voice shook with rage as he continued to advance on her. And then she swung the rolling pin in front of him and he stopped dead in his tracks. 'I *swear* if you don't get out this very minute, I shall wrap this around your head,' she warned. Hearing the distress in his mistress's voice, Rags had come to stand beside her, his hackles rising as he growled threateningly.

'All right, all right, keep your hair on.' Gilbert scowled as he backed off. By the look on Daisy's face, he had no doubt she meant every word she said, and he had no intention of getting his head caved in. 'I'm going, though why you have to be so hoity-toity I'll never know. We could have some very good times together if you'd let yourself go a bit.'

She took another threatening step towards him, lifting the rolling pin higher, and he swayed away unsteadily and was swallowed up by the darkness.

Daisy hastily locked and bolted the door again before sinking down onto a chair at the side of the table, allowing the tears that were pricking at the back of her eyes to pour down her cheeks. Why, oh why had her father ever got involved with the widow? If he hadn't, she wouldn't be forced to have anything to do with Gilbert. She could hardly tell her father what a nuisance he was making of himself though, not when he seemed so happy.

Once she'd composed herself, she made her way upstairs to get changed into her nightclothes before getting into bed and lying under the covers until she heard her father's footsteps in the yard. She hurried down to unlock the door for him.

'What's this? Since when have you had to lock the door?' he enquired.

'Oh, I was just being on the safe side.' Daisy forced a smile. 'There's been a lot of break-ins around here lately, and I feel safer with it locked if you're not in.'

Again, Jed felt guilty for leaving her alone so much, but what was he to do? He was completely under Victoria's spell.

The following morning over breakfast her father asked tentatively, 'I was wondering if we might invite Victoria and her sons to come here for Christmas dinner, love? Do you think you could manage to cook for so many? Lewis is due back from university today for the Christmas holidays, and Victoria's cook is going away for three days from Christmas Eve, so Victoria is in a bit of a flap. She has many attributes, but I don't think cookin' in one of 'em.'

'Oh!' Daisy was shocked. She and her father usually had a quiet Christmas dinner together after attending church in the morning, but how could she refuse him? He looked so hopeful. 'I, er . . . suppose I could manage it, but she'll have to understand that my Christmas dinner will be very plain compared to the meals she is used to being served.'

'I'm sure she won't mind that in the least.' He was beaming now. 'And it'll be nice for us all to be together, won't it?'

Daisy forced a smile. She didn't have much choice if she didn't want to upset him, but already she was dreading it.

On Saturday, as he had promised, Jed finished work at lunchtime and he and Daisy took the cart into the market at Nuneaton.

As they drove down Queens Road her father told her, 'I'll just go and get Fancy stabled at the inn, pet, then I'll come and meet you in the market square. I shouldn't be long.'

Daisy was glad to have a few minutes to herself. She had already knitted a warm scarf and gloves for her father for Christmas, but she also wanted to get him a new pipe and some tobacco.

Once she had what she wanted she made her way through the throngs of people to the market square. Everywhere she looked people were rushing about buying last-minute food and presents for Christmas, and to one side of the square the Salvation Army band was playing Christmas carols, which added to the happy atmosphere. She stood listening to them and shortly after her father joined her and they went on the hunt for a tree. They didn't have to go far and soon they had chosen the one they wanted and carried it back to put it in the cart.

'We'd best go an' order a nice fat goose now,' her father said.

Daisy shook her head. 'It's all right, Daddy, I already ordered one from Mr Piece, the village butcher.'

'Aye, but there'll be more of us now,' he pointed out worriedly. 'Will it be big enough? I don't want to skimp.'

'It'll be more than big enough,' Daisy promised. 'So now you can take me for a cup of tea and a mince pie before we have a scout around the stalls.'

It was late afternoon before they set off for home again and the light was fading fast, but Jed knew the roads to and from the town like the back of his hand, so there was no risk of them getting lost. As Fancy trotted along it began to snow again and Daisy pulled her shawl over her head and giggled. 'Looks like we're set to have a white Christmas.'

Once they got home, they unloaded the tree and bags from the cart, then Jed went to bed Fancy down in her stable while Daisy went inside to put the kettle on. Entering the kitchen she was shocked to see Gilbert sitting in the chair at the side of the fire as if he owned the place.

'What are you doing here again?' she hissed.

Gilbert looked at her remorsefully. 'I came to apologise for the way I behaved the other night,' he said contritely. 'I'm afraid I'd had rather too much to drink and I let my feelings run away with me. I do care about you, Daisy.'

He'd decided to try a different approach with her, but Daisy was no fool and she saw straight through him.

'Well, I'm very sorry but I don't have any feelings for you, Gilbert, only disgust after the way you behaved.' She didn't want her father to hear what was going on between them and just wanted him to leave. If her father discovered there was ill feeling between them she knew it would ruin his Christmas and that was the last thing she wanted to do.

Unfortunately, Jed appeared seconds later so Daisy quickly began to unpack the baskets.

'Hello, lad. What brings you here?' her father said with a smile.

'Oh, I was just passing by and thought I'd call in,' Gilbert said innocently.

'Did you now? That's very nice, isn't it, Daisy? It's snowin' out there so you'll need a nice hot drink inside of yer before you venture back out.'

Daisy took the hint and went to place the kettle on the hob as her father made the fire up. Recognising the visitor, Rags came to stand beside her and growled.

Jed looked at him in surprise. 'Why, Rags boy, what's wrong?' Glancing towards Gilbert he apologised, 'I'm sorry, lad. It ain't like him to be like this.'

Gilbert shrugged as Daisy glared at him. She carried a mug of tea to him and plonked it down unceremoniously.

Jed was more bemused than ever now and hoping to lighten the mood he said quickly, 'Tell your mother I'll be along for dinner tomorrow at the usual time, would you? I've no doubt I've got to help this young lass o' mine set the tree up tonight. It's somethin' we do together every year, ain't it, Daisy?'

She forced a smile and continued to unpack the shopping until at last Gilbert finished his drink and rose to leave. 'I'd best be off now before the weather gets any worse. There's a dance on at the village hall on Christmas Eve. Would you fancy coming along, Daisy?'

'No, thank you,' she answered primly. 'I shall be busy preparing the meal for the next day.'

'Perhaps I could come and help you?'

'I can manage perfectly well by myself, thank you,' she answered more tartly than she had intended to. She could feel her father's eyes on her and blushed.

'In that case I'll get off. Goodbye, both. I'll see you on Christmas Day, if not before.'

Jed shook Gilbert's hand as Daisy inclined her head and at last he went out into the snow, which was coming down faster than ever.

'Did I detect a bit of an atmosphere between you two?' Jed looked so worried that Daisy felt guilty. She supposed she had been rather short with Gilbert.

'Sorry, Daddy, I'm just a bit tired,' she muttered.

Instantly he was beside her. 'I'm sorry, pet. I know you've worked hard since your mam passed. I should have got someone in to help run the house instead of expectin' you to step into her shoes.'

'I'm happy to do it,' she assured him. 'Now I'll get some dinner on the go and then we'll put the tree up, shall we? Can you stand it in a bucket of earth for me?'

'I'll do that now.' He glanced towards the window. 'I'd best get the chickens into their coops an' all else we'll never find 'em if this snow keeps comin' down. I shan't be goin' out tonight, so we can 'ave a nice cosy night in by the fire.'

Feeling happy again, Daisy hummed as she put some pork chops into the oven and started to peel the potatoes. She and her father had spent such a lovely afternoon together. It was just a shame that she'd had to come home to find Gilbert there. *Still*, she thought, *he's gone now and hopefully he's got the message this time and won't trouble me again.*

They spent a pleasant night dressing the tree and Daisy went to bed in a good mood. Very soon it would be her twenty-first birthday and then Christmas Day. She still wasn't keen on Mrs Peake and her sons spending Christmas with them, but she had decided she would make the best of it for her father's sake. Hopefully, the friendship he and the widow had started would fizzle out soon, and then things could get back to the way they had been.

On that happy thought she snuggled down into her bed and was soon fast asleep.

Chapter Seven

'Happy birthday, sweet'eart.' It was Christmas Eve morning and Daisy and her father were sitting at breakfast when he handed her a small, prettily wrapped package.

'What's this?' Daisy was smiling as she took it from him and began to tear at the paper.

'I went into the jeweller's in town when we were there the other day. But don't worry, he assured me that if you don't like it, you can take it back and change it.'

Daisy stared down at a small velvet box and opened the lid. Inside was a dainty gold locket on a delicate chain and she gasped with delight.

'Oh, I love it, Daddy.' She lifted the necklace out of the box to admire it, but Jed wasn't finished just yet.

'The other thing I'd like you to 'ave is this. I were waitin' till you come of age to give it to you. I know yer mammy would 'ave wanted you to 'ave it.' He pushed a thin gold band across the table and tears sprang to Daisy's eyes. 'But, Daddy . . . this was Mammy's wedding ring. Don't you want to keep it?'

'It should be you who has it,' he said quietly.

Daisy slipped it onto her finger and sprang out of her seat to fling her arms about his neck and give him a resounding kiss on the cheek. 'I shall treasure it for always,' she promised.

'Now let's finish our breakfast while it's still hot, eh? I'm plannin' on closin' early today.'

'Good. I might set you on preparing the brussels sprouts ready for tomorrow if you do,' Daisy teased.

The morning passed in a blur as once again she cleaned the house from top to bottom before baking yet another batch of mince pies. She'd already made dozens but as fast as she cooked them her father ate them. Next, she iced the Christmas cake before slipping into the village to collect the goose from Mr Piece. It was so large that it barely fit in her basket and so heavy that by the time she got home she felt as if her arms had been almost torn from their sockets. *I don't know about being enough to feed us, I reckon this could feed the whole village*, Daisy thought with amusement.

Later that afternoon she once again donned her warm clothes and made for the churchyard, gathering two large bunches of holly with deep red berries along the way. Flowers were hard to come by at this time of year, but Daisy still liked to visit the graves and let her loved ones know she hadn't forgotten them. Once she arrived, she picked her way amongst the gravestones until she came to the resting places of her mother and brother. Gently she wiped away the snow, which was still falling heavily, from the gravestones with her mittened hands and stared at the names carved into the cold black marble. *Mauve Armstrong. Beloved wife and mother.* And on the second slightly smaller one, *Alfred James Armstrong. Beloved son and brother. Safe in the arms of Jesus.* Daisy fervently hoped that this was true.

She laid the holly in front of them and a tear slid down her cheek as memories of Christmases past flooded her mind. 'Do you remember how we always used to go and gather holly to put in the house every Christmas Eve, Mammy?' she whispered, but silence was her only answer.

A mist was floating across the churchyard and as she stared at the headstones rising above it, she felt as if she was the only person left on earth for there was not another living soul in sight. 'And, Alfie, can you remember how you always kept me awake on Christmas Eve because you were so excited about what Father

Christmas might bring you?' Already the snow was beginning to cover the holly she had laid and her fingers, even in their woollen protection, were numb.

Suddenly she raised her head and sniffed at the air and just for a moment she caught the faint whiff of the rose water her mother used to dab behind her ears. It was gone as quickly as it had come but it brought her comfort. She may not be able to see her mammy and her little brother but they both lived on in her heart so they would never truly be lost to her. With a sigh she turned and retraced her steps, wishing with all her heart that she could turn the clock back.

Her father was in the kitchen when she got home. 'Been to the churchyard have yer, pet?'

When she nodded, he smiled. 'I guessed that was where you might be. Now come and get warm by the fire, I've got a pot of tea mashin'.'

They spent a pleasant afternoon together but as it began to get dark her father rose from his chair. 'I'd best go an' get changed. I'm off to dinner wi' Victoria this evenin'. As it happens, she's invited you to come along too if you've a mind to. Lewis is back from university an' she wants us to meet him.'

'Oh, I won't if you don't mind.' Daisy swallowed her disappointment; she'd been hoping they'd spend the evening together, but she managed to raise a smile. 'I've got so much to do before tomorrow, but you go and enjoy yourself.'

He sighed, feeling guilty again. Half of him wanted to be with Victoria and yet the other half felt bad for leaving his daughter alone on such a special night.

'Well . . . if you're sure.' He sounded uncertain, but Daisy waved her hand at him.

'Go on, get ready and be off with you. I shall be perfectly all right. In fact, I've got so much to do I probably won't even miss you.'

An hour later he stepped out into the snowy night and as the door closed behind him, loneliness closed in on Daisy like a heavy blanket.

Once, not so long ago, Christmas Eve had been one of the happiest evenings of the year, when the family were all together, tucked in by a cosy fire in their home, with work and the rest of the world seemingly miles away. But now her mother and Alfie were lying in the cold earth in the churchyard and her father . . . Daisy took a firm grip on herself to stop her thoughts from going any further. *Pull yourself together, Daisy Armstrong. Daddy works hard and he deserves to have some time to himself so stop being so selfish and get on with what needs to be done.* And that was exactly what she did.

Chapter Eight

Daisy was up early the next morning to put the enormous bird into the oven and by the time her father rose she had a fire burning brightly and a pot of porridge bubbling on the stove.

'Merry Christmas, sweet'eart,' he said jovially as he handed her a parcel wrapped in plain brown paper and tied with string. 'I'm sorry about the wrappin' but you know I ain't no good at that sort 'o thing.'

Daisy eagerly opened it and gasped with pleasure as she found the prettiest shawl she had ever seen inside. Made in soft blues and pinks and trimmed with a luxurious fringe, it was so fine that it felt like silk.

'I know it ain't very practical, particularly in this weather,' her father told her with a smile. 'But I thought come the spring and summer you could wear it for church or if you went anywhere nice.'

'Oh, Daddy, it's just beautiful, thank you,' she told him, pleasure shining in her eyes. She handed him his gifts then and he was tickled pink with them.

'You take after yer mam fer bein' good at knittin',' he declared as he admired his gloves and scarf. 'An' this new pipe is just the job. Thanks, pet.'

As they had their breakfast he asked, 'Are yer sure you won't come to church this mornin'? It don't feel right goin' without you.'

'I'm quite sure.' She took his empty dish and planted a kiss on his cheek. 'I've got more than enough to do here. I don't want to let you down.'

'You could never do that.' He was solemn for a moment, before hurrying away to get into his Sunday best. He just hoped that the roads were still passable as he was going to collect Victoria and her sons in the trap before attending the service.

Half an hour later Jed left and the kitchen became a hive of activity. Daisy laid the table with her mother's best lace cloth and all the best china and cutlery before placing a bowl of holly in the centre. She stepped back to assess her work and smiled. Admittedly it was nowhere near as grand as the dining room at Victoria's house, but it was warm and cosy and everything in the room had been scrubbed or polished until it gleamed. The cats and Rags were fast asleep in front of the fire. None of them seemed very keen to venture outside into the snow and she didn't blame them.

An hour later she put a large tray of potatoes and stuffing to roast in the oven with the goose and began to cook the vegetables. She had prepared them all the night before and now there was nothing else she could do but pray that everything would be satisfactory. She wanted to make her father proud. She hoped Lewis wasn't like his younger brother. They had seen each other a few times in church but had never really spoken apart from to say hello. Still, whatever he was like she would only have to put up with them for a few hours so she was sure she could manage – provided Gilbert behaved himself.

Once she was sure that everything was cooking nicely, she hurried upstairs to get changed into her Sunday best gown. Finally, she brushed her hair and fastened it with a ribbon at the nape of her neck, before turning to survey herself in the mirror. A young woman with dimpled cheeks and a heart-shaped face looked back at her. Her eyes were very blue, as her mother's had been, and her long, dark hair had a tendency to curl, especially when it was damp.

Now there was nothing left to do but wait for everyone to get back from church. They were slightly late because of the bad weather and Daisy began to panic. What if the dinner burned? But she needn't have worried because at last she heard the trap pull into the yard and then the door opened and Victoria breezed in in a gust of expensive French perfume, followed by her two sons. 'Your father is just putting the horse in the stable and said to tell you he will be in directly. Merry Christmas, my dear. Oh, and this is Lewis, you already know Gilbert, don't you?'

As Lewis stepped forward and shook Daisy's hand, she took an instant liking to him. He was very handsome and had a nice smile, so it would have been difficult not to. Unlike his mother and brother, he was fair-haired with deep brown eyes that reminded Daisy of the colour of treacle.

'Nice to meet you, Daisy,' he said.

'It's nice to meet you too,' she murmured, blushing as he bent down to stroke Rags who had come up wagging a greeting.

'Oh, and a little gift for you.' Victoria handed Daisy a small package.

'Er . . . thank you very much.' Daisy was shocked. She certainly hadn't expected anything and wondered if perhaps she had misjudged the woman. She quickly opened it to find four lace-trimmed handkerchiefs beautifully embroidered with her initials.

'Thank you again, they're lovely,' she muttered, feeling ridiculously embarrassed.

Luckily her father appeared at that moment and she didn't have to say any more.

'Well now, this is nice, isn't it?' he said jovially as he crossed to the fire to warm his hands. 'And something smells delicious.' Turning his attention to Victoria, he asked, 'Would you like a glass of sherry to warm you up, my dear? Daisy, would you take Victoria's hat and coat, please?'

Daisy dutifully did as she was asked as the guests all took seats in front of the fire and she hurried off to check the dinner once more. Soon after she announced, 'The meal is ready if everyone would like to take a seat at the table.'

Once they were all seated, she carried the dishes of food to the table and finally she placed the goose in front of her father, who sharpened his knife and began to carve.

Everyone helped themselves to the various vegetables, stuffing and gravy, and once she was sure they all had everything they needed, Daisy joined them as her father poured them all a glass of wine. He was smiling broadly and the reason why became clear when he stood up to say heartily, 'I'd like you all to raise a glass to this beautiful woman sitting to the side of me, who has made me the happiest man on earth by agreeing to become my wife.'

Daisy's mouth gaped and she felt the colour drain from her face. It was what she had feared and she was hurt that her father hadn't warned her.

Victoria smiled up at him batting her eyelashes and Gilbert laughed. 'I've been expecting this. Congratulations, both.'

Lewis nodded and stuttered, 'Er, yes . . . of course.' Although he looked almost as shocked as Daisy was.

Jed raised his eyebrows and looked at Daisy, and feeling that she should say something she muttered, 'C-congratulations.' But inside she was crying. How was she ever going to accept this woman in place of her mother? She knew deep down that she was being selfish – after all, her main concern should have been for her father's happiness and Victoria did seem to make him happy. But although the woman had always been pleasant to her, there was something about her that Daisy didn't like. It had been hard enough having to just see her occasionally, but it was going to be so much worse if she was going to have to live under the same roof as her.

'So, we'd best make it official, hadn't we?' Her father laughed as he fumbled in his pocket and withdrew a small velvet box. Inside, on a bed of satin, was a small sapphire ring surrounded by a halo of tiny diamonds. Victoria looked at it and Daisy quite clearly saw a flash of disappointment cross her face. Oblivious, her father took the ring from the box and went to slide it onto her finger.

'Oh dear. I fear it is a little snug, darling,' Victoria told him. 'Perhaps we could take it back to the jeweller when they reopen after the holidays? And while we're there we could perhaps look to see if there is anything I like better? After all, an engagement ring is such a personal thing, isn't it?'

'Er . . . yes, of course, if that's what you'd prefer,' Jed told her, although Daisy could see the hurt on his face. He snapped the box shut and put it in his pocket, and they all turned their attention back to the lovely meal Daisy had cooked. But Daisy's appetite had disappeared and she merely pushed the food about her plate.

'So, when is the grand event to be?' Gilbert asked as he loaded his fork with a slice of succulent goose.

'Oh, we haven't thought that far ahead yet,' his mother told him as she stroked Jed's hand. 'He only proposed to me this morning before we left for church. But I was thinking of the spring. There's nothing nicer than a spring wedding, is there? And at our time of life there's no point in having a long engagement. What do you think, my dear?'

Jed looked at her adoringly. 'The spring sounds fine to me. After all, we don't need much time to plan it if we have a nice quiet affair, do we?'

'A quiet affair?' Victoria looked horrified. 'I'm sure we can do better than that. I thought we could have the service at St Lawrence's followed by a reception at the Kingsholme Inn in Nuneaton. They have a wonderful room upstairs that would easily seat as many guests as we care to invite. I shall get caterers in to do the meal, of course. And following the reception, I thought we could go abroad for our honeymoon. Perhaps France or Italy. What do you think, darling?'

'I, er . . . hadn't planned on a honeymoon,' Jed admitted, looking vaguely uncomfortable. 'I have so much work on, you see, and I don't like to let my clients down.'

She giggled girlishly and waved her hand. 'You work far too hard. But in that case, I suppose we could perhaps steal a few days in London instead and take our official honeymoon later in the year?'

'We'll see,' he said quietly.

'And where will we all be living after the wedding of the year?' Gilbert enquired with a grin.

'Again, we haven't thought that far ahead,' his mother answered.

Both Daisy and Lewis were staring down at the table not quite knowing what to say. She was relieved when everyone finished and she could clear away the plates. To her surprise Lewis rose to help her.

'That was a bit of a shock, wasn't it?' he whispered as they piled the dirty pots onto the draining board.

Daisy nodded, although if she was honest, it wasn't really. She just hadn't expected it so soon.

'It's such a shame you don't have a separate dining room, Edward,' Victoria said behind them. 'It doesn't seem right to have to sit, cook and eat all in one room. Only the servants eat in the kitchen in my home.'

The colour returned to Daisy's face with a vengeance. She had worked tirelessly for days to make the room clean and comfortable, and to make the meal as good as it could be, but it seemed it still didn't meet Victoria's exacting standards.

'Take no notice; everywhere looks lovely and the meal was delicious,' Lewis whispered, and Daisy smiled at him before carrying the Christmas pudding and a large jug of thick, creamy custard to the table.

'Oh . . . is there no cream or brandy sauce?' Victoria asked. 'Custard is so working class, don't you think?'

Daisy was getting annoyed now. 'I'm sorry, I never thought to get any cream or brandy sauce. Father and I prefer custard,' she said somewhat shortly. 'After all, we are working class, and proud of it.'

'Then perhaps I'll just try a little pudding, but only a small amount. We women do have to watch our figures, don't we?'

'You have a perfect figure,' Jed assured her, and she simpered prettily at him.

When at last the meal was over Jed took Victoria into the small sitting room to discuss their wedding plans.

Lewis again helped Daisy to clear the table as Gilbert threw himself into the chair in front of the fire and placed his feet on the brass fender.

'So, the old dear got her man yet again, eh, bro?' he said, chuckling as if Daisy wasn't even in the room. 'I could have told you weeks ago she'd set her cap at him, and what Mother wants, Mother usually gets.'

Lewis ignored him as he asked Daisy, 'And how do *you* feel about this wedding?'

'I suppose I'm a little shocked,' Daisy admitted with a sigh. 'But if it's what they both want it isn't our place to stand in their way. I just worry that . . . Well, your mother leads a very different life to us. She doesn't have to work and she has servants to wait on her, whereas we are very much what she just termed working class. Do you think she'll be able to adjust to our way of life?'

Gilbert chuckled as he bit the end off a cigar before lighting it and blowing a haze of blue smoke towards the rafters. 'Happen she hasn't got much choice.'

Lewis frowned. 'And just what is that supposed to mean?'

Gilbert gave a nasty little grin. 'You'll see.' And he went off to join the happy couple in the sitting room.

Meanwhile, to Daisy's surprise, Lewis pitched in to help with the washing up. 'There's no need really,' she told him, but he insisted.

'How much longer are you at university for?' she asked after a time, hoping to direct their thoughts away from the forthcoming wedding. She already suspected that Lewis wasn't any happier about it than she was.

'I've got two more exams to sit when I get back after the holidays and fingers crossed, if I pass them, I should be home early in March.'

'And then what would you like to do?'

He grinned. 'I'd like to be a veterinarian and get my own practice eventually, much to my mother's disgust,' he chuckled. 'She really can't understand why I would want to get my hands dirty, but I've loved animals ever since I was a child.'

'I think that would be a grand job to do,' Daisy told him. 'And good luck with your exams. I'm sure you'll pass them.'

Once all the pots had been washed and dried and put away in their rightful places, Daisy made a tray of tea, which they carried through to the sitting room, along with a large plateful of her delicious mince pies.

'Lewis was just telling me that he hopes to become a vet,' Daisy said as she poured the tea into her mother's delicate china cups and saucers.

Victoria sniffed her disapproval as she took a drink from Daisy. 'I really can't think *why* he should want to do such a menial job,' she complained. 'He has the brains to be an accountant or a barrister or anything he chooses.' Fixing her gaze on Daisy, she asked, 'And why have you never worked, my dear? Are you qualified for anything?'

Jed jumped to her defence. 'Daisy was as bright as a button at school.' He smiled at her affectionately. 'She, too, could have been anythin' she wanted, I'm sure. But after we lost her mammy and little brother, she took over runnin' the house. An' a right fine job she's done of it an' all. I really don't know what I'd have done wi'out her.'

Gilbert was scoffing the mince pies as if they were going out of fashion, so Daisy slipped away to get some more, grateful for the chance to escape, if only for a few minutes. She could hardly wait for their visitors to leave. She needed time to come to terms with the fact that her life was never going to be the same again.

Chapter Nine

At last they were gone. Her father had left to take them home and Daisy sank into a chair, tears sliding down her cheeks. Rags nuzzled her hand as if he could feel her pain and disappointment, and she kissed the top of his head as she cuddled him to her.

'Don't worry, old boy,' she told him gently. 'Victoria has made it more than clear that she doesn't like you and I don't think she likes me much either, but I'll look after you.'

They sat together in companiable silence in the glow of the fire until she heard her father return. She rose to put the kettle on to boil again. After all the sherry and wine he had drunk, she knew he'd welcome their nightly cup of cocoa once he had settled Fancy down for the night.

When he entered the kitchen some minutes later and shook the snow from his hat and coat, he looked at her sheepishly. 'Thank you for making such an effort today, pet,' he said quietly. 'The meal was grand an' I'm sorry if our announcement came as a bit of a shock to you. I realise now I should 'ave prepared you.' When Daisy shrugged, he went on, 'I don't want yer to think that Victoria can ever replace yer mammy. Mauve was the love o' me life an' when I lost 'er I thought I would die too fer a time. But the thing is . . . a man 'as needs. I get lonely an' miss the companionship of someone to snuggle up to of a night. Try to understand. It'll change nowt atween you an' me, yer should know that. You'll always be the most important thing in me life, but one day you'll meet a young man that'll turn yer head an' you'll start your own life an' I'll be all alone. Will yer try to understand?'

Daisy crossed to him and put her arms about his waist and for a moment they stood quietly. Eventually she said, 'Go and sit by the fire and get warm. The cocoa will be ready in a minute.' There were so many questions she would have liked to ask but she felt now was not the time. Everything was just too raw so the questions could wait until another day.

'I've told Victoria I won't see her tomorrow,' he told her when they both sat with steaming mugs in their hands. 'I thought it might be nice fer us to 'ave our last Boxing Day alone together, just the two of us.'

She managed to raise a smile. That was something at least.

'I noticed that you an' Lewis seemed to get along all right?'

She nodded. 'Yes, we did. I like him much more than Gilbert.'

'Between you an' me I agree with you.' Jed shook his head. 'I reckon because Gilbert's the baby his mother has spoilt him. I've already told 'er she should set 'im on managin' one of her empty shops in the town. It seems daft fer 'em not to be tradin' an' they're losin' money. But I reckon that young man is a little work-shy.'

Little more was said as they finished their drinks and once Daisy had washed the mugs, she wished him goodnight, and lit her way to her room with a candle.

She slept badly that night as she tried to imagine herself living in Victoria's large house. She presumed that's where they would be living, for the woman had made it very clear that their home wasn't nearly grand enough for her. She wondered what she would do with her days. If there were servants, she supposed she could offer to go and work in one of the shops. At least it would get her out of the house each day. But that was still a long way off. They had the wedding to get through first and she was already dreading it.

61

The next day, Daisy made another trip to the churchyard. The snow was still falling thickly and drifts were forming, but she felt the need to go.

'Oh, Mammy,' she whispered when she reached the grave. She began to quietly cry, her tears feeling like icicles on her cold cheeks. 'How can I ever accept that woman in your place? And what will Granny and Grampy think when I write to tell them that Daddy is to wed again?'

She stayed until her hands and feet had no feeling, and only then did she leave to make her way back to the house that her mammy had loved. The streets in the village were deserted as she passed through. Even Ansley Colliery, which was usually noisy with the tramp of the miners' boots coming and going on their way to and from shifts, was closed. Tomorrow everyone would be back at work and people could return to their usual routines. But Daisy's life would never be the same again.

Two days Later, Jed took a morning off work to return to the jeweller's with his new fiancée. They arrived back two and a half hours later and Daisy stared at the ring Victoria had chosen. It was a huge solitaire diamond on a slim gold band and nothing at all like the one her father had chosen for her.

Jed had paled when he saw the price – it was the most expensive ring in the shop – but then he had reasoned she would wear it forever, so if it made her happy, he would pay the price.

'It's, er . . . very big,' Daisy said quietly.

'As soon as I saw it, I just knew it was the one,' Victoria purred with a simpering smile at Jed. 'It was as if it was meant to be, for it fits like it was made for me.'

'So long as it makes you happy,' her father answered.

'Oh, it really does!'

'Good, then it was worth every penny. But now, my love, I should take you home. I have an order for buckets and bowls from the ironmonger I really must make this afternoon; I don't like to keep my customers waiting.'

Victoria inclined her head to Daisy, who was rolling pastry for a meat pie, and flounced out to the trap, the peacock feathers on her hat dancing as she moved.

When they were gone Daisy chewed on her lip. It was blatantly clear that Victoria had very expensive tastes and she wondered if her father would be able to meet her expectations. He made a good living, but he surely couldn't be anywhere near as rich as Victoria's late husband. But then, she would have inherited everything from him, surely, so it wasn't as if she would be coming to the marriage penniless.

The next morning, Daisy set off to replenish the pantry at the grocery shop in the village. As she was selecting carrots from outside, she became aware of some women talking in the shop. She didn't take much notice until her ears pricked up when she heard her father's name mentioned.

'Ah, the silly bugger 'as fell fer 'er charms 'ook, line an' sinker from what I've 'eard.' She recognised the voice as Mrs Blakely's, the village gossip. 'She set 'er cap at 'im an' she reeled 'im in. It wouldn't be so bad, but they reckon her debts are pilin' up. The maid walked out yesterday, by all accounts, cos she hadn't been paid fer months, an' the butcher's refused to deliver any more meat till she settles 'er bill. What does that tell you, eh? I've also 'eard that the bank has foreclosed on them two shops standin' empty in Nuneaton cos Mr Peake were be'ind wi' the payments. Jed Armstrong won't know what's 'it 'im when the truth comes out. But there'd be no point in tryin' to warn 'im, poor sod. Yer

63

know what they say, there's none so blind as them that don't want to see. I saw the cook from the widow's 'ouse this mornin' an' she reckons she came home yesterday wi' a diamond the size of a rock on 'er finger an' that wouldn't 'ave been cheap, would it?'

Colour burned into Daisy's cheeks and, clutching the carrots, she walked into the shop. The talking stopped immediately and an uncomfortable silence settled.

'Mornin', love. We 'ear you're to 'ave a new mammy,' Mrs Blakely said eventually, as bold as brass.

Daisy stared at her calmly with her head held high. 'You only ever get one mammy, Mrs Blakely. As far as I'm concerned no one could ever take her place, but I am to have a new stepmother.'

'Then I 'ope you'll all be very 'appy together,' the stout little woman told her.

Daisy handed the grocer her list and she stood primly with her eyes straight ahead while he collected what she needed. When her basket was piled high, she paid him quickly and with a curt nod at the assorted women she left the shop as fast as her feet would carry her, feeling humiliated. What would her father say if he knew what was being said? she wondered.

The snow had thankfully stopped and the paths were treacherously slippery, but Daisy hardly noticed as she hurried for home. How could she tell him? It would break his heart and he seemed so happy, so who was she to spoil it for him? And so, she decided that the best thing to do was to keep her own counsel.

That evening when her father visited Victoria, he finally brought up a subject that had been preying on his mind. They had already gone to see Reverend Bailey and the date for the wedding was set to be the first Saturday in April, but as yet they hadn't discussed where they were to live.

'So, my dear,' he said tentatively over dinner, which he noticed wasn't quite as grand as it normally was. 'I suppose you will want me and Daisy to come here and live after we are married. I can quite understand why, after all, this place is so much grander than ours.'

Victoria placed her knife and fork down and dabbed at her lips with a snow-white napkin. '*Dear* Edward,' she said fawningly. 'You are *so* kind to think of me. But no, it would make sense if the boys and I were to come and live with you. After all, I don't like to think of you having to traipse back and forth to the forge each day to work. I thought perhaps I could put my house up for sale after the wedding. There's no point in it standing empty.'

'Are you sure?' He was trying to hide the relief from his face. He had never felt quite comfortable in such luxurious surroundings, and he knew Daisy didn't either. 'But what about your servants? I only have four bedrooms and there would be nowhere for them to sleep.'

'Don't worry about that. As it happens, I have already let the maid go and I think the cook will go to live with her daughter. She should have retired years ago, if truth be told. And as for Jackson, the groom . . . Well, I'm sure he will be able to find himself another position. But I will, of course, want to bring some of my furniture and my curtains with me. Will that be a problem? I just think I will feel more at home with some of my own things about me.'

'Of course, you must bring whatever you like,' he assured her. 'I want you to feel comfortable. I can store anything of mine in the barn.'

He could hardly wait to get home and give Daisy the good news. At least this way she would be able to stay in the home she had been brought up in. He asked Victoria tentatively, 'And are you planning on selling this place?'

'I have an agent coming to value it this week,' she told him and again he was relieved. 'But now I must update you on the wedding plans. I've been to discuss my bouquet and the arrangements to decorate the church with the florist. I'm afraid they're going to be rather expensive as I've chosen white orchids and gypsophila, but I reasoned we're only going to get married once, so I don't want to skimp. I shall be going to London tomorrow to be measured for my wedding gown and I've already booked the room above the Kingsholme for the reception. I've also ordered the invitations.'

'I see.' Jed looked slightly uncomfortable, before suggesting gently, 'But don't you think it would make more sense to just have a quiet affair? We could have the reception at the Lord Nelson in the village. It's not as if it's the first wedding for either of us, is it? Planning a big affair is making so much work for you.'

'Oh, I don't mind in the least.' She flashed him a suggestive smile that made his legs turn to jelly as she placed her hand on his knee and squeezed it gently. 'In actual fact, I'm quite enjoying it.'

Jed wondered just how much all of this was going to cost, but as she continued to stroke his leg he felt himself becoming aroused and knew that she would be worth it, so he said no more. The wedding night couldn't come quickly enough for him.

Chapter Ten

Over the next weeks Gilbert became a regular visitor to the house and although Daisy wasn't comfortable with the situation, she knew there wasn't a lot she could do about it. He was becoming more and more suggestive and had made it clear that he found her attractive, but Daisy tried her best to ignore his unwanted attention.

Early in March, Victoria informed them all that Lewis had passed his final exams. He would be returning home in time for the wedding, which Daisy felt happy about. They'd got on well at Christmas, and she was looking forward to seeing him again.

Spring was her favourite time of the year. The garden and the surrounding countryside were slowly coming back to life after the long, cold winter, and she was able to get out and potter in the garden again. Crocuses and daffodils were peeping through the earth and the tender green buds on the trees were slowly unfurling. Out in the vegetable garden she had already planted cabbages, leeks, onions and carrots, and the borders were full of flowers, all ready to burst into glorious life.

The only dark spot on the horizon was the forthcoming wedding, and the nearer it got the more she dreaded it, although she realised that it was inevitable now – her father was completely under Victoria's spell. Daisy hadn't seen too much of her recently as she'd been too busy organising the wedding and she dreaded to think how much it must all be costing her father. She suspected the gown alone, which Victoria had already had numerous fittings for in London, must have cost more than her father could earn in months, and yet he had never once complained, so Daisy said nothing.

As usual, at mid-morning Daisy made her father a mug of tea and carried it across to the forge. As she opened the door the heat from the huge furnace almost took her breath away. The forge was warm and cosy to work in during the winter but as the weather improved the heat could become unbearable. Jed was shovelling more coal onto the fire – a never-ending job because it had to be kept at a very high temperature to allow him to heat the metal enough to mould it into whatever shape he needed.

He paused to mop the sweat from his brow and smiled. 'Ah, just what the doctor ordered, pet.' He took the mug and had a long drink. 'So what 'ave you been up to this mornin'?'

Daisy looked about at the various buckets and bowls he had made. 'I've been out digging the rest of the vegetable patch,' she told him. 'But I have to pop out to the village now to get some groceries.'

He nodded, then suddenly looked awkward. 'I, er . . . don't know if I mentioned it yet, but Victoria is having some of her furniture brought over this afternoon. We've employed a couple of chaps from the village to bring it on a cart. I dare say she'll come along to show 'em where she wants it to go. Anythin' she wants taken out can be stored in the barn till we decide what to do with it. I've cleared an area an' thought perhaps you could show 'em where it has to go.'

Daisy tried hard not to show her dismay. She loved every stick of the furniture they already had. Each piece had been lovingly chosen over the years by her parents. But she supposed it was only natural that Victoria would want to have some of her own things about her, so she nodded. 'Yes, I can do that. What time are they coming?'

'I shouldn't think it will be till later on.' Jed drained the rest of his mug and handed it back to her. 'Right, I'd best get on. I'll see you at lunchtime, pet.'

She left to fetch her basket and bonnet and made her way into the village. She was gazing into the baker's window wondering if she should treat her father to one of the cream cakes he was so fond of, when a friendly voice sounded over her shoulder. 'Morning, Daisy.'

Turning, she saw Lewis fast approaching and she smiled at him. 'Good morning, how are you? Daddy told me you were coming home. Congratulations on passing your exams. I dare say you'll be looking to start work at a veterinary surgery now.'

'Well, that was the general idea,' he said glumly. 'But I've had no luck whatsoever up to now. None of the practices I've approached need another vet at present. I reckon I might have to look around for something else to do until a position comes up. I can't be doing with just sitting around the house all day like Gilbert does.'

Daisy said nothing. She completely agreed with him. Gilbert was a layabout and if the rumours that were flying around were anything to go by, he was getting himself a rather bad reputation.

'I'm sure something will turn up,' she said instead. 'And what are you up to today?'

'Not a lot,' he admitted. 'So if there's anything you want doing I'd be happy to help.'

Daisy grinned. 'I've been digging the vegetable patch over this morning, or some of it anyway. I've already planted half of it.'

Lewis looked astonished. He had been brought up by a woman who didn't believe in getting her hands dirty and yet Daisy seemed happy to turn her hand to anything that needed doing. She was pretty, too, and he wondered why some young man hadn't snapped her up long ago.

'Anyway, I must get on,' she told him. 'Daddy just told me that your mother is sending over some of the furniture she wants to keep this afternoon, so I have to get back to show the men where to put anything she wants taking out.'

'In that case I'll come over with them later. You know what they say, "many hands make light work". Goodbye for now, Daisy.' He lifted his hat and walked on, feeling uneasy. Poor Daisy clearly loved her home, but knowing his mother as he did, she would probably change the whole place beyond recognition. The only good thing was that his mother's house was very much bigger than her future husband's so there was no way she would be able to take everything, otherwise they would have no room to move around.

It was mid-afternoon when a cart loaded with furniture arrived at Daisy and Jed's home, with Victoria in her smart chaise close behind it. She breezed into the kitchen without even knocking, as if she already owned the place, and Daisy, who was taking a tray of scones from the range oven, looked up startled.

'Oh . . . Victoria, good afternoon. Daddy said to expect you.'

As Victoria stared at her, her eyes were cold. 'You shall soon have to get used to calling me Mother,' she said.

Daisy frowned. She would never call any woman mother but her own, but she didn't argue for now.

The woman turned and crooked her finger at the men standing by the cart. 'Come in.'

The two men, who Daisy recognised from the village, appeared in the doorway and, taking their caps off, nodded towards Daisy as Victoria stood looking about the room.

'Hmm, well you can take that out for a start,' she said imperiously, just as Lewis arrived to join them.

'The *dresser*?' Daisy looked dismayed. 'But my daddy made that for my mammy when they were first married!'

Victoria shrugged and forced a smile. 'Then it's time you had a change. Oh, and get those pots off it would you? I'd like to use my own china. I hope you don't mind?'

Daisy bit her lip as she began to remove all her mammy's precious china and place it on the table.

'Hold on, Mother,' Lewis said, seeing Daisy's distress. 'The dresser obviously means something to Daisy so couldn't you at least keep that?'

'No, I could *not*,' his mother told him haughtily. 'And please don't interfere in things you know nothing about, dear. Our furniture is far superior to anything in here and I'm sure Daisy won't mind. Why would we settle for this when we have so much better?' She gestured at the dresser.

Within minutes the china and cutlery had been removed from the drawers and Daisy watched with a sinking heart as the two men began to heft the dresser out of the door.

'Where do you want it put, or is it going to be burned?' Victoria turned her attention back to Daisy and in that instant Daisy started to really dislike her.

'No, it is *not* going to be burned,' she ground out as she blinked back tears, and following the men she asked them, 'Could you put it over here in the barn for me, please?'

'O' course we can, love,' the older of the men answered, feeling sorry for her.

Daisy led them into the barn. 'Just over there by the wall, if you would, and then I'll fetch a sheet to cover it so it doesn't get damaged.'

By the time she got back to the kitchen there was a fine oak court cupboard in the dresser's place. It was a beautiful piece but to Daisy's mind it looked completely out of place in their humble

71

home, but again she didn't say anything. Victoria would soon be the lady of the house, after all, so she would have the major say in things. It was going to be hard to get used to.

The next things to go were the table and chairs, again to be replaced by the ones from the bride-to-be's kitchen. It was considerably larger than the one Daisy was used to and dwarfed the room a little, but Victoria seemed happy with it.

'Hmm . . .' The woman looked around thoughtfully. 'Those awful chairs to either side of the fireplace will have to go too,' she announced. 'And that settle. I shall bring the ones from my day room another time, so they can stay for now.' Next she swept into the small parlour. 'Right, that can go. Is there anything in it?' She pointed to the small sideboard that stood against one wall and Daisy rushed forward to empty it. Within no time at all that too had gone to join the table, chairs and dresser in the barn, and a much bigger, ornate mahogany one, which she recognised from Victoria's dining room, stood in its place.

Next to be carted away was the three-piece suite that her mother had been so proud of, and at this point Daisy knew she could stand no more without getting upset. 'I-I shall be upstairs if you need me,' she told her future stepmother in a choked voice, and she shot past Lewis and up the stairs.

'Go easy, Mother,' Lewis urged in a concerned voice. 'This is Daisy's home you're pulling apart!'

'Oh, don't be so ridiculous, dear. It's only furniture.' She continued to bark orders at the men until eventually there was not a stick of the original furniture left in the room. Even the old log basket to the side of the fireplace had been replaced with a highly polished brass one.

'Hmm, that's better,' she said when everything had been set out to her satisfaction. 'Although these awful curtains will have to go. I shall bring some of my velvet ones to put in their place. Whoever made these was clearly a novice at sewing and the material is so cheap! Now, I think we should start upstairs. I want everything brought down out of the three bedrooms that you, me and Gilbert will be using. Daisy's can stay as it is.'

During the afternoon the men returned to Victoria's house twice more to reload the cart and by teatime the place was almost unrecognisable. Daisy stayed in her room, unable to look, until finally she heard her father enter the kitchen. The men and Lewis were just carrying in the last of the bedroom furniture as Daisy appeared from the stairs' door, her eyes red and swollen from crying. Victoria appeared not to notice but Jed did, and he looked concerned.

'Are you all right, pet? You look a bit peaky.'

'I'm fine, Daddy. Just a bit of a headache.' Daisy crossed to peck him on the cheek.

Victoria frowned. He smelled of smoke and was grubby from the day's work and as he made to put his arm about her, she stepped away.

'Forgive me, Edward, but this is a new gown and I don't want you to get it dirty,' she simpered, looking at him disapprovingly. Her late husband had never been seen without his hair slicked down with brilliantine and a starched white shirt and collar on. But then, he had been a gentleman whereas Jed was merely a manual worker. It was going to take her a lot of getting used to.

'Of course.' His eyes swept the room and just as Daisy's had, his stomach sank. It didn't look like his home anymore and he wasn't sure he liked the changes. Victoria's grand furniture looked out of place in his much humbler dwelling, but he supposed he would have to get used to it.

'All the new bedroom furniture is in place too,' she informed him. 'Apart from the beds, of course, and we can't bring those just yet. We have to keep something to sleep on.' She tittered as

73

if she had said something highly amusing but for once Jed didn't respond. She went on, 'Everything that was in your wardrobe and drawers is in a pile on the floor. I'm sure Daisy will go and put them away for you.'

Daisy looked at Lewis and saw that he was scowling so she quickly lowered her eyes.

'And now I think I've done all I can for one day.' In actual fact, Victoria hadn't done anything apart from dish out orders as far as Daisy could see. 'So I'll be off, darling. Don't be late for dinner, will you? Oh, and do be sure to have a bath before you come.' And with that she swept from the room followed by the men she had employed to help, leaving only Lewis, who was twisting his hat in his hands and looking extremely uncomfortable.

'I can only apologise for my mother's behaviour today, Daisy,' he said haltingly. 'I'm afraid when she's on a mission she tends to get carried away. Would you like me to stay and help you put your father's clothes away?'

'There's no need for you to apologise, and thank you, but no, I can do Daddy's clothes.'

'In that case I'll get off and leave you in peace.' Lewis nodded towards Jed, who looked grim-faced.

After he'd gone, Daisy and her father stared around. They both felt as if they were in someone else's home. Rags slunk back into the kitchen almost on his belly. He had fled the moment Victoria had arrived, as had the cats. It was as if they could sense that she didn't like them.

'They put Mammy's lovely dresser in the barn,' Daisy said with a catch in her voice.

Feeling as if he was trapped between the devil and the deep blue sea, Jed put his arms around her, and she laid her head on his chest and sobbed broken-heartedly.

Chapter Eleven

It was the day of the wedding and as Daisy got ready there was a sick feeling in the pit of her stomach. The only room in the house that resembled the home she had known and loved was her own bedroom – Victoria obviously thought she wasn't important enough to bother changing anything in there. Daisy was glad. It was the only room where she felt comfortable and she sometimes thought her father felt the same, for he didn't seem to be particularly happy with the changes Victoria had made to the rest of the house.

The parlour now had gilt-framed mirrors and pictures hanging on the walls, rather than the cheap sketches that her mother had cherished. Daisy had packed them carefully away in boxes in the barn, never to be parted with. She just prayed that the rats didn't get to them. The cats managed to keep the population down somewhat, but it was impossible to be rid of them altogether. The kitchen was also changed. As well as the fancy court cupboard and the huge table and chairs, there were now two velvet-covered wing chairs on either side of the fireplace, which looked completely out of place. Expensive rugs that Daisy was almost afraid to step on covered the floors and rich velvet and damask curtains, which were far too big, were draped at the windows. Only her bedroom curtains remained and, although the flowers on them were faded, she only had to close her eyes to picture her mother sitting at the side of the fire stitching them.

A few weeks before, Jed had tentatively suggested that his wife-to-be might like to have Daisy as her attendant at the wedding, but to Daisy's relief, Victoria had shrugged the idea away saying that there really wasn't enough time to get a suitable gown made. Daisy would have preferred not to attend the wedding at all but she didn't want to let her father down.

Her father had insisted she had a new gown for the wedding, and now she stared at her reflection. The dress was a pretty shade of pale blue with wide petticoats and a full skirt, and trimmed with lace at the neckline and the cuffs. It was made of a soft satin that gleamed in the spring sunshine pouring through the window, and her father had even treated her to a new bonnet trimmed with silk flowers and tied beneath the chin with a blue ribbon to match her dress.

Of course it would be nowhere near as grand as the bride's, which Victoria had told her had a fashionable bustle at the back. But Daisy didn't much care about fashion, and she loved the dress, although she wondered how often she would get to wear it.

The night before, Daisy had carried the tin bath in from the yard, and she and her father had taken turns to wash their hair and bathe. Daisy grinned as she wondered how Victoria would manage with such primitive washing facilities. Her own house sported an indoor bathroom where hot water was fed through a pipe from the kitchen straight into the bath. Already Victoria had suggested Jed should look at having something similar built when they returned from their honeymoon, but as yet he hadn't agreed to it. He wasn't sure that he'd be able to afford it even if he wanted to – not until Victoria had sold her house and they had some more money. The wedding was going to be a very lavish affair and then there was the added expense of a week in London following the reception, which Victoria had insisted upon.

'But, darling,' she had purred as she leant against him. 'How can we possibly begin our married life in the same house with all our children around us? I want us to at least have a little time alone.'

So Jed had eventually agreed, just as he had to all her other demands. It would be down to Daisy to clean and cook for Lewis and Gilbert while the newly-weds were away. Daisy didn't mind – she had never been afraid of hard work – but she did wonder what arrangements Victoria had made for a cook and cleaner for when they got back. She couldn't imagine her stepmother doing anything for herself and Daisy wouldn't be able to do all of the work herself with three more people in the house. Still, she hadn't yet raised the matter. There would be time enough for that when her father and Victoria got home.

'Daisy . . . come an' 'elp me wi' this blessed cravat, would yer, pet?'

Daisy grinned; her father was a bag of nerves. She hurried along the landing to help him and found him standing in his room with a frown on his face and sweat on his brow. He looked very smart in the new suit and waistcoat that Victoria had insisted he should have, but he didn't look comfortable.

'Ah, here you are,' he said as Daisy appeared and he blinked as he stared at her. 'Bye 'eck! You gave me a turn there, pet. I thought it were your mammy standin' there for a moment. You look beautiful.'

Daisy smiled as she began to tie his cravat. 'You don't look so bad yourself.'

'This is the first new suit I've 'ad since I married yer mammy,' he grumbled. 'An' I can't wait to get out of it already. This bloody cravat 'as got a mind of its own an' I'm all fingers an' thumbs.' He stood quite still until the cravat was tied to Daisy's satisfaction then taking her hands, he looked deep into her eyes. 'Yer know 'ow much I love yer, don't yer?' There was a catch in his voice. 'An' I don't want yer thinkin' that you'll mean any less to me once I'm wed to Victoria. You'll allus be the most important person in me life. Yer mammy would be proud if she could see yer now.'

'I know,' Daisy answered in a wobbly voice. 'Now come along, we don't want to keep the bride waiting, do we?'

Side by side they left the house and headed off for the church. It was a beautiful day with not a cloud in the sky and as St Lawrence's came into view, they were both shocked to see how many people were congregated there.

'Crikey, I reckon she's invited everyone within a five-mile radius,' Jed commented, his voice cracking with nerves. Daisy saw Gilbert amongst the crowd and when he spotted her, he made a beeline towards her, eyeing her appreciatively.

'May I say you look particularly pretty today?' he said in a smarmy voice.

'Thank you,' Daisy replied coolly as she sailed past him into the church.

Lewis was going to give his mother away and Daisy wondered how he was feeling. She'd seen quite a lot of him over the last weeks because he'd still had no luck getting a job in a veterinary practice so Jed had set him on doing some of the simpler jobs in the forge. To his surprise Lewis had taken to it. He was a quick learner and Jed had told him that should he decide it was something he would like to do full-time he would be more than happy to take him on as his apprentice. Of course, being a blacksmith was a far cry from the job he had planned so he hadn't made a decision yet, but Jed was hoping that he'd join him.

The church was resplendent with huge vases of flowers placed in every nook and cranny, their scent filling the air, and as Daisy walked down the aisle to take her seat at the front of the church, the bells began to peal. She stared up at the stained-glass windows with tears in her eyes. From today onwards life would never be the same, but for her father's sake she was determined to make the best of the situation.

Slowly the church began to fill and the organist took his seat as the vicar and Jed took their places. The organist began to play, and a hush fell on the assembled crowd – the bride had arrived. As one everyone turned to watch her progress down the aisle on the arm of her son and they had to admit that she looked truly beautiful. The cream silk gown and matching hat she was wearing were magnificent and she carried herself regally.

Daisy stood quite still throughout the service, and soon it was over. The ring was on Victoria's finger and the new Mrs Armstrong looked like the cat that had got the cream.

'I just wonder 'ow long this one'll last?' Daisy heard someone behind her whisper. 'The last two both met wi' unfortunate ends, bless 'em. An' poor Jed, eh? She would only have gone fer 'im cos there weren't anyone better on the scene.'

Daisy gulped as she kept her eyes fixed on her father. He was leading his new wife back down the aisle and they emerged from the gloom of the church to a hail of rice. She just had the reception to get through now then thankfully it would all be over. She noted her father was beaming from ear to ear and looked as proud as punch, and although she had her reservations about Victoria, she hoped he would be happy.

'Daisy, you can come with me and Gilbert in the trap,' Lewis told her, and she smiled her thanks.

The reception proved to be just as lavish as Daisy had expected. There was a three-course meal, and the champagne and wine flowed like water, but eventually it was time for Lewis to take the newly-weds to the station to catch the train to London.

Before he left, Jed sought Daisy out to give her a cuddle. 'You look after yourself now,' he told her solemnly. He had never left her before and she couldn't help but smile.

'Daddy, I shall be perfectly all right. It's not as if I'm going to be on my own, is it? I have Gilbert and Lewis here to keep an eye on me. You just go and enjoy yourself and I'll see you next week.'

She followed the bride and groom out to the waiting trap, amused to see that someone had decorated it with tin cans on string to rattle behind it and a 'Just married' sign across the back. Jed helped Victoria up into her seat and as Lewis urged the horse on everyone threw more rice and shouted good wishes after the couple as they rattled away.

'That's it then.' Gilbert grinned as he sidled up next to Daisy. 'We're officially related now.'

'Yes, I suppose we are,' Daisy agreed solemnly. 'You're now my stepbrother.'

He leered at her. 'Legally, yes, but that doesn't mean we couldn't become close in a different way,' he whispered suggestively as he tried to put his arm about her.

He'd had an awful lot to drink and Daisy was worried he was going to make a spectacle of them both. 'I suggest you go back inside and get a waitress to make you some strong coffee.' Daisy shrugged his arm away, her expression leaving him in no doubt that she was more than annoyed with him. 'I'm going home.' It would be a long walk from there back to Ansley but she would have walked twice the distance if it meant getting rid of Gilbert. As it turned out she didn't have to because as she was climbing the Cock and Bear hill, Lewis pulled up beside her in the trap.

'Want a lift?'

'Ooh, yes please.' Daisy's new shoes were pinching, so she was more than grateful for the offer, especially as Gilbert wasn't with him.

'Where's Gilbert?' he asked once they were on their way.

Daisy shrugged. 'The last I saw of him he was heading into town.'

'He's no doubt got a card game on somewhere.' He shook his head. 'That brother of mine is bone idle. I blame my mother because she's always spoilt him. He's never done a day's work in his life.'

Daisy chose not to comment. She wasn't sure what to say, although she agreed with him.

As soon as they drew up outside the house, Daisy hurried in to let Rags out while Lewis went to stable the horse and give him a rub down.

Rags greeted her ecstatically but as Daisy stared around the room, which no longer looked like home, the enormity of the change that was about to take place in her life got the better of her and she had to gulp back tears. Her father would be well on the way to London with his new wife now and she could only pray, after all the gossip she had heard about Victoria, that she would treat him right.

By the time Lewis came in she had the kettle on and had lit the fire, for although it was spring it could still be chilly at night.

As Lewis stood by the door looking uncomfortable, she realised this was going to be as big a change for him as it was for her.

'I, er . . . wondered if it was all right for me to go up and get changed?' he asked uncertainly.

'Of course it is.' Daisy flashed him a warm smile. 'This is your home now. You can go wherever you want. You don't have to ask my permission.'

'It just feels a bit strange.'

She nodded. 'I know, it does for me too, but I dare say we'll get used to it. Anyway, when you've changed, I'm making a cup of tea if you'd like one and then I'll do us a bit of supper.'

'Oh, after that huge meal I shan't want a lot.' He returned her smile. 'But thanks for offering, and don't worry, I shall pull my weight about the place. I shan't expect you to wait on me.'

Half an hour later as they sat together at the kitchen table enjoying a cup of tea, Daisy asked him, 'When will your mother be putting your house up for sale? And what will she do with all the stuff that's left in it?'

'You know as much as me.' He sighed. 'Every time I've brought the subject up, she's snapped my head off and told me she'll do it when she's ready.'

'Perhaps it's hard for her to leave?' Daisy suggested, although she didn't imagine that Victoria was the sort of woman who would become emotionally attached to a house.

Lewis snorted with laughter. 'I doubt that's the reason. Mother doesn't get emotional about much.'

'Ah well, I dare say she'll do it when she feels ready.' Rags had slunk across to Lewis and laid his head on his lap. Daisy was pleased to see that Lewis was gently stroking him.

'I don't think your mother likes Rags much,' she said quietly.

'She doesn't believe in pets,' he informed her. 'Ever since I was little, I've been begging her to let me have a dog or a cat, but she wouldn't hear of it. I think my father would have, though, if he hadn't been so under the thumb.' He shook his head. 'Unfortunately, my mother is a very strong-minded woman. I just hope your father will be able to stand up to her otherwise she'll be ruling the roost in no time.'

Daisy frowned. Up to now her father had been like putty in Victoria's hands and she could only hope that now they were married he would be firmer with her. But only time would tell.

Chapter Twelve

A week later Lewis harnessed Fancy to the trap and went to collect Jed and Victoria from the station. It was late morning and Daisy had a roast beef dinner cooking, which would be ready for the newly-weds when they got home.

Gilbert was still in bed, and she sighed as she stared up at the ceiling. The last week hadn't been easy, for Gilbert seemed to think she was there to wait on him hand and foot, which she had no intention of doing. He seemed to sleep most of the day then stay out most of the night, rolling in at all hours and setting Rags off barking. His clothes would be flung all over the place, and for the first part of the week Daisy had put them away for him, but now she was leaving them where they were, much to his disgust.

As if her thoughts had conjured him, the door at the bottom of the stairs opened and he appeared, unshaven and looking very much the worse for wear.

'Oh, my head,' he groaned as he stumbled his way to the table. 'Get me some tea.'

'There's some in the pot, get it yourself,' Daisy said coldly. He was wearing crumpled trousers and a vest with his braces dangling around his knees, and as he snapped them across his shoulders, he glared at her. 'You wouldn't dare talk to me like that if my mother were here.'

Daisy laughed. 'Oh, believe me, I would.'

'And where are my clean shirts?' he whined.

Daisy raised an eyebrow. 'Where did you put them?'

'I threw them on the floor in my bedroom to be collected and washed and ironed.'

'Then that's where they'll still be.' Hands on hips she glared back at him. 'If you think I've got time to go fetching and carrying your dirties, you've got another think coming! I don't mind washing and ironing them for you if you bring them downstairs but I'm not a skivvy.'

Gilbert pouted like a spoilt child. 'What's for breakfast?'

'Whatever you feel like making for yourself. Lewis and I had ours hours ago. In fact, the dinner's cooking now.'

With a groan Gilbert fetched a mug and poured some of the stewed tea from the pot into it before grimacing. 'Ugh, this is lukewarm and stewed.'

'So? Make another one.' With an unsympathetic glance Daisy lifted her skirt and went out to feed the chickens, who were pecking amongst the cobblestones in the yard. It had been a funny old week one way or another, she mused, as she scattered the corn for the hungry birds. Lewis had been a great help. Every morning he fetched the coal and the logs in for her and he wasn't afraid to help with the washing and drying up either, whereas Gilbert had been a different kettle of fish altogether.

One morning, she had walked in on the brothers having a bitter argument.

'But if you don't lend me the money I'm done for,' she heard Gilbert plead. 'I lost at cards last night to George Bailey and you know what a reputation he's got! He'd break your knees as soon as look at you if you crossed him.'

'Then you shouldn't have upset him, should you?' Lewis was unbending. He'd helped his brother out of too many scrapes in the past, but now he'd decided it was time to leave him to stand on his own two feet.

Daisy had scuttled by them, her cheeks burning, and minutes later Gilbert had thundered out of the house with a face like a black cloud, not to be seen again until the early hours of the following morning, sporting a rather nasty-looking black eye and a split lip.

Once back inside, Daisy looked around the room critically. She had polished everything that stood still, even the floor was gleaming. She wanted everything to be just perfect for when the couple returned home.

Gilbert had slouched off upstairs in a sulk and Daisy hoped he would stay there. With Rags at her heels she went back out into the garden to pick a bunch of flowers for the table and once she had arranged them there was nothing to do but wait.

Over an hour later the trap entered the yard and Daisy flew out to meet it, eager to see her father.

'Daddy!' She flung herself into his arms and he kissed her cheek soundly. 'Have you had a wonderful time?'

His face fell slightly and after glancing at his wife he answered, 'Yes, it was very nice, thank you.'

He turned to help Victoria down from the trap and after a nod at Daisy she sailed past her into the kitchen where she proceeded to remove her bonnet and gloves. As always, she looked immaculate in a pale-green two-piece travelling costume. Her eyes flicked around the room but she made no comment as she asked, 'Where is Gilbert?'

'He's up in his room. Would you like me to call him for you?'

As it happened, she didn't have to, for he appeared at that moment looking considerably tidier. He had brushed his hair and put on a shirt and cravat but there was nothing much he could do to hide the fading bruise around his eye or his split lip.

'Oh, my *poor* darling.' Victoria was all concern. 'Whatever has happened to you?'

'It's nothing.' He glanced at Daisy as if he was daring her to contradict him. 'I just, er . . . fell over in the dark one evening coming home.'

'I do hope Daisy put some raw steak on it for you.' The woman stroked his cheek tenderly as Daisy hurried away to make some tea while her father carried their luggage in. They certainly seemed to be coming back with a lot more than they had gone away with. But she knew the woman's reputation for shopping, so she wasn't really surprised.

'I hope you're hungry,' she said brightly, hoping to get off on the right foot. 'I've got you a nice roast beef dinner ready.'

'That sounds just the job.' Her father smiled but Victoria made for the stairs.

'I'm afraid I'm getting a headache after all that travelling,' she said. 'So keep mine warm for me, would you, Daisy? I shall have it when I've had a little lie-down.'

Daisy felt a little disappointed. She had hoped they could all eat together, but she said nothing.

While they ate, Jed told them all about the sights they'd seen in London, and though Gilbert was still grumpy and barely listened, Lewis and Daisy listened with interest.

'The meal was wonderful, pet,' Jed told Daisy when they had finished. 'But Lewis tells me another big order from the hardware shop came in while I was away so I think I'll go and get changed and make a start on it. There's no point in sitting about all afternoon now I'm home.'

'I'll help you,' Lewis offered. 'Unless Daisy needs a hand with the pots?'

Daisy smiled gratefully at him as she began to load them onto a tray. 'I shall be fine, thank you.' She noticed that Gilbert hadn't offered yet again. Instead he'd slunk away to his room without a word.

By the time Victoria came down it was nearing teatime. 'Where is Edward?' she asked, scanning the room.

'Oh, he and Lewis went to start on an order some time ago.'

Nodding towards her luggage, which was still stacked at the side of the door, Victoria said sweetly, 'That will all need unpacking.'

Daisy steeled herself, took a deep breath and said, 'Perhaps you'd be better to unpack it yourself. And then you'll know where everything is.'

'Unpack it myself? But my maid always did that sort of thing when I was back in my own home!' Victoria was clearly indignant at the idea, but Daisy merely gave her a sweet smile.

'I dare say she did, but you're not in your old home now and you don't have a maid, do you? Actually, I was wondering about that. Now there are three more people in the house will you be employing someone to help with the washing, ironing, cleaning and cooking, or will you be helping me?'

'*Me?*' Victoria's hand flew to her throat and she began to fiddle with her pearl necklace. Daisy had never seen it before and guessed it was one she had purchased in London. 'Why . . . I wouldn't have a clue how to go about such menial tasks. I've never had to do them.'

'There's a first time for everything. I'll teach you,' Daisy said cheerily as she lifted two mugs from the table. 'If you'll excuse me, I'm going to take this tea over to Daddy and Lewis. I'm sure they'll be ready for it by now.'

Victoria narrowed her eyes as she sank into a chair. 'What, you mean Lewis is over in the forge again? I do hope he isn't thinking of making this a permanent pastime, after all the money his father and I spent on his education.'

'It's hardly a pastime and there's nothing wrong with being a blacksmith,' Daisy pointed out as she headed for the door. She was already getting annoyed with the woman, but she tried to calm down. After all, things could surely only get better?

When Lewis and Jed returned to the house late that afternoon, Victoria was still seated in the kitchen, and looking none too happy.

'Hello, sweet'eart.' Jed bent to kiss her, but she turned her cheek and his face fell.

'Oh, Edward *really*! Do get changed out of those *filthy* clothes. You *smell* of smoke!'

'That's probably cos I've been workin' next to a hot furnace all afternoon,' he said with a frown. But he went off to wash and change just the same.

By the time he came back Daisy was placing a pile of sandwiches and a fresh sponge cake she had made on the table and again Victoria expressed her disapproval. 'It's so common to have the main meal at lunchtime,' she griped. 'In our house we always had dinner in the evening.'

'Ah, but Daisy cooked especially at that time for us today cos she thought we'd be hungry when we got back. And anyway, I am common, as you know.' His eyes settled on the luggage still standing to the side of the door then. 'Shall I carry that lot up to our room for you?'

She sniffed. 'I suppose so. I asked Daisy to put it away for us, but she refused.'

'Yes, I did,' Daisy said defensively. 'Because as I told you if I put it away you won't know where anything is.' She turned to her father. 'And I also asked if Victoria was thinking of getting a maid to help in the house now there are so many of us, or if she would like to help me herself?'

'Well, as soon as the other house is sold, I'm sure we can arrange something,' Jed answered as his wife quickly averted her eyes. 'Speaking of which, now that we're 'ome there don't seem much point in delayin' the sale, does there? Would you like me to get the agent who went out to value it to put it on the market for you?'

'No, no, there's no need to rush,' she said in a fluster. 'There are still things back there that I need to sort and then I'll instruct the agent myself.'

'As you wish, my dear.' He sat down at the table with Lewis and they tucked into the sandwiches.

Victoria eyed Rags, who was sleeping peacefully in front of the fire, with contempt. 'I'd like you to get a kennel built for that . . . that *dog* now that we're home, Edward,' she said frostily. 'It won't hurt him to sleep outside in the better weather. It's *so* unhygienic having it in here!'

At this point Daisy was so incensed that she forgot all about trying to make an effort and ground out, 'Rags isn't an *it*!'

Victoria sucked in her breath and her cheeks reddened as she turned on her husband. 'Edward, are you going to let her speak to me like that? Surely, *I* am the lady of the house now, so what I say should go!'

Jed stared between the two women with a look of bewilderment but thankfully it was Lewis who saved the day when he piped up, 'Mother, I'm sure you'll get used to Rags if you just give him a chance. He's a friendly chap and he's very old. It wouldn't be fair to change his routine at this stage in his life. You wouldn't want his death on your conscience, would you?'

Victoria swallowed. She could have said that there was nothing that would give her more satisfaction than to see the mangy old beast dead, but she realised she was going to have to handle this situation carefully, so she sighed, 'Very well. I shall *try* to get used to him.'

She was rewarded with a dazzling smile from Jed, who had felt for a moment like he was stuck between the hammer and the anvil.

As soon as he had eaten his fill, Jed carried the cases up to their room and stared about him. It didn't feel like his room anymore. The old dressing table that he had bought for Mauve from a second-hand shop in Nuneaton many years ago now stood covered over in the barn with the rest of his late wife's treasures. When he closed his eyes, he could still see the look of pleasure on her face the day he had brought it home on the back of the cart and unloaded it for her. She had loved it and over the years she had polished it to a mirror-like shine. All through the spring and summer she would keep a vase of wildflowers on it but now the gleaming rosewood one that had taken its place was covered in fancy glass bottles of expensive French perfume.

With a sigh he crossed to the window and flicked aside the heavy damask drapes that had replaced the old, flowered cotton ones. His second marriage was not working out at all as he had hoped. On their wedding night, after booking into the expensive hotel Victoria had insisted they stay in, he had soon come to realise that despite the suggestive looks and kisses he had received before the wedding, Victoria was not at all keen on the physical side of marriage. She had lain quite still during their lovemaking, her stiff stance telling him more loudly than any words that this was something to be endured rather than enjoyed. At the time he had hoped it was because they had had a big day and she was tired, but things hadn't improved. Still, he told himself as he tried to look on the bright side, she was having to make many adjustments so things might improve with time. He could only hope so.

Chapter Thirteen

May 1881

Over the next month things did not improve and soon Daisy was worn out. Victoria was reluctant to do anything to help around the house and no longer even attempted to be pleasant to her. With three extra people in the house, Daisy often worked from early in the morning until late at night, a fact that was not lost on Jed, who was growing increasingly concerned.

'Can't you leave that for today, pet?' Jed asked one sunny morning early in May as he caught Daisy busily scrubbing sheets in the laundry room.

'They won't do themselves, Daddy.' She smiled as she rose from the tub and wiped the sweat from her brow. 'And I want to get them on the line before I go shopping, although I don't have much money left for that.'

The household bills had risen alarmingly and there was something Jed needed to do. In fact, he decided, there was no time like the present.

He strode purposefully back into the house where he found Victoria sitting reading a book.

'Victoria, I'd like a word.'

She stared at the old leather apron he was wearing with distaste before nodding. 'Go ahead.'

Jed took a deep breath. 'I don't want yer to feel like I'm pushin' yer, pet,' he began tentatively. 'But the thing is I used up most o' me savin's on the weddin' and our trip to London. I've noticed that Daisy is lookin' tired an' so I'm thinkin' that the sooner we can get your house sold the sooner I could get someone in to 'elp 'er out a bit.'

To his astonishment Victoria's face suddenly crumpled and she lowered her head.

'Why, pet, whatever's the matter.' He rushed over and took a seat at the side of her.

'Oh, Edward . . . I-I'm *so* ashamed,' she said tearfully. 'You see . . . the thing is, there is no house to sell. I didn't know how to tell you.'

'What do you mean?'

She gulped. 'It seems that when my husband died, he left us horribly in debt. The bank has foreclosed on the house and all the shops, so I'm left with . . . with nothing apart from the furniture that I brought with me. I've tried to tell you, but I could never bring myself to do it. I'm so sorry!'

Jed was shocked. He hadn't married the woman for her money, far from it, but he had hoped that what she brought with her would help to keep her in the manner she was accustomed to.

'So what will we do now?' she asked in a small voice as he sat there trying to take it all in.

'It appears there ain't a lot we can do,' he told her. 'But you should 'ave told me afore. Had I known this I'd never 'ave allowed you to organise such a swanky weddin'.' He thought for a moment. 'There's no way we can afford to get any help in for Daisy now, so unfortunately, you're goin' to 'ave to pitch in. An' Gilbert will 'ave to get out an' find a job an' all. There's no reason why he shouldn't. He's young an' healthy.'

Victoria looked distraught as she wrung her hands. 'But he isn't trained to do anything. And I wouldn't have a clue how to cook and clean!'

'Then you'll 'ave to learn,' he told her in a strict voice. It was the first time he had addressed her like this and she began to cry even harder.

'Oh, Edward, I'm *trying*, but everything is so different here,' she sobbed.

He instantly felt contrite. 'I know, my dear. Don't worry. Things will work out. We'll just have to tighten our belts a little and pull together more. Now if you'll excuse me, I must get back to work. Lewis is proving to be quite a hit with the local farmers and I have some of Farmer Brady's horses coming in to be shod. I'm teaching Lewis how to do it now because since word has spread that he's a qualified vet, they all want advice from him at the same time, and there don't seem to be enough hours in the day.'

He patted her hand then stood up and strode away grim-faced. He could understand why his wife had been hesitant to tell him about the mess her late husband had left her in, but if only she had there was no way he would ever have allowed her to plan such an extravagant wedding and honeymoon. Still, it was done now and Jed was a great one for taking things in his stride, although he hoped that Victoria would start to help about the house a little more. It wasn't fair to leave all the extra work for Daisy to cope with alone.

Lewis, however, was turning out to be a willing worker and better still, he was thoroughly enjoying what he was doing. Only that week he had informed his mother that he'd agreed to do an apprenticeship with Jed. She hadn't been very happy with the idea. Unlike his mother, Lewis didn't mind getting his hands dirty and Jed was delighted to have him. Hopefully now he'd have someone to pass the business on to as he had once hoped to do with his son.

When he entered the forge, he told Lewis about the conversation with Victoria. There didn't seem much point trying to hide it.

Lewis was horrified. 'I had a sneaking feeling that might be the case,' he admitted. 'I'm so sorry, Jed.'

'Don't be. It ain't your fault, son. An' it ain't as if I married your mam fer her money. I just wish she could have told me afore the weddin' an' we could 'ave 'ad a quieter do.'

'Hmm.' Lewis's eyes twinkled. 'I don't think my mother would have been very happy about that,' he chuckled. 'As you've discovered, she has rather expensive tastes. I think that was my father's undoing. He couldn't keep up with her.'

'Well, she'll 'ave to curb 'er spendin' now,' Jed said grimly.

Three days later, as Daisy stood ironing with the flat iron, Victoria lifted one of the neatly folded petticoats, sniffed and flung it back onto the ironing board just as Jed entered the room.

'Do that again,' she instructed rudely. 'There are still some creases about the hem! My maid always made a much better job of them than that!'

She was unaware that her husband had come to stand behind her with a stony expression on his face, but before he could say anything Daisy beat him to it.

'In that case I suggest you do the rest of your ironing yourself.' Her eyes were flashing. 'And while you're doing it, *I* can start to get the dinner on because I notice that you haven't bothered to!' And with that she slammed the iron down and strode away.

'Why! How *dare* y—' Victoria's words died on her lips as she turned to follow Daisy's progress across the kitchen only to find Jed glaring at her.

'That sounds like a very good idea to me,' he said ominously quietly as he held his wife's gaze. 'In fact, in future it wouldn't hurt you to take on your own washing as well. Daisy has more than enough to do.'

Victoria's eyes welled with tears. 'Oh . . . but, *darling*, I've never ironed an item in my life. I wouldn't know where to start.' Normally her tears melted him but today he remained grim-faced.

'We all have to start somewhere, and I reckon now is as good a time as any.'

Realising that he was going to stand his ground, Victoria stifled a sob and raced towards the staircase. 'I can't believe you're being so hard on me,' she cried and disappeared.

Daisy chewed on her lip wondering what she had started. 'I'm sorry, Daddy,' she began, but Jed held his hand up to stop her flow of words.

'There's no need fer you to be sorry fer anythin', pet.' He shook his head and ran his hand through his thick thatch of hair.

'Trouble in paradise?' A sarcastic voice said and looking around Jed saw Gilbert standing in the kitchen doorway with his jacket slung carelessly across his shoulder. He had obviously heard some of what had gone on.

Jed narrowed his eyes at him. As always Gilbert looked immaculate in his dandy suit and gaily coloured waistcoat. No doubt he'd been drinking with his pals in Nuneaton.

'You could say that,' Jed snapped. 'Your mother has to learn that she ain't a lady o' leisure anymore. She married a workin' man so she's got to pull her weight. An' so 'ave you. When are you gonna do somethin' about gettin' a job? Cos I'll tell you now, me lad, I don't intend to keep you for much longer fer nothin'.'

Gilbert's smirk disappeared and was replaced by a frown as he turned on his heel and stormed out again.

'Good riddance to bad rubbish, that's what I say,' Jed bellowed.

Daisy suddenly wished she had just ironed the petticoat again. Things between herself and her new stepmother had been bad enough before but now she had a feeling they were about to get much worse.

Chapter Fourteen

Just as Daisy had feared, from that day on things between her and Victoria went steadily downhill. When Jed was present Victoria would be civil to her, but when he wasn't she ignored her.

It was now early in July and the weather was so hot that Daisy spent half her time rushing to and from the forge with jugs of lemonade for Jed and Lewis. The heat they had to work in was almost unbearable and Daisy often wondered how they managed it. Today she was busy working in the vegetable garden when suddenly a pair of arms came about her from behind and she started. Turning swiftly, she found herself staring up at Gilbert and colour flooded into her cheeks. She could smell beer on his breath and he was unshaven, having stayed out all night.

'Just what the hell do you think you're doing?' she hissed, her eyes flashing.

'When are you going to stop playing hard to get?' he leered. 'I bet you wouldn't push my goody two-shoes brother away so quickly, would you? I've seen the way you look at each other. Both you and your precious daddy seem to think the sun shines out of his arse.'

Daisy flushed. 'And you're talking out of yours! I've never heard anything so stupid!'

He grinned and leant forward to twist a curl of her hair around his finger.

She furiously slapped his hand away. 'I suggest you go and lie down until you've sobered up,' she growled. 'If Daddy sees you in this state you'll be in trouble.'

Rags, who was lying at the side of the vegetable plot, growled deep in his throat and Gilbert chuckled. 'And I suggest you tell your friend there to mind what he's doing otherwise he just might have a little accident.'

Daisy's hands curled into fists and it took all her willpower to stop herself from smacking his hateful face. 'Don't you *dare* threaten him,' she warned, her voice ominously low.

He laughed. 'Oh, stop being so bloody prim and proper. We could have a good time if you'd only let yourself go a bit. No wonder you're not married – I reckon you must be frigid. You'll end up an old maid if you carry on this way.'

'I'd sooner that than end up married to someone like *you*,' she retaliated hotly.

'Who mentioned marriage? You don't really think someone from *my* background would marry a skivvy like you, do you? Girls like you are only good for having a roll in the hay with!'

When Daisy took a threatening step towards him, he laughed and sauntered away leaving her fuming. Over the last couple of weeks, he had crept up on her more than a few times and she was tired of it now, although she had no idea how to stop it. She knew that if her father discovered what was going on there would be ructions and she was trying to avoid that. Things were strained enough as it was.

'Come on, Rags,' she said. 'Let's go and get a nice cold drink, eh? We can finish this tomorrow.'

Rags obediently waddled after her as she made for the kitchen. Thankfully there was no sign of Gilbert, and Victoria was having afternoon tea with a friend, so for now at least she had the place to herself, which was just as she liked it. As she thought back to what Gilbert had said she felt herself blushing again, for not all of what he had said was untrue. She had come to realise that she *was* fond of Lewis – more than fond if she was honest with herself. He was the only man she had ever felt drawn to, and she suspected that he liked her as well. But as yet they hadn't taken things any further. Just the thought of him made her smile again and she returned to her chores feeling a little better.

Later that evening, as Daisy served dinner, the atmosphere in the kitchen was frosty. Gilbert took a seat without a word and Victoria seemed edgy. Her former home had been sold the week before and the rest of the contents had been auctioned to pay off some of her late husband's debts. The reason for her mood soon became clear when, as they were eating, she suddenly looked at Jed with a dazzling smile to say, 'Darling, when I was having tea with Mrs Byron-Tate this afternoon she mentioned that she's going to London for a few days next week.'

'Oh yes.' Jed kept his attention on the perfectly cooked lamb chops on his plate.

'Yes and . . . well, I was wondering if I might go with her? I think a few days away would do me good and there are a few things I need to buy.'

Jed looked up. 'What sort of things?'

'Well, the autumn will be upon us in no time so I could do with being measured for a new gown for a start.'

'A new *gown*! Why the wardrobe is—'

'Armoire,' she gently corrected him.

'All right then, the *armoire* is already *bulging* with your gowns. I'm having to hang my things on a nail on the back of the door,' Jed pointed out.

'Yes, but they're all last season.' Her smile was gone now as she headed towards a sulk. 'You wouldn't want your wife to be seen in out-of-date clothes, would you?'

Jed shook his head. 'Sorry, my dear. I'm afraid it's out of the question at the moment. There are still some outstanding debts of your husband's that I have to settle, so I'm afraid we can't afford it.' Jed had already discovered that a few days in London with Victoria could be very costly indeed.

'Then when *will* we be able to afford it?' she demanded petulantly.

As Jed looked at her calmly, he suddenly wondered why he had ever been so besotted with her. The woman he had courted had been nothing like the one he now found himself married to. She would never hold a candle to Mauve and already he was regretting his decision. Not that there was anything he could do about it now. He was just going to have to get on with it.

'It could be some time afore I could even think about it,' he said quietly.

Her eyes blazed as she threw her napkin down onto the table. 'It's *before* not *afore*!' she stormed.

Now his anger rose to meet hers. 'You didn't seem to mind how I spoke afore we were wed,' Jed responded hotly. 'You knew then I were a workin' man, so stop tryin' to change me. I am what I am an' I'm too old to change now!'

Daisy dared to glance up from her plate to find Gilbert grinning as he lolled back in his chair. He was clearly enjoying the exchange and her dislike of him grew even more. Lewis, on the other hand, was looking deeply uncomfortable.

'Look, why don't you both calm down a little?' he suggested at which his mother rose so abruptly that she almost overturned the chair before stamping away upstairs.

'That's one way to get out of helping with the washing up,' Gilbert chuckled, and his brother glared at him.

Daisy laid her knife and fork down, her appetite gone, and the rest of the meal passed in silence. As soon as it was over, Jed went upstairs to try and smooth things over, feeling that he should at least try, and Gilbert went out to meet friends leaving Daisy and Lewis alone.

'I'm sorry about that.' Lewis looked embarrassed. 'I know my mother can be difficult and as for Gilbert . . . well!'

'It's all right,' Daisy assured him. It wasn't his fault. He'd tried so hard to make everything run smoothly since moving in, unlike his mother and brother, and he was already proving to be an invaluable help to her father.

Without being asked he started to clear the unfinished meals from the table and they worked together in a companiable silence.

Gilbert returned home late that evening to find his mother sitting at the side of the dying fire looking morose. Her hair was loose about her shoulders and she was in her night robe.

'What are you doing up so late?' Gilbert questioned as he wobbled across the kitchen, smelling strongly of ale and whisky.

'I couldn't sleep,' she answered miserably.

He took a seat opposite her. 'So, having seconds thoughts about this marriage, are you?'

She shrugged. 'I suppose I am, but then I had to get out of the house before they repossessed it, didn't I? Unfortunately, Edward was the only available choice at the time.'

'I did tell you to hold fire, didn't I?' Gilbert said smugly. 'Some other mug would have come along, probably better off than Jed, if you'd waited.'

Her lips quivered as she looked at him. 'And where would we have lived in the meantime?'

Gilbert didn't have an answer to that but after a moment he said quietly, 'Things could change if something were to happen to him. As his wife the house and the business would be yours and you could make whatever changes you wanted.'

'In case you'd forgotten, Edward is still a relatively young man and in the prime of health.'

'So was Father.' He grinned.

She shook her head. 'No, it's too soon.'

Gilbert nodded. 'Very well, have it your own way, but if things get unbearable just give me the nod.' And with that he rose and staggered off to bed leaving Victoria staring thoughtfully into space.

The following morning the postman brought a letter and Daisy's face lit up as she saw the Irish stamp on it, although it didn't look like her granny's handwriting. She had been washing the breakfast pots and her father and Lewis were now working in the forge, but Gilbert and his mother were still in bed. It wasn't unusual, they rarely got up until late morning. Hastily drying her hands on a piece of huckaback, she sat down at the table and slit open the envelope. Inside was a single sheet of paper.

Our Dear Daisy,

I is so sorry to be havin to rite this but I needed to let yu know that yur granny is unwell. The doctor thinks she might have had a mild stroke although she is a bit beter now. If you cud manage a visit I reckon it wud cheer her up to be sure. I ain't much of a leter writer as you can see so excuse me spelin,

With luv

Grampy xxx

Daisy's face crumpled as she thought of the granny she adored and she flew out of the kitchen and across to the forge where Jed and Lewis were shoeing some of the pit ponies.

'Daddy, it's Granny.' Daisy's face showed her deep distress. 'I just had this letter from Grampy and he thinks a visit from me might do her good.'

Jed instantly stopped what he was doing and taking the letter from her quickly scanned it and frowned. 'You must go, pet,' he told her tenderly.

'But how will you all manage if I do?'

Jed smiled. 'Don't you go worrying about that; Victoria will have to pull her weight until you come back. It's overdue, to be fair. When can you be ready to go? I'll take you to the train in the trap.'

Daisy shrugged. Everything was happening so fast. 'Half an hour?'

'Half an hour it is.' Jed gave her a reassuring smile. 'Just go and get yourself ready and pack your belongings. Oh, and stay as long as you need to. We'll all be perfectly all right here.'

Daisy nodded and shot back across to the house to get changed and hastily pack a bag, and within no time she was outside where she saw Lewis waiting with the trap. 'Slight change of plan. I told your father I'd take you,' he said with a smile. 'I'm not quite confident to be shoeing the horses on my own just yet but pop over and say goodbye to him and I'll wait here for you.'

Daisy threw the carpet bag into the trap and rushed back to the forge where her father pressed some notes into her hand. 'Some money for travelling,' he told her. 'And a bit extra in case the old couple are a bit short.'

'Thanks, Daddy.' She stepped into his open arms and hugged him but then he put her from him. 'Go on now, there's no time to lose. And have a safe journey.'

She hurried back to the trap and within seconds they were off.

When they reached the station Lewis offered to carry her bag onto the platform for her, but she shook her head. 'No, it's all right, really, but thanks for the offer.' She hopped down from the seat and retrieved her bag before asking worriedly, 'Are you sure you'll all manage?'

Lewis chuckled, thinking how pretty she was with her hair loose about her shoulders. 'We'll manage just fine. Between you and me I reckon this will be just what my mother needs. While you're there to wait on her hand and foot she'll let you – don't think I haven't noticed how she treats you. But now she'll have to get off her backside and do her bit, won't she?'

Daisy couldn't help but grin. 'All right then. Thanks for the lift. See you soon.' And with that she lifted her skirt and hurried off to the ticket office.

Lewis watched her go feeling strangely bereft. It was odd, he thought, that she hadn't even left and yet he was missing her already.

Chapter Fifteen

It was late that evening when Daisy arrived at her grandparents' cottage. Grampy had Granny sitting in a chair by the fire with a blanket over her knees and he grinned as he told Daisy, 'I think she's slightly better cos she's done nothin' but moan about having to sit about today! She's chewed me ears off, to be sure, an' I can't do nothin' right.'

'Well, I'm here now so I'll take over,' Daisy told him as he gave her a cuddle.

Granny looked pale and her grampy looked worn out and she was glad she had come. She also found it was nice to be away from the tense atmosphere at home, although she would rather have come under happier circumstances.

She made them all some thick cheese sandwiches and cocoa for their supper and as they were eating her granny asked, 'How are you gettin' along wit' your new stepmammy, acushla? I'm so sorry we couldn't make it to the weddin'. I hope your daddy understood, but I reckon the journey would have been a bit too much for us at our age, to be sure.'

'Of course he understood,' Daisy assured her. 'And, er . . . we're getting along all right.'

'Are you now?' Her granny raised her eyebrow. 'An' how about tellin' me the truth? I've allus been able to read you like a book an' I know there's somethin' amiss, so I do.'

'Well . . . I suppose it's just taking some time getting used to having other people in the house,' Daisy said cautiously. She didn't want to risk upsetting her. 'Me and Daddy have been on our own for such a long time.'

Bridie McLoughlin sniffed. 'But it must be nice to have somebody to share the workload?'

'Oh, Lewis is being a great help,' Daisy said quickly. At least that was the truth.

'*And?*' Her grandmother stared at her. 'What about this wealthy widow your daddy married? And don't go tryin' to pull the wool over me eyes, now! I hoped that she'd bring some of her servants with her to take some of the work off you!'

'Actually . . .' Daisy lowered her eyes and started to pick nervously at a loose thread in her skirt. 'It turns out she isn't quite as wealthy as she thought. It seems her husband left her in a lot of debt, so she had to let her staff go.'

'But she helps you, right?' Granny was scowling now and Daisy felt tears burning at the back of her eyes. She could think of nothing to say so she remained silent.

Bridie sighed. 'So now you're runnin' around waitin' on her too, are you? And what about the other son? Gilbert, ain't it? Does he work or do anythin' to help?'

The colour rose in Daisy's cheeks and Granny slammed her hand on the arm of the chair. 'It's like I said to your grampy: it all happened too fast. Your daddy should have taken longer to get to know her properly. Sounds to me like he's taken on a load o' trouble. I wanted to say somethin', after all, as I said to your grampy, "Marry in haste, repent at leisure". But how could I? He would have thought we just didn't want him to put someone in your mammy's place, God rest her soul. She must be turnin' in her grave knowin' that things ain't right. Still, there's no need for you to put up wit' it. There's allus a home here for you wit' me an' Grampy.'

'I can't leave Daddy,' Daisy said in a wobbly voice. 'But I do appreciate the offer, Granny. Things aren't that bad really!'

'Hmm, we'll see.' Granny crossed her arms and glared into the fire. 'Let's just hope your daddy comes to his senses an' starts to put his foot down wit' her. Sounds to me like she needs a good swift kick up the arse!'

Daisy couldn't help but smile and thankfully the subject of her daddy's new wife was dropped, for then at least.

The next two weeks passed peacefully. Daisy hadn't realised how tired she'd been and it was almost like a holiday for her. Gradually her granny improved and took over the running of the house again until finally, after almost a month, Daisy felt she was well enough to be left.

'I think it's time I was heading home,' she told Granny one evening as they sat outside the back door enjoying the flowers in the garden.

'Aw, really?' Granny's face fell. 'I'll miss you, so I will.'

'I'll miss you too.' Daisy looked at her grampy, who was contentedly smoking his pipe, and her granny, whose knitting needles were clicking. 'But I'll come back again soon, I promise.'

The older woman smiled at her fondly. 'Just remember, there's allus a place for you here wit' us if you ain't happy. It'd certainly make young Patrick Donnelly happy if you stayed. He's rarely been off the doorstep since you arrived. It's time you were thinkin' o' settlin' down wit' a nice young man, now.'

Daisy blushed. Patrick lived with his parents in a cottage about half a mile along the lane. He had made it more than clear that he was keen on her, but Daisy didn't feel in the least romantically inclined towards him, so she just chuckled, hoping to bring the conversation to a close, then slipped inside to make them all a last hot drink before they retired.

Three days later, she set off for home early in the morning after a tearful goodbye with her grandparents. She arrived late that evening and the first person she saw as she approached the cottage was Lewis. He was feeding the chickens and when he caught sight of her his face lit up and he rushed to meet her at the gate, Rags wagging his tail beside him.

'Daisy, welcome home. We've missed you.'

Daisy felt herself blush as he took her hand, and a little tingle ran up her arm. 'Thank you. How are things?'

He sighed as he opened the gate for her. 'Er . . . let's just say not running as smoothly as they do when you're here.'

'Oh dear, that sounds daunting,' Daisy answered as they walked across the yard and entered the kitchen. There was no sign of Gilbert, which was no surprise – he was rarely in of an evening – but her father was at the kitchen sink unsuccessfully tackling a towering pile of dirty pots while Victoria was relaxing on a chair to one side of the fireplace.

'Ah, you're back.' Like Lewis her father looked delighted to see her and, wiping his wet hands down the side of his legs, he rushed to give her a hug.

Daisy glanced towards Victoria just in time to see her lip curl with contempt at the sight of his affectionate demonstration. '*Really*, Edward, she isn't a child,' she reproached him.

Jed ignored her as he held Daisy at arm's length. 'How is your granny?'

Daisy dropped her bag onto the floor and stifled a yawn – it had been a very long day. 'She's much better, thank goodness, and she sends her love.'

'Good, now you sit yourself down an' I'll make us all a nice cup o' tea, shall I? Yer look like you could do wi' one.'

As he bustled away Daisy glanced around the room and her heart sank. It didn't look as if it had been cleaned since she had left and she had no doubt the rest of the house would be the same, so she would have her work cut out over the next few days trying to get everything back to rights.

'I've been unwell,' Victoria piped up as she saw the expression on Daisy's face.

'Oh yes? What's the problem?' Daisy didn't believe her for one minute. As she'd discovered, Victoria tended to develop an ailment whenever there was work to be done.

'I, er . . . I've had a very upset stomach.'

'She 'as an' all, so I've 'ad to be 'ead chef an' bottle washer.' Jed chuckled. 'That's probably what upset 'er stomach. I'm all right fryin' a bit o' bacon and an egg but I ain't much good at anythin' else. It's probably all the fatty food she's been eatin' that's made her ill.'

'It probably is,' Victoria said with a scathing glance at Daisy. 'In fact, I think I might go up early. I'm not feeling at all well.'

Once she was gone Jed looked at Daisy apologetically. 'Sorry you've 'ad to come back to such a mess, pet. Victoria 'as tried but . . . well, she just ain't as 'andy about the 'ouse as you are. But me an' Lewis will give you a hand to try an' get it back to rights, won't we, lad?'

Daisy smiled. 'There'll be no need for that, Daddy,' she told him. 'You work hard enough as it is. I'll soon have everything back to normal. But not tonight, I'm so tired I reckon I could sleep on a washing line, so I think I'll go up after this cup of tea, if you don't mind. Leave those pots for now. I'll do them in the morning.'

They sat and shared the pot of tea together and were just finishing when Gilbert came in looking dishevelled.

He glanced at Daisy and said quickly, 'Oh, you're home. Good break, was it?' And before she could answer he shot away upstairs leaving them all to stare after him.

'It's unusual fer 'im to be back this early!' Jed remarked. 'Happen there were no card games this evenin'. It's just as well because' – he lowered his voice – 'he's been tappin' me up fer money all week. I've 'eard the silly young sod owes Mickey Jameson.' He shook his head. 'Bad mistake that. Mickey would break yer kneecaps as look at yer if yer upset 'im. He ain't a man to be messed wi'. Even so, I've turned Gilbert down; sometimes you 'ave to be cruel to be kind and I reckon it's time he learnt to stand on his own two feet. His mam ain't in a position to 'elp 'im out financially anymore an' I'm hopin' this'll make Gilbert realise that it's time to get himself a job.'

Lewis sighed. 'I hear what you're saying, but I wouldn't bank on it,' he said. 'Gilbert is bone idle and I despair of him sometimes.'

Soon after Daisy left the two men chatting and went to her room, and once she had snuggled down in bed was almost instantly asleep.

The next day the job of cleaning the house from top to bottom began. As well as that, there was baking to be done and dinner to prepare, but as usual Victoria and Gilbert didn't put in an appearance until just before lunchtime. When they did come downstairs Daisy noticed that Gilbert was sporting a black eye.

'Crikey, what happened to you?' she asked.

'Oh, I, er . . . went flying on the way home in the dark and smacked my eye on a rock.'

After what her father had said last night, Daisy was sure he was lying, but it was no concern of hers.

Jed and Lewis came in for their lunch break almost an hour later.

'Farmer Perkins brought his mare in this mornin',' Jed told them as he tucked into the pile of sandwiches Daisy had made. 'And he reckons Nuneaton is crawlin' wi' police. It seems they fished Mickey Jameson out o' the River Anchor in the park this mornin'. Dead as a dodo he were an' they suspect foul play. Funny, I were only talkin' about 'im last night, an' all.'

'How awful.' Daisy placed a pot of tea on the table. 'I mean, I know the man had a terrible reputation but what an awful way to die.'

Jed nodded in agreement and the talk moved on to other things.

Later that evening when Daisy was carrying the rubbish to the bonfire by the orchard, she noticed a sack pushed into one side of it. Curious she hooked it out and opened it. The clothes Gilbert had been wearing the evening before were crammed into it. She frowned, wondering who could have put them there. But then she realised that it could only have been Gilbert. *Why would he do that?* she wondered. Reaching into the sack, she pulled out the colourful waistcoat and gasped. There was a dark stain down the front of it. Examining it more closely, she realised it was blood. But whose could it be? She chewed on her lip for a moment then, making a decision, she shoved the waistcoat back into the sack and took it to the barn where she hid it in a corner behind some bales of straw before going back to the kitchen.

She noticed that Gilbert spent most of the time in his room, which was strange for him, but she didn't voice her concerns, although she knew that from then on, she would be watching him very closely indeed.

Chapter Sixteen

On a beautiful afternoon in August, Daisy headed for the orchard to pick some apples for the pie she intended to make for their pudding that evening. Lewis and her father had taken the trap into the town to get feed for the animals and Victoria was visiting a friend, so Daisy assumed she was alone, which made a nice change. As she strolled beneath the fruit trees, she sighed with contentment. The grass was covered in wildflowers, and bees and butterflies were everywhere she looked. The orchard had always been one of her favourite places. The banging and hammering from the forge couldn't be heard from here and now the peace of the place washed over her.

Sinking to the grass she decided to rest for a minute, and as she studied a bee that was busily collecting nectar from a flower, a smile played over her lips as her thoughts turned to Lewis. Unlike his brother, Lewis was gentle and kind. She still suspected that he had feelings for her as well but neither of them had said anything yet, although she hoped that in the not-too-distant future he would. When she was close to him, she got butterflies in her stomach and if they happened to touch, her body tingled. She shivered pleasurably, wondering what it would be like to kiss him. She'd never felt like this about anyone else and wondered if it could be love. Having never known love before she could not tell.

Suddenly someone plonked heavily down beside her making her start. She had been so lost in her daydream that she hadn't been aware of anyone else but as she turned her head the smile disappeared as she saw Gilbert lolling back on one elbow grinning at her lasciviously.

'Oh, I-I didn't hear you coming,' she muttered as she made to rise.

He caught her arm and dragged her back down. 'No need to rush off, is there?' he leered, his eyes fastened on the swell of her breasts beneath her blouse. 'It's not very often you and I get time to ourselves so why don't we make the best of it, eh?'

'Unlike you, *some* of us have work to do!' she told him haughtily as she tried again to stand. But once more he pulled her back down, more roughly this time, and a little bubble of unease started in the pit of her stomach. She could see his fingerprints on her arm and she scowled at him. 'Just leave me alone, can't you?' she hissed.

'Oh, I could, yes . . . but I don't want to. So why don't you relax a little? You don't want to be a prude, do you?'

Suddenly he stood up and lunged at her, pushing her flat on her back. She tried to scream but he had knocked the wind from her and she could only croak. Then before she could stop him, he was on top of her, his mouth coming down on hers, and she groaned as she felt his wet tongue trying to prise her lips open. She bucked and writhed beneath him but that only seemed to excite him more and she began to panic. She managed to wrestle her head to one side and let out a blood curdling scream.

'That's it, me beauty, you scream.' He chuckled as he ripped at the buttons on her blouse. 'There's no one around to hear you. And I do like a girl who puts up a bit of a fight.'

The buttons flew into the grass and then he was tugging at her chemise and she felt the air on her bare breasts. The sight of her seemed to excite him even more and as his lips fastened on an exposed nipple he started to breathe heavily. '*I've . . . been . . . waiting . . . for . . . this,*' he gasped as one hand began to yank her skirt up. Daisy was still screaming for all she was worth but eventually she realised he was right. There was no one to hear her, no one to help and she started to sob, heart-wrenching sobs that came from deep inside her.

She felt the thin cotton of her knickers rip as he pushed them to one side and still she fought, but his strength was far greater than hers. And then he was parting her legs with one of his own and before she could do anything to stop him, he was on top of her and yanking at the buttons on his flies. As he released his manhood, she felt it hot and throbbing against her bare skin and terror robbed her of her voice. He was still sucking and biting noisily on her nipples and the pain was becoming unbearable, but there wasn't a thing she could do about it. She had thought things could get no worse but suddenly he positioned himself right next to her most private part and she felt a searing pain as his manhood pushed into her, robbing her of her virginity and her pride.

The pain and humiliation were excruciating, but the fight had gone out of her and she lay there praying for death. In a few short minutes, Gilbert had stolen any happy future she may have had. No decent man would ever want her now; she was soiled goods.

Unbidden a picture of Cassie Bates, a young girl from the village, floated in front of her eyes. Just the year before Cassie had been raped on her way home from a dance at the village hall. The rape had resulted in a pregnancy and her family had turned her out onto the streets. Cassie's body had been found floating in the canal beneath the bridge on Clock Hill in Hartshill several days later. With nowhere to go and no one to turn to, she had taken her own life and had been buried in unconsecrated ground in the churchyard of St Lawrence. Now Daisy could well understand why the girl had done it, for if death had come knocking at that moment, she would have welcomed it with open arms.

Gilbert was grunting and groaning as he bucked up and down, but suddenly he gave a sickening groan and flopped on top of her panting.

Swallowing the vomit that was rising in her throat, Daisy lay quite still, terrified that he might do it again. For what seemed like an eternity he lay there until his breathing returned to normal, then he rolled off her and began to rearrange his clothing. Daisy gathered her torn blouse across her bare, throbbing breasts and, as he rose, she stared at him with hatred glowing in her eyes.

'I hope you *die* for what you have just done to me,' she spat. 'And you *will* when I tell my father!'

'Oh, going to tell Daddy, are you?' He smirked as he tucked his shirt into his trousers. 'Are you quite sure about that? I shall just tell him that you led me on, and who do you think he would believe? Think what it would do to our parents' marriage. It would be over before it had begun. Do you *really* want to make him choose between you and my mother? It would break his heart.'

Sitting up abruptly Daisy leant over and was violently sick in the grass.

'I suggest you keep what just happened to yourself.' His voice held a threatening note now. 'Who knows . . . the next time you might actually enjoy it!'

Daisy swiped the back of her hand across her mouth and the words she shot at him were like daggers. 'If you ever . . . *ever* . . . lay your hands on me again I will kill you!'

He shrugged and strolled away leaving Daisy sitting there feeling sore and nauseous. She waited until he was out of sight then somehow managed to stagger to her feet and back to the cottage. There she filled a bowl with hot water and after carrying it to her room she scrubbed herself until she was so sore she couldn't bear to do it any longer. But she still felt dirty, and tears ran down her cheeks as she realised she always would.

A picture of Lewis's gentle face swam in front of her eyes and she cried even harder. She had hoped there might be a future for them, but now that could never happen and she let out a moan of despair at her lost dreams. Despite her anguish, she was painfully aware that Lewis and her father would be back soon and there was work to be done, so she quickly changed the torn blouse and underwear and tidied her hair before going downstairs again. Somehow, she was going to have to go on as if nothing had happened, because Gilbert had been right when he'd said she'd destroy the family if she told her father. Personally, Daisy would have been only too happy to see the back of both Victoria and Gilbert, but she didn't want to break her father's heart, so for his sake, somehow, she would have to try to put all this behind her.

The rest of the day passed in a blur as Daisy tried to go about her business, but by the time the evening meal had been served she knew that she must rest. Every inch of her ached and her breasts were tender with black bruises and bite marks.

'Are you feeling all right, Daisy?' Lewis asked as he helped her to clear the table. She hadn't been her usual cheery self since he and Jed had returned from town.

'Actually, I don't feel that well,' she told him in a subdued voice.

He immediately took her arm and led her to the stairs. 'In that case, you go up and rest. We can see to the clearing up.'

She gave him a grateful smile and slowly climbed the stairs to her room where the tears started once again. Thankfully, Gilbert had gone out shortly after he had raped her, which was just as well. She didn't know how she could have coped had he been there at dinner laughing at her. Slowly and painfully, she undressed and put her nightgown on before slipping into bed where she lay hugging her pillow and fighting the urge to run away. If only she had taken her granny up on the offer of staying in Ireland with them,

115

but it was too late for regrets. The damage was done and nothing could change that.

It was almost a week later when Jed took her to one side to ask, 'Is everything all right, pet? I've noticed you seem a bit down and you haven't spoken a word to Gilbert for days. Has he done something to upset you?'

Daisy swallowed before replying quietly, 'No . . . I just . . . I just don't like him. I try, really I do, for the sake of peace in the house, but I can't stomach him.'

Jed sighed and nodded. He had never seen his girl so subdued, even following the death of her mother. 'Between you and me I don't like him either,' he admitted. 'I think almost every argument Victoria and me 'ave ever 'ad 'as been either about 'im or money.' He put his arm about her and gave a rueful grin. 'Unfortunately, Victoria still resents the fact that she can't 'ave as many frills an' furbelows as she used to when she was married to her last 'usband. An' that son of hers don't 'elp, holdin' his hand out fer money all the while. Like chalk an' cheese 'im an' Lewis are. There's nothin' I'd like better than to give Gilbert a good swift kick up the arse an' tell 'im to go an' get a job. But that's got to be down to 'is mother, ain't it? We're tryin' to merge two families 'ere an' it was never goin' to be easy, although I still 'ope things will get better wi' time.'

'I'm sure they will, Daddy,' she told him. She couldn't bear to see him looking so sad but even for his sake she couldn't bring herself to look at, let alone speak to Gilbert.

Before they knew it, they were into September and suddenly, after the intense heat of the summer, the days had a nip in the air. Daisy was seriously concerned and found it hard to concentrate on anything, for her courses were now over two weeks late. She was normally as regular as clockwork. As she pegged the wet clothes onto the line strung across the yard one cold Monday morning, she suddenly felt sick and raced for the toilet, which was set at the end of a cinder path in the small garden to one side of the house. Once inside she sat and lowered her head into her hands praying that the nightmare might be over, but when she dropped her knickers there was no change and she felt sicker still. Could it be that she was pregnant with Gilbert's child after the horrific rape that still haunted her day and night? The family had all noticed how quiet she had been in the previous weeks. She wasn't sleeping well and there were dark circles beneath her eyes. Still, she tried to console herself, it could just be that she was late for another reason. All she could do was wait and see.

September moved on with no change in her condition and when she missed her courses again early in October, she knew that her worst fears were going to be realised. For weeks she had avoided Gilbert like the plague, but now she steeled herself to talk to him, and the chance came the following day. Lewis and her father were working in the forge repairing some farm equipment and Victoria was out visiting, so when he rolled down the stairs shortly before lunchtime following yet another night's drinking, she raced to shut the door and turned to confront him.

He raised his eyebrows as she came to stand in front of him. 'Want a bit more of what I gave you last time, do you?' he leered, stretching his hand out to her.

Furious, she slapped it away. 'You won't feel so cocky when you hear what I have to tell you,' she warned him.

He frowned. 'What do you mean?'

'I'm *pregnant*!' she said bluntly and had the satisfaction of seeing the colour drain from his face.

'*What!* You . . . you can't be!'

'Oh, *yes* I can. I've missed two courses now so what are you going to do about it? It's not something that I'm going to be able to hide for long.'

He looked dumbstruck but after a moment he scowled. 'And how do I know that it's mine?'

She gritted her teeth as she advanced on him with her fists clenched. 'Don't you *dare* say that to me! I was a virgin when you raped me, as you well know!'

He gulped. It wasn't the first time he had found himself in this situation. The first girl he had got pregnant was Eunice Barnes, a farmer's daughter. On the night he had met her up in Hartshill and she had threatened to tell her father what had gone on, things had turned nasty, and it had ended very badly. The second had been Cassie Bates.

'So, what are we going to do now?' She glared at him, bringing his attention sharply back to her. 'And don't say we'll get married. I wouldn't marry you if you were the last man on earth!'

'Oh, *shut up*, you silly little cow, and let me think a minute.' He leant on the back of the chair and stared into the fire before saying eventually, 'We're going to have to get rid of it!'

'Get rid of it?' As it dawned on her what he was suggesting, she shook her head. 'Oh no . . . not that! I won't be visiting old Dolly Watts anytime soon.' Dolly was an old woman who lived on the outskirts of the village. It was a well-known fact that many a young woman who had found themselves in an unfortunate position had trod the path to her door. It was also well known that many of them had died after Dolly had butchered them and Daisy had no intention of that happening to her.

'So, what *do* you suggest then?' he asked angrily.

They stood there for a few moments until a sudden thought occurred to him. 'Didn't I hear you once tell me that there was a home for unmarried mothers in Ireland near your grandparents' place?'

'Er . . . yes. But how will that help us?'

'Well, you don't *want* this baby, do you?'

She shuddered. 'How could I ever want something that was forced on me in that way?'

'So, we can tell your father that your granny is ill again and that you're going to care for her for a few months. Instead, you'll be in the home. Then when the baby is born a new home will be found for it and you can come back and no one will be any the wiser.'

Daisy stared at him uncertainly. The idea didn't appeal to her at all, but she couldn't think of a better alternative.

'You could write to your father while you were there,' he hurried on as the idea took shape. 'And he would never know that you weren't writing from your granny's.'

'But what about Granny and Grampy? Wouldn't they wonder why I wasn't writing to them for months?'

He chewed on his lip. 'Hmm . . . I know, you could write a few letters before you leave and I could post them at intervals.'

'And what if they reply? Wouldn't it seem strange for them to be writing to me here if I was already supposed to be staying with them?'

'Don't worry about that. I'll just have to make sure I get to the postman each morning before anyone else does. It shouldn't be hard. Your father and Lewis are always at work early and my mother rarely shows her face till late morning.'

'I suppose it *could* work,' she agreed uncertainly, although there was nothing about the plan that appealed to her.

Seeing her wavering, he hurried on. 'There'd be no need for you to leave before the end of November or early in December, surely? You won't even be showing until then, will you?'

'I don't suppose so, but how would we go about booking me in?'

He waved his hand at her. 'Don't get worrying about that. I'll see to everything. I might even say that I'm going travelling for a while and take you there myself.'

Daisy sighed. 'All right, I'll think about it,' she said dejectedly. She hated deceiving her father but surely that was better than breaking his heart?

'Fine, but don't take too long about it,' he said unpleasantly.

Daisy stared calmly back at him and in that moment, she knew that she would never, even if she lived to be a hundred, hate anyone as much as she hated him!

Chapter Seventeen

Over the next few weeks, Daisy's breasts became sore and by the end of November she was having to loosen the waistbands on her skirts, although she had been so unhappy that she had lost weight everywhere apart from her waist and stomach. Her father had noticed that she didn't seem to be herself but had put it down to the fact that she was simply overworked. Victoria was still doing very little to help in the house.

'I think it's time to make the arrangements,' Daisy whispered to Gilbert one day when they had a quiet moment alone in the kitchen. She'd hoped to be able to wait until after Christmas but was terrified of her father noticing her expanding waistline.

He nodded. 'Very well, I'll get on to it straight away,' he responded, only too glad to get her out of the way.

'But won't Daddy and Victoria think it's fishy if we leave together?'

He shook his head. 'No, I'll tell them that I'm travelling to Ireland with you and going on from there.'

Unhappily, Daisy agreed. The thought of spending a whole day in this man's company filled her with horror, but what choice did she have?

'It's all arranged,' Gilbert told her early in December. 'We leave in a week.'

As the day of their departure approached Daisy alternately looked forward to getting it all over with and dreaded what was about to happen.

Lewis seemed particularly sad that they wouldn't be spending Christmas together and told her so, but Daisy had tried to harden her heart against him over the last weeks. There was no point in letting him in now. Should he ever find out what had happened with his brother she had no doubt he wouldn't want to touch her with a bargepole, and she couldn't risk seeing the look of disgust that would surely show on his face.

All too soon the morning for them to leave rolled around. She said a tearful goodbye to her father – Victoria was still in bed – and Lewis drove her and Gilbert to the train station. While Gilbert was unloading the luggage from the back of the trap, Lewis took her hands in his and the familiar tingles ran up her arms.

'Is there any chance you might be home for Christmas?'

She shook her head. She hated lying to him, but what choice did she have? 'It will all depend on how Granny is. I won't come back until I know she's on the mend.'

'I understand, but I'll miss you. Christmas won't be the same without you,' he said softly.

She stared back at him with tears in her eyes. There was so much she wanted to say but at that moment Gilbert approached with a large bag in each hand and they said their goodbyes before making for the station platform.

Once they were seated in a carriage, Daisy gave way to the tears she had been holding back.

Gilbert eyed her with contempt. 'I don't know what you're so upset about,' he said unfeelingly. 'It's not as if either of us want this child.'

'This wouldn't be happening if it wasn't for what *you* did,' she spat at him with such loathing that he looked away. 'And what's going to happen when I've had the baby?' she enquired. She had never looked that far ahead before.

'I've already told you. The sisters assured me that the baby will be found a home and you can come back here.'

She nodded and stared from the window. She didn't want to be in his company and could hardly wait to get to Ireland. The sooner she was there the sooner it would be over.

The majority of the journey was made in silence but the ferry crossing was horrendous. It was bitterly cold and the combination of the rough seas and Daisy's condition meant she spent most of the journey hanging over the rail on deck being sick into the sea. The ferry bobbed about on the waves like a cork in a bottle and at one stage Daisy wondered if she would survive. But at last, they drew into the harbour in Dublin and Gilbert helped her down the gangplank. Her legs seemed to have developed a life of their own.

Once on solid ground, he hailed a cab and they were soon on the last leg of the journey. At one point they passed so closely to Daisy's grandparents' cottage that she could see the smoke from their chimney rising into the sky. She would have done anything to feel her granny's gentle arms about her. It was dark by that time and the cab was rocking from side to side as the horse trotted along, adding to her persistent nausea.

At last the cab pulled up in front of an enormous pair of metal gates surrounded by a high brick wall.

'This is it, gov,' the driver shouted down to them. 'The sisters' home for unmarried mothers.'

Daisy cringed with shame as she realised that the driver would know why she was there. Gilbert climbed down to ring the large bell and after a few moments a tiny man appeared from a small gatehouse. He was dressed in a long dark overcoat with a cap pulled low across his eyes and he peered through the gates at them.

'Miss Armstrong, my man, we're expected,' Gilbert told him pompously.

After fiddling with a huge bunch of keys the old man unlocked the gates and Gilbert climbed back into the cab. Daisy peered through the gloom looking for the first glimpse of the nunnery that was to be her home for the next few months, but there was nothing to see but bare trees forming a canopy above them as they drove down the long drive. At last the place loomed ahead of them and shivers ran up her spine. It was a large, forbidding-looking building with a flight of stone steps running up to two enormous oak doors, which were flanked by windows that stared blankly into the stormy night. Daisy swallowed nervously, thinking it looked more like a prison than a home. With an effort she pushed the thought away.

'I'll wait here for yer, gov,' the driver said as Gilbert grabbed Daisy's bags.

They climbed the steps together and Daisy's heart hammered in her chest when he rang the bell. It clanged inside and soon they heard the hollow sound of footsteps approaching. The door inched open to reveal an elderly nun in a black serge habit. On her head she wore a black wimple and a white coif surrounded her face. Around her neck was a starched white collar and a long chain on which hung a crucifix. Daisy shuddered as the nun fixed her with gimlet eyes.

'Daisy Armstrong?'

When Daisy nodded the nun ushered her into the hallway. Gilbert followed and almost instantly another nun appeared and took Daisy's arm.

'Come with me,' she said tartly. Meanwhile Gilbert was being shown into an office with 'Mother Superior' written on the door.

Daisy started to panic as she was led up a steep staircase to the first floor. At the top of the stairs the nun opened a door with a key from a large chatelaine that hung about her waist, and after locking it again once they'd passed through, they proceeded along a long corridor until they reached another door.

'In here!' The nun's eyes were cold as Daisy walked through the door and found she was in a large, stark bathroom. There were a number of tin baths against a wall – one of them was full. Along the other wall was a row of toilets with no doors. Daisy shuddered, imagining having to use them in view of others. However, she had no time to think on it before a voice sliced through her thoughts. '*Strip off!*' Another nun had joined them. She was enormous with hands like hams and as she began to roll up the sleeves of her habit a cold finger raced up Daisy's spine.

'Why?'

The larger of the two nuns stepped forward and without warning slapped Daisy's face so hard that her head snapped back on her shoulders.

'While you are here you will do as you are told without question!' she barked. 'Otherwise, it will be all the worse for you.'

Daisy's cheek stung as she began to remove her clothes. She tried to hide her naked body with her arms as the nuns stared at her with looks of distaste on their faces.

'Get in there!' The smaller nun pointed to the full bath and Daisy tentatively lowered her foot over the side, gasping as she realised the water was icy cold.

'B-but it's freezing.' Her teeth were beginning to chatter and her breath floated in a cloud in front of her. But before she could say anymore the larger nun stepped forward and pushed her into the bath so hard that Daisy's head disappeared beneath the surface. She sat up coughing and spluttering, but the humiliation had only just begun.

While one nun grabbed a large bar of carbolic soap and began to scrub Daisy's skin until it felt raw, the other took up a large pair of scissors, grabbed Daisy's lovely hair and began to hack at it, throwing handfuls of it onto the bathroom floor.

Throughout the ordeal, Daisy was crying and shaking violently. She wanted to fight them but she would be no match for the two of them, so instead she sat as still as she could and tried not to scream. It felt as if she was caught in a nightmare and for the first time she wondered if she had done right in agreeing to come here.

At last, just as Daisy feared she would pass out, the nuns grabbed one of her arms each and hoisted her unceremoniously out of the bath.

'Dry yourself,' the larger one ordered, throwing a rough towel at her.

As Daisy began to rub at what was left of her hair, she began to cry harder. She had never been a vain person, but she had loved her long hair and now all she was left with were tufts that stood up across her scalp.

Next, she was given a shapeless shift to put on. It reached down to her ankles and would have wrapped around her twice so the nun threw a piece of string towards her to tie it up at the waist. It was a drab brown colour and resembled one of the sacks that her father kept in the barn back at home. She was then given a pair of wooden clogs that were so big she wondered how she would ever manage to walk in them.

'Right, now you will see the Mother Superior and then you will come back here and tidy this mess up.'

The nuns marched her out of the room and back down the stairs where she looked for a sign of Gilbert. She wanted to tell him that this had all been a huge mistake and that she had changed her mind about staying here but he was nowhere to be seen.

When they reached the Mother Superior's office one of the nuns rapped at the door. A voice bade them to enter, and she pushed the door open and nudged Daisy inside.

Unlike the rest of the place, inside this office there was a cheery fire burning in the grate and thick velvet drapes hung at the windows. Expensive rugs were arranged across the highly polished wooden boards and a deep leather wing chair stood next to a mahogany desk, behind which sat a nun with a stern expression on her face.

'Thank you, Sister Monica-Joan.'

She pushed Daisy forward to stand in front of the desk. The woman had a file open in front of her and after looking at it for a moment she raised her eyes and stared at Daisy.

'Daisy Armstrong?' she barked.

'Yes!'

The woman scowled. 'You mean, "*Yes, Mother Superior!*"'

Daisy swallowed. 'Yes, Mother Superior.'

'Hmm.' The woman steepled her fingers and contemplated Daisy over the top of them. 'And you admit to the heinous crime of incest?'

'*What!*' Daisy was so shocked the words seemed to stick in her throat. 'What do you mean . . . *incest*? I am here because my stepbrother raped me and got me with child. I was told that once it is born, you can find the baby a good family and I can go home and try to put this all behind me.'

The woman smirked. 'Yes, most of the mothers here try to come up with a story that absolves them of any blame! But the report I have from your father is completely different.'

Daisy blinked, hardly able to believe what she was hearing. 'B-But my daddy doesn't even know I'm here. I came to save him any upset.'

The woman bent her head to the file in front of her again before continuing, 'You have been placed here for your own safety after tempting your father and brothers to perform incest with you. This report goes on to say that you are the same with any male that you meet and so he feels that it is in your best interests to be here, in a place of safety.'

'*No!*' Daisy shook her head. 'My daddy would *never* say that – none of that is true. My stepbrother, the man who brought me here today, is to blame. He forced himself upon me. I-I want to go home *now*! I came here voluntarily but I've changed my mind!'

At this the woman actually smiled, but it was a cruel smile that didn't reach her eyes. It reminded her of Victoria's.

'I'm afraid it's too late for that. Here, see for yourself, your father's signature on the report.'

Daisy staggered forward and as she gazed down at the file in front of her, she shook her head vehemently. 'No, that isn't my daddy's signature.'

Almost as if she hadn't heard her the nun continued. 'Only your father can get you out of here now. But I should warn you, those who come in because of incest usually remain here. It is too unsafe for their families to release them back into the community and the sooner you realise that, the better it will be for everyone. You have committed the ultimate sin and now you and your unborn child will pay the price. Take her away, Sister Monica-Joan.'

'No!' Daisy whirled on the nun with fury in her eyes. 'Get *away* from me! I won't stay here, do you hear me?'

The door behind the nun suddenly slammed open and two more nuns appeared. The three of them bore down on Daisy and dragged her out into the hallway kicking and screaming.

'We'll put her into the padded cell. That should calm her down,' one of them said as they dragged her along the hallway, her feet slipping on the shiny tiles – she had lost her clogs somewhere along the way.

Eventually they came to a door through which she could see stone steps that led down into darkness. The nuns hauled her down them, her knees scraping painfully on the way. At the bottom of the stairs was a large door with bars in the small window at the top of it and after unlocking it, they threw her inside. She fell heavily, knocking the air from her lungs, but she was up in seconds and pounding on the door as the key turned in the lock.

'*Let me out! Come back!*' she screamed, but already she could hear the nuns' footsteps receding as they climbed the stairs, then there was only an unearthly silence that seemed to settle around her. She screamed until she felt as if her lungs were on fire, but finally she sank down onto the floor as exhaustion and despair washed over her.

Hatred rose like bile in her throat as she realised that Gilbert had tricked her. Did he have any intention of ever coming back for her? She doubted it. But then she felt a glimmer of hope. Her daddy would soon wonder why he hadn't heard from her and he would come looking. But then she remembered the letters she had left with Gilbert. No, he wouldn't know she was missing; he would believe that she was living happily with her granny and grampy for months to come! And the Mother Superior had told her that only her daddy could ever get her out of this place. She had no doubt that Gilbert would be quite happy to leave her there to rot forever.

Lowering her chin, she began to sob, and once she had started, she found that she couldn't stop.

Chapter Eighteen

Daisy had no idea how long she was left in the cell. She tried to sleep as much as she could, although there was no bed or bedding so she was forced to curl up on the uncomfortable floor. At last she heard the sound of footsteps and a glimmer of light appeared through the small window in the top of the door. Seconds later there was the sound of a key in the lock and the door swung open.

'Ready to behave now, are you?' It was Sister Monica-Joan, and Daisy nodded numbly. 'Good, then come along.'

Daisy ached in every limb and her lips were cracked, and in that moment, she would have paid a king's ransom for a glass of water.

Somehow she managed to drag herself up the stairs and once at the top she was again led to the bathroom where she was told, 'If you want to eat get yourself cleaned up now! I'll be back in two minutes and if you aren't ready, you'll go to bed with no food.'

Daisy realised that it was evening once more. She had been left in the cell for at least twenty-four hours. Hurriedly she tidied herself as best she could and when the nun came back, she beckoned for her to follow. They went back downstairs and through a labyrinth of corridors, all painted in the same drab green, until they reached a large room that Daisy realised must be the dining hall. There were a number of girls there, many of them pregnant, and they glanced at her with dull eyes as they shuffled forward in a queue towards a table where nuns were serving them food.

'Get on the back of the queue and think yourself lucky I'm allowing you any supper,' the nun said.

Although Daisy wanted to scream at her, she meekly did as she was told. She was too thirsty and hungry to do otherwise. On the end of the table was a pile of tin dishes and Daisy followed the other girls to collect one. When it came her turn to be served, a much younger nun with a pretty face slopped a spoonful of unappetising stew into her bowl. It was watery and there were dollops of overcooked vegetables and gristly meat slopping about in it, but by then Daisy was so hungry she would have eaten anything to get rid of the gnawing pains in her stomach.

She took a seat at one of the long tables and helped herself to a slice of stale, grey-looking bread. She would have started to eat immediately but the girl sitting next to her gently squeezed her hand beneath the table as if to warn her, and glancing about Daisy saw that the rest of the girls were standing as the Mother Superior entered and took her place at a table at the top of the room.

'We have to do prayers first,' the girl whispered and Daisy quickly rose and gave her a grateful smile.

The next ten minutes were spent in prayer as Daisy's stomach rumbled ominously. By the time they were allowed to eat, a layer of fat appeared to be floating on the surface of the food and it was only lukewarm, but Daisy ate it anyway. She noticed that the nuns on the top table were being served slices of beef and a selection of vegetables and she thought how unfair it was.

Once they had eaten the girls were each given a cup of weak tea with no sugar and then there were yet more prayers before they began to form orderly lines.

'Armstrong, follow the girl in front of you,' an elderly nun told Daisy. 'You will be in her dormitory.'

Daisy was relieved to hear that. The girl who had warned her about the prayers was the only friendly face she had seen in the place. They were led through a number of locked doors and allowed to use the bathroom before being taken to their rooms.

Daisy was mortified at having to sit on the toilet with everyone able to see her but no one else seemed to take any notice. They were used to it.

'Right, girls, into your nightgowns now,' the elderly nun barked. 'Lights out in ten minutes.'

Daisy headed for the end bed where she found a rough cotton nightgown laid out for her. There were six beds on each side of the room and as the girls changed, she noticed that some of them looked close to their time if the size of their stomachs was anything to go by. Once they had all changed and folded their clothes on the chairs to each side of the beds, the nun appeared again and they said yet more prayers before clambering under the thin blankets. When the nun was satisfied they were all where they should be she left, taking the candle with her and leaving them in darkness.

Only then did Daisy allow the tears to flow as she thought of the terrible trick Gilbert had played on her. Worse still was the fact that she had fallen for it hook, line and sinker. How could she have trusted him? But soon she felt a ray of hope. She could write to her father and tell him what had happened. Of course, it would cause trouble in the family, which was what she had tried to avoid, but even so she had no doubt that once her father knew what had happened, he would come and fetch her.

'Are you all right?' a little voice whispered through the darkness.

Turning on her side, Daisy saw the shape of the girl who had spoken to her in the dining hall. 'Yes . . .' she answered in a wobbly voice. 'Thank you.'

'So what's your name?'

'I'm Daisy, Daisy Armstrong.'

'Nice to meet you, Daisy. I'm Niamh, Niamh Murphy.'

'And when is your baby due, Niamh?'

'Oh sure, I reckon I'll be another three months at least. And you?'

'Mine's not due till the end of April or the beginning of May.'

'You've still a way to go then,' Niamh said sympathetically. 'But just try to keep your head down and do as you're told, and it won't be so bad.'

'I've got no intention of staying here,' Daisy told her heatedly. 'I was brought here under false pretences but I'm going to write to my daddy tomorrow and when he knows where I am he'll come and get me.'

'O . . . oh!'

'Why do you say it like that?' Daisy was concerned now.

'Did no one tell you? We're not allowed to write to anyone while we're here. Nor receive any letters.'

'*What?*' Daisy was horrified. 'But that can't be right, surely? We're not prisoners!'

'We may as well be,' Niamh whispered dejectedly. 'And the nuns can be wicked buggers if you cross 'em, so they can. When I was first put in here, I spent half my time in the padded cell for answering back and not doing what they told me. But they managed to knock that out of me in the end. I soon learnt it's easier to just behave, so it is. But anyway, try an' sleep now. If Sister Monica-Joan hears us chattin' our heads will be for the chop for sure. Goodnight, see you in the morning.'

When silence settled around her Daisy lay there staring into the darkness. Her one hope of getting out of this hellish place had just been taken away from her, but she wasn't done yet. Somehow, she told herself, she would escape.

At some point she slept, only to be woken by the sound of someone groaning. She lifted herself onto her elbow and rubbed the sleep from her eyes just as a nun she didn't recognise burst into the room holding a candle.

'What's to do?' the nun said angrily as she approached a young girl who looked to be no older than fourteen or fifteen. She was leaning forward in the bed gripping her stomach as tears coursed down her cheeks.

'I-I t'ink me baby's comin', Sister,' she sobbed. 'An' I t'ink I might 'ave wet the bed. Is sorry I am!'

'You *stupid*, *evil* girl,' the nun scolded. 'Your waters have broken. How often are the pains coming?'

'E-every few minutes, I t'ink!'

'In that case you'd best come with me to the delivery room. Come along now.'

The young girl began to cry harder. 'But I's afraid, Sister!'

'And so you should be. You're a sinner and now is the time to pay the price for your sin.' There was not an ounce of sympathy in the woman's voice as she crossed to the bed and unceremoniously yanked the girl out of it. 'Come along an' just pray that you survive the birth.' She looked around at the rest of them. 'And you lot get back to sleep, but don't forget this. It will be your turn soon.'

The poor girl was bent almost double and trying not to cry out as pains wracked her body, but the nun continued to haul her towards the door and soon there was only silence again.

'The poor little bugger. May our Lord look on her kindly,' one of the girls said as she made the sign of the cross on her chest. Slowly the girls lay back down and silence reigned, although few of them slept.

At six a.m., one of the nuns came to wake them. This time it was the younger, prettier nun that Daisy had seen in the dining room.

'Good morning, girls.'

'Good morning, Sister Patricia,' they chorused.

'Come along to the bathroom and when you've washed, I will be back to take you down to the chapel for morning prayers. Twenty minutes now, girls.'

Daisy tacked onto the end of the queue as it shuffled along the corridor to the bathroom. There were some old towels and bars of carbolic soap there so she washed as best she could and dampened down her stubbly hair, holding back tears as her hands ran across it. Her daddy had always loved her hair and he would be heartbroken if he could see what they had done to it. There was a large bruise on her cheek from where the nun had slapped her. It was tender when she touched it, and she promised herself she would try to be good today.

Once they were ready Sister Patricia led them downstairs to a chapel at the back of the huge building. It was quite beautiful and under other circumstances Daisy would have loved the stained-glass windows and perfectly embroidered altar cloths. But as things were, she could only see this part of the building as an extension of her prison.

At last, the prayers were over and they filed into the dining hall. This morning they were served with bowls of thin porridge that ran off the spoon. It was unsweetened and Daisy couldn't help but think of the thick, creamy porridge dripping with honey that she made for herself and her father back at home. What she wouldn't have done for a dish of it right then. The thin porridge was washed down with stewed, unsweetened tea and once again she saw that the nuns were eating much better than they were – rashers of crispy bacon and eggs with thick yellow yolks.

When breakfast was over, a nun approached her and ordered, 'Come with me, the Mother Superior will tell you where you will be working.'

Daisy hadn't realised she would have to work, although she didn't mind. At least if she was busy, it would keep her mind off what was happening to her. The nun glided ahead of her with her hands tucked into the sleeves of her habit, her feet making no sound on the tiled floors. When they reached Mother Superior's office they were invited in and once more Daisy stood before her.

The woman glowered at her. 'Ready to behave now, are you, Armstrong?'

'Yes, Mother Superior.' Daisy had to force the words out, for they seemed to stick in her throat.

'Good! I have decided that for the rest of this week you will work in the laundry. Go with Sister Augustus and she will show you where to go.' The woman returned to her paperwork, clearly dismissing her.

'Yes, Mother Superior . . .' Daisy paused before hurrying on. 'I was wondering . . . would it be possible to write to my father?' Although Niamh had told her it wasn't allowed, she felt she had to at least try.

The woman's head snapped back up and she stared at Daisy as if she had asked for the moon. 'Write to your *father*?' She inhaled deeply. 'That's *quite* out of the question. It was he who placed you here as I clearly told you. Why ever would he wish to hear from you? The poor man! You are the lowliest of sinners. No decent man is safe from your immoral advances, that's why you are here. On top of that you are not even a Catholic, but a heathen. Now go quickly before I give you another stretch in the padded room, and never ask for privileges again, do you hear me?'

'Y-yes, Mother Superior.' Daisy meekly bowed her head and followed Sister Augustus from the room, but inside she was fuming. No matter what any of the girls who were incarcerated here had done, surely none of them deserved to be treated like this.

Once again, she was led through the never-ending corridors until at last, at the back of the house, Sister Augustus led her into a steamy room where some heavily pregnant girls were leaning over deep stone sinks and dolly tubs, sweat pouring down their flushed faces. Others were either feeding wet washing through heavy mangles or ironing with large, flat irons that they were heating on the fires.

At least it's hot in here, Daisy thought. It was the first time she had been warm since she had arrived.

As they entered another nun came to meet them, eyeing Daisy with disdain. 'Yet another sinner to join us, Sister Augustus?'

'Yes, Sister Agatha-Mary. This is Armstrong. May I leave her with you?'

'Of course.' Daisy detected a cruel gleam in the woman's eye. 'So, Armstrong . . .' She was holding a split cane and Daisy would soon discover why. Should any of them place so much as one foot out of line they would feel the length of it. 'We'll start you off on the coppers.' She grinned wickedly. 'Best be careful, though, the water is red-hot.' She pointed to a long pair of wooden tongs. 'You hook the sheets out of the water and rinse them thoroughly in those sinks there. When they are done to my satisfaction some-one else will come and put them through the mangle and you take the next one out. But it will be woe betide you should I find so much as *one* mark on them. If there is, you will scrub it until it's perfect. We wash these sheets for one of the finest hotels in Dublin so they have to be immaculate. Do you understand?'

'Yes . . . Sister Agatha-Mary,' Daisy added hurriedly. She had thought Sister Monica-Joan was bad enough, but this nun was even worse.

And so her first day in the laundry began and by the end of it Daisy was almost dropping with exhaustion. She had thought she worked hard back at home, but that had been easy compared to this. By six o'clock that evening, when they were taken to the chapel for yet more prayers, she could barely put one foot in front of another. Her back was aching, and her hands were red and cracked from continually being in hot water. There were times during the service when Daisy had to force herself to stay awake and it was a relief when they were finally taken to the dining hall for their supper and allowed to sit down.

During the afternoon one of the girls had collapsed, gripping her stomach, and in minutes she had been lying in a pool of blood as she screamed in pain. As Daisy had looked on in horror two nuns had rushed in and dragged her away and that was the last she had seen of her.

'What do you think happened to that poor girl who collapsed this afternoon?' Daisy whispered to Niamh as they sat together tackling the lumpy mashed potato and what looked like a sausage that had been served to them. Tonight, she noted, the nuns were being served crispy lamb chops.

'I don't know,' Niamh whispered back. 'I just hope the poor lass survives, so I do. There's many girls that come in here who do not.'

'And what about the girl that went into labour in our room last night?' Daisy stared at Niamh from the corner of her eye.

'Aw well, it's sorry I am to tell you that neither she nor her babe survived the birth.'

As hungry as Daisy was, suddenly she couldn't eat another morsel. 'What? You mean they both *died*?'

Niamh nodded. 'Sadly yes, but at least she's at peace now.'

Daisy took a deep breath. This place was supposed to be a sanctuary. But as far as she was concerned it was hell on earth, and somehow, she was determined to escape.

Chapter Nineteen

Over the next two weeks, Daisy did as Niamh had suggested and obeyed the nuns, although she had come to hate the majority of them. It hurt her to know that her grandparents were just a stone's throw away and had no idea she was even here. She knew that if she could only have got word to them, they would have been here in the blink of an eye to rescue her.

By keeping quiet and listening, she had discovered that the home was actually a very profitable business. It was set in twenty acres of rolling countryside and the nuns kept a herd of milking cows. With the milk the cows supplied, some of the girls spent gruelling hours in the dairy making cheese, while others cared for the animals. The laundry took in washing from hotels, which made the nuns a very good profit, and the vegetable garden not only supplied the home but the excess was sold to the same hotels. The fruit from the large orchard was made into jams and pies, and again sold on. The worst, though, was what Daisy learnt about the newborn babies' fates.

'I was sent to work in the nursery one day and I heard Sister Consumpta talking to a couple who had come all the way from America to adopt a baby. I saw the money change hands meself,' Niamh confided to Daisy in a hushed voice one night as they lay in bed following an exhausting day in the laundry. It was the only time they got to speak to each other properly, as during the day they were under constant supervision, and the nuns could appear at any moment.

Daisy was horrified. 'They're selling babies! But I thought the nuns adopted the babies out to childless couples out of the goodness of their hearts!'

Niamh snorted and shook her head. 'They don't do anything for nothing, to be sure. And the amount of girls that don't survive birth here is terrible. All they care about is the babies. Have you noticed that patch of bare ground next to the orchard?'

Daisy nodded mutely, hardly able to believe what she was hearing.

'That's where the girls and the babies that don't survive are buried. Usually at night when we are all in bed. They have no coffin, no service, nothing. God rest their souls. They're just wrapped in an old sheet and thrown into the grave as if they are worthless. The nuns won't even allow a doctor to tend girls if there are complications during birth. They say that Sister Maria is a midwife but I have grave doubts about that. No doubt the latest mound of earth there holds little Maureen an' her babe who died the night you arrived.'

Appalled, Daisy shook her head. 'But if this is the case, we must tell someone.'

'Oh yes, and who do you think would listen to us?' Niamh scoffed.

Daisy thought for a moment. 'What about the priest who comes to take mass every Sunday? Surely he would do something if he knew what was going on?'

'He's as thick in with the Mother Superior as can be, to be sure,' Niamh told her solemnly. 'And I've no doubt she's lining his pockets too. Haven't you noticed how comfortable the Mother Superior's quarters are compared to ours? She doesn't have to be cold, for sure, there's always a fire burning in her office, and the nuns don't have to eat the slop they serve us. I'm tellin' you, they're all corrupt, every last one of 'em, except perhaps Sister

Patricia. I don't think she's been here long enough to get brought into their evil schemes.'

Daisy could hardly believe what she was hearing. For her the long hours of prayer each day were the worst. She had been brought up as Church of England and she remembered her mammy telling her once that Daddy's religion had caused a problem when they first met. She had been a practising Catholic and the two shouldn't have wed. It was the only thing about Jed that Mauve's parents hadn't liked, especially when her mammy had decided to forego her religion and change to his. They had been so much in love that her mammy couldn't bear anything to get in the way of them being together. And so Mauve had turned her back on the Catholic faith and become Church of England and eventually her parents had accepted it and come to love her choice of partner.

Now Daisy was being forced to follow the Catholic faith whether she liked it or not. What Niamh had just told her made her feel even more resentful towards the nuns who preached about sin, for surely, they were more evil than any of the unfortunate girls who found themselves here.

'How did you come to be here?' Daisy questioned tentatively.

Naimh sighed. 'I've been a fool.' There was a catch in her voice. 'I lived wit' me family in a house just outside Dublin. Twelve of us there were, ten weans an' me mammy an' daddy in a two-up, two-down cottage where the walls ran wit' damp. Me daddy is fond of the drink, so sometimes we lived from hand to mouth, but he ain't a bad soul all in all. Me mammy took in washin' an' ironing an' that helped keep us all. Anyway, when I got a bit older, I got a job in a hotel as a chambermaid an' that's where I met Liam Kelly. Oh, he were just the handsomest man I'd ever seen an' the first time I clapped eyes on him me heart were lost. He stayed in the hotel two days a week an' told me he were there on business. Talk about the gift o' the gab! Liam could have charmed the birds out o' the trees. He started to buy me pretty trinkets an' I thought the sun shone out of his arse. Anyway, we started an affair. He told me that he were going to marry me an' I believed every word that dropped out o' his mouth. But then I found out about this baby an' when I told him, he promised he'd do right by me. Then the followin' week he didn't arrive at the hotel.'

A muffled sob reached Daisy from the darkness, then Niamh went on. 'I spoke to the manager an' said weren't it unusual for him not to be there? He told me that Liam were a card shark. He made his livin' roamin' the country an' I never saw him again. I found out later he were already married an' all. I hid me condition from me mammy an' daddy for as long as I could but then when they found out they brought me here. Mind, I have high hopes they'll fetch me out again once the baby is born.'

'Oh, Niamh, you poor thing.' Daisy's heart broke for her.

'An' what about you?'

'My stepbrother raped me,' Daisy said brokenly

Niamh sighed. 'Ah well, we are where we are an' all we can do is hope we get out o' this hellhole one day.'

'Oh, I *will*,' Daisy said with gritty determination.

Early the following morning another of the girls in their room went into labour and the nuns took her away as the rest of them trudged to the rest rooms to wash in the icy cold water.

'Poor little bugger,' Niamh said with a sad shake of her head. 'Shelagh is just fourteen years old an' still nowt but a child herself. Her daddy raped her and then dumped her here, the bastard!'

There was no more time to talk then as they were led down to the dining room and yet another exhausting day began. Daisy's hands were calloused and red raw but she was getting used to it.

Just before lunchtime Sister Augusta came to say to her, 'Come with me, Armstrong. Sister Consumpta is ill, so we need someone to look after the girls in the labour ward.'

Daisy panicked. 'But what will I have to do? I don't know anything about childbirth.'

The nun's lip curled with contempt. 'Then it won't hurt to see what lies ahead for you, will it? Now come with me.'

Daisy meekly followed the nun to another room. There were four beds in it, two of them with terrified girls lying in them. She recognised one of them as the girl from her dormitory. She was rolling and crying out with pain, while the other watched her fearfully.

'Shelagh here is near her time,' the nun told Daisy unfeelingly. 'All you have to do is watch and when you see the baby's head coming ring that bell there. Sister Agatha-Mary will come for the delivery then.'

Daisy gulped. 'But how will I know?'

The nun ripped the sheet from the girl's bed exposing her swollen stomach and her most private parts. 'You have eyes, don't you? Now do as you're told and no more lip!' And with that she stormed away, leaving Daisy glaring after her.

Eventually Daisy approached the bed and took the girl's hand gently in her own. 'It's all right, Shelagh. I'm here with you,' she said soothingly, although her heart was beating a tattoo in her chest. 'Everything is going to be all right.'

'*Mammy, Mammy!*' The girl was screaming in agony and Daisy had never felt so useless in her life. She couldn't believe the nuns could be so cruel as to leave this poor soul in the care of someone who knew absolutely nothing about birth.

'Have they given you anything for the pain?'

The girl shook her head and the older girl in the other bed grunted. 'Huh! You don't get not'ing to help you in this place, for sure. All they care about is getting a live baby at the end of it, the cruel bastards!' She gasped then as one of her own contractions started and Daisy turned her eyes back to Shelagh.

There was a bowl of water with a rag in it at the side of the bed, so she wrung it out and started to gently wipe the sweat from the young girl's forehead. There was nothing else she could do for her apart from be there. The screams seemed to go on forever and Daisy's nerves were stretched to breaking point when at last Sister Agatha-Mary appeared.

Leaning over she slapped the girl's face and growled, 'Stop that hideous noise *immediately*! This is the price of sin, my girl. I bet you won't be so keen to canvas your wares to men again, will you?'

She felt around the girl's stomach before looking to see if anything was happening between her legs, then she began to roll her sleeves up, telling Daisy, 'Fetch me that trolley over there. She's taking too long and needs some help to hurry everything up.'

With her heart in her mouth, Daisy rushed to do as she was told. She stared down at the evil-looking scalpels lying on the trolley as she wheeled it over to the bed.

All she could do then was stand back and watch as the nun lifted a scalpel and cold-heartedly began to slice at the poor girl's most private parts.

Shelagh screamed piteously as blood began to leak out of her, but the nun ignored her. 'That should do it,' the woman said as she wiped her hands and sure enough soon after Shelagh screamed again and a little head appeared between her legs.

Daisy felt ready to faint but she held on to Shelagh's hand and forced herself to try and stay calm.

'The head is crowning,' the nun said with satisfaction. 'I think it just needs a little more help.' So saying she lifted the scalpel again and widened the cut she had already made.

Shelagh was only semi-conscious now and Daisy knew she would never forget this horrific experience for as long as she lived. Worse still was the fear that in the not-too-distant future she would have to go through the exact same thing. It was a terrifying thought.

Everything seemed to happen at once then as the baby emerged in a gush of blood and fell onto the bed between its mother's legs.

The nun quickly cut the cord and hanging the baby upside down by its feet she slapped it soundly on the backside. As a mewling cry filled the room, Daisy felt a lump form in her throat as she stared at this beautiful little new life. It was a baby girl and although she was drenched in her mother's blood, anyone could see that she was a little beauty.

'Oh, Shelagh, you have a beautiful baby daughter,' Daisy whispered, but the grip on her hand had loosened and as she looked into the girl's pale face, she was horrified to see that her eyes were rolling in her head.

'S-sister, I think something is wrong,' she gasped fearfully, but the nun was more interested in inspecting the baby.

'She's in God's hands now,' the woman answered unfeelingly. 'He will decide if it's time to welcome another sinner into heaven. I'll look at her after she's delivered the afterbirth, but here, make yourself useful and get this child cleaned up. There's water ready over there and some clothes for it.'

Daisy stared helplessly between the baby that had been dumped into her arms and the mother, who looked as though she was dying with blood still pouring from her at an alarming rate. But Daisy had no idea how she could help her, so she took the child and bathed it. The gentle bathing revealed a halo of downy blonde hair and a rosebud mouth and once she had dressed her and the child had fallen asleep, Daisy lay her in a drawer lined with a thin blanket and hurried back to Shelagh's side.

The afterbirth had now come away but she was still bleeding profusely, so doing the only thing she could think of, Daisy grabbed a towel and pressed it hard against her, hoping to lessen the flow. By the time the nun returned it did seem to have slowed a little, but Daisy was still gravely concerned.

'I think she needs a doctor,' she told the nun.

The woman glared at her. 'Oh, you're a midwife now, are you?' She narrowed her eyes at Daisy as she lifted the sheet from the cold floor and flung it across the girl. 'Leave her be and go and see how Caitlin there is doing.'

Daisy did as she was told as the nun carried the baby away to the nursery. The other girl's contractions were coming much more quickly now and she looked afraid. It was no wonder, Daisy thought, after watching what young Shelagh had just suffered.

'You'll be fine,' she said softly.

Caitlin stared back at her through pain-filled eyes. 'Oh aye, after what I just saw over there? You really believe that, do you? Why, we're nothing to these nuns. They treat their cattle better than they do us, to be sure.' She groaned and gritted her teeth as another contraction tore through her and once again all Daisy could do was comfort her. Shortly after another nun appeared and nodding to Daisy she snapped, 'You get back to the laundry. You're not needed anymore.'

Daisy staggered away, appalled at the cruelty she had just witnessed, and she knew that should she survive her own baby's birth, she would never forget this horrific day for as long as she lived.

Chapter Twenty

'Aw Daisy, what's wrong?' Niamh whispered in the darkness that night as she heard Daisy crying in the next bed.

Haltingly, Daisy told her what she had witnessed that day and Niamh sighed. Her own time was drawing close and just the thought of having to give birth in this godforsaken place filled her with dread.

'W-we have to get out of here,' Daisy said in a wobbly voice.

'There's not much chance o' that, to be sure,' Niamh answered resignedly. 'The nuns watch us like hawks, so they do. But try not to worry, Shelagh will probably be much better tomorrow.'

It was then that the most amazing thing happened, and Daisy gasped as she felt her baby move for the first time. It was only in that moment, as her hand dropped to her belly, that it struck her there was a real live little human growing inside her. Up until then she had tried not to think of it, and when she had she had wished it gone. But suddenly things were different. No matter that she hadn't wanted it, or even the way it had been conceived, this was her baby and the child couldn't be blamed for what Gilbert had done to her.

'I-I just felt my baby move,' she said incredulously.

Niamh chuckled softly. 'You'd best get used to that, for if it's anything like mine it won't stop now. I sometimes t'ink mine is playing football inside o' me, to be sure.'

For the first time Daisy wondered if the baby would be a boy or a girl. Would it have fair or dark hair? What colour would his or her eyes be? And what would become of it once she had given birth and the nuns took it away to the nursery? How could she know that they would find her baby a good home where it would be loved and treated well? So many questions swirled through her mind, but she could answer none of them.

Her thoughts were interrupted by a groan from the girl in the bed by the door and within seconds the door flew open and Sister Monica-Joan appeared and whisked her away.

'Phew, that's another poor bugger ready to drop,' Niamh hissed. 'The nursery will be full this week at this rate, so it will.'

They fell silent, their thoughts on the babies lying so helpless up in the nursery waiting for their new parents to come and claim them, until eventually they slept.

It was mid-morning the next day as they toiled in the laundry that one of the girls whispered, 'Look yon.'

Daisy quickly glanced at the open door that led into the yard just in time to see two of the nuns hurry past carrying a small shape wrapped in a bloody sheet.

'Holy mother!' Niamh quickly genuflected as the colour drained from her cheeks. 'That's another poor soul headed for the graveyard. May she rest in peace!'

Sister Bernadette advanced on her then and before Niamh was even aware of what was about to happen, she raised the split cane that barely left her hand and brought it whistling down across Niamh's backside.

'That's enough chatting, get back to work. And you over there, girl. Shut that door!'

Niamh yelped in pain and jumped at least a foot in the air. The shapeless shifts they were forced to wear were no protection against the cane and already she could feel a weal rising across her bare backside and something warm dripping down her leg.

Another nun entered at that moment to have a hurried word with Sister Bernadette, then she turned to Daisy. 'You, dry your hands and come here! You're to go with Sister Agatha-Mary.'

Daisy quickly did as she was told and when she was hurrying after the nun in the corridors she dared to ask, 'May I know where we're going, Sister?'

'We have three babies up in the nursery,' the nun replied. 'And we need someone to look after them until their new parents arrive.'

'B-but I've never looked after a baby before.' Daisy was nervous. What if she did something wrong?

The nun chose not to answer her and they moved on in silence until they came to the room where she had seen Shelagh give birth the day before. As they passed, she quickly glanced in but there was no sign of the two girls who had been there the day before.

The nursery, as it was called, was a drab, comfortless room with little cheer. A number of small wooden cribs stood against one wall and in three of them were tiny babies, two of them crying lustily.

'They want feeding,' the nun told her, glancing at the infants with distaste. 'You'll find the feeding bottles and the milk over there and make sure you put a few drops of this in the bottles each time you feed them. No more than a couple of drops, mind. It will keep them quiet.'

Daisy stared down at the small phial the sister had placed in her hand, horrified to see that it was laudanum. She could remember the doctor had prescribed it for her mother to help with the pain shortly before she had passed away. They were actually drugging the babies just to keep the poor little mites quiet!

'B-but won't this harm them?' she asked uncertainly.

The nun's lips drew into a hard, straight line. 'Not so long as you stick to the dose I told you. Just do as I say or it will be the worse for you. You'll find clean bindings over there. Put the dirty ones in that bucket and later take them to the laundry.' And with that she sailed away leaving Daisy to stare after her in disbelief. How could anyone be so cruel and heartless to helpless newborn babies?

Quickly she made up two bottles hoping she had done it right. There was no way of warming the milk so they would just have to have it cold. She went first to the baby who was crying the loudest. It was a baby boy and he had clearly been crying for some time because his face was red and his tiny hands were bunched into fists.

The minute Daisy held the rubber teat on the glass feeding bottle to his little lips he latched onto it and sucked for all he was worth. The bottle was drained in minutes and Daisy then made her first attempt at changing a binding. She wasn't very good at it but at least he was clean and dry, and after giving a big burp his eyelashes fluttered and he fell asleep. Quickly she went on to the next baby, very aware that she would be in trouble should the sister discover she hadn't given the first any laudanum. This next baby was a girl with dark hair and brown eyes. She could only think that she must be Caitlin's baby unless the girl who had gone into labour in the night had had a girl too. She knew that Shelagh had had a girl – how could she ever forget it? The horror of that birth would stay with her for the rest of her life.

A little later a nun appeared to relieve her of her baby minding duties while she went down to lunch, which consisted of sandwiches made of grey, doughy bread with scraps of cheese inside them. They were so dry that Daisy had to drink water just to swallow them, but she ate them all the same. Anything was better than hunger pains and she seemed to be hungry all the time now.

'Where's Niamh?' she whispered to a girl from their room when she saw that her friend was absent.

The girl glanced fearfully towards the nuns to make sure they weren't looking before whispering back, 'They've taken her off to

150

the delivery room. I reckon that whack from the cane made her go into early labour, poor soul.'

Daisy felt sick. Niamh was only seven months pregnant. It was far too soon for the baby to be born and the chances of it surviving were slim. As soon as the meal was over, she hurried back to the nursery and the nun left her to tend the babies. Two of them were crying again for a feed and as she left the nun told her, 'Put a drop more laudanum in their bottles. Keep the little sinners quiet. Oh, and have the boy ready to leave in the morning. His new parents will be coming for him. You'll find a shawl and a new nightgown in that drawer over there.'

Daisy quickly saw to the babies' needs and once they were settled again, she dared to peep out into the corridor. The delivery room was just a few doors along and inside she could hear someone groaning in pain. It sounded suspiciously like Niamh and her heart sank. She listened for a while longer and when there was no other sound, she crept along the corridor and peeped inside. Sure enough, there was Niamh on one of the beds. She was deathly pale and gripping her stomach as contractions tore through her.

Daisy rushed to her side. 'Oh pet!' She had never felt so useless in her entire life. 'What can I do to help you?'

'A-a drink . . . please.'

Daisy quickly lifted the glass of water from the small table at the side of the bed and held it to her friend's lips.

'What are you doing here alone?' she asked when Niamh had drunk her fill.

Niamh bit down on her lip so hard that she drew blood as another contraction gripped her. 'They're not bothered about me,' she gasped. 'The baby is coming too soon and I heard them say they don't expect it to survive. If they're not going to have a baby to sell I t'ink they don't care what happens to me either.'

At that moment Sister Monica-Joan appeared and glared at Daisy. 'And just what do you think you are doing here?' she demanded.

Daisy was so upset for Niamh that she didn't care if she was in trouble. 'I heard her crying out so I came to see if there was anything I could do,' she said boldly.

'Get *back* to the nursery,' the nun told her angrily. 'I'll take over here.'

Daisy had no choice but to do as she was told but once she was back with the babies, she paced the floor restlessly as she heard her friends screams of agony grow louder. Then suddenly the cries stopped, abruptly followed by the mewling cry of a newborn. Niamh's baby had been born. After what felt like an eternity, but was in fact only a matter of minutes, Sister Monica-Joan appeared and thrust a tiny form wrapped in a bloodstained towel at her.

'Get this child bathed and keep it warm,' she said callously. 'I fear it's too small to survive but we'll do what we can.'

'And Niamh?' she asked fearfully.

The nun shrugged. 'She's in God's hands now. Or should I say the devil's. Our Lord wouldn't accept a filthy sinner like her into heaven.'

Bitter words sprang to Daisy's tongue, but she swallowed them back. She could be more help to Niamh if she said nothing and took care of her baby.

As soon as the nun had gone, her footsteps echoing hollowly in the corridor outside, Daisy gently unwrapped the little bundle in her arms. Tears sprang to her eyes. It was a little girl, the tiniest thing she had ever seen, barely the length of her hand. Her chest was rising and falling alarmingly fast, and Daisy had no idea what to do for her. Pulling herself together with an effort, she dried her tears and began to gently wash the infant and tie a binding on her. Throughout the child didn't even whimper and Daisy laid her down gently while she hastily made a bottle for her. She then settled in the only chair in the room and pressed the rubber teat to the baby's lips. It was soon apparent that she was too weak to feed so Daisy began to drip milk into the infant's mouth. Unfortunately, she was also too weak to swallow and the milk dribbled out of her mouth and down her chin, so Daisy laid her against her shoulder and gently began to rock her to and fro.

'Come on now, little one,' she urged softly. 'You have a wonderful mammy who will love you all the world if you'll only be well.' She began to sing a lullaby as the baby lay nestled beneath her chin and she was still there some time later when Sister Patricia appeared to relieve her while she went down to prayers.

'You can stop singing, Daisy. I'll take over now.' She was the only nun who ever addressed her by her Christian name. The kindly nun took the child and quickly weighed her saying with a sigh, 'She doesn't even weigh four pounds.'

'Do you think she'll survive?' Daisy asked worriedly.

The sister shrugged. 'We can only do what we can and leave it to our Lord.'

Daisy's head shook as bitter tears stung the back of her eyes. 'And her mother . . . Niamh?'

'I think she'll be fine. But go and say a prayer for this little one and have your supper now. I'll see to what needs to be done.'

Daisy staggered from the room feeling as if her heart was breaking. Then, just as she reached the top of the stairs her own baby began to kick. Her hand dropped protectively to her stomach and she prayed as she had never prayed before that such a terrible fate was not awaiting her child.

Chapter Twenty-One

When prayers and the evening meal were over, Daisy volunteered to go back to the nursery. At least there she could be close to Niamh.

Sister Monica-Joan was only too happy to allow it. It meant that she could get a good night's sleep in her own bed. 'You do realise that you'll only be able to nap in the chair when you're not seeing to the babies?'

'I'm quite happy with that,' Daisy assured her. When all was said and done, it was much easier than the back-breaking work in the laundry, and she liked looking after the little ones.

'Very well.'

Daisy climbed the stairs and as she passed the delivery room she was relieved to see that Niamh was there and alone. She slipped inside and approached the bed. Naimh was still very pale but looked a little better than she had earlier. 'My baby. What is it? They wouldn't tell me, they just whipped it away without even letting me see it.'

'You had a baby girl,' Daisy told her, her voice cracking.

Niamh's thin face broke into a smile. 'And how is she?'

Daisy's heart broke afresh as she gently took her friend's hot hand in hers. 'I'm afraid . . .' She gulped and was unable to go on for a moment. 'I'm afraid she is very tiny but there is hope. And I'll tell you now, from the moment they brought her to me I showered her with love and told her all about her wonderful mammy. She has fair hair and blue eyes and reminds me a little of you.'

Niamh squeezed her hand. 'Bless you.' Her voice was clogged with tears that now rolled slowly down her cheeks. 'The truth of it is, even if she does survive, I will never get to know her. They will sell her on to anyone who has the money to pay for her, so they will. At least, though, I might be able to get to meet her before she goes.'

The two girls sat silently for a time, each lost in their thoughts, until Daisy sadly made her way back to the nursery.

Daisy slept little that night. It seemed that each time she managed to doze off in the chair, one of the babies would wake and she would have to jump up to see to their needs. But she didn't mind. And then suddenly it was morning and Sister Agatha-Mary came to take over while she went to wash and go to morning prayers, then went on to breakfast.

When she went back to the nursery Sister Agatha-Mary pointed to the boy child. 'Have him ready to leave in an hour,' she ordered.

Daisy immediately got him ready for a bath with warm water that was sent up from the kitchen. With his hair clean and brushed and standing up in downy little tufts all over his head and dressed in the fine nightgown and shawl the nun had instructed her to dress him in, he looked beautiful, and Daisy's heart ached as she cuddled him to her for one last time and thought about his mother who had died bringing him into the world.

'I wish you a loving home with kind parents who will always care for you,' she whispered as she kissed his soft cheek. He was so little and defenceless, much like we girls who are trapped here, Daisy thought.

When the sister returned, she heard voices in the corridor.

'Do wait in here, my dears,' she heard the nun say in an ingratiating voice and seconds later she appeared and almost snatched the baby from Daisy's arms.

She carried him into the room next door and Daisy heard a woman say, 'Oh look, Charles, isn't he just adorable?' She was very well spoken and Daisy couldn't resist peeping through a slight gap in the door.

'He's very healthy,' the nun assured them in the same sweet voice. 'And I have no doubt he will bring you years of love and pleasure, to be sure now.'

'Oh, I'm sure you are right,' the man agreed.

Daisy saw him take a large envelope out of his pocket and hand it to the nun. 'If you would like to count it, I think you will find it's the correct amount.'

Daisy noted that he and his wife were superbly dressed – it was obvious they were very wealthy people. He wore a thick over-coat and a shiny top hat over a pin-striped suit, and she wore a navy velvet travelling costume with a matching hat trimmed with peacock feathers that danced as she moved, making them appear to have a life of their own.

The nun opened the envelope and Daisy spotted a thick wad of bank notes. So Niamh had been right when she had said that the nuns sold the babies for profit.

'Oh, I'm sure it will be right,' the nun simpered. 'But now you'll want to get your little treasure home in time for Christmas. I don't wish to detain you.'

Daisy shot back into the nursery just in time as the group left the room, the wealthy woman holding the baby in her arms. She could hear them talking as they disappeared from view, and she crossed to the window and stared through the bars. A fine carriage drawn by four magnificent black horses was wait-ing outside the front doors. Minutes later the group appeared and once the man had helped the woman and child up into the carriage, he climbed in beside them and it rattled away down the drive.

Daisy turned and looked at the three sleeping baby girls that were left. It would be their turn to leave soon, if the littlest survived that was.

It was much later that day before she dared to venture to the delivery room again where she found Niamh dressed and sitting on the side of the bed.

'What are you doing up so soon?' Daisy questioned worriedly. Niamh was ghastly pale and there were dark circles beneath her eyes.

'Huh! You don't get to lay about in this place for long, to be sure,' Niamh said with a shake of her head. 'Sister Monica-Joan is sending me back to work in the laundry this afternoon.'

'But you're not well enough!'

Niamh shrugged. 'Sure, it'll be better than lyin' here wit' too much to t'ink about,' she said quietly. 'How is my baby?'

'She's holding her own and taking a bottle now, against all the odds,' Daisy assured her. 'And at least when your family realise that you've had the baby they'll come and fetch you out,' Daisy said, hoping to raise her spirits.

Niamh snorted. 'Huh! You t'ink so, do you? I don't. I did at one point but I've given up hope. My guess is they'll leave me here to rot. An unpaid worker for the nuns.' And then, 'Do you know what day it is?'

Daisy frowned as she shook her head. Time had no meaning in this place. Each day rolled into the next.

'It's Christmas Eve, so it is.'

'Oh!' Daisy realised with a little shock that it was her birthday and Christmas Eves gone by flashed into her mind. Happy times when her mammy and brother had been alive and her mammy had made her a birthday cake, then later times when she and her

157

daddy had eaten mince pies and roasted chestnuts on the fire with Rags curled up at their feet. Happy times that could never come again.

The memories only made Daisy more determined than ever to get out of there.

'Never mind.' She patted Niamh's arm. 'This will be the first and last one we'll ever spend here,' she promised.

'Oh yes, sure about that, are you?' Niamh sounded defeated. Her spirit had died when the nuns took her baby daughter away from her.

'Yes, I am!' Daisy stuck her chin in the air. 'This time next year we'll be far away from this hellhole, you'll see.' And with that she hurried back to the nursery to see to the babies.

The majority of Christmas Day was spent in prayer taken with Father O'Leary in the chapel, but at least that day the girls were given a fairly reasonable meal of goose, potatoes and vegetables. The next of the baby girls in the nursery was due to go to her new home the following day, and as Daisy lay in bed that evening, she wondered what the new parents would be like.

She reported back to the nursery straight after prayers and breakfast, such as it was, the next morning, to find Sister Monica-Joan in a fluster.

'This one has cried on and off all night,' she declared angrily.

Daisy tried not to smile. Normally when the nun was in charge of the babies you didn't hear so much as a whimper from them because they were drugged up with small doses of laudanum. But of course, she wouldn't have dared to risk drugging the baby when the new parents were due to take her home.

'Take over,' the nun ordered. 'And have her ready to leave for eleven o'clock.' She glided away, hands tucked into the sleeves of her habit, her steps silent, making her appear like some giant crow floating along the landing.

Daisy took great care in preparing the baby for her new home and when she was bathed and changed into the pretty nightgown she looked like a little angel.

'I pray you will be loved,' she whispered as she gently planted a kiss on her smooth skin. Minutes later she heard Sister Monica-Joan on the landing and, as before, she led the new parents into the room next door before coming for the baby.

Once again Daisy couldn't resist taking a peek through the slightly open door. This couple looked, if anything, even wealthier than the last, although she noted that the woman didn't seem particularly interested in the child. It was the man who crossed to take the babe into his arms.

'Do you have any other children?' Sister-Monica Joan asked him.

He shook his head. 'I'm afraid not. My wife preferred not to have any, but I wanted at least one, so we decided to adopt.'

'Then I hope she will make you very happy,' Sister Monica-Joan purred falsely. 'And now, er . . . the little matter of the money, if you please?'

'Oh, of course.' The man balanced the child in one arm while he withdrew a thick envelope from his pocket with his other hand, and handed it to her.

The nun smiled graciously before hastily tucking it away in the deep pocket of her habit.

'May I say, Sister, I greatly admire the work you and the other nuns do here. To help so many young women is admirable.'

'Oh, we do our best to care for the poor souls,' she answered.

Daisy almost choked. *Did their best – poor souls!* Oh, how she would have liked to tell him of how they were all really treated: bullied and abused and made to feel like scum! But of course, she couldn't, so she crept back to the nursery to watch the baby depart from the window.

It was then that a thought occurred to her, and her breath caught in her throat. Would it be possible to escape somehow in one of the carriages that came for the babies? All the other vehicles that came into the grounds were searched before they were allowed out again, but not those. Only the week before one of the girls had been found hiding amongst the clean sheets that were collected for the hotel and she had been dragged out kicking and screaming. No one knew what had become of her since then. She hadn't been seen and Daisy shuddered to think of it. The nuns had descended on her like a pack of wild dogs and beaten her to within an inch of her life before dragging her away.

'Let that be a lesson to any others of you who might be planning on trying to escape,' Sister Mary had ranted.

For the first time Daisy felt a ray of hope before turning her attention to the other two babies left in the nursery . . . for now! She picked up Niamh's baby and held her close. Though she loved all the babies, this one was special to her, and she was determined to do all she could for her.

Chapter Twenty-Two

Ansley Village, December 1881

Halfway between Christmas and New Year Gilbert returned home to find his mother sitting at the side of the fire in her normal position while a woman from the village put a large meat pie into the oven.

'Darling . . . I've missed you.' Victoria rose from her seat to embrace him as the woman put her coat on.

'Will that be all, missus?' she enquired. 'Only I've to get back. All you've got to do now is take the pie out when it's cooked and dish it up.'

'Yes, that'll be all, Mrs Smith,' Victoria told her with a dismissive wave of her hand.

'Who was that?' Gilbert enquired as he placed his bag down and undid his coat. It had started to snow and was bitterly cold outside, although it was as warm as toast in the kitchen.

'Oh, I persuaded Edward to allow me to have someone in to help around the house.' His mother grinned at him. 'I think he finally realised that I had no intention of doing it, and the work started to pile up after Daisy left. She's a widow from the village. But tell me, has everything gone to plan?'

He nodded. 'Yes, she went into the home like a lamb to the slaughter and I paid a young chap to post the letters to her father at regular intervals before I went travelling. It occurred to me that he might smell something fishy if he saw an English postmark. Have they been arriving?'

'Oh yes, as regular as clockwork. Edward has no idea whatsoever. As far as he's concerned, she's staying with her grandparents. But tell me, how have you been?'

He helped himself to a jam tart that Mrs Smith had left cooling on a rack on the table. 'I've been fine,' he told her with a grin. And in truth he had. After leaving Daisy at the nunnery, he had travelled from place to place trying his hand at cards with no conscience at all for what he had subjected Daisy to. He had won some games and lost a lot but the amount he had won had enabled him to stay in hotels until his luck changed, and then he had just moved on to another place before the people he owed money to could catch up with him. 'And how have things been here?'

She pouted and shook her head. '*Dreadful* if you must know! Things are so much worse than I had feared. Even after selling the house and your father's assets we discovered that there was still a substantial amount of money owing to the bank, so Edward is having to pay it off. He's not at all happy about it, I assure you.'

Gilbert grinned again. 'Well, that's his problem, isn't it? You knew when you married him that this could happen. In fact, that's *why* you married him, if I remember rightly. It's just a shame he was the only available man in the area at the time. It would have been so much better if you could have latched on to someone with money.' He glanced around before asking, 'And where's that mangy mutt? Did you finally manage to get rid of it?'

She shook her head. 'Edward has started taking him into the forge with him every day and of course I can do nothing to him when Edward is about. But what will happen to Daisy when she's had the baby? She won't come back here, will she?'

Gilbert laughed. 'I don't think there's much chance of that happening. I had to pay them to take her in because she isn't a Catholic, but from what I could gather, once the girls are left there, they can't come out again, even after giving birth, unless a member of the family goes for them. And we're hardly likely to do that, are we?'

'And the letter I wrote to Daisy?' she queried.

'The Mother Superior has instructions not to give it to her until she's had the brat.'

'But what if they write to us asking for money to keep her there?'

He laughed. 'You don't think I'd be so foolish as to give them our real address, do you? No, relax. Daisy is gone for good, so you can stop worrying on that score. She'll rot in that place, and even if she doesn't, she'd never dare to show her face around here again after what you've written to her.'

'Good,' she responded callously. 'She and Lewis were growing a little too close for my liking. He's done nothing but mope since she left.'

He looked solemn. 'But how are you and Jed getting along? You don't look too happy.'

'I'm *not*!' she said bluntly with a toss of her head. 'He is just so . . . so *common*! I can hardly bear having him touch me!'

'Hmm, then if things are that bad, perhaps we should think about doing something about him once the debts are paid off? We could sell up here and with the money move away from this dump to somewhere where you could meet someone of our own class who can give you the lifestyle you're accustomed to.'

'But wouldn't that look a bit suspicious so soon after your father dying?'

He chuckled. 'Just leave it to me. No one suspected that Father had been helped on his way, did they?'

'Well, no,' she admitted. 'But if Edward were to develop the same symptoms—'

Gilbert stopped her mid-sentence. 'I've told you, just give me the nod when we're clear of debt and leave everything else to me. We should get a fair price for the house and business. More than

163

enough to move somewhere slightly more salubrious where you'll meet a better class of person. Now, what about some tea? You can manage that for your favourite son, can't you?'

Laughing, Victoria went to do as he asked.

When Jed and Lewis came in from the forge that evening after a back-breaking day's work, Jed's welcome to Gilbert wasn't as warm as his mother's had been.

'Oh, so you're back!' He went to wash his hands at the sink.

'Looks like it,' Gilbert drawled insolently.

But the smirk was wiped off his face as Jed went on, 'Well, now you've been an' had your fun it's time you buckle down to some work. I can't afford to keep shirkers here!' He glanced at Victoria, who flushed and averted her eyes, before going on. 'Me an' Lewis are snowed under wi' work, more than enough to keep us all busy, so you've got a choice. Either you go out an' get a job o' your choosin' or you join us in the forge. It's as simple as that! I ain't prepared to keep you 'ere any longer if you ain't payin' your way!'

'Some welcome home that!' Gilbert sniffed sarcastically.

Jed shrugged. 'Take it or leave it. If you ain't 'appy to abide by the rules you know where the door is.'

'Don't you think you're being a little hard on the boy, Edward?' Victoria butted in.

Jed rounded on her. '*Hard* on him? Why, he's bone idle. An' may I remind you he *ain't* a boy, he's a young man.'

Seeing how angry he was, she fell silent and rose to put the dinner out.

As they ate the atmosphere was strained. Lewis tried to lighten the mood by questioning his brother about where he had been. 'I've always wanted to tour Ireland,' he said. 'Is it as beautiful as they say?'

'I suppose so.' Gilbert pushed his food about the plate in a sulk and eventually Lewis gave up.

'I think I might go out for a while,' Gilbert told his mother when they had all finished.

'Oh, should you, darling?' She glanced towards the window. 'It's still snowing.'

'Let him go,' Jed interrupted as he sucked on his clay pipe. 'Happen he can ask about if there are any jobs goin'.'

Gilbert jumped out of his chair in a temper and after dragging his coat on, he barged out, slamming the door so hard behind him that it danced on its hinges.

'Now look what you've done.' Victoria sniffed and dabbed at her cheeks. Normally she only had to turn on the tears and flutter her eyelashes and Jed was putty in her hands, but tonight it had no effect.

Realising this, she glared at him. 'I must say, I think you are being *very* unreasonable.' And with that she too marched from the room and up the stairs.

Lewis looked embarrassed. 'I'm sorry about that, Jed,' he muttered. 'I'm afraid both my mother and Gilbert are used to getting their own way.'

Jed sighed and shook his head. He was missing Daisy dreadfully and couldn't wait for her to come home. He had received her last letter just a week before but from what she had said it could still be some time before she would be happy to leave her granny. It was only since she had been gone that he had realised just how much she had done for him. From the day her mother had died, Daisy had taken over running the house, as well as all the other things she had done, without complaint. Whereas Victoria . . . Well, she was probably the only woman in the world who couldn't even boil an egg. And as for cleaning . . . he shuddered just to think of the state the place had got into before he had finally agreed to allow a cleaner to come in. But then, he shouldn't have expected so much from her.

He said as much now to Lewis but the young man shook his head. 'That's no excuse. She knew when she married you that you were a working man, and other women have to adapt to their circumstances so why shouldn't she? If she never tries, she'll never learn, will she?'

The subject was dropped but when Jed went up to bed, he found her as usual with her back to him. Early in their marriage he and his first wife Mauve had agreed never to go to sleep on an argument and it was an agreement they had always stuck to. In fact, she had once told him, with a twinkle in her eye, that the making up was almost worth having an argument for. But as he had soon discovered, Victoria was a different kettle of fish altogether, and turning her back on him had become a regular occurrence. But tonight, he was just too tired to care so after slipping into bed he put the candle out and went to sleep without a word being spoken. Let her sulk!

Much later that evening Victoria heard Gilbert return and after grabbing her robe she tiptoed down to the kitchen. 'You were right,' she told her son in a hushed voice. 'I don't know how much more of living like this I can stand. Give it another couple of months and then we'll put the plan into action. I don't care what people say, because once Edward is gone, we can sell up and move away and make a new start somewhere else. London, perhaps? I have far more chance of meeting a more suitable husband there.'

Chapter Twenty-Three

Ireland, February 1882

Despite the odds, Niamh's baby did survive, but as she was the only baby left in the nursery since the other little girl had been adopted, Daisy had been assigned to work in the dairy shortly after Christmas. She had hoped it would be slightly easier work than the laundry, but this hadn't proved to be the case. In fact, by the time the girls were dismissed to attend prayers in the chapel each evening, Daisy's back felt as if it was breaking. She had never realised that producing butter and cheese was such hard work, especially in the quantities the girls were expected to turn out.

Daisy's job was producing the butter, which involved hours and hours of turning the milk in a churn until it solidified and could be made into butter pats. Sometimes by evening her arms ached so badly that she could hardly lift them, and she could barely straighten up. She had never been large, but she had lost weight everywhere since being there, apart from her stomach, which now looked incongruously out of place on her small frame.

Each day was the same and Daisy could hardly wait for her baby to be born. The child seemed to kick from morning till night, as if he or she could hardly wait to come too. And then one evening early in February, as Niamh and Daisy made their way to the chapel across the snow-packed yard, Sister Patricia appeared in the doorway and told Niamh, 'You're to come with me. Mother Superior wishes to see you immediately.'

'B-but I ain't done nothin' wrong!' Niamh paled at the thought of why she might be being summoned.

The nun smiled at her. 'I'm sure you haven't. But come along, we don't want to keep her waiting, do we?'

Niamh cast a last anxious glance at Daisy, who shrugged and moved on to the chapel. She had never enjoyed the lengthy services, but this particular evening it was impossible to concentrate, and her eyes kept straying to the door for a sign of her friend.

When the prayers were over and Daisy was sitting in the dining hall with her measly meal in front of her, Niamh finally reappeared and went to stand in the queue to get her own supper. Daisy could see that she'd been crying and her heart began to race. Eventually Niamh came to stand beside her and they bowed their heads in prayer before finally being allowed to sit down and begin their rapidly cooling meal.

'What's wrong?' Daisy hissed softly when she was sure none of the nuns were looking.

'I-I'll tell you when we get to our room after lights out.'

Daisy had to be satisfied with that for now. It was only later when they had tucked down into their beds and Sister Monica-Joan had left them in darkness that she dared to ask again, 'So come on . . . tell me what's happened.'

Niamh took a deep breath. 'It's good news and bad news, so it is,' she confided with a hitch in her voice. 'The good news is me daddy came to see Mother Superior today an' he's comin' to take me home tomorrow.'

'But that's *wonderful*,' Daisy told her, although already she was wondering how she would cope without her friend.

'The bad news is the reason I'm goin' home. Me mammy has passed away an' I have to go home an' look after the little 'uns. I reckon he would have left me here to rot if he didn't need me help.'

'Oh . . . I'm so sorry, Niamh. About your mammy, I mean. But won't it be great to get out of here?'

'Aye, it will,' Niamh admitted. "Ceptin I won't have much of a life, I don't t'ink. An' I-I won't get to see me baby again.'

On quite a few occasions she had managed to sneak into the nursery to see her little girl, who was now thriving, and it was clear Niamh adored her.

Daisy didn't know how to answer so she asked, 'What time will you be going?'

'Daddy's coming straight after breakfast. But here, I want you to hide this.' She reached into the darkness and placed a scrap of paper in Daisy's hand. 'That's me address in Dublin an', God willin', if you ever manage to get out of here you must come and find me. Hide it somewhere safe, better still memorise it.'

'Thank you,' Daisy said humbly. Niamh had turned out to be a good friend. 'I shall miss you.'

'Well, let's hope it won't be for too long. Once you've had the baby you can concentrate more on your escape, so you can.' Their hands joined in the space between the bed and Daisy squeezed Niamh's fingers as she felt tears smarting at the back of her eyes. They stayed that way for some minutes until finally they snuggled down in the cold sheets and Daisy fell asleep from sheer exhaustion.

Niamh, however, waited till all was quiet and after creeping from her bed she silently made her way to the nursery, praying that she wouldn't be intercepted on the way. Thankfully all was quiet and once she arrived at the nursery door, she was relieved to find the room empty apart from her own baby and a little boy who had been born just that day. Creeping over to the cot she stared down at her daughter and her heart filled with love as she committed every tiny detail of the child's face to memory.

'Hello, me little precious,' she murmured as tears started to roll unchecked down her cheeks. 'It's me, your mammy, an' I've come to say goodbye. Not from choice, may I tell you.' She stroked the baby's cheek tenderly. 'If it were up to me, I'd be takin you home wit' me, so I would, an' I'd never let you go, but sadly I can't do that. I wanted you to know, though, that I love you wit' all me heart an' I'll *never* forget you. Have a good life, me darlin'.' Leaning over she planted a gentle kiss on the baby's head and crept away as quiet as a mouse, her heart breaking all over again.

The next morning dawned all too soon. Daisy and Niamh sat side by side at the breakfast table as they always did, until eventually Sister Patricia arrived to tell Niamh, 'Your daddy is here to fetch you.'

They had said their goodbyes in the dormitory that morning, aware that they might not have another chance. So now Niamh gave Daisy a sad little smile and quietly walked away, leaving Daisy feeling as if there was a hole in her heart the size of a giant boulder.

The next month passed painfully slowly and Daisy had never felt more alone. But at least she knew there were now only a few weeks left until her baby was due. She tried not to think of what would happen to it once it arrived and just went about her work mechanically.

One day at the end of March, as Daisy was turning the handle on the butter churn late in the afternoon, she felt a warmth between her legs and was suddenly seized by a searing pain, which had her doubling over. She'd had a dull, throbbing backache all night and now she looked up in terror as Sister Agatha-Mary descended on her.

'And what's wrong with you, Armstrong?' she asked unsympathetically, but then spotting the puddle that had formed between Daisy's legs she told her, 'Ah, your water's have broken. We'd best get you up to the delivery room.'

'B-But the baby isn't due for another four or five weeks at least!' Daisy was panicking now. It was happening too soon and she knew all too well what that could mean.

The nun shrugged. 'Babies have a habit of coming when they're ready. Especially sinful little bastards like the one you are carrying. Come along now. You had the fun and now you must have the pain. Maybe it will make you think twice before you fornicate again.'

Gripping Daisy's arm, the nun hauled her roughly across the room and towards the stairs. Twice on the way up Daisy had to stop and grip the banister rail until a pain had subsided. She was afraid. She had known that childbirth would be painful, but she had never dreamed it would be this bad and she knew there was worse to come.

Once in the delivery room the nun told her, 'Get up on the bed and let's have a look how far along you are.'

Daisy did as she was told, flushing with humiliation as the nurse hoicked her drab shift up and bent to gaze at her most private parts. 'Huh! You could be hours yet,' she told her unsympathetically. 'Just stay there and keep the noise down! This is the price of your sin. Perhaps in future you will think back to this.'

As she glided from the room, panic set in. Daisy had never felt so alone and tears began to course down her pale cheeks. She had no idea how long she lay there but gradually the light faded and the pains grew worse until she felt as if a band of steel had been placed about her stomach. The pain was unbearable and she screamed as she prayed for it to end. But still no one came to her and suddenly she felt the need to bear down. *But I can't*, she thought desperately as she fought the urge to push. *There's no one here to help the baby if it comes.*

'S-sister . . . anyone, please help me!' she shrieked, but no one came and now the urge to push was so strong that all she could do was go with it. She felt as if she was being rent in two, and as she put her hand down between her legs, she felt a tiny head emerging. Her baby was being born. Thankfully, at that moment Sister Patricia appeared and Daisy sobbed with relief. She was the only nun in the whole place that showed any kindness to the girls and Daisy thanked God for her presence.

The sister took in the situation at a glance and quickly rolled her sleeves up. 'It's almost here,' she encouraged as she took her place beside the bed. 'On the next pain push for all you're worth and it should be over.'

Daisy nodded and as the pain came again, she did as she was told, grunting with the effort. She felt something slither out of her and the pain receded as if by magic. But there was no sound of a newborn baby's cry and she stared at the nun with frightened eyes.

'What is it? Is it a boy or a girl? And why isn't it crying?'

The only light in the room now was from the flickering candle that Sister Patricia had brought in with her and the flame was casting dancing shadows across the walls as an icy feeling spread up Daisy's spine.

'I-it's a girl,' the nun told her in a shaky voice. 'But I'm afraid she isn't breathing.' Daisy leant weakly up on one elbow and saw that the nun was pressing gently on the baby's chest as she tried to get a response from her. Next, she lifted the baby by its heels and smacked it hard on its back, but still there was no response and Daisy started to cry again. Time seemed to stand still as the nun continued to do all she could to get some response from the child but eventually she lay her gently on the bed then wiped the sweat from her brow.

'I'm sorry, Daisy, but it's no use. I've tried everything I know. I'm afraid she's gone; God bless her little soul.' She began to say a prayer as Daisy looked on in horror. This was her worst nightmare come true. Admittedly the baby had been forced on her and she had never truly wanted it, but now seeing the little soul lying there so weak and defenceless she felt as if her heart would break.

'B-but she can't be.' Her voice cracked as she gently stroked the tiny limp hand. The baby's skin was as smooth as silk and she looked perfect. Lifting her, the nun wrapped her in a towel and handed her to Daisy.

'I shouldn't let you see her really, let alone hold her,' she told Daisy worriedly. 'So don't go telling Sister Monica-Joan, will you?'

Daisy was too upset to answer as she gazed at the baby in her arms. She was still covered in blood but Daisy could see that her hair was fair. She had long eyelashes that curled on her little cheeks and she looked for all the world as if she was just fast asleep and might wake up at any minute.

Sister Patricia was now delivering Daisy's afterbirth, looking concerned. Daisy was still bleeding profusely and the nun knew from past experience that if she couldn't manage to stem the flow, Daisy's life would be seriously at risk.

Daisy, meanwhile, was so intent on trying to memorise every single inch of her daughter's face that she wasn't even aware of the danger she was in.

'I wanted her to be called Mauve after me mammy,' she whispered.

The sister was too busy doing all she could to stop the blood to answer. She wedged a towel between Daisy's legs just as Sister Monica-Joan appeared in the doorway.

'Oh, it's over, is it?' she said brusquely, frowning as she saw the newborn babe in its mother's arms. 'And what were you thinking of, Sister Patricia, allowing the sinner to hold the child? Don't you think it will be tainted enough?'

'I saw no harm in her holding the baby as it was born dead,' the younger nun told her.

Sister Monica-Joan tutted. 'That's a shame, so it is, when we have a list of would-be parents waiting for babies to be born. Still, it's just another price for the sinner to pay. Get rid of it, Sister Patricia,' she said unfeelingly. 'I'll take over here.'

Sister Patricia approached Daisy and gently took the baby from her arms before sadly leaving the room. Daisy could only watch her go. She felt numb and was so quiet that Sister Monica-Joan said, 'Oh, I thought you'd gone as well for a minute there.' She glared at her as she lifted the blood-soaked towel and placed another in its place. 'And there's every chance you still could if this bleeding doesn't slow down. Still, it's in God's hands now. If you don't recover it will be one less sinner in the world.'

Daisy didn't react to the vicious words. She was past caring. She would never forget that tiny face for as long as she lived, and death would be a blessed release from the pain and misery she was feeling.

Chapter Twenty-Four

For two weeks Daisy hovered between life and death but at last the bleeding slowed and although she was weak, she finally began to mend.

'You should be able to get back to work by the end of the week,' Sister Monica-Joan informed her callously one evening when she presented her with her meal on a tray. 'It's not as if we have time to be running about after the likes of you sinners all the time.'

Daisy simply lay there without answering. What was the point? For the first few days after the baby's birth, she had drifted in and out of consciousness, only aware of the sound of a baby crying in the next room after yet another of the girls had given birth. It had tormented her, for she knew that she would not even have that memory of her baby to cling to now. The poor little mite had never even drawn her first breath let alone cried. Despite her despair, day by day Daisy grew a little stronger and now she was able to get out of bed, albeit on wobbly legs, to use the bucket they had placed in the room for her to use as a toilet.

It was a typical showery April day, and she lay watching the raindrops lash against the window through the bars that covered it. There was nothing else to do – nothing to relieve the boredom, so she didn't mind the thought of returning to work. At least if she was busy, she wouldn't have so long to think and remember the ordeal she had gone through.

She often wondered if her father or Lewis ever thought of her. She thought of Rags, too, and hoped he was well, and for the first time she wondered if she would ever see any of them again, or if she was destined to be a prisoner in this place forever.

Two days later, Sister Patricia came to say, 'Daisy, Mother Superier wishes to see you in her office immediately.' She was still the only one of the nuns who had ever called her by her Christian name or shown her an ounce of compassion and Daisy would never forget her for that.

Daisy eased herself to the edge of the bed and once she had managed to sit up and the dizziness had subsided, she dared to place her legs on the floor. They felt like jelly but she persevered and managed to stand before walking slowly behind the nun.

'Lean on me,' the woman offered when they reached the head of the stairs and Daisy did so gratefully until at last, they were in the hallway. Sister Patricia knocked on Mother Superior's door and when she bade them to entre, they went inside. The warmth in the room wrapped around Daisy like a blanket as her bare feet sank into the soft carpets.

'Ah, Armstrong.'

Daisy stood before her desk feeling weaker by the second.

'I have received a letter for you from your stepmother. I have read it and although, as you are aware, I do not usually allow the girls here to receive mail, I feel you should have it. I take it you can read?'

When Daisy nodded, she passed an envelope to her and Daisy withdrew the sheet of paper and began to read.

Dear Daisy,

It is with regret that your father and I have just discovered your deceit and that you are not, as you told us, at your grandparents' home, but in a home for unmarried mothers in Ireland. Of course, we are gravely disappointed in you!

Gilbert has admitted to us that he is the father of your baby, that you threw yourself at him and he was too weak to spurn your advances. He also admitted to being a part of the deceit when you wrote the letters to your father making us believe that you were caring for your grandmother. He now deeply regrets his part in this but admits that he didn't know how to cope with the situation. Because of your wanton behaviour, your father feels that he no longer wishes to call you his daughter and has asked me to write and tell you that you are not welcome here. We have been corresponding with your grandparents who also feel the same, so please, when you leave the home, do not upset them by darkening their doorstep. As far as they are concerned, they no longer have a granddaughter. You are a young woman so we have no doubt that when or if you leave the home, you will be able to make a life for yourself elsewhere.

It is sad that it has had to end this way, but we are now a strong and happy family unit and do not want the shame of having to see you again.

Sincerely

Victoria Armstrong.

As the cruel words sank in Daisy felt as if the floor was rushing up towards her and had it not been for Sister Patricia, who came forward to take her arm, she would have stumbled. But that wasn't all for Mother Superior then went on, 'I also received a letter from your stepmother telling us that she and your father are no longer willing to pay for your stay here. Normally what would happen to other girls in these circumstances is that we would keep them here and they would work to pay for their keep. But they are Catholic girls while you are not even of our religion. And so, I would like you to leave immediately. We do not wish to keep heathens amongst us. Sister Patricia will give you the clothes you arrived in and then I would like you off the premises as soon as possible.'

'B-but where will I go?' Daisy asked in a shaky voice.

Mother Superior shrugged. 'That is of no concern to me. I believe many of our girls who have left under these circumstances end up on the street corners of Dublin earning their living the only way they know how. Once a sinner always a sinner, I'm afraid. And now kindly leave.'

Daisy was so shocked that she was hardly aware of Sister Patricia taking her arm and leading her from the room. Under normal circumstances she would have been delighted to gain her freedom, but after reading the letter, she was heartbroken. How could her daddy believe Gilbert and turn his back on her like that? And her granny and grampy. They were her whole world and now she knew with no shadow of a doubt that she would never be welcomed by any of them ever again. The pain was even worse than that she had felt on the day she had given birth to her stillborn child and she wished at that moment that she had died too.

'Here we are, in here.' Sister Patricia led her into a room where shelves of clothes were packed into bundles with girls' names on them. She went along the shelves examining the labels until she said, 'Ah, these are yours.' She handed the bundle to Daisy. 'I will give you a few minutes to get dressed then I will see you to the front door.' She paused, her face troubled as if she wanted to say something more but then, thinking better of it, she left, closing the door gently behind her.

Daisy untied the string that bound her clothes with shaking fingers and shook them out. They were creased but after the shapeless shift she had become accustomed to wearing they looked luxurious. It felt strange to be getting into underwear and petticoats again, and when she came to put on the gown she had arrived in, she realised with a little shock how much weight she had lost. It hung off her. The shoes and stockings felt even stranger after the hard wooden clogs. Lastly, she put on her coat and bonnet. She was ready to go, although she had no idea where to. Opening the small bag that her clothes had been in, she saw that there were still a few shillings in her purse. It was a pitifully small amount with which to be embarking on a life on her own, and she wondered what would become of her.

Sister Patricia appeared and gave her a gentle smile. 'Are you ready, Daisy?' Personally, she felt that the girl was far too weak to be turned out, but it would be woe betide her if she tried to go against Mother Superior.

'Yes . . . and thank you. You have been the only person, apart from Niamh, who has ever shown me any kindness in here. And just for the record, I swear to you on my life that I was brought here under false pretenses. My stepbrother raped me, I never, ever led him on.'

Just for a second, she thought she saw the hint of tears in the nun's eyes before she ushered her out into the hallway and towards the front door.

Once outside on the steps Sister Patricia took Daisy's hands in hers and said, 'We have advised the gateman that you will be leaving. He will let you out . . . and may God go with you.' With that she went back into the convent while Daisy took her first, faltering steps towards freedom.

Just as the nun had told her, the small gateman was waiting to open the gates for her and he watched her pass through them without a word.

Suddenly she was on the lane that led to the home and she realised that she was free – really free! But her freedom had come at a price: the loss of her family. As she stood there clutching her bag and chewing nervously on her lip, she panicked. Where was she to go? Her grandparents lived temptingly close, and she wondered if she should go there and try to tell them what had really happened. But then pride reared its head and she began to walk ever so slowly in the opposite direction towards Dublin. They must have been so hurt to turn their backs on her as they had, and the last thing she wanted was to inflict any more pain on them. She loved them too much for that.

Thankfully the rain had stopped, although the sky was leaden and grey and the air was damp. Even so, after all the months of being locked away and treated like a prisoner, the open fields had never looked more lovely and she drank in the sight of them. The lane was muddy and covered in puddles and within minutes the hem of her skirt and her boots were sodden. She was still very weak from loss of blood and she had not gone very far when she had to stop and lean against the trunk of a tree as dizziness overtook her.

She had been there for a short while when she heard a cart trundling towards her and when it appeared she saw an elderly gentleman at the reins with winter vegetables piled in the back of it.

He drew up alongside her and frowned. 'Are you all right, pet?' he asked kindly and tears stung her eyes. It had been a long time since anybody had cared apart from Sister Patricia.

'I-I'm trying to get into Dublin,' she told him, although she refrained from telling him where she had just come from.

'Then it's your lucky day, to be sure. I'm headin' there now, so I am. Hop up here on the bench beside me an' we'll be there in no time. Which part o' Dublin were you wantin'?'

It suddenly struck Daisy that she did have somewhere to go after all. Hadn't Niamh told her that if ever she were to get out of the home, she could go to her. The address was imprinted on her brain and she told him, 'I'm going to the village of Blackrock. My friend lives just outside it. I believe it's on the coast.'

'It is that,' he agreed. 'An' not too far from the market I'm headin' for. I'll give you directions when we arrive. It shouldn't take you too long to walk there.'

Daisy thought that was just as well. She felt as weak as a kitten and was just thankful to be sitting down again, although climbing up to the bench seat had felt like climbing a mountain. As they moved on it started to rain again and reaching into the back of the cart the man picked up a sack and handed it to her. 'Here you are, lass, it ain't posh but it'll keep the worst off you if you put it over your head and shoulders.'

'Thank you.'

Daisy huddled beneath the sack feeling a little more optimistic. At least she had somewhere to head to, but it wasn't like going home and her heart broke afresh as she realised she could never go home again. She had never dreamed that her daddy would turn his back on her, but love was a powerful thing, and he clearly loved his new wife. Victoria had wanted rid of her from the day they had wed and now she had got her way. But, oh, how she wished she could have had just ten minutes alone to tell him what had really happened. Perhaps then things might have been different. Still, she consoled herself, at least she was away from the dreadful home. And soon, hopefully, she would be reunited with Niamh. That was something to look forward to. She just prayed the girl would stand by her promise of giving her shelter. If she didn't Daisy didn't know what she would do!

At last, the cart rattled over the cobblestones of Dublin town. Up ahead she could see the stalls of a small market, which was where the kindly farmer was heading. When he drew the horse to a halt he jumped down and helped Daisy to the ground.

'Here we are then, lass.' He frowned as she wobbled danger-ously and held on to the side of the cart for a moment. 'Are you sure you'll be all right now?' He looked at her with concern.

She forced a smile. 'Yes . . . thank you, you've been very kind.'

'Right.' He pointed ahead. 'Follow the street to the very end, then turn right and keep going. The road will take you back out of the town and if you stay on the coastal path, it will bring you to Blackrock. It's not so far as the crow flies.'

She took the sack from her shoulders and handed it back to him and after thanking him once more she set off on wobbly legs. Just as the man had told her, she eventually came to the coastal path and set off along it, leaving the town behind her. The wind was bitterly cold and it was still raining so she was surprised to find that she was sweating. To the side of her the Irish sea was choppy and grey, thundering onto the beach in great crested waves, but Daisy felt too ill to notice. Normally she would have loved being close to the sea but today she just needed to get somewhere she could rest.

Soon she was gasping as the sweat rolled down her face and every step was an effort. And then at last a row of terraced cottages came into sight and she prayed that these might be the ones that Niamh lived in, for she wasn't sure how much further she could go. The address Niamh had given her was number four Sea View Terrace. Daisy had thought how grand that had sounded but as she drew closer, she saw that this wasn't the case. The cottages were dilapidated and tiny, but she didn't care so long as they could offer her shelter.

The doors of each cottage were firmly closed against the cold, and there was not a soul in sight, although there was smoke ris-ing from the chimneys. Heartened that this might be the right place, Daisy found number four as waves of dizziness washed over her. She could hear the sound of children inside and leant heavily against the door frame before knocking on the door weakly. And as if in answer to her prayers it opened and Niamh's face appeared.

'Why, Daisy!' She looked delighted but shocked. 'How did you get here?'

Daisy opened her mouth to answer but then blackness rushed towards her and she fell forward into Niamh's arms and knew no more.

Chapter Twenty-Five

When Daisy finally opened her eyes, she found herself in a tiny room lying on a straw mattress to the side of a fireplace. Niamh was bending over her, tenderly bathing her forehead with cool water from a bowl and as Daisy blinked blearily up at her she sighed with relief.

'Oh, lass! You gave me a rare turn there, so you did! I thought for a while you were a goner, to be sure!'

Daisy opened her mouth to speak but it was so dry that no sound came out, so she just lay back against the pillows as Niamh rushed away to get her some water. On the floor nearby, two little girls and a small boy with serious expressions sat cross-legged, and she managed to smile at them – they looked frightened. Niamh came back with the water, and held Daisy's head while she gulped at it. She was sure nothing had ever tasted so good.

'Now then, sip it, don't gulp, you'll make yourself sick,' Niamh scolded but she was smiling.

Daisy looked down and was surprised to see that she was dressed in a thick cotton nightgown and she could see her clothes spread across a wooden clothes horse drying by the fire.

'I-I'm so sorry to be a bother,' Daisy croaked.

Niamh laughed. 'Don't be so daft. It's right welcome you are. But I'm longin' to know how you got out o' that place.'

Daisy opened her mouth to explain, but Niamh held her hand up. 'No, not now. Later will do, when your strength has come back a bit. I'll tell you now, you were burnin' up when you

184

arrived, I could have fried an egg on your forehead, so I could.'
She turned to the two little girls, who were like peas in a pod, and
told them, 'Keep your eye on Daisy for me while I go an' finish
makin' the dinner. Daddy will be in soon – that's if he doesn't
call into the inn on his way home – an' you know what he's like if
his dinner isn't on the table.'

When she'd gone, the girls cautiously approached Daisy and
she managed another smile. 'And what are your names?'

They were both blue-eyed and blonde and one of them told her,
'I'm Roise, and this is Aoife. We're twins, so we are, and we're
seven years old.' She pointed to their brother who was also fair-
haired and told her solemnly, 'An' that's our Riley. He's nine. How
old are you?'

'I'm twenty-two.'

'Ooh, that's very old, so it is,' the little girl responded.

Daisy found herself smiling again. 'How long have I been
here?'

'You came yesterday an' our Niamh has been lookin' after you.
She t'ought you was going to die, so she did!'

Niamh bustled back in, wiping her hands on a bit of rag and
scolding them, 'Now, girls, what do you t'ink you are doing? I told
you to keep an eye on her, not chew her ears off, the poor soul.'

'I don't mind – really,' Daisy defended them. She was still very
weak but was already feeling so much better than she had.

The door opened and an older boy appeared. Unlike his sisters
he had dark hair and eyes and he was very tall and handsome.

'This is me big brother Declan,' Niamh introduced him and
he gave Daisy a smile that could have charmed the birds off the
trees.

'Nice to meet you, Daisy. It's good to see you looking a little
better. Our Niamh was worried sick about you yesterday, to be
sure. She stayed up all night wit' you.'

'Oh, I'm so sorry I . . .'

'Don't be!' Niamh glared at her brother. 'You would have done the same t'ing for me. I sleep down here any road. There ain't enough room upstairs for all of us. An' it used to be worse. There were ten of us weans at one time but t'ree of 'em died.'

The door opened again, letting in a blast of bitterly cold salt-laden air and another boy appeared, this one looked to be slightly younger than Declan.

'An' this is our Ryan,' Niamh told her with a smile at the lad, who looked very much like his brother.

He smiled and nodded towards Daisy before heading for a door that she later learnt led up to the bedrooms. It was such a tiny house that Daisy wondered how they all managed to fit in it.

'Ryan works on the docks unloadin' an loadin' the ferries,' Niamh informed her friend. 'And Declan works at the brewery makin' Guinness. That's why he allus stinks so!' The little girls giggled and Daisy had a warm feeling inside. This family didn't have much but it was obvious they cared about each other.

'How many more of you are there?' Daisy asked.

'Oh, there's just Daddy an' our Erin to come now. She's fourteen an' works in a tailor's shop in Dublin town sewin'. She's a dab hand wit' a needle. Takes after our mammy, she does. Daddy works at Jacob's biscuit factory, which has its perks cos the workers are allowed to buy the broken biscuits for a song, so they are.' She chuckled. 'At least when he goes off the rails an' his wages go over the bar we have biscuits to eat if not'in' else.'

Already Daisy's eyes were closing so after tucking the blanket more securely about her Niamh left her to sleep.

The next time Daisy woke she saw a man smoking a pipe on the other side of the fireplace surveying her solemnly.

'Ah, here you are.' Niamh hurried over to her. She had been washing pots at the sink and there was no sign of the children now so Daisy guessed it must be late. 'Do you t'ink you could manage to eat a little broth now? We need to build your strength back up. Oh, an' this is me daddy, Nolan, by the way. Daddy, meet Daisy.'

The man inclined his head and Daisy blushed. He looked to be about the same age as her own father and was still attractive for his age: tall with thick, dark curly hair and deep-brown eyes.

'How do you do?' Daisy said politely. 'I'm so sorry to impose on you like this but I didn't know where else—'

He held his hand up. 'There's no need to apologise. Niamh had told us all about you before you arrived an' it's welcome you are.'

'I-I won't stay longer than I have to,' Daisy promised.

Again he shook his head. 'Let's just concentrate on gettin' you better, lass, eh? Then we'll decide what you're to do.'

She gave him a grateful smile and minutes later Niamh came back with a dish of broth that smelled delicious.

'So now, let's get you propped up a bit an' see if we can get some o' this inside you.' She hoisted Daisy up on her pillows as Nolan tapped his pipe out on the hearth and rose to his feet.

'Right, it's off to bed for me. See you in the morning, girls.' And with that he disappeared through the stairs' door and they were finally alone. Daisy was so weak that she could barely hold the spoon but Niamh helped her patiently. After the awful meals they had been served back at the home the broth was so tasty that Daisy could have happily cleared the whole bowlful, but after a few spoons she found that she had had enough.

'Aw well, at least we got a bit down you,' Niamh told her brightly. 'Now we're on our own you can tell me how you came to be here. Did you manage to escape?'

'As it turned out I didn't have to . . .' Daisy went on to tell her about the letter she had received from her stepmother and the other one that had been sent to the Mother Superior.

'So, the long and the short of it is they threw me out,' she ended in a choky voice. It was still very hard to accept that her whole family had turned their backs on her for something that hadn't been her fault. She had never once led Gilbert on or given him the least encouragement, in fact it had been quite the opposite. And yet her father and stepmother had chosen to take his word over hers.

'And your baby?' Niamh asked hesitantly.

'Born dead.'

Niamh quickly made the sign of the cross on her chest and sighed sadly. 'Quite a few o' the babies that are born there are, an' it's no wonder when you t'ink how the poor mothers are treated. Still, at least you're out o' there now. It's over.'

'But it isn't for me, is it?' Tears were trickling down Daisy's cheeks. 'I've lost everything and everyone I cared about. My home, my daddy and my grandparents. I don't know what I'm going to do.'

'Then I'll tell you.' Daisy frowned at her. 'You're goin' to stay here wit' us for as long as you like. Perhaps when you feel stronger you could get a little job or just stay here an' help me. God knows there's always enough to do wit' my lot. Washin', cookin', cleanin', it's never-endin'.'

'And how are *you* feeling?

Niamh's eyes filled with tears as she thought of the tiny daughter she had been forced to give up. 'Oh, t'ings ain't so bad. Daddy refuses to even let me mention the baby so I have to try an' put it all behind me, though I'll never forget her.'

Daisy squeezed her hand. 'Let's both just take one day at a time for now, eh?' she suggested. The last thing she wanted was to be a burden on the family.

Over the next week Daisy grew a little stronger each day until she was well enough to sit in a chair for a few hours with a blanket across her legs. She felt dreadful watching Niamh run around after her, doing all the work, but vowed she would make it up to her as soon as she was able. She would never forget what her friend had done for her in her hour of need and shuddered to think what might have happened had she not been able to come here. She was still heartbroken about the way her father had turned his back on her and also surprised to find that the thought of never seeing Lewis again was painful. They had grown close when he'd moved into the cottage and she found herself thinking of him more and more. But if Gilbert had convinced him that the pregnancy was all her fault, she supposed he couldn't be expected to have any sympathy for her.

Already she had grown fond of Niamh's family. They had all been so good to her, even Niamh's father.

'I reckon he's been on his best behaviour since you arrived. He ain't passed his wages over the bar once. He must be tryin' to make a good impression,' Niamh laughed one morning as she was helping Daisy to wash and dress. 'An' long may it last.'

The statement worried Daisy somewhat. She had seen the way Nolan looked at her and noticed how attentive he was towards her. She had seen that look before on Gilbert's face and she hoped she was wrong. Nolan was a nice man but old enough to be her father and she had no intention of becoming romantically involved with him.

Her hair had begun to grow back now and formed a halo of soft curls around her face, and although she still looked frail and thin the bloom was returning to her cheeks. She hoped soon she would be well enough to find work of some kind, so she tried her best to eat whatever Niamh put in front of her to build her strength up.

They were nearing the end of April and Daisy could now sit outside the door as the weather had drastically improved. The view was breathtaking with rolling green fields surrounding the humble cottages and the sea stretching away like a never-ending blue carpet in front of them. Now she was able to help Niamh do little jobs about the house, and although she still had to rest frequently, she began to feel better day by day.

Eventually the time came when she told Niamh, 'I think I might take a walk into Dublin tomorrow to see if there are any jobs going.'

Niamh instantly looked worried. 'But it's a fair stretch; are you sure you're up to it?'

As it happened Daisy didn't have to go searching for a job because that evening when Erin got back from work, she told her, 'The pie an' mash shop a few doors down from where I work is lookin' for someone to work part-time.'

'Really?' Daisy was immediately interested. She still hadn't regained her full strength so a part-time job would be ideal for now. 'Do you think they'd consider me?'

'Don't see why not.' Erin smiled at her. 'You could walk into work wit' me tomorrow if you like an' I could introduce you to Mr and Mrs Kelly who own the shop.'

And so the next morning Daisy was up bright and early, trying to make herself look respectable.

'Now, don't go pushin' yourself,' Niamh warned, clucking around her like a mother hen. 'If you get part o' the way an' find the walk is too much turn around an' come straight back.'

Daisy laughed and pecked Niamh on the cheek and she and Erin set off. Admittedly, she felt exhausted by the time they reached the high street, but she was also excited about the prospect of getting a job.

'That's the Kellys' shop just there. Come on, let's go an' see what you t'ink of 'em.'

Erin led the way and Daisy followed, hoping that she would be successful. If she could only earn some money, she would be able to give Niamh some to cover her board, but better still she would hopefully be able to save some too, and then she could decide what she wanted to do. After all, she couldn't expect Niamh's family to keep her forever.

'I'm ready,' Daisy told Erin, and taking a deep breath and lifting her head high she entered the shop.

Chapter Twenty-Six

Ansley Village, April 1882

It was purely by chance that Jed saw the postman heading for his house at the end of April as he hurried from the forge. He would usually have been hard at work, but for the last few days he'd been forced to keep making a rush for the toilet with an upset stomach. He couldn't understand it: normally he was as strong as an ox but lately he'd been feeling really off colour.

'Anythin' there for me, Fred?' he asked cheerily.

The postman nodded. 'There is, Jed. A letter an' it's got an Irish postmark.'

'Ah, that'll be from our Daisy. It's funny, though, I had one from her only a few days ago. I hope nothin's happened to her granny.' He took the letter from the man before making a dash for the toilet situated beside the house. He was sitting there with his trousers around his ankles when he glanced at the envelope and realised it was Bridie's handwriting.

Frowning, he slit it open and withdrew the paper inside.

As he began to read the colour drained from his face and his mouth gaped open. None of what Bridie said made any sense. Dragging his trousers back up he stuffed the letter into his pocket, hastily buttoned his flies and marched into the kitchen.

'Where's Gilbert?' he demanded shortly, looking at Victoria, who was sitting in her usual seat while Mrs Smith cleaned up around her.

She straightened in her chair and glared at him. She'd have something to say to him later for speaking to her like that – and in front of the char lady, indeed!

'As you should know, he's at work,' she answered frostily.

At Jed's insistence, Gilbert had taken a clerk's job in the local bank, and he hated every single minute of it.

'And what time will he be home?'

'I should think about five thirty. But why do you want to know?'

Without bothering to answer, he turned and strode back to the forge where he asked Lewis, 'Would you get Fancy and the cart ready for me, lad, please? I have to go into town, it's important.'

Lewis looked concerned. 'Is there something wrong, Jed? Would you like me to come with you?'

'No, lad, you stay here an' finish that repair for Farmer Baker, if you would. I'll tell you all about it when I get back.' And with that Jed hurried back to the house to quickly get changed into some more respectable clothes. He knew Victoria well enough to know that she wouldn't appreciate him going into town in his work clothes.

Meanwhile Lewis quickly harnessed Fancy and went into the barn to drag the cart out. As he was hauling it towards the door a sack hidden behind some bales of straw caught his eye and, curious, he went to see what was in it. What he found made him frown. It was one of Gilbert's best outfits but there was something dark and dried all over them and as he looked closer, he recoiled with horror when he realised it was blood. But whose blood was it? he wondered. And why had Gilbert hidden the clothes? What was he covering up? Quickly he checked the pockets of the trousers and frowned as his hand closed around something. It was a leather wallet with the initials MJ on the front of it.

He heard Jed emerge from the house at that moment and hastily stuffing the clothing and the wallet into the sack, he put it back where he had found it and went to the cart. He had it hitched up to Fancy in minutes and Jed drove off in a hurry, leaving Lewis to wonder just what the hell was going on. And what about the clothes he had found? MJ. The initials meant nothing to him until he suddenly remembered the murder of Mickey Jameson! But no, surely his brother couldn't have had anything to do with that? He knew Gilbert had owed Mickey money but that wouldn't be enough reason to kill someone. And what if he were to question him about it? He could be stirring up a hornet's nest and as much as he disliked him at times, Gilbert was still his brother and he didn't want to see him dangling at the end of a rope. He decided that it might be as well to tread carefully for now. But one thing was for sure, he would be keeping a very close eye on Gilbert in future!

All the way into town, Jed's heart was pounding with panic and anger. He would have liked to push Fancy into a fast trot but mindful that she was an old horse he let her go at her own pace. As soon as he arrived, he tethered the horse and strode towards the bank with a face as dark as thunder.

'I wish to see Gilbert Peake – now,' he told a young man sitting at a desk. 'And tell him it's important.'

The young man frowned. 'Er . . . our manager doesn't like staff having personal visits during working hours, sir,' he sputtered.

Incensed, Jed slammed his fist down onto the desk so hard that the inkwell danced. 'I said *now*!'

'Yes, sir . . . excuse me.' The young man hurried away through a door behind the desk only to return minutes later with the manager, who recognised Jed immediately.

'Ah, hello, Mr Armstrong. What brings you here today?' he asked pleasantly. Jed had been a good customer over the years.

'I need to see my stepson and it's urgent.' Jed tapped his foot impatiently.

The manager shook his head. 'I would like to see him too,' he answered with a frown. 'But he hasn't turned up to work again today and if he doesn't pull his socks up very soon, I'm afraid I shall have no choice but to dismiss him. It really isn't good enough!'

'I see!' Jed was even more furious now, although he realised it wasn't the manager's fault. 'In that case, rest assured I shall be havin' words with him when he comes home. I'm sorry for disturbing you. Good day.'

Once outside he glanced up and down Queen's Road, wondering what to do. Common sense told him that Gilbert could be anywhere, so eventually he climbed back onto the cart and started the journey home.

Back at the house he unharnessed Fancy and gave her a rub down before turning her out into a small paddock to the side of the orchard to graze. He felt sick with worry but there was nothing he could do until Gilbert decided to show his face.

'Where have you been?' Victoria asked the second he stepped back into the kitchen. 'If you've been into town, I could have come with you. There's a bonnet I have my eye on in the window of the milliner's.'

Jed merely glared at her before stamping upstairs to get changed. He had work waiting to be done but he knew it was going to be hard to concentrate after what he had read in the letter.

'Is everything all right, Jed?' Lewis asked cautiously when Jed went back to the forge.

Jed scowled as he lifted the heavy leather apron and tied it about his waist. And suddenly the anger disappeared like mist in the morning and in its place was merely dread.

'No, it ain't, Lewis, it's far from all right,' he admitted in a shaky voice. 'I had a letter from my mother-in-law this mornin' an' it appears that Daisy ain't there.'

Lewis looked confused. 'But I thought Daisy was looking after her granny because she's been sick?'

'So did I but it seems she never arrived! That's why they wrote; they're worried because they haven't heard from her. And it doesn't sound as though they were expecting a visit, neither.'

Lewis's face fell. 'So where is she then . . . and how come you've been receiving letters from her?'

Jed shrugged. 'I have no idea where she is, that's the trouble. I can only think that she must be sending the letters from wherever she's staying. But why would she do that? Pretend to be at her granny's, I mean? And why did Gilbert tell us that he'd taken her to the door if she never arrived? I'm tellin' you, that brother o' yours 'as some questions to answer when he gets in tonight. I went to the bank to speak to him but surprise, surprise, he never turned in for work today an' it seems from what the manager said that it's a common occurrence.'

Lewis chewed on his lip. He had a few questions of his own he wanted answering, and his stomach churned as he thought of the bloodstained clothing he'd found in the barn. Could it be that it was Daisy's blood? Had Gilbert done something to her? But soon common sense took over and his heart rate slowed a little. No, of course it couldn't be that. The initials on the wallet had clearly read MJ. And Daisy wouldn't still be sending letters home if anything had happened to her, would she?

The two men started work again but neither of them could concentrate fully and the day seemed to drag by interminably slowly.

The forge was a nice place to work in the cold weather, cosy and warm, but now that the sun was shining it was unbearably hot and they worked on with the outer door wide open – not that it did much to cool the place. Daisy had always said that the furnace was like a hungry dragon that needed feeding coal on the hour.

They finished work early that afternoon, which was rare for them, and when they entered the kitchen Victoria looked up from her seat in surprise.

'Are you going to tell me what's wrong now?' she asked peevishly. 'It's apparent that something is.'

Jed told her briefly about the letter from Ireland and she frowned. She had hoped to keep up the deception for a little longer.

'Well, obviously wherever Daisy is she doesn't want you to know,' she answered unfeelingly. 'And she is a grown woman so I don't see that there's much you can do about it if she doesn't want to come home!'

Jed merely glared at her as he paced the floor waiting for Gilbert to put in an appearance. He then went on to tell her what the bank manager had said about her son's poor attendance, and she pouted.

'Perhaps you are to blame for that! After all, Gilbert never wanted that job in the first place. It was you who insisted he should work.'

'And why shouldn't he?' Jed snapped, his eyes flashing. 'Why should he be allowed to spend his time swanning about expecting me to keep him? He's a grown man, for goodness' sake, it's just a shame he can't act like one. He's been thoroughly spoilt!'

Victoria's nostrils flared. 'Huh! You're a right one to cast blame for that,' she retaliated. 'There's no one more spoilt than your Daisy!'

'How can you even *say* that?' Jed was furious. 'Why, my Daisy did more work here in a day keeping the house running smoothly than you do in a month! I've even had to bring a village woman in to keep on top of the work because you won't do it!'

'I didn't realise you only married me because you wanted a skivvy!' Victoria decided to try a different tack. 'You knew when we were walking out together that I had maids to do the house-work for me and I expected to have the same here.' A solitary tear slid down her powdered cheek but once again it had no effect on her husband whatsoever. In fact, if anything it seemed to make him angrier still.

'Why don't you get washed and changed, darling,' she suggested with a sweet smile. 'You know I don't like to see you in your dirty clothes and smelling like a furnace!'

He glared at her and at that moment they heard the gate opening and closing. It was Gilbert coming home.

Lewis wasn't sure if he was relieved or scared. His mother and Jed were clearly on the edge of a major row and he hoped it wouldn't erupt further now his brother had appeared.

'Evening, all.' Gilbert stepped into the kitchen as if he hadn't a care in the world.

'Busy day, was it?'

Failing to notice the sarcasm in Jed's voice, Gilbert nodded. 'Oh, you know! So so, no more than usual.' He crossed to the sink to swill his hands.

'That's funny. It looked busy when I went in this morning.'

Gilbert's smile slipped. 'Oh! You don't usually go into the bank until Friday. Was there any particular reason?'

'There was, as it happens. I wanted to speak to you, but I was told that you hadn't shown up . . . *again*, according to the manager. But that isn't what I wanted to speak to you about. We'll sort that later. What I want to know is what this is about.' He thrust the letter from Bridie into Gilbert's hand.

As the young man read it, his Adam's apple bobbed nervously up and down in his throat. 'So, er . . . what's this to do with me?' he asked eventually.

Jed struggled to contain his urge to thump him.

'It's got *everything* to do with you, you stupid little bastard!' Jed shouted angrily, making Victoria flinch. '*You* were the one who went with her to Ireland and you told me that you'd taken her direct to her granny's door. So, what I want to know is . . . why did you lie to me and *where* the bloody hell is Daisy?'

'I, er . . . I have no idea.' Gilbert was having to think quickly now.

'But you *must* have. You said you'd seen her to her granny's door when she's never even been there.'

'Well, er . . .' Gilbert's mind was working overtime. 'The truth of it is, once we got to Dublin, Daisy told me she had somewhere to go but she wouldn't say where. She just said to tell you she had arrived at her granny's safely and then she went her own way. I only told you what she'd told me to! And she must be all right, mustn't she? Otherwise, she wouldn't have been writing to you. She clearly just doesn't want you to know where she is.'

Suddenly Jed's shoulders sagged and as a wave of dizziness swept over him, he dropped heavily onto the nearest chair and buried his face in his hands. He had no reason to think that Gilbert was lying but this didn't sound like something Daisy would do. She had always been as honest as the day was long and had never lied to him before, so what could be so terrible that she had started now? There was only one thing he could do. If Gilbert was saying that he had last seen her in Dublin, then that was where he must begin his search.

Meanwhile, Lewis waited for his chance to get his brother alone and it came late that night when everyone else had gone to bed. As usual Gilbert had gone out early that evening and Lewis lay awake listening for him to come in. As soon as he heard the back door open, he pulled on his trousers and crept downstairs just in time to see Gilbert sprawl into the fireside chair.

'I want a word with you,' Lewis said sternly, and Gilbert looked blearily up at him. He had clearly had too much to drink as usual.

'Can't it wait till morning?' he muttered drunkenly. 'I've had enough with the old man getting on at me earlier without *you* starting!'

'No, I'm afraid it *can't* wait!' Lewis stood in front of him, his hands on his hips and his eyes flashing. 'I want you to explain why

I found a sackful of your best clothes hidden in the barn. And, may I add, covered in blood!'

Gilbert looked startled. Lewis could only be talking about the clothes he had thrown away on the night he had murdered Mickey Jameson, but he had put the sack onto the bonfire so how had they ended up in the barn?

'I, er . . . have no idea what you're talkin' about,' he blustered. The police had called off the search for Mickey's murderer as far as he knew and the last thing he needed was someone to get them to reopen the case.

'If I thought for one minute that you had harmed a single hair of Daisy's head I would murder you with my bare hands,' Lewis growled.

Gilbert felt relief flood through him. Thank goodness, Lewis had clearly not linked him with Mickey's death. 'Don't talk so fuckin' daft, man,' he said defensively. He'd thought that Lewis had feelings for Daisy for some time now, but he had just confirmed it. 'I haven't hurt her. Why would I? It was like I told Jed, we got to Ireland and went our separate ways. God knows where she is. She's probably shacked up with some bloke somewhere.'

'Why, you filthy-minded little *scum*!' Before Gilbert knew what was happening Lewis had punched him hard in the face and blood spurted from his nose. 'Now tell me or I'll shake you like a dog would shake a rat. If that isn't Daisy's blood on your clothes, whose is it? And why was there a wallet in your pocket with the initials MJ on it?'

Suddenly sober again, Gilbert had to think quickly. 'The blood was mine, if you must know,' he said heatedly as he pressed a handkerchief to his nose. 'I got drunk one night and went my length on the way home. That's when I had the black eye. You know what him upstairs is like. I'd never have heard the last of it if he'd seen the state I was in, so I thought it would be easier to just dispose of the clothes. And as for the wallet I found it in the town. I don't know why I even bothered picking it up really, there was nothing in it!'

Lewis eyed him warily for a moment, his fists clenching and unclenching. 'It did occur to me that Mickey Jameson was killed on the night that happened so I just hope you're telling the truth,' he ground out. 'Because as sure as eggs is eggs if I find you're lying you won't live to lie again.' And with that he stormed back upstairs leaving Gilbert to stare after him. All in all, it hadn't been the best of days.

Chapter Twenty-Seven

Blackrock, Ireland

'Eh, come an' put your feet up, lass. You look worn out, so you do!' Niamh pulled a chair out from the table and Daisy sank onto it with a grateful sigh.

She had been working at the pie and mash shop for a while now and she was exhausted. Mr and Mrs Kelly were nice people but they expected a hard day's work from all their employees, and as Daisy still wasn't back to her full strength it had taken its toll. They had agreed that she would work four days a week: Wednesday, Thursday, Friday and Saturday, which were their busiest days, and already Daisy was heartily sick of the sight of pie and mash. She had never dreamed that so many different pies existed. There were steak and kidney, chicken and mushroom, chicken and ale, pork and lamb to name but a few. Mr Kelly made them all himself, starting at five o'clock each morning so the first batch would be ready when the shop opened.

'They must be makin' a fortune, to be sure,' Erin said one morning as she and Daisy walked back home after work, and Daisy didn't doubt it. She was on her feet from the time she arrived until the time they closed the doors at five thirty. The kitchen at the shop was downstairs so Daisy spent a lot of her day running up and down the stairs fetching each fresh batch as they were baked. In between she waited at the counter or did any extra jobs Mrs Kelly needed her to do.

Some days they gave Daisy the pies that hadn't been sold to take home, which was a great help for Niamh, who had to manage the housekeeping money.

Tonight her wages were tucked in her pocket and all the hard work felt worth it. When she got back home, she laid two shillings on the table.

Niamh shook her head. 'That's far too much,' she objected. 'You don't eat enough to keep a bird alive, so you don't, so there's no way I'm takin' all that off you.'

'I insist,' Daisy told her with a smile. 'You said yourself the other day that Roise and Aoife need some new boots. I'm sure you'd be able to get them each a good second-hand pair off the rag stall with that if you can find their sizes.'

The two little girls nodded eagerly. 'So you could, Niamh,' they told their sister. 'We both have blisters from our old boots, so we do.'

Niamh melted. She could never say no to her little sisters, especially as they were still missing their mammy so much. 'Very well, we'll go to the market next week,' she promised, and with a grateful smile at Daisy she put the money in the tin on the shelf.

As the little girls ran outside to play, Daisy chuckled. 'I still can't tell those two apart. I don't know how you manage to.'

'It's easy when they're standin' up, so it is,' Niamh confided as she carried a cup of tea over to her. 'Roise is fractionally taller than Aoife. But it's harder if they're sittin' or lyin' down. But here, get this down you, dinner will be ready soon.' She grinned. 'I reckon your comin' has had a good effect on this family. Daddy ain't stopped off once at the inn since you've been here an' neither has our Declan. Between you an' me, I reckon they both have a soft spot for you.'

Daisy forced a smile as she sipped at the hot drink. Their attentions hadn't gone unnoticed and she found it concerning. She liked them but that was as far as it went, and she didn't want to give either of them the wrong idea. She had no wish to get romantically involved with anyone. Unbidden a picture of Lewis's kind face flashed before her eyes and she felt her colour rise. Now why did I suddenly think of him? she wondered, and quickly went on to tell Niamh about some of the people she had met in the shop that day.

Almost an hour later Nolan arrived home from the biscuit factory carrying a bag of broken biscuits in one hand and a bunch of wildflowers in the other.

Smiling nervously, he held the flowers out to Daisy. 'I, er . . . thought you might like these, lass.' In that moment it would have been hard to say who was the most embarrassed, him or Daisy.

'Er . . . why, er . . . thank you,' Daisy stuttered.

When the twins started to giggle Daisy felt like crawling under the table but luckily Niamh saved the day when she told them all, 'Right, you lot, come to the table if you want your meal. I ain't stood here slavin' over the hob all afternoon for it to be ruined, for sure.'

Declan was the first to take a seat, glaring at his father all the while.

'Actually, I had some pie at work, Niamh, so I won't have any, if you don't mind,' Daisy said hastily, and rising she placed the flowers on the wooden draining board and escaped outside.

It was a beautiful evening, although there was still a nip in the air. She stood for a few minutes before deciding that a walk along the beach might be just what she needed to clear her head, so she set off in that direction. Very soon she was wandering along the shoreline with her boots dangling from her hand as she paddled in the surf. The sea was calm, although there was a breeze down there that tossed her hair into a mass of tangled curls. Daisy's hair had always grown fast and already it almost touched her shoulders and it was hard to remember how awful it had looked after the nuns had hacked at it in the home. She shuddered at the memory before forcing herself to think of the flowers that Nolan had picked for her. He was a lovely man and he had shown her nothing but kindness ever since she had arrived so unexpectedly at his home. But now Daisy feared that he might be seeing her as a replacement for his wife and she didn't know what to do about it. She didn't want to hurt his feelings, but she looked on him as a father figure rather than a husband. And then there was Declan; he too had gone out of his way to be nice to her. He hadn't asked her out as yet, but she had a horrible feeling that he would and then what would she do? Suddenly she thought of Lewis again and soon the tears came. She missed him and her daddy and Rags, and knowing that none of them ever wanted to see her again was still painfully raw.

After a time, she sank onto the sand to think. It seemed there was only one sensible option. She must find somewhere else to live and avoid any problems. But where could she go? She was so lost in her thoughts that she didn't realise how long she had been gone until she suddenly became aware of a small figure racing along the beach towards her. It was Riley, Niamh's youngest brother.

'Here y'are.' He gave her a cheeky grin. 'Our Niamh's worried sick, so she is, so she sent me to find you.'

'I'm sorry, I didn't mean to worry anyone.' Daisy quickly rose and after brushing the sand from her skirt they walked back along the beach together.

'Me daddy an' our Declan have just had words,' the child told her solemnly. 'Though I don't know what it were about.'

Daisy sighed. She had been right to think of leaving and she determined to do just that as soon as she could find somewhere cheap to rent. A room somewhere, perhaps? There was no way she could afford to rent a whole house or cottage. *I'll start to look in my dinner break on Wednesday*, she thought. Then again, perhaps it would be better to walk into Dublin the next day while the family were at church.

Thankfully, when they got back to the cottage, Nolan was sitting quietly at the side of the fire smoking his pipe and reading his newspaper and there was no sign of Declan. Daisy breathed a sigh of relief and kept out of the way as much as she was able to.

Once everyone had gone to bed that evening and she and Niamh were alone having a cup of cocoa, Daisy told her friend of her plans. 'I was thinking that it's time I found myself a room in Dublin somewhere,' she said. 'I think I've imposed on you and your family for long enough. But I'll never forget what you've done for me. I dread to think what might have become of me if you hadn't taken me in when I was ill.'

Niamh looked horrified. 'Ah, but we love havin' you here, so we do,' she protested.

'Thank you, but look around. You're crammed in and me being here as well is only making things more difficult for you.'

Niamh gave her a knowing look. 'It ain't nothin' to do wi' overcrowdin', is it? It's cos me daddy an' our Declan have set their caps at you, ain't it?'

Daisy glanced towards the wildflowers that Niamh had put in a jar on the windowsill, and flushed. 'Well, I, er . . . don't want to make problems,' Daisy said quietly. 'And they're both lovely but after what happened with Gilbert, I don't want anything to do with men, not for a long time at least.'

Niamh sighed. 'I know what you mean.' They were both thinking of the babies they had lost and the pain was still raw. 'All I can say is that you must do what's right for you, but please don't go until you've got somewhere decent to stay. There are some right slums in Dublin, so there are. Why don't you let me help you find somewhere? I know the town better than you. We could walk into town while the men are at work.'

'I'd appreciate that.' Daisy squeezed her hand. In Niamh she had found a true friend and she thanked God for her. Meeting her had been the only good thing to come out of the sorry mess she had found herself in and she knew they would be friends for life.

The next morning Niamh and Daisy set out for Dublin along the coastal path. Even though it was spring it was windy and by the time they reached the road they were both cold.

'Let's treat ourselves to a cup o' tea,' Niamh suggested when they reached the high street.

They were sitting in a café enjoying their drink when Daisy glanced up and Niamh saw the colour drain out of her face as she slopped the contents of her tea all over the table.

'Holy Mother, what's wrong wit' you?' Niamh said as she dabbed ineffectively at the spills.

'S-sorry.' Daisy had shrunk down in her chair. 'But that's my granny over the road. The one standing outside the greengrocer's.'

Niamh followed her friend's gaze and saw a little, homely looking grey-haired woman with a basket on her arm rooting amongst the carrots.

'So perhaps you should go and have a word wit' her?'

Daisy shook her head. 'No, she mustn't see me. She's washed her hands of me and I'm too ashamed to face her.'

Niamh scowled and looked furious. 'Sure, so perhaps it's time you told her what really went on, then!'

'No!' Daisy was adamant.

She could never make Niamh understand how much the family disowning her had wounded her and she didn't want to make things worse. She loved her granny with all her heart and she knew that should she have to face her now she wouldn't be able to bear the look of disgust on her face.

Niamh fell silent. She was clearly not happy with Daisy's decision but there was nothing she could do about it.

Eventually Daisy's granny went into the shop and a short time later she came back out with her purchases in her basket and went on her way along the busy street.

'I suppose we should get on and look at some rooms now,' Daisy said quietly when her granny was out of sight.

They left the café and headed for the back streets where there were rows of terraced houses with front doors that opened directly onto the street. They didn't look at all salubrious, but Daisy supposed beggars couldn't be choosers.

In the window of one of them was a sign saying 'Room for Rent' so Niamh knocked at the door.

It was opened by an old man who looked as if he hadn't bathed or shaved for at least a month. Even from the pavement they could smell the ripe scent of stale urine as he peered at them.

'Yes?'

'We've come to enquire about the room you have to rent,' Niamh told him.

He smiled, revealing a set of tobacco-stained teeth. 'Ah, then come in.' He ushered them into a tiny hallway that smelled even worse than he did. The paint was peeling and the wallpaper was hanging off the walls. A staircase led directly up from the hall and he pointed towards it. 'The room is up there. The second on the right. I t'ink you'll like it.'

Both Daisy and Niamh doubted that very much but they were here now, so it seemed silly not to have a look. Daisy went first, followed by Niamh and the old man and when they reached the room, he shoved the door open and ushered them inside.

'Here we are. What to do you t'ink of it?'

Anyone would have thought he was showing them into a room in a palace but the one they found themselves in was as far from a palace as it was possible to be. An old, tarnished brass bed covered in grubby blankets stood against one wall, and threadbare curtains hung at the windows, which were so dirty that it was impossible to see out of them, and Daisy was horrified to see rat droppings on the bare wooden floorboards. A small table, which was leaning dangerously to one side, stood against the other wall with a wooden chair against it and there was a chest of drawers that was so scratched and worn it was hard to see what wood it was made of. The walls had huge damp patches and the smell was even worse than downstairs.

'So?' He looked at them hopefully, rubbing his grimy hands down his filthy waistcoat. 'It's a bargain for two shillin's a week, so it is!'

Niamh stared at him. 'Two shillin's! Why, you must be jokin', to be sure. I wouldn't give you sixpence to stay in this dump!'

He bristled with indignation. 'Wh-what?' he sputtered. 'Why, you'll not find better or cheaper. I tell you what, I'm feelin' generous so we'll make it one and sixpence. How would that do you? It only needs a bit of a tidy up!'

'We'll leave it, thank you!' Niamh responded. She sailed out of the room and clattered down the stairs with her nose in the air, Daisy close on her heels.

They spent another two hours scouring the rooms for rent but found little better and by lunchtime Daisy was feeling despondent.

'I don't expect a palace on what I can afford to pay, just somewhere clean and dry,' she told Niamh miserably.

'We'll find it,' Niamh said optimistically. 'And in the meantime, it ain't as if you ain't welcome where you are. You're hardly livin' on the streets – though I'll admit our place ain't posh. Come on, we'll get home now an' try again tomorrow.'

Feeling depressed, Daisy nodded and they made their way back to Niamh's little cottage.

Chapter Twenty-Eight

Ansley Village

'What are you doing?' Victoria asked the next morning. She had been woken by Jed opening and shutting his drawers and he was now packing some clothes into a well-worn carpet bag.

Jed didn't even look in her direction. 'I'm going to Ireland to look for my daughter, of course.'

She pulled herself up onto her pillows and stared at him. 'You're *what*?'

'You heard me.' Jed was in no mood to pander to her that morning. He had been awake half the night worrying about Daisy.

'But how long will you be gone for?'

He shrugged as he snapped the bag shut. 'How long is a piece of string? For as long as it takes, I suppose.'

'But how will I manage for money while you're gone?'

He shook his head. He might have known that would be her main concern rather than Daisy. 'Don't worry, I've left money on the mantelshelf, more than enough to keep you for a few weeks if need be.'

'Actually . . .' she said in a wheedling voice, 'I was going to ask if I could perhaps go to London for a few days next week with Mrs Byron-Tate. She'll be staying in her townhouse in Mayfair and I thought a little break might do me good. She's told me I would be most welcome.'

He stared at her as if he was seeing her for the first time. He could hardly believe what he was hearing. Here he was, almost out of his mind with worry over his daughter, and all Victoria could think about was going on a little holiday. Most women would have insisted on going with him, but not his wife.

'I'm afraid you'll be needed here until I get back,' he said shortly.

She pouted, but Jed didn't have time for her selfish nonsense that morning and lifting the bag he left the room without a backward glance, leaving her to sulk.

Downstairs he found Lewis toasting bread on the fire. He pointed towards the table. 'There's a pot of tea ready to be poured, and I want you to eat some of this before you go. It won't do you any good travelling on an empty stomach. I'd like to come with you to help you look for Daisy, but I dare say you'd rather I stay here to keep on top of the jobs in the forge?'

'If you wouldn't mind.' Jed found himself wondering how two brothers could be so different. Lewis was always willing to lend a hand with anything that needed doing and now word had spread that he was a qualified vet it had brought even more work to the forge. But Gilbert . . . He frowned just to think of him; he was utterly selfish and lazy. The only thing he did for them was make them a cup of tea before he went out each night. A griping pain started in Jed's stomach and he winced. He hadn't felt well for weeks but there was no time to think of himself now. Daisy must be found.

He tried to eat some of the toast that Lewis had buttered and put in front of him, but it tasted like cardboard and seemed to stick in his throat. 'Sorry, lad,' he apologised as he pushed the plate away. 'I think I'm too worried and wound up to eat anythin' just yet. But don't worry, I'll get somethin' on the way.'

'Just see as you do,' Lewis told him, much as a father would have told a child.

Jed shook Lewis's hand. 'Take care, lad, an' keep your eye on everythin' for me. I'll be back as soon as I'm able, hopefully wi' Daisy.'

'I will,' Lewis promised. 'Take as long as you need. Goodbye for now.'

And so, Jed set off on the first stage of his long journey.

It was evening before the ferry pulled into Dublin and once on dry land Jed set off for the cottage where his first wife had been brought up. His stomach was in knots and he prayed that by some miracle he would find Daisy there and this nightmare would be over.

It was a long walk but the cottage finally came into view with smoke rising lazily from the chimney. His in-laws gave him a rapturous welcome and almost dragged him over the doorstep.

'It's good to see you, lad.' Connor shook his hand so hard that Jed thought it might drop off. 'Come away in now while Bridie makes you a cup o' tea.'

Jed gratefully sank into a chair as Bridie bustled about preparing a pot of tea for him.

'So, this is a nice surprise, it surely is,' Bridie told him. 'But why isn't our Daisy wit' you? Did you get our letter? It isn't like her not to write, so it isn't. But we haven't heard from her in months.'

As Jed slowly told them about Daisy being missing her grandparents were horrified.

'Her stepbrother came with her to Ireland and said he had brought her here to you,' he explained. 'But when your letter came, I realised that he was lying and he told me that Daisy had left him when they arrived in Dublin.'

'So where is she?' Bridie whispered.

Jed shrugged. 'I have no idea. That's why I've come; to find her hopefully.'

'I'll help you,' Connor promised. 'But how are you and your new bride, lad?'

Jed sighed and for the very first time he made a confession. 'I think I made a mistake,' he said quietly. 'Victoria and I aren't suited at all; she's findin' it very difficult to adjust to bein' married to a workin' man. She's used to havin' servants, see?'

Bridie frowned. Jed looked so miserable that her heart went out to him.

'I should 'ave known that I could never replace Mauve,' he went on brokenly. 'But I was so lonely. I had Daisy, admittedly, but I'm a man an' I missed havin' a warm body snuggled up to me of a night. You must 'ave been horrified when you heard I was gettin' married again, an' thought I was betrayin' Mauve's memory, an' all I can say is I'm sorry.'

'You don't have to apologise to us, lad, not at all,' Connor assured him. 'I'll admit it felt strange to think of someone in our Mauve's place when Daisy first told us you were gettin' wed again, but you're still a relatively young man, an' a man has needs, so he does. Our Mauve wouldn't have wanted to see you miserable and on your own; she was a grand lass.'

'She certainly was,' Jed agreed as memories flooded back.

While he'd been speaking, Bridie had been studying him carefully. 'Have you been ill, lad? You're looking a bit peaky, so you are.' She was sure he'd lost a good deal of weight and his skin seemed to have a yellowish tinge to it.

'I have been feelin' a bit off colour for the past few weeks,' he admitted as he ran his hand through his hair. 'Nothin' serious, just an upset stomach an' occasional vomitin'.'

'Hmm.' Bridie frowned. 'Well, perhaps a break from work is just what you needed,' she said practically. 'Although I wish it could have been under happier circumstances. I won't rest easy till I know our girl is safe and well.'

Both men nodded in agreement and Bridie smiled. Hopefully Jed would be with them for some days now and happen some good home-cooked food would put some weight back on his bones and a bit of colour back into his cheeks.

'Right, lad, you must be worn out after your journey,' Connor said as he packed his pipe with tobacco. 'But what I suggest is we start lookin' for Daisy at first light an' we'll start in Dublin, seein' as that's where your stepson said he left her. She's a bonny lass an' someone will remember seein' her hopefully.'

'Speakin' of your stepsons, how are you gettin' on with them?' Bridie was curious.

'The older one, Lewis, is a fine chap.' Jed smiled. 'He's a qualified vet but he's workin' with me in the forge an' seems to be enjoyin' it. But the other one – *Gilbert* . . .' He shook his head and grimaced. 'He wouldn't know what a good day's work was if it were to 'it him in the face! He's bone idle an' spoilt rotten into the bargain.'

'Ah well, you allus get one bad apple in a barrel,' Connor commented.

Bridie bustled away to fetch Jed a steaming dish of Irish stew and dumplings along with a loaf of freshly baked soda bread to go with it.

'Now, you get that down you,' she ordered bossily. 'And make sure you clear the dish, do you hear me? Then you can get a good night's sleep an' start to search for our girl first thing, cos I tell you now I won't rest easy in me bed till I know she's safe, to be sure!'

Chapter Twenty-Nine

Blackrock, Ireland

The next morning when Niamh rose, she found Roise and Aoife were poorly. They were both hot to the touch and had a rash.

'What do you think this is?' she asked Daisy worriedly as she sat them by the fire and tucked blankets around them.

'I'm no nurse but I remember some of the children in the village coming down with a rash like this.'

The girls were covered in what appeared to be little blisters and they were scratching at them furiously.

'And what was it?' Niamh was concerned.

'The doctor called it chickenpox.' Daisy smiled. 'I remember because I thought what a funny name for a disease it was.'

'And is it serious?'

'I don't think so,' Daisy assured her. 'I think once the rash has come out, they're already over the worst. Didn't you mention yesterday that they'd both been off their food for a few days? That was probably the start of it. If I remember rightly, the children were advised by the doctor to dab calamine lotion on the spots to ease the itching. Any apothecary should sell it. I could walk into town and get some, if you like?'

'Would you?' Niamh was fussing over her sisters like a mother hen. 'I am sorry to trouble you but I don't want to leave them, an' I'm sorry we can't continue the search for a room for you either. Will you be all right goin' into Dublin on your own? There's an apothecary on the high street.'

'Of course I will. In fact, I'll go now,' Daisy answered. 'Is there anything else you need while I'm there?'

Niamh shook her head, so Daisy hastily dragged a brush through her hair and set off. It looked set to be another lovely day but as she strolled along the coastal path, her heart was heavy. She missed her family and still hadn't accepted that she would never see them again. Somehow, she was going to have to make a life on her own but, as yesterday's search for a room had already proved, it was going to be harder than she'd expected.

Once she reached the town she went straight to the apothecary and bought some calamine lotion for the children. Next, she went to the baker and treated the two poorly little girls to a sticky bun each before heading back.

Could she have known it, as she took the coastal path to Niamh's cottage at one end of Dublin, her grampy and daddy were entering on the other side of town to begin their search.

Later that night, once the girls had been dabbed with calamine lotion and put to bed, Niamh told her father of Daisy's decision to get a room.

He frowned. 'What? So you're thinkin' of leavin' us then, lass?'

Daisy looked embarrassed. 'I can't expect to stay here indefinitely. You've already done more than enough for me,' she pointed out.

He laid his knife and fork down, leaving the fish dinner Niamh had cooked for him. 'But it's welcome you are here, I t'ought you knew that.'

Daisy blushed and looked away, not quite knowing what to say as he stood up, collected his coat from the hook on the back of the door and left.

'Eeh, he'll be headin' for the pub now, to be sure,' Niamh said despondently.

Daisy felt guilty as she quietly began to clear the pots from the table. Now more than ever she knew that it was time to go. The last thing she wanted to do was cause any more trouble for Niamh.

Daisy was lying on her straw mattress by the fire when Nolan came rolling home. The rest of the family had retired upstairs some time ago, so when the door opened, Daisy kept her eyes tightly closed and pretended to be asleep. She heard Nolan sink into the chair at the side of her, so close that she could have reached out and touched him, and her heart began to hammer in her chest.

'Daishy . . . Daishy, wake up, lash, I needs to talk to you, sho I do!'

He sounded very drunk and knowing that she had little choice Daisy slowly opened her eyes and looked up at him, pulling the blankets up to her chin as she sat up.

'Ah, here you are, me lufely girl.' He reached out to touch her hair, but Daisy shrank away from him.

'I-I think you should go up to bed,' she suggested quietly. She didn't want to wake the others.

He nodded. 'An' so I shall, me lufely, but not till I've talked to you. You shee, the thing ish, I've been meanin' to ask you somet'ink for a while, an' now seems the right time.' He gave a drunken little grin before going on, 'As you know, I losht me lufely wife a short time ago.' He shook his head sadly. 'A grand girl she was, to be sure. But the t'ing is, life hash to go on. Now, I know I'm a bit older than you . . .'

Daisy thought that was rather an understatement. He was at least as old as her daddy.

'. . . but there's a lot o' life left in this old dog, so there ish. So I was t'inking it might be right for the pair of ush to get wed. You haven't anywhere to go an' I needs a mother for me children. Oh, I know you're a fallen woman like my Niamh but I's prepared to overlook that. So, what do you t'ink o' the idea, lass? I'd be good to you, so I would, hand on me heart!'

Daisy felt like a rabbit caught in a trap as she lowered her eyes. 'I'm sure you would, Mr Murphy,' she said formally. 'And I'm honoured that you've asked. But the thing is I don't want to get married for a long time . . . if ever. You see, I'm *not* a fallen woman, as you put it. I never willingly laid with a man; my stepbrother raped me.'

She waited for a response but when none was forthcoming, she dared to glance up only to find Nolan's head had lolled back against the chair and he was fast asleep. She wasn't even sure he had heard what she said or even if he would remember what he had asked her the next morning. He began to snore softly, and under other circumstances Daisy would have found it amusing but as things stood, she knew that the sooner she left the better it would be.

Her decision was reinforced when Declan was the first down the following morning to get ready for work. Daisy stirred when she heard him enter the room. She'd had a restless night keeping one eye on Nolan but at some point, she had dropped off and he must have staggered to bed.

'Morning, Daisy,' Declan greeted her as he filled the kettle from the pump at the sink. He threw some wood onto the fire and once it was blazing merrily, he placed the kettle into the flames.

'Had a good night, did you?' he asked as she sat up and knuckled the sleep from her eyes.

Daisy nodded. She could hardly tell him what had happened with his father the night before.

He sat down in the chair his father had vacated and said quietly, 'It's not often that we get the chance to have a minute alone. I'm glad we have now though, cos there's somet'ing I've been meanin' to ask you.' He licked his dry lips nervously before going on. 'You see the t'ing is . . . I like you . . . More than like you, if truth be told, an' I were wonderin' . . . would you be my girl?'

Daisy's heart sank as she looked into his handsome face. 'Oh, Declan . . .' She didn't know how to let him down gently. He was a truly lovely young man, but she didn't want to get involved with anyone.

'I do like you, more than like you,' she said stumblingly. 'But more as a brother. I'm not ready to be anyone's girl, not for a long time, and I've no doubt there'd be many of the local girls who would be proud to walk out with you . . . I'm sorry.'

His face fell. 'Aw well, it were worth a try,' he said resignedly. 'But the t'ing is, I don't want anyone else so I'll keep tryin'. Yer might well change your mind as time goes on.'

He went to prepare the teapot and much to Daisy's relief left for work soon after. She sat up and hugged her knees as she contemplated her predicament.

She was still sitting there when Niamh appeared, yawning and rubbing her eyes.

'Ah, you're awake.' She helped herself to a cup of tea before coming to sit by Daisy. 'Sleep well, did you?'

Daisy nodded, deciding not to say anything about what had happened with Niamh's father and brother. It would only worry her.

'Not bad, how are the twins today?'

'Sleepin' like babies, t'ank the Lord.'

Nolan appeared at that moment looking very much the worse for wear.

'Be Jesus I have a ragin' headache, so I do,' he declared as he too helped himself to some tea.

Niamh looked at him scathingly. 'Serves yourself right so it does. In the Pig an' Whistle all night, were you?'

He scowled. 'I might have called in for a few jars. Ain't a workin' man allowed a drink?' he answered petulantly. Thankfully he didn't even glance at Daisy and she hoped he had forgotten about his proposal. He took a few swallows of the fast-cooling tea, then set out for work, much to Daisy's relief.

Daisy looked at Niamh and frowned. She was flushed and there were beads of sweat on her forehead. 'Are you feeling all right?' she asked.

'I do feel a bit off, to be honest wit' you,' Niamh admitted.

'Oh dear! I have a horrible feeling you're coming down with it too now!'

'Oh no!' Niamh looked horrified. 'But I can't be ill. I have the whole family to look after, so I do!'

'Not while I'm here, you don't.' Daisy wagged a finger at her. 'So, what you're going to do now is get yourself back to bed and leave everything to me. I'm perfectly capable.'

Niamh reluctantly did as she was told as Daisy set to preparing breakfast for those that wanted it. Nine-year-old Riley was the next to put in an appearance, and the minute she saw his flushed face, she knew that he, too, had come down with chickenpox.

'Off to bed, now,' she ordered him. 'I'll bring you some porridge just as soon as it's ready.'

For the rest of the day Daisy was rushed off her feet, running up and downstairs caring for the four invalids, and doing housework and cooking in between.

In the mid-afternoon, eighteen-year-old Ryan came home from work early looking flushed and unwell so Daisy packed him off to bed as well. Now there were five invalids to care for. She just hoped she didn't come down with it too.

Daisy made a large pan of chicken soup for their dinner. Her mother and granny had always told her it was a great cure for everything. By that time spots were beginning to appear on Niamh and Riley and their temperatures were sky high.

'I don't want anyt'ing to eat,' Niamh said irritably when Daisy carried a bowl of soup up to her.

'That's too bad because I won't leave until you've eaten at least some of it,' Daisy told her firmly, plonking the tray across her lap. 'You've got to keep your strength up.'

'You're a bully, Daisy Armstrong, so you are!' Niamh muttered. But she sat up and ate a little.

Thankfully, within two days Roise and Aoife were back to their normal, mischievous selves and their spots were fast fading. Although the same couldn't be said for the other three family members who were covered in them from head to foot. Niamh was the worst affected and she complained constantly. 'I tell you, I shall be scratching meself raw at this rate, so I shall,' she moaned, and Daisy couldn't help but laugh at her.

A few days later, at least two of the three invalids were well on the mend, much to Daisy's relief. However, being at their beck and call and running the house had meant she hadn't been able to work at the pie shop, and had also put paid to any hopes of finding a place to live. Hopefully, though, there would be time for that when Niamh was well enough to take the reins again. She was just grateful she had been there to help after all Niamh had done for her.

Sometime in the afternoon, when the patients were resting, Daisy took the twins down to the beach. She was convinced the fresh air would do them the power of good and the three of them enjoyed every second of it: paddling, catching crabs and building sandcastles. It made Daisy realise how much she was going to miss them all when she did finally leave. They had become like a second family to her, and she would never forget their kindness. She knew she needed to make a new life for herself, but the trouble was it was proving very difficult to forget the other life she had shared with her daddy . . . and Lewis!

Chapter Thirty

Kilmainham, Ireland, June 1882

As Jed and Connor entered Bridie McLoughlin's spotless little kitchen late one afternoon, one look at their downcast faces told her all she needed to know.

'No luck then?'

The two men shook their heads. 'Not a sign of her, nor anyone that's seen her, and we've walked miles as me poor old feet are tellin' me.' Connor sat down and groaned as he yanked a boot off. 'Would you just look at that. I've got blisters on me blisters.' He yanked the other boot off and dropped both by the chair.

Jed looked on with concern. Connor was getting on a bit now and he feared all the searching was too much for him. The trouble was, he wouldn't hear of letting Jed continue by himself. He was a stubborn old devil.

'Why, look at your ankles,' Bridie scolded him. 'They're all swollen. I'm goin' to put me foot down now an' insist you have a day off, so I am! You're not a young man now, you know, Connor McLoughlin, although you still try to act like one.'

'Oh, cease with your naggin', woman. You're worse than a fishwife, to be sure,' he retorted, but there was a twinkle in his eye despite his words. It was easy to see how much they loved each other, and Jed envied them as he thought back to the precious years he had spent with their daughter. He knew he would never experience the same closeness and affection with

Victoria, but he had made vows to her, and he was going to stand by them.

Bridie put the dinner out for the men and glanced at Jed. He had been there for three weeks and he looked much better, despite his deep concerns for his daughter. He had some colour back in his cheeks and his appetite, which had been almost non-existent when he had first arrived, had come back with a vengeance. He was no longer feeling sick or tired, either, and she put it down to all the fresh air he had been getting. He and Connor had walked miles, scouring everywhere they could think of, stopping at every farm and smallholding they passed, asking everyone they met if they had seen a young woman fitting Daisy's description. But so far it had been to no avail. They had searched Dublin town asking for her there too, but again had met with a blank wall. It was as if Daisy had vanished from the face of the earth, and they were all sick with worry for her.

As the men came to the table to eat the lovely meal of fresh fish and home-grown vegetables and potatoes, Jed said the words she had been dreading.

'I'm afraid I'm going to have to think of going home soon.' He sighed. 'I can't expect young Lewis to keep the business running all on his own for much longer. He's learnt a lot since he joined me in the forge but there are still jobs he can't do on his own, an' the last thing I need is for the business to go under.'

'Don't worry, lad, I'll keep searchin' for Daisy, so I will,' Connor assured him. He and Bridie missed Daisy almost as much as Jed did. She had always been the apple of their eye.

'I know you will.' Jed gave him a grateful smile. 'I just keep prayin' that she'll be there waitin' for me when I get home. We'll have one more day searchin' for her tomorrow an' then I'll catch the ferry home the day after. I wrote to Victoria a few days ago to tell her to expect me.'

Bridie nodded sadly. She'd miss him when he left, but she accepted that he had a life back in Ansley.

The next morning Jed and Connor set off again, this time in the direction of Carrysfort, which was a short distance from Blackrock. They stopped at every cottage and farm they passed but the answer to their question was always the same: no one had seen hide nor hair of Daisy. They returned to Bridie that evening tired and disheartened.

'We called to see Liam Doyle this morning at Brooke Farm,' Connor told his wife over dinner. Today she had cooked them bangers and mash with thick onion gravy, one of Connor's favourites. 'And sad I was to find that he had just lost Aisling. He was waiting for the undertaker to arrive, so we didn't linger.'

'Well, it were a well-known fact that he worked the poor woman almost into the ground,' Bridie said with a shake of her head. 'Poor lass, since her little ones flew the nest the majority of the work about the farm fell on her shoulders. Liam was always too busy caring for his cattle to help do anything else and young Daniel can't be much help to him, bein' an invalid.' She peeped at Jed from the corner of her eye. 'And are you still planning to return home tomorrow?'

He nodded. 'I shall have to.'

'Then let's just hope Daisy is there waiting for you safe and sound when you get back.'

The next day, bright and early, Jed said his goodbyes and set off for Dublin. It was a beautiful day with seagulls wheeling in the blue sky above him. Under different circumstances he would have enjoyed his surroundings, but today his heart was heavy.

As he passed a huddle of little terraced cottages in Blackrock, he smiled to see two identical little girls playing in a small yard at the back of their home. He briefly considered stopping to ask them if they might have seen anyone fitting Daisy's description, but then thought better of it. They were only children after all. They waved to him as he passed, and he waved back and went on his way.

'I heard tell they're buryin' Aisling Doyle tomorrow,' Erin told Daisy and Niamh that evening when she got back from work. 'An' I heard a woman in the shop sayin' that Liam is lookin' for a hired help to live in.'

Daisy's ears pricked up immediately. Now the invalids were better, she was about to start looking for a new job – sadly, someone else had been given her old one in the pie shop.

'What sort of help?' she asked. A live-in position might solve all her problems.

Erin shrugged. 'Like a housekeeper an' someone to do jobs about the farm, I should imagine.'

Noting Daisy's interest, Niamh frowned. 'I wouldn't even consider workin' for Liam Doyle if I were you,' she warned. 'He's a right old slave driver by all accounts. That's why his wife never had anyone to help her for long, so it is. Aisling were a lovely woman but no one would put up wit' him. Since his older kids left to get married there was only him, his wife an' their youngest son Daniel, but he's no help cos he's an invalid.'

'Even so it would be better than nothing till something else came along,' Daisy pointed out.

Niamh shook her head. 'I can't stop you enquirin', for sure. But why don't you wait a couple of days an' let Aisling be put to rest first? Sure, it would seem disrespectful if someone were to step into her shoes before she's even been laid in the ground.'

Daisy waited for three days before she set off for Brooke Farm. Niamh had reluctantly given her clear directions and after a brisk walk, the farm came into view. The farmhouse was bigger than she had expected, and as she approached a large, five-barred gate leading into the farmyard, a sheepdog came hurtling out of a kennel and began to bark at her.

'It's all right, boy, I'm not going to hurt you,' she said soothingly as memories of Rags tore at her heart. Tentatively she put her hand over the gate and offered the dog her palm, and after a moment he stopped barking and licked her. She was standing there stroking him when a great bear of a man with a bushy grey beard and moustache appeared from the kitchen doorway.

'What do you want?' he asked abruptly, with no trace of a welcome in his voice. 'This is private property, so it is!'

'I'm sorry, sir, I didn't wish to disturb you,' she said politely. 'But I've been staying with a friend in the area who said you might be looking for a housekeeper.'

'An' what if I am?' he answered, eyeing her up and down shrewdly.

'I'm looking for work and I thought you might consider me?'

'*You?*' He looked surprised. She was only a slip of a girl. He needed someone who would pull their weight about the place like his Aisling had done.

'I'm a good worker,' she hurried on. 'I kept home for my daddy for a number of years and I'm stronger than I look. I can cook too.'

He scowled at her English accent. 'Can you now?' He stroked his beard and narrowed his eyes. 'You're not from around here, are you?'

'No, sir,' she agreed. 'I was brought up across the water.' She didn't want to tell him that her grandparents lived close by. Somehow, she had to put that part of her life aside and start afresh.

'So, what brought you to Ireland then?'

Daisy hadn't expected so many questions and she flushed as she searched for words.

'You been up at the home for unmarried mothers, have you? Sure, that's what brings most young lasses this way.'

Her mouth opened and shut. She thought of lying but decided against it. 'Yes, sir . . . I have.'

'Ah, so your family have washed their hands of you, have they?'

She bowed her head and nodded miserably. He was more astute than she had thought.

'And do you have the brat in tow?'

'No, sir.'

'Hmm. Well, if I were to give you a trial you would have to live in, and I can't offer much in the way of wages, not if I'm going to be keeping you.'

When she didn't argue, he went on. 'I'd need someone who can start straight away.'

Seeing a glimmer of hope she nodded eagerly. 'I could do that. Tomorrow, if you like!'

Again, he scowled. 'Board and keep and t'ree shillings a week. That's me offer, take it or leave it.'

It was hardly more than she was earning for four days in the shop but at least she would be independent and not relying on Niamh's family to keep her. 'I'll take it,' she told him.

He nodded. 'Right, so be here at six o'clock sharp in the morning. And be warned, I don't like latecomers! One of the first jobs is helping to milk me cows. Have you ever done that before?'

She shook her head. 'No, but I'm a quick learner and I have worked in a dairy.'

'I'll see you in the morning, then. Oh, an' what's your name.'

'Daisy, sir. Daisy Armstrong.'

As she turned and walked away, he frowned. He could vaguely remember a chap enquiring about his missing daughter on the day Aisling had died, but he couldn't remember for the life of him what her name was now. He shrugged. Well, it didn't much matter.

'How did you get on?' Niamh was waiting for her when she got back to the cottage.

Daisy smiled. 'He's giving me a trial.'

Niamh sighed. 'All I can say is, good luck to you. You'll need it workin' for him, so you will. When do you start?'

'Tomorrow morning. I've to be there for six o'clock.'

Niamh's face fell; she was going to miss having her friend around. 'So soon? You know there'll always be a place here for you if things don't work out, an' I've an idea they won't. Farmer Doyle is a hard man, though his son is nice enough.'

'How old is his son?' Daisy asked.

Niamh frowned as she tried to think. 'I reckon Daniel must be about twenty-two or twenty-t'ree now.'

'And what's wrong with him? Didn't someone say he was an invalid?'

'He is that,' Niamh told her. 'I t'ink he's got a dicky ticker or somet'ing like that. I heard me mammy an' daddy speakin' of him once an' they reckoned no one t'ought he'd reach his teens, poor t'ing.'

Niamh gave Daisy a hug. As much as she would miss her, she could understand why she was going. Daisy had eventually confided to her that she had rejected both her daddy and Declan and there had been an uncomfortable atmosphere between them, and Niamh knew that Daisy wanted to avoid that. She went back to washing dishes at the sink but when Daisy lifted a cloth and went to start drying them for her, she shook her head and snatched it off her.

'Oh no, you don't.' She wagged her finger at her. 'If this is to be your last day wit' us, I want you to take it easy. Take the twins an' Riley down to the beach if you want to do somet'ing. They could do wi' runnin' some o' their energy off, to be sure.'

And so Daisy did just that and soon she had her skirt tucked up into her knickers and was paddling in the waves with the children as they giggled and splashed each other. When they tired of that they collected shells and combed the rock pools for crabs and by the time they got home they were tired but content.

'They'll sleep well tonight,' Niamh commented with a smile.

After dinner that evening the men went to the pub and once the children were all in bed Niamh and Daisy were able to spend some time together in front of the fire. Despite the lovely weather they still needed one of an evening because the breeze from the sea could be nippy.

'Just remember, we're here if you need us,' Niamh told Daisy seriously. 'Don't you go takin' no shit from Farmer Doyle, now! Start as you mean to go on an' show him you'll stand for no nonsense, an' you might stand half a chance o' gettin' on – though knowin' him, I wouldn't bet on it.'

Daisy chuckled. Surely the farmer couldn't be as bad as Niamh had made out?

Chapter Thirty-One

'According to the letter I received from Edward he should be home today,' Victoria said to Gilbert with a worried frown. 'You don't think he will have found Daisy, do you?'

Gilbert chuckled as he lolled in his chair drinking tea. Lewis had been at work in the forge for hours, but he had just rolled out of bed, once again feeling rather the worse for wear after attending a card game that had gone on until the early hours of the morning.

'There's no chance,' he assured her. 'The convent will be the last place he would ever think to look, and now that we're no longer paying for her, I expect they'll be keeping her there as an unpaid worker. No, you need have no concerns on that score. No one comes out of that place unless their family goes to fetch them, so she'll rot in there.' He scowled. 'I reckon you'll have some explaining to do, though, when Jed learns that you took all the money he left us for food and bills to go gadding off to London with Mrs Byron-Tate.'

Victoria sniffed peevishly. 'Why *shouldn't* I have a little pleasure? I'd go mad stuck in this godforsaken hovel if I didn't get away from it for a few days now and again.' She gave him a sly look. 'And as it happens it was a very productive little break.'

'In what way?'

Knowing that she had her son's full attention, she made a pretence of examining her nails. 'I just happened to meet a rather

231

charming and, may I add, very wealthy widower while I was there. Mrs Byron-Tate and I attended a dinner party at a friend of hers one evening, and he was there. He's a very well-known politician and he owns the most charming house in Mayfair.' She gave a smug little grin. 'I believe he was quite taken with me, so if something should happen to Edward . . . well, let's just say with Daisy out of the way as well, I could sell the forge and the house lock, stock and barrel and move to London.'

Gilbert chuckled. 'Sounds like you have it all planned. Does that mean you want me to go on with . . .?'

She nodded. 'Yes, but it must look like an illness so don't overdo it. He must have a gradual decline.'

Late that evening, as Victoria was thinking of retiring, she heard a key turn in the lock and Jed appeared looking much better than he had when he had left, although he was obviously tired.

'Oh, darling.' She rose graciously to greet him, the new taffeta gown she'd bought in London rustling. She could afford to be a little kinder to him now that she had the next husband lined up. 'How wonderful it is to have you back.' She made a great show of looking over his shoulder and frowned. 'But where is our dear Daisy? Didn't you find her?'

Jed shook his head miserably. 'It were like lookin' for a needle in a haystack. Me an' Connor scoured miles wi' not one sign of her. It's like she's just vanished into thin air.'

'Oh, you poor darling, how awful.' Victoria managed to look concerned, although her heart was singing. 'Come and sit down, dear. I'll make you a drink, you must be tired.'

'I am,' he admitted, glancing around. 'Where are the lads?'

'Oh, Lewis is in bed and Gilbert went out. He had some business to attend to, I believe.'

Jed could guess what sort of business that would be but he said nothing. It wasn't often he caught Victoria in a good mood nowadays and he intended to make the most of it. Rags, who had followed him in from outside, came to lay his head in Jed's lap. He appeared to have lost weight. 'Why was the dog locked outside?'

'Oh, he wasn't locked out. I'd just let him out to go to the toilet before I went to bed. I was about to let him back in when you arrived.' It was a complete lie. Poor Rags had slept outside every night since Jed had left, and had it been left to her the mangy mutt would never have set foot inside again. But of course, she couldn't say that to Jed. For some reason he loved the animal. More was the pity.

As she poured boiling water over the tea leaves, he asked, 'I don't think I've seen that gown before. Is it new? It's very pretty.'

'Oh, this old thing.' She waved her hand. 'I've had it for ages and decided it would still be all right for wearing around the house.' She was keen to change the subject. Jed was clearly more observant than she had given him credit for. 'Now, tell me how Bridie and Connor are. We have so much catching up to do!'

Jed didn't learn of Victoria's trip to London until the following day, when Mrs Smith appeared in the forge as he and Lewis were shoeing a horse.

He stopped what he was doing to glance up at her. 'Good morning, Mrs Smith, what can I do for you?'

'Sorry, Mr Armstrong, but your missus has told me to ask you for some money for shoppin' – food shoppin', like.'

He looked confused. 'But I left her enough money for at least a few months' housekeeping and bills in the tin on the mantelshelf before I set off for Ireland.'

'I know you did, but she took that when she went to London.'

Jed looked stunned and not a little disappointed. So even though his wife had known he was worried sick and looking for his daughter, she had chosen to go off enjoying herself?

'I see.' Fumbling in his pocket he produced some coins and passed them to the woman. 'There you are. I'm afraid that's all I have on me at present, but you should be able to get what we need for now with that.'

After she'd gone, Jed looked at Lewis. 'Why didn't you tell me your mother had gone off galivanting?'

'I was in bed when you got back last night and I assumed she would have told you herself. I did ask her not to go, but you know what Mother is like when she gets an idea into her head.'

'I'm learning fast,' Jed replied, feeling more than a little let down. It seemed that Victoria was even more hard-hearted and selfish than he had thought.

'I know you're worried sick about Daisy,' Lewis went on. 'But I have to say you're looking a lot better than you did when you left.'

'Funnily enough I'm feeling better,' Jed admitted. 'It must 'ave been all the fresh air I was gettin' walkin' about tryin' to find Daisy.'

Lewis thought again of the bloodstained clothes he had found in the barn and his stomach churned. Gilbert had sworn he had tumbled in a drunken stupor, yet knowing his brother as he did, Lewis still didn't believe him completely. But one thing he did know – if ever he found out that those bloodstains were connected in any way to Daisy's disappearance, he would kill his brother with his own bare hands because he was missing her as much as Jed was, and he knew he wouldn't rest easily till she was home safe and sound again.

Chapter Thirty-Two

Brooke Farm, Ireland

'Now you take care o' yourself, d'you hear me?' The two girls clung to each other early the next morning and Daisy had to blink back tears. She would never forget what a good friend Niamh had been to her – she had even got up at this ungodly hour to see her off.

'I will, and don't worry, you're not getting rid of me completely. I shall be here to see you every day off I get.'

'Huh!' Niamh snorted. 'I wouldn't bet on that. Knowin' Farmer Doyle, they'll be few an' far between.'

Daisy had packed her carpet bag and said her goodbyes to the rest of the family the night before, so after placing a gentle kiss on Niamh's cheek, they tearfully parted.

It was time to begin the next chapter of her life but oh how Daisy wished she could return to the one she had had before the widow stole her father's heart.

As she approached the farm gate sometime later, the dog again rushed from his kennel, but this time there was no growling and his tail was wagging. Farmer Doyle appeared and beckoned her to follow him. Daisy had hoped to be shown where she was sleeping and to put her things away before she started work, but it appeared the farmer had other ideas.

He led her into a large milking shed. 'Right, now watch carefully, I shall expect you to be doin' this without any help in a couple of days, so I will.' This was her surly greeting but she hadn't really expected him to roll the red carpet out for her. With a silent sigh, she dropped her bag at the side of the door.

He sat down on a small three-legged stool next to a large brown-and-white cow with soft, velvet eyes, and placed a bucket beneath her huge udders. He began to pull and squeeze each teat rhythmically and Daisy watched in fascination as a steady stream of creamy white milk splashed into the bucket. When he was satisfied that he had taken all the cow had to give, he slapped her gently on the rump and she moved along through a door into a paddock and another cow took her place.

'This one here is Buttercup,' Farmer Doyle told Daisy shortly. 'An' she can be a bit of a madam, so you'd best leave her to me till you get the hang of things. She can give you a rare kick if the mood takes her, to be sure!'

Daisy didn't much like the sound of that, but she didn't say anything.

When he had milked four of the cows, Farmer Doyle beckoned Daisy over to try her hand at a fifth one, but first he placed the bucket he had filled safely to one side and replaced it with an empty one.

She sat on the stool and gently caught two teats, one in each hand, as she had seen him do, but her first two tugs on them yielded nothing.

Farmer Doyle snorted in disgust. 'Pull 'em harder, girl, you ain't ringin' bells,' he snapped. And so Daisy did just that, only to find the milk spurting all over her hand. It wasn't as easy as he had made it look.

'*Aim* at the bucket,' he said frustratedly.

This time she had a little more success – until the cow kicked out and sent the bucket flying. But Daisy wasn't one to give up easily, so she quickly retrieved it and tried again. Slowly but surely, she began to get the hang of it.

Farmer Doyle nodded. 'Not too bad for a first attempt,' he said grudgingly. 'Though you'll have to get faster else it'll be time to milk the first one again afore you've finished the last.'

He started to milk the cow behind her. At last all of the cows were done, although Daisy noted Farmer Doyle had milked more than twice as many as she had. Still, she consoled herself, it had been her first attempt.

Once the cows were contentedly grazing in the paddock, she lifted her bag and followed the farmer across the yard, where chickens were pecking amongst the cobbles, into a large kitchen. A young man was standing in front of a range stirring something in a pan and he turned his head to smile at Daisy.

At least he seemed friendly, she thought.

'Is that breakfast ready yet, lad?' the farmer barked.

The young man nodded. 'Aye, it is, Daddy, sit yersens down now.'

The farmer gestured to Daisy to take a seat as the young man carried a large dish of porridge to the table and plonked it down. He was tall with dark hair and deep-brown eyes and Daisy thought he could have been handsome if he hadn't been so painfully thin. He was no further through than a bean pole and his face was sunken and sallow.

'This is me son, Daniel,' the farmer introduced him brusquely as he spooned porridge into a bowl. 'An' makin' porridge is about all he's good for. He's as weak as water, so he is.'

A look of hurt flashed across Daniel's face, and Daisy felt sorry for him, but she didn't say anything.

'If you've had no breakfast, help yersen to some o' this cos there'll be nowt else to eat till lunchtime,' the farmer warned as he began to slurp at his spoon.

Daisy did as she was told and found that the porridge was quite tasty, especially when she added a little sugar.

'This is very nice,' she told Daniel.

Obviously unused to praise he flushed to the very roots of his hair, while his father scowled at him.

When they had eaten the farmer pushed a mug of tea towards Daisy and she asked, 'What would you like me to do next?'

'Open your eyes, girl, an' look around you. Have you any need to ask? Since my Aisling died, this place has gone to pot. She kept it neat as a new pin, so she did, so stick in and get it back to scratch. Then when you've done that collect the eggs – be warned some of 'em like to lay in the hay barn. Then you can get some lunch on. Daniel will show you where things are. I'll be back to eat at one o'clock sharp an' I'll expect it to be on the table – I don't like to be kept waitin'. After lunch you can tackle the washin'. It's been pilin' up, so it has, an' you can make a start on gettin' the rest o' the house back to rights an' all before you start dinner. I'll be wantin' that at six, no later. When that's done you can help me wi' the evenin' milkin' afore you wash the dinner pots an' make me some supper.'

'What time do I actually finish work?' Daisy asked with a frown. They had worked her hard at the convent but even there the girls finished work at six in time for prayers in the chapel.

'You start at six in the mornin' an' finish when all the jobs are done,' he said coldly. Then he belched loudly, stood up and left the room.

'Sorry about that. Daddy's a bit of a slave driver, so he is,' Daniel muttered, looking embarrassed.

Daisy was feeling angry but Daniel couldn't be blamed for his father's rudeness, so she forced a smile. 'Don't worry. I've never been afraid of hard work, but before I start could you perhaps show me where I'm to sleep? I'd like to take my bag to my room.'

Daniel nodded and led her into a large hallway where a staircase led up to the first floor. By the time they reached the top of the stairs, he was gasping for breath, and she noticed a slight bluish tinge to his lips. They were on a long landing that ran either side of them and he pointed to the right. 'Daddy said you're to have the room at the end there. I'm afraid it will need a very good clean. Mammy only used it for storin' odds an' ends. Me an' Daddy sleep this side.'

Daisy went to the end of the corridor and gasped with dismay when she opened the door. The room seemed to be full to the brim with lengths of material, old pieces of furniture, old carpets and boxes piled high. The single bed was also covered in boxes, and there was hardly room to walk around the room as it was so full.

Daniel caught up with her and he, too, looked dismayed. 'It's even worse than I feared,' he admitted. 'But don't worry, I'll help you to empty it. We'll clean it out an' stack everything in the barn.'

Daisy rolled her sleeves up. There was no time like the present. 'Let's just carry everything out onto the landing,' she suggested. 'And then we can move it from there.'

They began to lift the boxes but she could see Daniel was struggling. 'It's all right. I can manage on my own.'

'Are you sure?'

She nodded. 'You just go and get on with whatever you were doing and we can shift this lot out to the barn later.'

Within an hour everything was neatly piled along the landing and the room looked like a bedroom again, although it was very dirty and obviously hadn't been used for years. Cobwebs hung from the ceiling and the air was full of dust motes that danced in the sun shining through the window. Daisy had unearthed a chest of drawers beneath all the junk and there was also a small table and a chair that could stay. Next, she went down to the kitchen to fetch a pail of hot water, some cleaning rags and a brush. Once back upstairs she set to and after another hour the room was spick and span. She'd found some curtains that would fit the window once they were washed and ironed and also some rag rugs that she intended to take outside to beat.

Standing back with her hands on her hips she surveyed her new room with satisfaction. It wasn't posh, admittedly, but it would certainly beat sleeping on a straw mattress downstairs as she had at Niamh's.

She hooked the rugs and the curtains under her arm and with the pail of dirty water and cleaning things in her other hand, she went back downstairs. It was time to make a start on the kitchen.

By the time Farmer Doyle appeared for his lunch the kitchen floor was shining, and the windows were sparkling.

He frowned as he looked at the loaf of bread and the block of cheese she had put on the table for him. 'Is this the best you can do for a hard-workin' man?'

Daisy stared at him coldly. 'I shall be cooking you a meal this evening,' she replied. 'You could hardly expect me to cook this morning as well as do everything else you told me to do. I only have one pair of hands!'

He looked taken aback – he clearly wasn't used to anyone answering back, but Niamh had told her to 'Start as you mean to go on!' and that was just what she was doing.

With a glare, he sat down at the table and hacked a slice of bread from the loaf.

Daisy, meanwhile, was making a pot of tea and once it was ready, she plonked it down in front of him. 'There, that should keep you going until teatime,' she told him shortly.

Daniel quietly sat down at the table with his father, stifling a smile as he helped himself to a small portion of bread and cheese.

While he was eating Liam Doyle glanced about the room and noted the sparkling windows and floors. This new girl was a bit mouthy for his liking, but she did appear to be a good worker, so he supposed he'd have to put up with it.

When he'd eaten his fill, he left to continue his chores and Daisy quickly helped herself to a small amount of bread and cheese, looking around at what needed doing next. She'd noticed that the range needed a good clean and the grate could do with black leading, but they could wait until tomorrow. Daniel had mentioned that he and his father were running out of clean clothes as there had been no washing done since his mother passed away, so she decided to get cracking on that while the weather was fine.

Daniel showed her to the washroom where she found a large copper with a number of shirts soaking in it. She lit the fire beneath it and grated some hard soap into the water, and once they were bubbling nicely, she slipped away to fill the stone sink with cold water to rinse the shirts in. In no time at all they had been rinsed, fed through the mangle and were flapping gently in the breeze on the line strung across the yard.

After that, she found a wicker basket in the kitchen, and went to collect the eggs, which proved to be easier said than done. It was a little like playing hide and seek as the hens seemed to have laid them all over the place but at last, she'd collected enough to hopefully keep her new employer happy.

Back in the kitchen she made pastry for a meat pie and some jam tarts. Daniel's mouth watered as she rolled it out. Neither he nor his father were very good cooks, and this would be the first decent meal they had had since his mother died.

Over dinner, Daniel praised her for the fluffy pastry but Liam just kept his head down and shovelled the food into his mouth.

As soon as they were finished, he stood, telling Daniel, 'You can start the washin' up. You're good for nowt else, to be sure. An' you' – he thumbed towards Daisy – 'come wi' me, the cows are ready to be milked again.'

Daisy bit her lip as she saw the resigned expression on Daniel's face. He was clearly used to being put down by his father and

241

she felt sorry for him. She wondered why he didn't stand up for himself. Still, their relationship was nothing to do with her – she was simply the hired help and it wouldn't do for her to interfere between father and son.

When the cows were milked and back out in the pasture, she filled buckets of water from the pump to wash the cowshed down, then hurriedly fetched the dry washing in off the lines and folded it. She would tackle the ironing the next morning, although she wasn't looking forward to it – ironing had never been one of her favourite jobs.

It was almost ten o'clock by the time she had finished her list of jobs and she was almost dropping with weariness. But, she consoled herself, at least she had somewhere to stay and was being paid a wage, albeit a small one.

Daniel and his father were still in the kitchen drinking the cocoa she had made for them when she bid them goodnight and, lighting a candle, she slowly climbed the stairs to her room, every limb aching.

Her first day at Brooke Farm had come to an end, and looking to the future all she could see were more days of hard work. She undressed and washed and dropped into bed, then cried herself to sleep as she thought of the family she loved, who she would never see again.

Chapter Thirty-Three

For the next three weeks Daisy worked ceaselessly from morning until night and when she finally dropped into bed each night, she was exhausted. The farmhouse now gleamed from top to bottom, but she never received a word of praise from Farmer Doyle, and as yet she hadn't received a penny in wages. There were times when she felt like going back to Niamh's and searching for another job, but worry for Daniel kept her there. She felt sorry for him and hated the way his father treated him. The farmer put him down at every opportunity and it was soon clear that Daniel had no self-confidence whatsoever.

'You should stand up to him,' she advised him one day after Liam had been particularly scathing to him.

Daniel shook his head and smiled sadly. 'Why? He's only telling the truth when he says how useless I am, isn't he?' he responded. 'I'm an invalid and very limited in what I can do about the place. I accepted that a long time ago, but it was easier when me mammy was alive. She was nowhere near as stern as Daddy. And anyway, you're a rare one to talk, so you are!' He grinned at her. 'He's almost worked you into the ground since you arrived, so he has. Don't t'ink I haven't noticed, and has he paid you even a penny piece yet?'

When Daisy frowned, he had the answer to his question.

'Hmm, I t'ought not and furthermore he won't if he can get away with it. He's as tight as a duck's arse when it comes to payin' out, to be sure. And what about a little time off? You haven't even had half a day to yourself yet.'

'You're absolutely right. I've been so busy that I haven't given it much thought, but rest assured, I will now, the very next chance I get.'

The chance came that evening as she was serving dinner. As always, after trailing in and leaving a set of muddy footprints all over Daisy's clean floor, Liam took a seat at the table without even washing his hands.

'You could at least take your boots off when you come into the kitchen,' Daisy complained as she laid a plateful of sizzling lamb chops and mashed potatoes in front of him.

He scowled at her before snatching up his knife and fork and beginning to shovel the food into his mouth.

Daisy watched with distaste as the gravy trickled into his beard before saying, 'Oh, and I should tell you that I shall be taking the day off this Sunday!'

This did get his attention and his head snapped up. 'I don't t'ink so. There's the milkin' to do an' the dinner to cook an—'

Daisy held her hand up to stop his flow of words. 'You'll have to manage a day on your own,' she told him firmly with her chin in the air. 'I wasn't asking, I was *telling* you. I've had no time off whatsoever since I came here and everyone is entitled to time off. Oh, and I shall also want paying before I go. I believe you owe me nine shillings now!'

He opened his mouth to tell her that she stood no chance but thought better of it. Although he wouldn't tell her, Daisy was the hardest worker he had employed for some long time, and he knew that if he let her go, he would be cutting off his nose to spite his face.

'I'll give you five shillin's,' he muttered.

She shook her head. 'No, it's nine shillings you owe me and I shall want it before Sunday.' Then she turned on her heel and went to fetch Daniel his meal.

Liam's nostrils flared as he glowered down at his plate and Daniel suppressed a smile. It was the first time he had ever seen anyone stand up to his father and it was long overdue. He just wished he had the courage to do the same. In fact, he and Daisy had struck up a friendship and already he was more than a little fond of her, although he could never let her know it. After all, what girl in her right mind would tie themselves to an invalid who could drop dead at any minute? He had already survived for far longer than anyone had expected him to, so he knew he was living on borrowed time, and every day was a bonus. It hurt him to see how hard his father worked Daisy, yet she never complained and all he could do was help her out wherever he could by doing little jobs like getting the coal in and preparing the vegetables for dinner. It wasn't much, but she was always grateful, which only made him love her more.

For the rest of the week, the thought of her day off put a spring in Daisy's step. By now, she'd become a dab hand at milking the cows and could do it almost as well as Liam. She actually found the job quite relaxing as she leant into the warm cows' sides and watched the milk squirting into the buckets. Admittedly, cleaning the milking parlour out after she had finished wasn't quite so enjoyable, but she took it all in her stride.

At last Saturday evening came around and as Daisy entered the kitchen after feeding the pigs, she saw Liam sitting at the side of the fire smoking his pipe. 'May I have my wages now please? Don't forget, I shan't be here tomorrow.'

He grunted and delved into the pocket of his greasy trousers. 'Here,' he said testily. 'That's all I have on me for now, so it is.'

Daisy stared down at the two shillings in her hand before saying calmly. 'Then I'll wait here while you fetch the rest, shall I?'

Colour flooded his cheeks so quickly that she feared he was going to have a seizure, but she stood her ground.

'What's the matter wit' you, girl?' he growled. 'Don't you trust me? You should have more than enough there.'

'I probably shall,' she agreed. 'But I want what's owed me. And in future I'd prefer it if you paid me weekly.'

He grunted as he pulled himself out of the chair and left the room. Moments later, he returned and slammed the rest of the money down so hard on the table that the sugar bowl danced. He wanted more than anything to tell her not to bother coming back, but he was reluctant to let such a hard worker go. The girl might be a little more spirited than he would have liked but she was certainly a grafter and girls like her were few and far between, as he had long since discovered. As Daisy dropped the money into her apron pocket, Farmer Doyle noticed the way Daniel's eyes followed her across the room and he smiled slyly to himself.

So that was the way the wind was blowing, was it? Daniel was taken with the lass. He could understand why. As well as being a hard worker, Daisy was a pretty girl and kind into the bargain. Admittedly, she was a fallen woman, but that shouldn't trouble Daniel too much. There wasn't much chance of him meeting any other lasses, and she would probably jump at the chance of securing herself a home for life. After all, there weren't many other chaps would want her when they learnt she had been a loose woman. If he could only get them to wed, he'd have a free worker for life. In a slightly better mood, he lay his head back and dropped into a doze.

The next morning Daisy was up even earlier than usual, and she slipped downstairs to have a bath and wash her hair knowing that Daniel and Liam would still be in bed. It took some time to boil enough water for the bath but once she had, she emerged feeling fresh and clean for the first time since she'd arrived. She emptied the bath and took it outside again then hurried up to her room to rub her hair until it was almost dry. It was now shoulder length and usually she tied it back while she was working, but today she left it loose to curl softly, and after putting on her best outfit she set off for Niamh's in a happy mood.

The sun was already shining, giving promise of a good day to come as she walked along the coastal path, and above her storm petrels and roseate terns, birds native to the coast of Dublin, wheeled and dived in the sky. She wished that she could have taken some sweeties for the little ones but there had been no chance to visit a shop, so she decided she would give them some pocket money to choose their own. After a brisk walk, the little row of cottages came into view and Daisy quickened her steps, thinking about how surprised Niamh would be to see her.

The welcome she received when she tapped on the door was every bit as good as she could have wished for as Niamh almost yanked her over the doorstep.

'Eeh, I've been that worried about you, so I have,' she told Daisy as she hurried to fill the kettle for some tea. 'Have you been all right? An' how is Farmer Doyle treatin' you?'

Daisy grinned as she brushed Aoife's hair and plaited it before doing Roise's. 'Oh, every bit as hard a taskmaster as you warned me he would be.'

'Our Niamh has got herself a boyfriend, so she has,' Aoife piped up.

Niamh blushed. 'Get away with you,' she scolded.

'Hmm, tell me more,' Daisy laughed.

'His name is Aiden, Aiden Callahan,' Aoife told her with a wide smile. 'We went into town to shop an' our Niamh dropped her basket wi' all the groceries in it, so she did. Anyway, Aiden helped her pick 'em all up an' he's been up here twice to see us now. Well, I think he came to see Niamh, really.'

'Oh, get away wit' you.' Niamh looked embarrassed. 'Me an' Aiden went to school together an' we're just friends, so we are. His daddy owns a shop in the town centre an' Aiden works there wit' him.'

Both little girls now had neatly plaited hair, so Niamh sent them out to play, saying, 'The men and Riley have gone off to watch a cricket match in Dublin this mornin', an' Erin stayed at her friend's last night, so none of us is going to church today. I dare say we'll be in bother with Father O'Brien but it can't be helped.' Her voice became solemn then and keen to steer the subject away from Aiden she asked tentatively, 'Now, tell me all about you. I don't suppose you've heard anyt'ing from your family?'

Daisy sighed and shook her head. 'Not a word, nor do I expect to. They don't even know where I am. I'm trying to come to terms with it now.'

'And do you think you'll be stayin' at Brooke Farm?'

Another shake of the head. 'For now at least, but I can't see me staying there forever. Once I've got enough saved, I might try for another job elsewhere.'

They sat and had tea together as they caught up on what they had both been doing in the time they had been apart, then Niamh surprised Daisy when she told her, 'I might come wit' you. See, me daddy is seein' a widow in Dublin town centre. She owns a little guest inn an' she ain't short of a few bob, by all accounts.'

Daisy giggled. 'Crikey, he doesn't believe in letting the grass grow beneath his feet, does he?' But she was pleased to hear that her leaving hadn't upset Nolan too much. 'That's good to hear but I just hope he doesn't jump in too fast like my daddy did with his second wife. But why would you think of leaving if you and Aiden are getting along so well?'

Niamh sighed as she poured them another cup of tea. 'Ain't no sense daydreamin'. I admit I like him . . . a lot. But once he finds out about the baby I had . . . Well, he ain't goin' to want me then, is he?'

'I wouldn't be so sure.' Daisy patted her arm.

'Aw well, what will be will be,' Niamh said quietly. 'You will stay for dinner, won't you? What time do you have to get back?'

'I don't!' Daisy grinned. 'I've got the whole day off, much to Liam's disgust. I took your advice and started as I meant to go on. We have some rare old ding-dongs, I don't mind telling you. So, I told him that I was taking the day off today. I think I've earned some time to myself. I haven't stopped working since I got there. It's even harder than they worked us up at the home.' She glanced down at her hands, which were rough and calloused.

'And what about the son . . . Daniel, ain't it?'

'Oh, he's lovely.'

'Is he now?' There was a twinkle in Niamh's eyes. 'Just *how* lovely?'

Daisy shook her head and grinned. 'There's nothing like that between us. We're just friends,' she assured her. 'The poor thing is very unwell. He doesn't have to do much before he's gasping for breath, but he does try, bless him. And it's nice to have someone there that I can get along with.'

As they prepared the dinner side by side Daisy almost felt as if she had never been away. Even so, she knew that she had done right by trying to be independent. It was nice to know that Niamh was here, though, like a safe harbour in a storm. Sadly, she was the closest thing to family that Daisy had now. Despite her brave words it had taken courage to stand up to Liam Doyle and who knew how long it might be before she got to spend time with Niamh again? With this in mind, she was determined to enjoy every minute of the day.

It was late that evening before she set off for the farm and as she approached, she was surprised to see that the oil lamp hadn't been lit in the kitchen. Hurrying now, she entered the room to find Daniel lolling in a chair with his chin on his chest.

Liam was sitting in his usual place with a mug of ale in one hand and his clay pipe in the other. 'Had a good day, have you?' he sneered. 'It's all right for some, swannin' off an' leavin' the work to everybody else.'

Ignoring him completely, Daisy quickly crossed to Daniel and as he lifted his head, she saw that his lips were a dull bluish–purple colour.

He lifted his hand and weakly pointed towards a drawer where he kept a small glass bottle of pills for when he had a bad turn. She hurried over and fetched him one, then rounded on Liam.

'Why didn't you get him his pill?' she demanded. 'You know he has to have one when he takes a bad turn. He could have died if I hadn't come back when I did!'

Liam shrugged. 'Well, that would have been one less useless mouth for me to feed, to be sure.'

Daisy was sickened. This was his son he was talking about, but he clearly had no affection for him. In fact, from what she had seen, Liam didn't care about anyone or anything apart from his beasts.

She turned her attention back to Daniel, pleased to see that he was looking slightly better, but what would have happened if she hadn't come back when she did? It didn't bear thinking about.

Chapter Thirty-Four

On a roasting hot day in July, Jed leant heavily on his anvil and wiped the sweat from his forehead. He had just fired up the furnace and although he had closed the doors on the enormous oven, the heat was almost unbearable. Even Rags couldn't stand to be in there but instead lay just outside the open doors with his head on his front paws as he watched his master. He had learnt that it was best not to stay in the kitchen when Jed wasn't around as Victoria would kick him out of the way every chance she got, so now he stayed away from her as much as he could.

'Are you all right, Jed?' Lewis asked with concern. Since he had returned from Ireland he seemed to have been going steadily downhill again and Lewis was worried. Now that he came to think about it, Jed's symptoms were much the same as his father's had been before he passed away, which was strange. Like his father, Jed was constantly rushing off to the toilet and on a few occasions lately Lewis had heard him being sick.

'Aye, I'm all right, lad,' Jed assured him. He had never been one for making a fuss but he had never felt this ill before. His appetite had gone and what he did manage to eat he usually threw back up again. But the fatigue was the worst part. He seemed to be constantly tired with no energy at all.

'Hmm, well I think it's time you made a trip to the doctor's all the same,' Lewis advised.

'Oh, it's probably because I'm still worrying about Daisy,' Jed confided. 'I can't remember the last time I had a good night's sleep. I just lie there trying to think where she might be. I doubt I'll rest easy till I've found her.'

'We could always go back to Dublin and search for her again,' Lewis volunteered.

'As it happens, I'm plannin' on doin' just that.' Jed took a long swallow of water. 'Your mother wants to go to Dublin at the start of August. The Prince of Wales opened the Royal Agricultural Exhibition there some years ago and a friend of hers told her that he goes there every year at that time. She's hopin' to catch a sight of him. An' there's just a chance that Bridie and Connor might have had word from Daisy by now.'

'But wouldn't they have written and told you if they had?'

Jed sighed. 'I suppose they would,' he answered dully. 'I dare say it's just me clutchin' at straws.'

In the house, Victoria was talking to Gilbert, who had only just rolled out of bed. Mrs Smith was not cleaning for them that week as she had come down with a bad case of the summer flu, and Victoria was not best pleased.

'How much longer do you think it will be?' she asked, keeping a wary eye on the door in case anyone should come in and hear them.

Gilbert chuckled. 'Oh, a few more months should do it. We don't want to rush things and arouse suspicions.'

'Hmm, I suppose you're right,' she said petulantly. Jed had almost cleared all her debts now so when something happened to him, she would be able to sell the business and the house and pocket all the proceeds – as long as Daisy didn't turn up. But Gilbert had assured her this wouldn't happen.

She had managed to talk Jed into letting her have two more short breaks in London recently and her friendship with the wealthy politician, Lord David Harlow-Green, was progressing nicely. She had no doubt that once she lived there permanently, he would be like putty in her hands, and after seeing his beautiful home she could hardly wait to be his wife. It was so much more civilised in London than in this back-of-beyond hovel and she knew a bright future lay ahead of her. First, though, she would have to wait for Jed to die and play the dutiful, grieving widow for a time. But not for too long, she thought, with a wicked little smile.

Lewis found himself watching his brother closely when they were in the house, and one evening shortly after his conversation with Jed, he noticed something strange. Every night once dinner was out of the way, Gilbert would make them all a cup of tea before getting ready to go out. It was odd because he had never bothered to do anything like that before they had lived there.

Lewis said nothing but when everyone had retired to bed, he started to search through the cupboards. His search turned up nothing untoward, which made him feel guilty. Gilbert would have to be very wicked indeed if he was doing what Lewis had suspected. He made a mental note to stop letting his imagination run away with him and climbed the stairs to bed with an easier mind.

At the end of July, Victoria and Jed set off for Dublin and when they arrived, they went straight to the hotel. Once they were settled, Jed planned to go and see Bridie and Connor.

'Why don't you come with me?' he suggested before he left.

Victoria shook her head. 'No, I won't if you don't mind. I spotted a rather nice milliner's shop on the way here from the ferry and after I've had some tea, I might take a stroll there. I can't turn up in front of the prince in a tatty old bonnet, can I?'

'But you got a new bonnet less than a month ago, and chances are you won't see the prince. Chances are the shop will be closed by now anyway,' Jed pointed out, trying to keep his patience. 'And Bridie and Connor haven't met you yet.'

She waved her hand airily. 'I know, darling, perhaps I'll find time before we head back home after the opening of the exhibition. I understand it's going to be very grand. Everybody who is anybody will be there. We might even be lucky enough to be presented to the prince if we're in the right place at the right time. Oh, and don't be too long. I would like you to take me out to dinner this evening. It will be a nice change from having to cook myself or put up with another of Mrs Smith's home-cooked dinners.'

Jed sighed and went on his way. When the cottage came into sight, he felt a lump form in his throat as he watched a plume of smoke drift lazily from the chimney into the clear blue sky. He had written to tell Bridie and Connor that they would be coming and even before he got to the gate Bridie rushed out to greet him.

'Eeh, it's good to see you, lad, so it is.' She gave him a big hug before looking over his shoulder. 'But where is your wife? I've cooked you both dinner, so I have. And I've been looking forward to finally meeting her.'

Jed instantly felt guilty. 'Sorry, Bridie, Victoria was feeling rather tired after the journey so she sends her apologies. I hope you ain't gone to too much trouble for us.'

Connor appeared from the barn and gave him a welcoming slap on the back.

'Is there any news of Daisy?' Jed asked tentatively.

Bridie's face fell. 'Not in' at all,' she said. 'Although I reckon her grampy here must have scoured every inch o' the country for miles around. But come away in now, there's the kettle boilin an' I'm sure you're ready for a cuppa.'

Jed spent a couple of happy hours with them before heading back to the hotel where he found Victoria dressed up to the nines.

'Ah, here you are at last.' There was a hint of irritation in her voice as she crossed to the most enormous hat box Jed had ever seen. 'What do you think of this? It will go beautifully with the gown I'm going to wear to the exhibition.'

'It looks, er . . . expensive,' he said apprehensively as she lifted the hat from a bed of tissue paper. It was pale green with a very wide brim lavishly decorated with peacock feathers.

Victoria pouted as she set it on her head. 'Oh, trust you to think of the price. Don't you like me to look nice?'

'Of course I do, but must you always choose the most expensive thing in the shop? You won't have many opportunities to wear it when we get home.'

'Of course I will,' she snapped. 'I can wear it to go to church on Sundays and it will be perfect for my trips to London.'

Jed gave up as he flopped tiredly into a chair. He knew when he was beaten, and he was so tired he could hardly keep his eyes open. 'Actually, I thought it might be nice if we had room service and dined in here tonight,' he suggested.

She shook her head adamantly. 'Oh no, darling. We simply *must* dine out. One never knows who one might meet in the better class of eateries.' She eyed him up and down. 'Although you will need to change. I don't want to be seen out with you looking like that.'

Jed slowly stood up and removed his tie before unbuttoning his shirt. 'As you wish. In actual fact, Bridie and Connor were disappointed you didn't come to meet them. Bridie had cooked dinner for us so I've already eaten. And there's been no news of Daisy at all.'

'Oh, can't you stop thinking about that *damned* girl for *one* minute,' Victoria snapped peevishly. 'Daisy went of her own free will, so why can't you leave her be? She's an adult and quite capable of looking after herself.'

'That *damned* girl, as you refer to her, happens to be *my* daughter,' he snapped back. 'And knowing her as I do, she would never just have upped and left without a word. There's something more to this an' if it takes till me dyin' day I'll find her, you see if I don't!'

Victoria felt a moment of panic. But then she thought of Daisy locked safely away in the unmarried mothers' home and relaxed. It was the one place Jed would never think of looking for her.

When they arrived at the opening of the exhibition the following day it was instantly obvious that Victoria wasn't at all interested in the agricultural displays. She had come solely in the hope that she would be presented to the Prince of Wales, but he was nowhere to be seen.

To make matters worse the sky was a heavy grey colour and it was drizzling, so very soon her new hat looked like a somewhat bedraggled peacock and was quite ruined. She had been sadly disappointed the year before when she had been unable to attend the exhibition, but now she realised that she really hadn't missed much at all and by the time they left she was in a sulk.

'Well, that was a waste of time,' she grumbled as Jed hailed a cab to take them back to the hotel.

'Not really, at least I got to see Bridie and Connor again,' he pointed out. 'An' I have told 'em that we'll have dinner with them this evenin'. It will be our last chance because we're booked on the early ferry home in the morning.'

'*Must* I come?' she whined with a long-suffering sigh.

But for once Jed put his foot down. 'Yes, you must, but you'll need to get changed first an' put some sensible shoes on. It's a bit of a hike along the coastal path to the cottage.'

Victoria was horrified. 'You mean we have to *walk* there?'

Jed's jaw set. 'Yes, it ain't so far as the crow flies.'

An hour later they set off, although Victoria didn't seem at all pleased to be going. She could see no reason why she should have to meet Jed's dead wife's parents.

By the time they were halfway there her cloak was heavy with rain and the bottom of her gown was sodden. She moaned nonstop but at last they spotted the little cottage and Jed drew her to a halt.

'Look at it. It's pretty as a picture, ain't it?'

'I suppose it is if you like that sort of thing,' she said drily. It certainly didn't look grand enough to her. In fact, it looked to be even smaller than Jed's house.

'Well, it's nice to meet you at last, lass,' Connor and Bridie greeted her when they arrived. 'Come on in out o' the rain. We've a hot drink ready for you an' dinner won't be long. There's a nice piece o' roast beef.'

Victoria walked into the cottage and sniffed. Just as she had thought, there was nothing grand about it, although she was forced to admit it was cosy.

For Jed, the next two hours were a nightmare. Despite Connor and Bridie doing their best to engage Victoria in conversation, she spoke only when asked a direct question and made it more than obvious that she didn't want to be there.

'Are you ready, Edward?' she asked Jed the moment he had finished his meal. 'We should be getting back now; I have the packing to do if we're leaving first thing in the morning.'

'Aye, o' course.' He cast an apologetic glance at Bridie before going to get his coat and Victoria's cloak. 'Thanks for the meal, it were grand,' he told the kindly old couple. 'An' please, if you hear anythin' at all about Daisy, let me know an' I'll do the same for you.'

'That goes wit'out sayin', lad. An' don't give up hope. She'll turn up, you'll see.'

The old couple saw their visitors off at the door and as they closed it on the cold night, Bridie looked at her husband. 'I reckon he's got hisself a bad 'un there,' she said sadly.

Connor could only nod in agreement. 'I'm afraid I 'ave to agree, lass.' He lifted his pipe and began to pack it with tobacco. 'No wonder our poor Daisy never seemed that keen on her.'

'You don't think that's why she's run away do you?' Bridie said fearfully.

He shook his head. 'No, our Daisy is made o' sterner stuff than that. She'd 'ave stuck it out for her daddy's sake.' He placed a gentle arm about his wife. 'Come on, me old wench, you sit there by the fire an' I'll make you a nice mug o' cocoa, eh?'

'That sounds just the ticket,' she told him and sank into the fire-side chair, not much caring if she never saw her new daughter-in-law again. She couldn't hold a candle to their Mauve for sure!

Chapter Thirty-Five

Brooke Farm, Ireland, September 1882

Suddenly it was autumn and if Daisy had thought life on the farm was hard before, it was now even harder. Every morning she would have to wrap up warmly to go to the cowshed before scuttling back to the kitchen to start the breakfast. Her relationship with the farmer was just the same as when she had arrived, although he was paying her now, albeit begrudgingly. Daniel continued to have good days and bad days and he often teased her, 'I'll go on forever!' Daisy prayed that he was right because he was the only friend she had at the farm.

On this particularly blustery day, as she milked the cows, she was practising what she would say to Liam when she managed to get some time with him, because she was sick of being paid a pittance. But nothing seemed right so she decided she would just say it straight out. She knew he wouldn't be happy about it, but now that she had a little bit of money saved, she could afford to walk away if he didn't like it.

Her opportunity came as she placed a large plate of bacon, egg and sausages in front of him. As always, he merely lifted his knife and fork and started to eat with not a word of thanks. He had no social graces whatsoever and his table manners were worse than the pigs outside in the sty.

'I've been meaning to ask you something,' she told him, trying to keep her voice steady, although she was shaking. 'The thing is,

I've been here a good while now and I think it's time you started to pay me a proper wage.'

That got his attention and his head snapped up. 'I *do* pay you a proper wage,' he argued, narrowing his eyes.

Daisy shook her head. 'No, I'm afraid you don't. I've been making enquiries in town and the average wage is between fifteen and eighteen shillings a week. I'll settle for twelve shillings, and that's cheap for what I do.'

'*Twelve* shillin's!' He stared at her as if she had taken leave of her senses. 'Are you *mad*, girl? I ain't made o' money, you know!'

Daisy shrugged and stood her ground. She had expected this.

Seeing her determined stance, he sighed. 'I'll tell you what I'll do, I'll raise it to five shillin's.'

Daisy crossed her arms and stared back at him. 'Twelve!'

He slammed his knife and fork down. 'All right then . . . eight!'

Another shake of the head from Daisy. 'If I left you'd need two people to get through the amount of work I do,' she pointed out. 'And you'd be having to pay two wages.'

Daniel had just entered the room and he stifled a grin as he heard them bartering.

'An' what if I refuse?'

'Then I'll go,' Daisy said matter-of-factly. 'It's your choice.'

Liam made one last attempt to lower her price. 'All right then . . . *ten*, an' that's me last offer. You're robbin' me an' taking advantage o' me good nature, so you are.'

'Make it eleven and you've got a deal.'

He growled. 'All right, *eleven*. It's bloody daylight robbery, to be sure.'

'And I want it paid regularly every Friday morning,' she warned him. 'No more having to keep chasing you for it or I'm off!'

'All right, all right,' he muttered, frowning.

Daisy breathed a small sigh of relief and glanced at Daniel, who gave her an approving smile.

The following day Daisy went with Liam on the cart into Dublin to buy food for the animals. Whenever she could she avoided Dublin because she was afraid she might catch sight of her granny again. She knew she wouldn't be able to bear it if the dear soul turned her back on her with disgust. But today it couldn't be avoided. They needed flour and a lot of other household items, and Daisy knew Liam would grumble if she asked him to buy them. It was a dull, overcast day, although thankfully it was dry, and they made the journey in silence. They rarely had much to say to each other and that suited Daisy.

Once they reached the town, Liam took the horse to the stables, telling her, 'Meet me back here in two hours. I have a mind to call in at the tavern for a jar or two of ale when I've done me business. Mind you ain't late, though, I won't hang about for you if you ain't here.'

'I'll be here,' she answered shortly and set off with her basket across her arm. Once she had everything they needed, she decided to head to the rag stall. The few clothes she had were getting pitifully ragged, so she decided she would spend some of her wages and treat herself.

There were a lot of women swarming around the stall searching through the used clothes and Daisy joined them. She managed to find two plain skirts that would be perfect for working in when they had been altered and she also found a white blouse that looked as if it had had very little wear. But there was nothing that caught her eye for best and as she paid the old woman in charge of the stall, she asked, 'Have you anything that would do for Sunday best?'

The old woman smiled, showing her toothless gums. 'It just so happens I might have the very thing. Come round here, lass.'

Daisy joined her at the back of the stall and watched as the woman rummaged through a bag before pulling out a very pretty dress.

'I went to a posh house the other day an' the maids there sold me these,' the old woman told her. 'There's not a mark on 'em, to be sure. They belonged to the lady o' the house but they're last season's so the maids said she didn't wear 'em anymore. They'd look perfect on a pretty young lass like you, so they would. Here, have a rummage through an' see if there's anything else that catches your eye.'

Daisy studied the gown. It was made of a very soft satin, perfect for the spring and summer. It was in a lovely duck-egg-blue colour with a full skirt and three-quarter sleeves and it was trimmed with cream ribbon.

'How much is this?' Daisy enquired worriedly. It looked as if it was going to be terribly expensive.

'To you, lass, two shillin's.'

'Oh!' Daisy stared at the gown uncertainly.

'I'll tell you what, I'll make it one an' sixpence. How would that be?'

Daisy beamed. 'I'll take it, and thank you.' She knew she'd got a bargain and could hardly wait to get the dress home to try on. 'And I don't suppose you have any shoes that might go with it?' She could hardly wear her old work boots with it.

The old woman chuckled. 'Let's have a look now. Ah, what about these?'

She held up a pair of dainty black leather button boots and Daisy's eyes lit up. She tried them on and discovered that they were about a size too big, but that didn't trouble her. Far better to be too big than too small and she could always pad them out with a little newspaper.

'I'll take them,' she said happily, parting with another sixpence. Next, she went to the haberdashery stall. Now that her hair had grown to a decent length, she had been tying it back with string, but she decided she would treat herself to some pretty ribbon, if they had any to match her new gown. Once again, she was lucky when she found a length that was almost a perfect match, so she paid for that too and added it to her basket. Finally, she went to find the second-hand book stall. Daniel loved reading and she wanted to treat him. She decided on a novel called *The Adventures of Tom Sawyer* by Mark Twain, and smiled at the thought of his pleasure when he received it.

She was just turning away with the book tucked safely into her heavy basket when she stopped dead in her tracks and the colour seeped from her face. Her granny was standing talking to another stallholder just feet away. Shock glued her to the spot for a few seconds as she stared at her granny's beloved face, but then gripping her basket she turned about and rushed away in the opposite direction.

At that same moment Bridie looked up and frowned as she saw a young woman almost running through the stalls. There was something familiar about her. Her hair was exactly the same colour as her Daisy's, although it was much shorter. Within seconds the girl disappeared into the labyrinth of backstreets bordering the market. Bridie had the urge to follow her, but then she pulled herself together. She wasn't as nippy on her feet as she used to be and the chances of catching up with the girl were slim. Anyway, she scolded herself, it was probably just wishful thinking on her part. And yet for the rest of the morning she couldn't get the image of the girl out of her head. What if it had been Daisy and she had missed the chance of finding her?

When Liam returned to the stables to collect the horse and cart, he found Daisy waiting for him. She had seemed to be in good spirits when they had set off from the farm, but now she looked strangely subdued and if he wasn't very much mistaken, she had been crying. Not that it bothered him particularly. As long as the girl continued to work hard, especially now he was having to pay her more money, he didn't much care how she was feeling. It might be time to have a word in Daniel's ear and suggest that he offered to marry her. That way he would get her to work for nothing.

They were passing through Blackrock on the way home when Daisy suddenly said, 'Drop me here. I have something I need to do.'

'What? But what about all the work that's waitin' back at the farm?' Liam blustered. He liked to get his penny's worth of flesh.

'I'll do it when I get back,' Daisy told him abruptly. 'An' I don't know how you can complain. I haven't had any time off for at least three weeks. I shan't be long.'

Growling, Liam drew the horse to a halt. 'Just make sure you ain't, else I shall dock the time out o' your wages,' he warned.

Daisy gave him a scathing glance before hopping down from the cart and racing towards Niamh's cottage.

Niamh was rolling pastry on the kitchen table when Daisy appeared and she looked up in surprise. 'Hello, I wasn't reckonin' on seein' you today.' Then seeing Daisy's tear-stained face she asked, 'Is everythin' all right, lass?'

'I-I just went into Dublin to do some shopping with Farmer Doyle,' Daisy gulped. 'An' while I was there, I saw my granny.' The tears came hard and fast again and wiping her floury hands down her apron Niamh hurried over to her and led her to a chair.

'An' did she see you?'

Daisy shook her head as she swiped tears from her cheeks with the back of her hand. 'I don't think so. I went in the opposite direction as soon as I saw her.'

'Perhaps you should 'ave approached her?' Niamh suggested tentatively. 'From what you've told me of her, I find it hard to believe that she'd ever turn her back on you, so I do!'

'But she has, the whole family has,' Daisy insisted. 'It was all there in the letter that Victoria sent to the home. I saw it with my own eyes.'

'Hmm.' Niamh still wasn't convinced, but she bustled away to put the kettle on. Daisy looked as if she could do with a cup of tea, poor thing. The loss of her family was eating away at her like poison in the blood.

Two cups of tea later, Daisy had managed to compose herself a little and she looked at Niamh sheepishly. 'I'm sorry to bring my troubles to your door.'

Niamh wagged a finger at her. 'You need never apologise to me. I'll always be here for you. We went t'rough hell together up at that godforsaken place, so we did. Now, will you be stayin' for dinner? There's more than enough to go round. We've got rabbit pie tonight.'

Daisy shook her head. 'No, thanks all the same, but I'd best get back. Liam wasn't at all happy that I came here in the first place and I promised I wouldn't be long.'

'All right, but just t'ink on what I said, would you? About speakin' to your granny, I mean. There's something that don't seem right about that letter to my mind. They've only heard Gilbert's lies an' perhaps if you were to tell 'em the truth about what really happened they'd—'

'*No!*' On that score Daisy was adamant. The only thing of her past life that was still intact was her pride and she knew she wouldn't be able to bear it if she was rejected again.

After saying their goodbyes, Daisy set off for the farm with a heavy heart. Even the excitement of finding a new gown was gone now.

Daniel was waiting for her when she got back, looking worried. 'Oh, here you are.' She could hear the relief in his voice. 'Where did you get to?'

'I just popped in to see Niamh on my way home,' she told him as she approached the table where Liam had dumped the shopping and the new clothes she had bought. 'Oh, and I got you this. I thought you might like it.'

When she took the book from the basket and handed it to him his whole face lit up. 'Y-you bought this for *me*?' He stared down at the book in his hands as though it were covered with diamonds.

She nodded.

'B-but *why*?' No one ever bought him presents.

'I thought you'd like it.'

Daniel was deeply touched. Daisy had a heart of pure gold, so she did. And she was beautiful into the bargain. Far too beautiful to ever look at an invalid like him.

'Thank you,' he said quietly. 'But what else have you been buying?' He laughed as he looked at all the packages. 'It looks like you've bought up half the stalls.'

'I treated myself to a new . . .well, a second-hand new gown from the rag stall,' she answered as she drew the gown out of the bag. 'I think it might be a little big for me but I can soon alter it.'

'Eeh, that colour will look a fair treat on you,' he said admiringly. 'Although I t'ink you'd look beautiful in a sack, so I do.'

When Daisy glanced at him, surprised, he blushed and hurried away to put the kettle on. You dope, he silently scolded himself. The last thing he wanted to do was scare her away, for he didn't know how he would go on without her now.

Chapter Thirty-Six

Ansley Village, October 1882

Shortly after Lewis and Jed had gone to start work in the forge, the postman arrived with a letter for Jed that bore an Irish postmark.

Victoria stared at it as Gilbert appeared from the stair doorway, yawning.

'A letter for Jed,' his mother told him. 'It looks like it's from those interfering in-laws of his. What do you think I should do?' She still had a fear that Daisy might be released from the convent and turn up at any minute.

'Open it,' he said without hesitation. 'And then burn it. Jed will never even know it arrived.'

Needing no encouragement, Victoria lifted a knife and slit the envelope and what she read made her pale significantly.

Dear Jed,

I've no wish to worry you unduly but when I was in the market in Dublin some days ago I glanced up to see the back of a young woman rushing away from me. She looked so like our Daisy, but I couldn't be sure, and by the time I'd pulled meself together she'd disappeared. Now I know it could be purely wishful thinking on my part but there was just something about her. She was the right build for Daisy and her hair was exactly the same colour as hers. It gave me a right gliff, so it did, and it's kicking meself I am that I didn't try to follow her. I don't even rightly know why I'm writing to tell you this except it gave me hope that she is still here somewhere, although why she should have cut us all out of her life, I have no idea. You can rest assured that me and Connor will be keeping our eyes peeled for her more than ever from now on and should I have any further news I shall write to you again straight away. I hope you are keeping well; it was concerned I was when you last came to see us to see you looking so peaky again!

Look after yourself, lad.
Much love
Bridie xxx

Victoria looked up at Gilbert and frowned. 'You don't think the nuns have let her go from the home, do you?' she asked fearfully.

Gilbert shook his head. 'Not a chance,' he assured her. 'She'll rot in that place, believe me. Now throw that in the fire and Jed will never even know it came.'

She did as she was told and as they watched the flames lick around it, she shuddered. Should Daisy turn up now all the plans she had made for her future would be scuppered. Jed's health was slowly declining, as they had planned, and now she went to London for at least a few days every month. Strangely, Jed didn't even object anymore. If truth be told, she suspected he was glad to see her go.

At her suggestion Jed had moved out of their bedroom to sleep in Daisy's room some weeks ago. She had told him that he was keeping her awake with his constant tossing and turning and he had seemed only too happy to oblige.

She, meanwhile, was enjoying her monthly breaks away. She had told Lord Harlow-Green that her husband was much older than her and on his deathbed, and she was fairly certain that when she was widowed, he would be only too happy to step into Jed's shoes. Victoria could hardly wait. With him she would have the lifestyle she craved and more money than even she could spend.

Much to her delight, one evening David had hosted a dinner party at his magnificent home in Mayfair and the Prince of Wales himself had attended. She would lie in bed and replay the evening over and over in her mind, but there was still a long way to go before her dreams could come true and she was fearful that if Daisy turned up back at the forge, she could ruin everything.

As if he could read her mind, Gilbert told her, 'Look, Mama, if Daisy was free don't you think this is the first place she would have headed for? It's just wishful thinking on that silly old woman's part. Forget about it.'

Despite Gilbert's reassuring words, however, she still felt apprehensive. How cruel it would be if her dreams were to be snatched away from her now.

Over in the forge Jed was forcing himself to carry on working as waves of dizziness came and went. He thanked God that Lewis had come to work with him when he had, for he was his right-hand man now and almost as good a blacksmith as Jed himself.

'Are you feeling ill again?' Lewis asked as he fed the ever-hungry furnace with yet more coal.

'I'm all right, lad, it'll pass.'

Lewis frowned. 'I think it's time you went to see the doctor. This has been going on for too long and you aren't eating enough to keep a sparrow alive. Don't think I haven't noticed.'

Jed gave a rueful grin. 'That's only cos I tend to bring it straight back up if I do eat much.'

'All the more reason to see the doctor,' Lewis persisted.

'We'll see,' Jed said wearily. Every day was an effort now and worrying constantly about Daisy didn't help. She was the first thing he thought of every morning when he opened his eyes and the last he thought of before going to sleep.

When they stepped out of the forge early that evening, the leaves were fluttering from the trees and they crossed a carpet of russet and gold as they walked to the house. While Jed paid yet another visit to the toilet, Lewis went into the kitchen, where he found his mother packing a small trunk.

'Off to London again, are you?' He raised an eyebrow. Knowing his mother as he did, he could guess at what the attraction was.

'Yes, dear.' She favoured him with a sweet smile. She was always in a good mood when one of her trips was imminent. 'I thought I might visit the art museum this time.'

'Hmm, I have to say I'm not so sure your timing is right. Haven't you noticed how ill Jed is looking? I've tried to get him to see the doctor. Perhaps you could try?'

Gilbert was lolling in a chair with his feet stretched out to the fire. He had lost his job at the bank some time ago and had made very little effort to find another one since, much to Jed's disgust.

'It's probably just some bug,' he told his brother lazily.

'Since when have bugs lasted for months?'

Gilbert shrugged. 'He's a grown man and able to decide for himself if he wants to see the doctor or not, and I don't think you should make Mama responsible for him.'

At that moment Jed entered the room looking worn out, Rags close to his heels. He stopped short when he saw the trunk.

'Ah, here you are,' Victoria giggled girlishly. 'Did I mention that I was going to London tomorrow, darling? And I'll be staying at Mrs Byron-Tate's this evening. You don't mind terribly, do you?'

He shrugged, he was past caring where she went or what she did; they rarely even spoke when she was home anyway, unless it was for her to demand something.

He and Lewis took it in turns to wash at the sink and once they had gone upstairs to get changed, Victoria stared at Rags with distaste.

'I wonder if we shouldn't start giving that mangy mutt a few doses of what Jed is having,' she suggested to Gilbert.

He grinned. 'I'll be more than happy to, but let's get one out of the way first, eh? Otherwise, it might look suspicious.'

She pouted as she kicked Rags out of her way and with a yelp he hurried beneath the table, not venturing out until Mrs Byron-Tate's grand carriage arrived to take Victoria to her house an hour later.

Meanwhile, the workers' meals had been left in the oven by Mrs Smith to keep warm. Sometimes Jed wondered what they would do without the kindly woman – she had kept the house going since Daisy had left. But he merely picked at his meal before giving it to Rags who wagged his tail delightedly.

'Not hungry, Jed?' Gilbert said pleasantly. 'Never mind, I'll make you a nice cup of tea before I get ready to go out.' It was still the only thing he ever did do to help about the place, so Jed let him get on with it.

Once Gilbert had left a short time later, Lewis asked, 'What are we going to do about Gilbert? He can't just sit around here forever expecting you to keep him.'

Jed shook his head. 'I've no idea, lad. I've given up trying because I'm afraid while your mother keeps giving him money, he'll never want to stand on his own two feet. Has she always spoilt him?'

Lewis nodded. 'Yes, she and my father were always arguing about it. Dad was like me and you, he believed a man should do a fair day's work for a fair day's wage. After Gilbert got expelled from school, Father employed him in some of his shops for a time but he rarely turned up so that didn't last long.'

Lewis leant his head back in the chair and looked around the room. There were signs of Daisy everywhere. In front of the hearth was a gay peg rug she had made. It was the only one Jed had not allowed Victoria to store in the barn. Lewis's eyes grew sad as a picture of her face flashed in front of his eyes. He was missing her more every day. He looked back at Jed and sighed. The poor chap looked ghastly, his face was grey with a yellowish tinge and he really had lost so much weight. Suddenly Jed leant forward, gripping his stomach, groaning.

Lewis was out of his chair in a moment. 'What's wrong, Jed?'

'Pains . . . in my stomach.' Jed gasped for breath. 'They haven't been this bad before!'

'Right, that's it.' Lewis strode towards the door and snatched up his coat. 'This has gone far enough. I'm going to get the doctor and I'm also going to fetch Mother home from Mrs Byron-Tate's.'

'Sh-she won't like that,' Jed groaned, but Lewis was determined.

'That's too bad, she'll just have to lump it! I'll not have her swanning off leaving you while you're ill. Now stay there in that chair until I get back and don't move, do you hear me?' And with that there was the slam of the door and he was gone.

It was almost an hour later when Lewis returned with the doctor, who had come straight from delivering a baby in the village.

'So, what's this then, Jed?' he asked as he placed his bag down and took out his stethoscope. 'Young Lewis here tells me that you haven't been grand for some time. Why have you left it so long to call me out?'

'I-I thought it would pass,' Jed told him, sweat standing out on his forehead.

'Hmm, so tell me the symptoms.'

As Jed told him how he had been feeling, Lewis saw the doctor frown, although he didn't comment. He began his examination and when he was done, he took Lewis to one side and told him in a low voice, 'This is most strange.' He had signed the death certificate for Victoria's late husband. They had been such a highly esteemed family and there had been nothing to prove he had died from anything other than natural causes, but now the doctor couldn't help but notice the similarity in his and Jed's symptoms and alarm bells were ringing. Could Mr Peake's death have been from something other than natural causes?

The doctor looked at Lewis. 'Do you keep any arsenic on the premises?'

Lewis frowned. 'I think there's some in the barn that Jed used to use to keep the rats down, but now the cat has had kittens, I don't think he has cause to use it very often, if at all.'

'So, he doesn't handle it regularly?'

Lewis shook his head and the doctor scowled. All Jed's symptoms pointed to arsenic poisoning but if he didn't handle the substance often it couldn't be that.

'And where is Mrs Armstrong?' The doctor enquired next, glancing around.

'Er . . . she was called away to London.' Lewis felt himself flush. He could hardly tell the doctor that he had just visited his mother's friend's house to tell her that Jed had taken ill and she had told him in no uncertain terms that she couldn't possibly delay her visit to London.

'I see.' The doctor placed his stethoscope in his bag. If he remembered rightly, Mrs Armstrong hadn't been very sympathetic towards her last husband when he had been ill either, but he supposed that was really none of his business.

'So, will there be anyone here able to take care of Jed until he recovers a little?'

'Oh yes, there's me and my brother and Mrs Smith who comes in to clean from the village each day. I'm sure she'll help out until my mother returns.'

'Good.' The doctor took a bottle from his bag and handed it to Lewis. 'This is a tonic, be sure to see that he takes it. It's about all I can give him for now, but should his condition worsen don't hesitate to call me out again.'

'Of course. Thank you, Doctor.' Lewis saw the man to the door before returning to Jed. 'Right, it's bed for you, and no arguing. Come on now.' He gently took Jed's arm and led him upstairs to the bedroom before going down to the kitchen again where he paced the floor with a worried frown on his face. He couldn't believe that his mother had refused to come home to care for her sick husband, but that was his mother for you. She and Gilbert had definitely been tarred with the same brush, both gut selfish.

Meanwhile, at the luxurious Byron-Tate residence, Victoria was anxiously pacing the bedroom floor. What would the doctor say when he saw Edward? she wondered. Would he smell that something was amiss? She'd have a word or two to say to Gilbert when she got home, that was for sure. He had obviously been a little overgenerous with the dose of poison he was giving Edward each day and the last thing they needed to do was arouse suspicion. Gilbert would have to lower the dose, which would mean Jed's demise would take longer than she'd hoped, but there was nothing she could do about that.

As she thought of Lord Harlow-Green and the gown she had ordered the last time she was in London, a smile touched her lips. It was quite magnificent and the most expensive she had ever owned. She would be going for her final fitting the very next day, although she dreaded to think what Edward would say when she presented him with the bill for it. He could be very mean. But still, she consoled herself, once she was Lady Harlow-Green she could have as many expensive gowns and jewels as she wanted, and she could hardly wait.

Chapter Thirty-Seven

Brooke Farm, Ireland, December 1882

'There, I think that's it,' Daisy told Daniel with satisfaction as she snapped the thread on the last stitch of her gown. On getting it home she had thoroughly washed and pressed it and every night since, when all the other jobs were done, she had sat at the side of the fire and made the alterations by candlelight. Now it had been taken in and shortened and she could hardly wait to try it on, although it was so smart that she doubted she would get to wear it very often. It certainly wasn't a gown for milking cows or cleaning out pigs in.

Liam, who was puffing on his pipe with a glass of whisky in his hand, had seen his son watching Daisy as she sewed, her hair looking silky in the firelight, with an adoring expression on his face. He was ready to put his suggestion to Daniel as soon as the opportunity arose.

It came sooner than he expected when Daisy suddenly yawned and stood up. 'Oh dear, I think I might turn in.'

'But what about your cocoa?' Daniel asked.

'Oh, I think I'll give it a miss tonight.' Daisy gave him a gentle smile. 'Goodnight, both.' And lifting her gown she went upstairs.

'She's a bit of a mouthy little cow but she's a good worker, I'll say that for her,' Liam said.

Daniel smiled. It wasn't often his father bothered to talk to him apart from to tell him how useless he was.

'She'd make someone a good wife, to be sure,' Liam went on cautiously. 'I wonder you ain't asked her yourself, lad. It'd be nice to have a grandson; an heir to pass the farm on to when owt happens to me and you.'

Daniel looked shocked. 'Why would Daisy look at me when she could likely have her pick of any chap she fancied?'

'Ah, but you're wrong there.' Liam wagged his pipe at him. 'Think about it. She came here almost hotfoot from the unmarried mothers' home, so she did. What decent chap would take her on once they knew that, eh? And think, if she could get her feet under the table here, she'd be set up for life and we'd keep a good worker.' He didn't mention that another benefit would be that he would no longer have to pay her any wages.

Daniel flushed. He had never ventured far from the farm, had never even kissed a lass before, especially one like Daisy.

'Well, what do you think o' the idea?' his father pushed. 'You know the old sayin,' "nothin' ventured nothin' gained".'

Daniel shrugged. 'I, er. . . I'll think on it.'

Seeing that there was no more to be gained for now, Liam rose and knocked the tobacco from his pipe.

'Just see as you do then. I'm goin' up now.' And with that he too went to bed leaving Daniel with a lot to think about.

He was forced to admit that he had been drawn to Daisy since the first time he had clapped eyes on her. But, he asked himself, what red-blooded male wouldn't be? It wasn't just her pretty face, it was her kind nature. To him she was perfect, but he still couldn't see her ever tying herself to someone like him – an invalid who was living on borrowed time. And yet he couldn't just dismiss the idea; it was too appealing. He had little sleep that night as he tossed and turned thinking about it.

Daisy was kneading dough at the table the next morning when Daniel asked, 'Do you mind me asking what happened to your baby?' Daisy had never spoken about her life before she came to the farm.

Instantly her eyes looked haunted and she paused before answering, 'My baby was born dead.'

'Oh . . . I'm so sorry. Did its father not want it?' he probed gently.

'No. And truthfully I didn't want it either,' she admitted in a voice so low he had to strain forward to hear it. 'I was raped, you see . . . by my stepbrother.'

Daniel was shocked. And suddenly the whole sorry story poured out of her: about her father's remarriage to Victoria, the brutal rape and the way she had allowed Gilbert to take her to the unmarried mothers' home to save her father shame and embarrassment.

'Unfortunately, he learnt about the baby anyway and washed his hands of me. He only heard Gilbert's side of the story saying I'd led him on, you see? Even my grandparents turned their backs on me and said they never wanted me to darken their door again. It's so hard knowing that they're only a stone's throw away.'

'Where?'

'Kilmainham,' she told him dully. 'I've seen my granny twice from a distance since I came out of the home and it's been so hard not to be able to approach her.'

'This Gilbert must be an evil bastard, to be sure!' Daniel said vehemently. 'But didn't you say your father's bride had two sons? Was the other one wicked too?'

'On no . . . Lewis is lovely,' she said far too quickly.

Seeing the flush that rose in her cheeks Daniel's heart sank. It was clear, whether she admitted it to herself or not, that she had feelings for this Lewis. 'Were you walking out together before all this happened?'

She shook her head. 'No, we were just very close. He's working with my daddy now in the forge.'

'I see. So, what are your long-term plans?'

'I thought I might move somewhere else and try my hand at another job when I have enough saved,' she admitted, and his heart sank even further.

'Oh no . . . you mustn't.' The words had burst from his lips before he could stop them.

She stared at him in surprise. 'And why is that?'

'It's because I-I have feelin's for you, an' I couldn't bear to see you go, to be sure.' He bowed his head in shame. 'Oh, I know I'm talkin' out o' turn. After all, as me daddy's allus told me, I'm useless, no good to man nor beast. So why would a lovely girl like you be wantin' to tie yourself to a chap like me, especially if you have feelin's for someone else? I can't even promise I'll be here this time next year.'

'You shouldn't talk like that, Daniel,' she told him sternly. 'You're a lovely person and I've no doubt there's lots of girls who would be proud to be seen with you.'

His eyes were veiled with tears as he shook his head. 'No, there wouldn't. And it's sorry I am that I ever said anyt'in'. Just try to forget that we had this conversation, eh?' And with that he rose and went to feed the chickens.

Daisy stared after him. His declaration had come as a shock to say the least. But even more of a shock was that she had been forced to admit to herself that there was someone who she cared for deeply. It was Lewis! Just the thought of him made her heart ache as she wondered what might have been if the rape hadn't happened. But it was no good thinking about that now, she scolded herself. Lewis had turned his back on her like the rest of the family. Why, he probably had a young woman he was walking out with by now! The thought was painful and she tried to push it from her mind as she got on with the kneading. The baking wouldn't do itself; more was the pity.

At the beginning of December the first snow fell and although the views were chocolate-box pretty, life on the farm got even harder. After lighting the fires each morning, Daisy had to go out and clear the snow from the door before beginning the milking. Once that was done, she had to break the ice on the buckets of water she had ready to clean the milking shed, and her hands were soon chapped and raw. Instead of being able to hang the washing out in the yard it now had to be strung up on lines hung between the beams in the kitchen, causing a damp atmosphere, and Daniel caught a chill. She kept him huddled in a blanket at the side of the fire and rubbed goose fat onto his chest every morning and night, but it didn't seem to be doing much good and she was concerned about him.

'I think we should call the doctor out,' she told Liam.

He shook his head and scowled. 'An' why would we waste good money on that when we already know what's wrong wit' him? He's allus worse in the winter months, so he is.'

She got a similar response a week later when she asked Liam if he could pick up a small Christmas tree.

'*A Christmas tree*?' He looked horrified. 'An' why would you be wantin' me to waste me hard-earned money on fripperies?'

'Because it's almost Christmas,' she told him with her chin in the air.

He snorted. 'Christmas Day is just another day when you live on a farm. The cows still have to be milked and the jobs are still there waitin' to be done, so they are.'

'Fine then, I'll pay for one myself,' she told him boldly. 'I'll give you the money when you next go into Dublin and would

280

appreciate it if you'd bring one back. Better still, I'll come into Dublin with you. There's some shopping I need to do and I want to get Daniel a gift.'

'You must want somet'in' to waste your money on,' he said with disgust.

A few days later they set off for Dublin. Liam hadn't intended to go until the following week, but the snow was still falling and he feared that if it kept on, they could be snowed in. It wouldn't be the first time.

Before they left, Daisy built the fire up and made sure Daniel had everything he needed until they got back.

The journey was slow. Snow was drifting in places already and Daisy huddled beneath a sack trying to get warm. At last they arrived, and while Liam went off to get food for the beasts, she made for the market to buy a small tree. She also stocked up on flour and any-thing else she thought they might need, and visited the second-hand book stall again, where she found a wonderful old leather-bound atlas of the world that she was sure Daniel would love.

It was no easy feat dragging the tree back to the cart, laden down with shopping as she was, but at last she got there, breathless and flushed from the exertion.

'Huh!' Liam snorted with disgust as he lobbed the tree into the back of the cart with the animal's food and they set off for home. By now the snow was almost blizzard-like and the return journey took even longer, but at last they pulled into the yard and Daisy hurried into the kitchen while Liam stabled the horse and put the cart away. It was only four o'clock in the afternoon, but it was already pitch dark outside. Once she entered the warmth Daisy's clothes began to steam in the heat and Daniel chuckled as colour rushed into her frozen cheeks.

'You look like you've just come out of the oven,' he teased.

She grinned. 'Wait till you see the tree,' she told him excitedly. 'I've bought some coloured crepe paper that we can cut into strips to decorate it and some tiny candles and holders, and I'm going to go and collect some holly to finish it off. You can help me do it this evening if you like.'

Daniel beamed. They had never been allowed to celebrate Christmas, even when his mammy had been alive. His daddy had always been too mean to let her spend money on what he considered to be extravagances, and so he was looking forward to it. Daisy had baked the Christmas cake weeks before, stealing a little of Liam's brandy to soak the fruit in, and she was going to decorate it with icing. They were going to have mince pies too and a fat goose for their Christmas dinner.

True to her word, as soon as she'd had a hot cup of tea, Daisy ventured out into the snow and came back half an hour later with her arms full of holly branches covered in shiny red berries. She then had to make the dinner and finish the rest of her chores, so it wasn't until much later that evening that they got the chance to decorate the tree.

Liam had moaned when she asked him to put the tree in a bucket of earth, but he had begrudgingly done it, and it now stood in all its splendour to one side of the fireplace, totally transforming the drab little room and Daniel could hardly take his eyes off it.

'You just wait until you see it when we've finished decorating it,' she promised, handing him the crepe paper and some scissors so he could cut it into strips.

Much later that evening Daisy stood back to study her work and felt pleased with the result. Back at home she and her daddy had each taken turns decorating their tree with the pretty glass baubles that he had bought for her mammy when they were first married. They had been Mauve's pride and joy and every year when Christmas was over, she had painstakingly wrapped each individual one in layers of newspaper before packing them in a box that would go into the loft until the following year. Daisy had nothing as fancy to work with here, but with her limited resources she thought the tree still looked very presentable. They had draped the crepe paper all around it in swags and with the holly tucked amongst its branches and the tiny candles twinkling it looked quite charming. There was a large bowl of holly on the table and another on the mantelshelf.

'It looks beautiful, so it does,' Daniel told her in awe, his eyes shining.

Liam snorted behind his newspaper. 'You sound like a couple o' kids, so you do,' he said testily. 'It's a pity you've neither of you got anyt'in' better to do wit' your time!'

Daniel and Daisy grinned at each other, but they didn't comment. It was only much later, as Daisy was damping down the fire and blowing out the candles before going to bed, that she grew sad as she thought of Christmases past. This would be the second one that she would spend apart from her family, and the realisation made her heart ache.

In her mind's eye she could still clearly see the last Christmas the whole family had spent together before her mammy and Alfie had passed away. It had been such a happy time. Her daddy had made Alfie a train set with little metal carriages and tiny wheels that really worked. It had been a testament to his skill as a blacksmith and Alfie had been so thrilled with it, he had cried with joy. For her there had been a pretty sweater that her mammy had knitted, and she had loved it. Such a happy time. But then suddenly there was just her and her daddy, but he had still tried his best to make Christmas a special time for her. With a sniff she pushed the memories away and made her weary way to bed.

On Christmas Day, Daisy rose early and got the fires lit. Her birthday the day before had passed unremarked, and she had tried very hard not to think about the last birthday she had spent with her daddy two years ago when he had given her her mother's wedding ring and the necklace. How she wished she'd had them with her when she'd left to go to the convent; mementos from happier times to comfort her.

Pushing these gloomy thoughts aside, she stuffed the goose with home-made thyme and parsley stuffing and popped it in the oven to cook slowly before going out to milk the cows. As Liam had rightly said, Christmas Day or not, the beasts still needed looking after.

The night before she and Daniel had peeled the brussels sprouts and potatoes together. The Christmas cake was now iced and there was also a batch of fresh mince pies as well as a Christmas pudding for after dinner.

By the time she had finished milking, Liam was outside feeding the pigs and hens, so she was alone when Daniel entered the kitchen, and she flashed him a bright smile.

'Merry Christmas, Dan.' When she crossed the room and planted a soft kiss on his cheek he blushed with pleasure.

'Merry Christmas to you, too,' he responded.

She went to fetch him his gift from the cupboard beneath the dresser and when she handed it to him his face was a mixture of pleasure and guilt.

'Why, it's beautiful,' he said in a choked voice. 'But I'm afraid I haven't been able to get out to buy you anyt'in'.'

'Oh, don't worry about that,' she told him airily. 'Just enjoy your book.'

He was already turning the pages and his eyes were wide. 'Why, I never realised the world was so big!' he declared in awe. 'All these countries. I shall be able to travel anywhere I want from now on wit'out even having to leave the room.'

Daisy was happy that he was so thrilled with his gift and set about laying the table with Daniel's mother's best cutlery and china, only ever used on special occasions.

The meal was cooked to perfection, even Daniel, who had the appetite of a bird, tucked in. Liam made no comment on it, but Daisy hadn't expected him to. It didn't stop him clearing his plate though, so that said volumes.

After the main course she served the pudding with a jug of thick, creamy custard and Daniel declared it was the best meal he had ever had, while Liam went off to sit by the fire and hide behind a newspaper.

'Now I'm going to help you wit' the washing up,' Daniel told her.

She shook her head. 'No, it's Christmas Day, go and put your feet up.'

'It's Christmas Day for you, too,' he pointed out. 'And so I insist. It's the least I can do after all the trouble you've gone to.'

'I wanted to make it a bit special for you,' she told him, and when he caught her hand, she saw all the love he felt for her shining in his eyes.

'You did that just by being here,' he said softly, and her heart did a little flip. He really was such a lovely, kind young man. She had no doubt that had he not been born with a bad heart he would have had the girls queuing up for him. As it was, it was highly unlikely he would ever get to meet any.

Suddenly she found herself thinking back to when Daniel had admitted that he had feelings for her. He had been true to his word and had not mentioned it since, but he had made it more than obvious that he cared about her. Would it be such a bad thing to be married to him? Her heart ached as a picture of Lewis's face flashed before her eyes, but common sense told her that nothing could ever come of the feelings she had for him now. At least married to Daniel she would have some sort of security and she was very fond of him. Not in the way she was of Lewis, admittedly, but maybe love would grow? Perhaps it would be worth giving it some thought. At least it would make Daniel happy, and he deserved some happiness in his life.

Chapter Thirty-Eight

Ansley Village

Back in Ansley, Christmas Day was not such a happy affair. With no Mrs Smith to do the cooking, Victoria had made a token effort to cook dinner, but it had been a disaster. The goose was overcooked, the brussels sprouts were undercooked and she had been in a bad mood all day.

Jed and Lewis decided to take a brisk walk after dinner and now that Victoria was alone with Gilbert, she told him, 'I don't know how much more of this I can take. Lord Harlow-Green is growing impatient, but I know Edward won't allow me to go to London any more than I already do. He's still angry about the amount I spent on my gown when he was taken ill.' She sniffed indignantly. 'I think he'd have me walking around in a serge skirt like the village women if I let him! If only the doctor hadn't come round sticking his nose in.'

It had shaken both her and Gilbert when Lewis had told them that the doctor suspected arsenic poisoning, and since then Gilbert had lowered the dose he was giving Jed each day.

'It's going to take forever to get rid of him at this rate,' Victoria complained. 'Surely there is *something* we can do to hurry his demise without it looking suspicious.'

Gilbert was lolling in the fireside chair smoking and he looked at her through narrowed eyes. 'Oh yes, so what do you suggest, Mama dear? I can hardly shoot him, can I? I don't want to end up dangling at the end of a rope.'

'I know that,' she snapped, as she paced up and down the kitchen like a caged animal. 'But couldn't we stage some sort of accident? He's said that he intends to go back to Ireland in the new year to continue his search for Daisy. Couldn't you go with him and sort of . . . oh, I don't know, push him into the sea when you're on the ferry or something?'

Gilbert laughed. 'I think you've been reading a few too many books, Mama. How am I supposed to do that?'

'Well, if you were to take the night ferry and suggest taking the air on deck when it's dark you could do it when he wasn't expecting it.'

Gilbert shook his head. 'Too risky. What if someone were to see me? Like I said, I don't want to end up being hanged. No, you're just going to have to be patient.'

Ignoring the mountain of dirty pots piled in the sink, Victoria stamped her silk-shod foot before storming upstairs leaving Gilbert staring into the fire.

Actually, an accident, or what could be made to look like an accident, wasn't such a bad idea. It was just working out how to do it and get away with it. After all, it wouldn't be just his mother escaping from this slum. She had told him that her new lover was more than happy to let him join them when they were finally able to be together.

Her first idea of tipping Jed over the side of the ferry was a non-starter as far as Gilbert was concerned. But what if he were to go with Jed and he engineered a different accident? There would be plenty of opportunities, especially on the cliff path leading to Kilmainham. Were Jed to accidentally slip off the sheer cliff he would have no chance of surviving a fall onto the rocks below. Smiling, he rose to help himself to another tankard of ale from the jug on the table. It was certainly worth thinking about.

On Boxing Day, after milking the cows and preparing a meal of cold meat, bread and pickles for Liam and Daniel, Daisy told Liam, 'I'm taking a few hours off. I have some gifts to deliver.'

Liam stared at her. 'What do you mean, you're takin' a few hours off? There's still jobs to be done, to be sure. You can't just go swannin' off whenever the fancy takes you, girl!'

'There's nothing needs doing till the next milking this evening,' she told him firmly as she pulled her coat on. 'And I shall be back in plenty of time for that. Your dinner is laid out ready for you.'

'But it's blowin' a blizzard out there, so it is. Will you be all right?' Daniel looked anxious as he stared at the fast-swirling snow through the window. 'I wish I were well enough to come wit' you to keep you safe,' he said mournfully.

She patted his hand as she wound a muffler she had knitted about her neck. 'I shall be fine, honestly. You just stay here in the warm and keep the fire stoked for me and I'll be back before you know it.'

'But how will you see where you're going in this?' he persisted.

She laughed as she pulled her mittens on. 'Oh, I know my way to Niamh's like the back of my hand.'

'I should t'ink you do, the amount o' times you go there,' Liam grumbled sarcastically.

'Actually, I think I could count on one hand how many times I've been there since I started working here,' Daisy snapped back. Then she smiled at Daniel and set off.

Before she had gone very far, she had to admit that Daniel had been right to raise his concerns. Snow covered many of the familiar landmarks she usually followed and the visibility was very limited, but she was fairly certain she was going in the right direction, so with her head bowed against the storm, she battled on along the cliff path, taking care to keep away from the edge. Below she could hear the waves pounding onto the rocks and she started to shiver. Perhaps this hadn't been such a good idea after all. But as she thought of the pleasure the twins and Riley would get from the little gifts she had bought them, she battled on.

More than once she stumbled but she knew she must be at least halfway there now. It would be as far to go back as it would to carry on, so she kept going. And then at last she saw smoke curling from the chimneys of the terraced cottages and breathed a sigh of relief. There had been times when she had thought she was lost, and her hands and feet were numb with cold, but she had made it. As she drew closer to the cottages, she smiled to see a large snow-man in Niamh's front garden with one of Nolan's old hats perched high on its head at a jaunty angle. It had two pieces of coal for its eyes and a large carrot nose and two long sticks poking out of either side to form its arms. It was obviously the work of the twins and Riley, but it seemed even they had chosen to stay inside this morning.

She rapped on the door and when Erin opened it, she gasped. Daisy was so thickly coated with snow that Erin wasn't even com-pletely sure who it was.

'Niamh, I reckon it's Daisy,' she shouted over her shoulder. Then grasping Daisy's arm, she hauled her inside. 'Come on in quickly. You're letting all the cold in, so you are!'

Niamh appeared behind her and chuckled. 'Crikey, kids, it's your snowman come to life, to be sure.' Then becoming stern she wagged her finger at Daisy. 'Sure, woman, it's mad you are to ven-ture out on such a day. Get yourself over by the fire and get those wet clothes off afore you catch your death o' cold.'

The water was already beginning to puddle around Daisy's sod-den boots and she guiltily glanced at the mess she was making. Niamh, meanwhile, was helping her to peel her outer clothes off before giving them a good shake and hanging them across the large wooden clothes horse. 'Sit yourself down, madam, while I go and get you a hot drink.' Despite her stern words her eyes expressed how pleased she was to see their unexpected visitor.

While she was gone Daisy opened the bag she had brought with her, and gave the twins and Riley a little parcel, each wrapped in brown paper.

'It's nothing much, mind,' she warned them. 'But I thought they'd keep you out of mischief for a few hours.'

The children crowed with delight when they opened their gifts. Each of them had a drawing pad of coarse paper and a packet of gaily coloured chalks. They instantly took their treasures to the table and were soon busily sketching.

'And I brought these for you,' Daisy told Niamh when she returned with a very welcome mug of steaming tea.

'Ah, you shouldn't have, lass,' Niamh scolded, but she ripped the parcel open excitedly all the same. 'Aw, why they're just beautiful, so they are. Did you knit them yourself?' She held up the bright red woollen scarf and matching mittens, and Daisy nodded. For Erin there was a bar of sweet-smelling lavender soap as well as small token gifts for the menfolk, which she left for them to open when they got home later in the day. Niamh then gave Daisy the small gift she had for her – a pretty silk scarf in shades of blue, which Daisy loved.

'And now tell me all that's been happenin' to you,' Niamh said as she plonked herself on the seat beside Daisy.

Daisy sipped at the sweet tea and shrugged. 'There's not much to tell really . . . except . . .' Lowering her voice she went on to tell her friend about the night Daniel had confessed his feelings for her.

'Hmm, so what are you goin' to do about it?' Niamh asked in her usual forthright way.

'Well, Daniel is a lovely chap and it's not as if I have any other prospects, is it? It would make him happy too, and that's important,' Daisy said uncertainly.

Niamh frowned. 'But you don't love him!'

'I admit, I don't. But perhaps that would come with time.'

'Huh! Personally, I still think you should go an' see your grand-parents before you go makin' any rash decisions,' Niamh said. 'Who knows, they might have had a change o' heart an' be ready to welcome you back into the fold, especially when they hear your side o' the story. An' what about Lewis? Don't think I ain't noticed how you go all dewy-eyed every time you mention him. How can you consider weddin' one man when you love another?'

Daisy's eyes were veiled with tears as she shook her head. 'Lewis is just a pipe dream. Life with Daniel could be real.'

'But Liam would just work you into the ground,' Niamh pointed out. 'He'd have you as an unpaid help for always once that ring were on your finger, an' God knows what sort o' life you'd have! Don't get me wrong, I've heard tell what a rum life Daniel has had wit' his daddy, so I have, an' I've no doubt he's a lovely man. But t'ink carefully, Daisy. This is the rest o' your life you're talkin' about. *Please* don't go makin' any rash decisions.'

Daisy sniffed back the tears and forced a smile, eager to change the subject. 'That's quite enough about me for now. How have things been for you?'

Niamh blushed prettily. 'Actually, they've been pretty good. Aiden an' me are walkin' out together now. I don't know if anythin' will come of it yet, o' course, but I do like him . . . very much, in fact. An' the best part of it is he knows all about the mistake I made an' the baby, an' he's happy to accept me as I am. He says everyone is entitled to make one mistake. But it's early days, so we'll just 'ave to wait an' see how t'ings pan out. He was takin' me to meet his mammy an' daddy this week but lookin' at the weather I reckon we'll have to put it off for a while. Still, there's plenty o' time, so there is.'

Daisy was pleased for her. 'That's wonderful. I really hope things work out for you. And what about your daddy?'

Niamh giggled. 'Oh, he's still smitten with the widow. I wouldn't be surprised if we didn't hear weddin' bells soon, to be sure. He's down at her inn now an' they seem to be gettin' along just fine. She never had any children of her own so she seems to be fair taken wit' the twins an' Riley, an' they like her too.'

'That's excellent, I'm pleased for him. If he does remarry that will give you the chance to do what you want.'

In a short pause in their chatter, Daisy glanced at the small tin clock on the mantelshelf and gasped with dismay. 'Oh dear, I didn't realise how long I'd been here,' she fretted as she hurried across to the clothes horse to collect her hat and coat. 'Liam will be angry if I'm not back soon.'

'Oh, sod Liam,' Niamh laughed. 'He's nowt but a slave driver anyway.'

Once Daisy was dressed in her outdoor clothes, Niamh followed her to the door and hugged her. 'I wish you could stay longer.'

'I'll come again soon, I promise.' Daisy opened the door and to her shock and horror was confronted with a wall of snow. 'Oh dear,' she gasped. 'It looks like we've been snowed in. Have you anything I can use to dig my way out.'

'Don't be so daft. You'll not be goin' anywhere today,' Niamh responded as she slammed the door shut again. 'You'd never make it back in this lot so I'm afraid it looks like you're stuck here for today at least.'

'But—'

Niamh held her hand up. 'No point arguin'. Liam will 'ave to understand. Daddy an' the lads will probably stay at the inn so you'll have to sleep here tonight an' we'll see what it's like tomorrow.'

Daisy hurried to the window to peer through the glass but all she could see was a white world. 'I think you're right,' she agreed resignedly. It had been a struggle to get here but the conditions had worsened further in the last few hours. 'But Daniel will be so worried.'

Niamh shook her head. 'He ain't daft, so he ain't, so he'll guess what's happened. Come away to the fire again an' let's make the best of it, eh? We've got plenty o' wood in to keep us warm, an' plenty o' food.'

Daisy thought her friend looked quite happy at this turn of events and deep down the thought of no more work for the rest of the day was quite pleasing, although she could only guess how peeved Liam would be if the late milking was left to him.

'Don't fret about that,' Niamh told her with a grin when she expressed her concerns. 'It might do 'im the world o' good an' make him realise just how much work you do about the place.'

And so with a sigh Daisy took her coat off again and they settled down by the fire for another good gossip.

Chapter Thirty-Nine

It was two days before Daisy was able to attempt getting home again because it snowed non-stop on the day following Boxing Day. But the morning after that Nolan and the boys finally returned and dug the snow from the door.

'I think I should try to get back now,' Daisy told Niamh.

'Then I'll come wit' you wit' me shovel,' Declan said. 'The roads are bad, so they are, an' I don't want you gettin' lost in a drift.' And so Daisy said her goodbyes and they set off.

'Niamh tells me you're walking out with a girl from Dublin,' she said as they trudged along.

He blushed. 'Aye, I am that, her name is Isla an' she's a bonny lass.'

'I'm pleased for you,' Daisy told him, relieved he had got over his crush on her. It seemed everyone was finding their love match but her, she thought enviously.

The walk back to the farm took them twice as long as it should have but at last the smoke from the chimney came into view. 'I can make it from here. Thank you so much for walking me back, Declan.'

'T'was no trouble at all, to be sure,' he answered. 'Good day, Daisy.'

He turned and started back the way he had come, and Daisy trudged on, slipping and sliding. At last, she crossed the yard and lifted the latch on the kitchen door. As she stumbled inside Daniel rose from his seat and rushed to greet her.

'Thank God,' he breathed. 'I've been worried witless, so I have. Are you all right?'

'Of course.' She stood for a moment getting her breath back. 'I suppose you guessed I got snowed in at Niamh's and I didn't dare attempt the return journey till it stopped snowing.'

He nodded. 'Aye, I thought as much, but I was also worried that you'd ended up in a drift.' His eyes grew teary as he suddenly flung his arms around her and clutched her to him. 'I don't know what I'd 'ave done if you hadn't come back, to be sure.'

Slightly embarrassed at his show of emotion, Daisy gently pushed him away. 'I'm sorry I worried you, but as you can see, I'm back now.'

At that moment Liam appeared through the kitchen door and glowered at her. 'An' where the bloody hell do you think you've been, girl?'

'You know exactly where I've been,' she snapped back.

'Huh! I don't pay you good money to gad about, so be sure I'll be stoppin' you two days money out o' your wages.'

'That's fine.' Taking her coat off she hung it on the nail behind the door before filling the kettle at the pump above the sink. 'But I'm back now so if you don't mind, I'll make a start on the dinner.'

He grunted in reply and slammed out again.

For the next two days Daniel followed her about like a puppy, as if he was afraid to let her out of his sight, and Daisy couldn't help but feel sorry for him. She was aware that she was the only person who showed him any kindness and it was clear that he'd missed her while she'd been away.

He was eager to know about everything happening with the Murphys, and as she told him of their blossoming love lives he sighed. 'It seems like there's love in the air for your friend and her family. I hope everything works out for 'em all, so I do. I only wish I had someone to care for me like that.'

Daisy glanced up to see him staring into the fire.

'I care about you, Daniel,' she told him gently, and when he looked back at her there was a wealth of sorrow in his eyes.

'Aye, I know you're fond o' me, lass. But what I meant was, I wish I had someone who *really* loved me. A wife, like other men have.'

Her heart ached for this gentle, caring man and the words slipped out before she could stop them. 'I'll marry you, Daniel . . . if you want me to, that is.'

His head swivelled and he stared at her as if he could hardly believe what he was hearing. 'D-do you mean that?'

She swallowed and lowered her eyes. 'Yes, I mean it.'

Suddenly he was out of his chair, pulling her to her feet and holding her against him. 'Aw, lass, you'll not regret this, I promise. There'll never be another could love you as I do. I knew you were the one for me the second I clapped eyes on you, but I never believed . . . What I mean is, I didn't think someone like you would ever consider me.'

'Why not?' She forced a smile to her face. 'You're a fine-looking young man.'

'But I'm also an invalid. Me heart could pack up at any time. Can you live with that?'

She nodded numbly. There could be no going back now.

'Daddy, Daddy, wake up,' Daniel shouted, and Liam, who had been dozing by the fire, started awake and blinked.

'Wh-what's to do? Can't a man 'ave a bit o' peace an' quiet, even in his own fireside chair after a hard day's work? Why, you near scared me to death, you useless big lummox!'

'Daddy, I've news for you.'

Daisy was a little concerned to see that Daniel's lips were turning a frightening shade of blue. Too much excitement wasn't good for him.

'It's me an' Daisy here. She's only agreed to be me wife, so she has, an' made me the happiest man in the world, to be sure!'

Liam looked shocked and for the first time since Daisy had known him, he gave a genuine smile as he rose from his chair and pumped his son's hand up and down. 'Why, that's *grand* news, lad, to be sure. Congratulations. An' when is the happy day to be?'

'Oh, er . . . we haven't thought that far ahead yet,' Daisy blustered. 'Perhaps in the summer?'

A frown creased Liam's forehead. 'The summer? But that's months away. Why wait?'

Daisy didn't know what to say.

'It's a bride's prerogative to choose her wedding day, so if that's when Daisy wants it to take place that's when it shall be. I have things I need to be doin' meanwhile.'

'Such as?' Liam asked.

'I need to get her a ring for a start, though that's goin' to prove to be difficult wit' me not bein' able to get into town.'

'Ah, now I can help you there.' Liam strode out of the room only to return minutes later with a small box that he pressed into his son's hand.

'This was your mammy's an' she treasured it, but I'm sure she'd want your future wife to have it if she were here.'

Daniel sprang the lid and a small diamond on a gold band winked up at him. 'Ah, I remember it well, so I do. She would only ever wear it for high days an' holidays. Thanks, Daddy.' Taking the ring from the box, he turned back to Daisy and gently placed it on the third finger of her left hand.

She stared down at it. It felt wrong on her finger, and she suddenly had the urge to cry. She forced a smile to her face and muttered, 'It's beautiful.'

Liam slapped his son on the back again and laughed. 'Well now, I reckon this calls for a toast.' Hurrying over to the dresser he took a half-bottle of brandy and three glasses from the cupboard beneath it and poured them each a measure.

'To the newly affianced couple,' he said, lifting his glass high. 'May they allus be as happy as they are this night!' Then he promptly drained the glass.

Daisy, meanwhile, took a sip and grimaced as the fiery liquid burned its way down her throat. The diamond on her finger winked and sparkled in the candlelight and she had to fight the urge to cry.

'I, er . . . won't have any more, if you don't mind,' she said in a small voice. 'I'm not really fond of strong spirits.'

'That's all right.' Liam chuckled. She had never seen him in such a good mood. 'Pass it here, lass, you know the sayin': "Waste not want not", eh?' He took the glass from her and tossed that drink back too.

'Right, er . . . it's been a long day.' Daisy quickly gathered her darning together and put it into her sewing box. 'I'll be going up now. Goodnight, both.'

'Ah, already?' Liam was pouring himself another stiff drink while Daniel was still struggling with the first one. 'But we've celebratin' to do, so we have!'

'Oh, I'm sure you can do that without me.' Daisy was backing towards the door, eager to escape. She turned and took the stairs two at a time as if the hounds of hell were snapping at her heels.

Once in her room she stood with her back to the door until her heart rate slowed to a steadier rhythm, then she crossed to the window and stared out at the snowy landscape. At last, the tears came, so fast and furious that she couldn't breathe as she stared down at the ring on her finger. If she were to tell Daniel that she had made a mistake she knew she would break his heart, but how could she lie with him when someone else held her heart?

'Oh, *Lewis*,' she sobbed as she hugged herself, the breath in front of her floating like lace on the air. '*Why* did you all turn your backs on me?'

Her only answer was the hoot of a tawny owl in the tree outside her bedroom window. She felt as if she was the only person left in the world. This would be her world from now on, day after day of hard work and drudgery, and as much as she cared for Daniel, it was a daunting thought.

Liam was his usual grumpy self when he came down to breakfast the next morning complaining of a headache. It was no wonder, Daisy thought, as she eyed the empty brandy bottle on the wooden draining board.

He grunted as she placed a plate full of sizzling bacon rashers and fried eggs in front of him and he shocked her when he said, 'An' mind you don't go losin' that ring now. It cost me a fair penny, so it did.'

'In that case perhaps you should have it back,' she snapped as she made to take it from her finger. 'I never asked for it!'

'No, no, keep it on,' he urged. 'Daniel will be upset if you don't wear it. I'm just sayin' have a care wit' it.'

Daniel came down shortly after with a wide smile on his face and crossing to Daisy he shyly kissed her on the cheek.

'We shall have to start making plans for our wedding soon. You'll need a new gown and—'

'No, she won't,' Liam butted in. 'Your mother kept hers wrapped in brown paper in the bottom o' the wardrobe. I'm sure Daisy could alter it to fit 'er. No point in wastin' us money on sommat as she's never likely to wear again.'

Daniel's face fell but Daisy squeezed his hand. 'It's all right, really. I should be honoured to wear your mother's gown. As your daddy said, I'm only likely to wear it the once.'

'All right, but which church would you like to be married in, and where shall we hold the reception?'

'The local church will be fine. We can book the service for midday when all the beasts have been seen to. An' as for a reception . . . Pah! What's the point? It ain't as if we 'ave many friends, is it?' Liam said.

Daniel looked worried. It sounded like his daddy was planning a very low-key affair for them, but he wanted the world for his Daisy. A fairytale day that she would never forget.

'He's right, Daniel,' she answered quietly. 'There's no point in making a big fuss. I'll just invite Niamh and the children to the service, if you don't mind, and after that we can come back here and I'll make us all a bit of lunch.'

'If you're sure?' he said uncertainly.

She nodded as she began to clear Liam's breakfast pots from the table. This would be her life from now on, but she could stand it if it made Daniel happy.

Chapter Forty

Ansley Village, January 1883

In the third week of January, the rain set in and slowly the snow began to disappear. The roads and lanes became slushy and lethal underfoot as it melted but everyone was just glad to be able to get back to some sort of normality.

Victoria had been in a vile mood for weeks, for the snow-covered rail tracks had prevented many of the trains from running and she had been unable to get to London for the New Year as she had planned. Jed had also been forced to cancel his trip to Ireland to resume his search for Daisy. But as he was washing his hands at the sink after coming in from the forge one evening, he commented, 'I should think the trains and ferries will be operating again now, so I've decided to go to Ireland next Monday.' He was feeling slightly better and felt able to tackle the journey.

'I'll come with you,' Gilbert offered quickly.

Jed frowned. It wasn't like Gilbert to be helpful.

'I was thinking I might be able to help,' Gilbert rushed on, seeing Jed looking doubtful. 'Two pairs of eyes have got to be better than one, surely? Plus, I know whereabouts in Ireland I left her when we first went there.'

'Well, I suppose . . .'

'Oh, Edward, don't cut your nose off to spite your face,' Victoria snapped. 'Take Gilbert up on his offer. Or perhaps you don't really want to find Daisy?'

'Of course I do!' He scowled at her, then looking at Gilbert he nodded. 'Very well, but we're not going to have a holiday. We're looking for my daughter.'

Gilbert grinned like a cat that had got the cream. 'Fair enough. I'll be ready to go whenever you like.'

Jed thought that would make a change from him lying in bed until dinnertime but he didn't comment. It would only cause another row and there seemed to be more than enough of those in this house lately.

'I assume you and Lewis will be all right keeping everything going here while we're gone?' He looked at Victoria.

Suddenly in a better mood, she smiled sweetly at him. 'Actually, darling, I think I might get away for a few days too. It's been so dreary stuck here all winter. A little break might do me good.'

'Hmm, London, I assume?'

When she nodded, he shrugged. 'As you wish.' He didn't really care where she went.

'Don't worry, Jed, I'll keep everything running smoothly,' Lewis promised him. 'Although I'd rather be coming with you to help search. Still, no point in all of us going.'

Jed gave him a grateful smile and sat down for his meal, which, as usual, the trusty Mrs Smith had prepared for them.

It wasn't until the next day, after Mrs Smith had left, and Jed and Lewis were in the forge, that Victoria was finally able to speak to Gilbert alone. 'Don't forget,' she hissed, 'whatever happens to him, and I don't care how you do it, just make sure it looks like an accident. And for God's sake don't let him go near that convent. If he ever discovers that she's been locked up there all this time I dread to think what he might do.'

303

On the evening before Jed and Gilbert's trip to Ireland, Victoria left to spend the evening at Mrs Byron-Tate's, and the next morning Jed and Gilbert waited in the village for the carrier cart that would take them into Nuneaton and the train station.

Jed was grim-faced with little to say to his stepson and only spoke when absolutely necessary. He was only allowing Gilbert to accompany him as he was hoping he might remember some small thing that could lead them to Daisy.

Although the thaw had set in, the trains were still delayed, so by the time they reached the port they had missed the early ferry and had no choice but to wait for the evening one.

'I wonder if we shouldn't wait for the morning,' Gilbert said worriedly as they stood on the dock looking out over the grey, heaving sea. He had never been the best of sailors.

Jed stared at him in disgust. 'You can do whatever you like, but I shall be goin' on the next one,' he told him shortly. 'This was never intended to be a joyride. Meantime I'm goin' to find somewhere to eat.' He set off, not caring if Gilbert followed him or not. The lad clearly had no backbone.

Scowling, Gilbert fell into step beside him. Perhaps the evening ferry wouldn't be such a bad idea. Maybe he could enact his mother's original plan and push Jed overboard. At least his mission would be complete early.

It was dark and bitterly cold as they boarded the ferry that evening and Gilbert was a bag of nerves, for more than one reason. First of all, he was dreading the journey, especially on such a stormy night – he was surprised the ferry could sail in such conditions. But he was nervous about his plan as well. Soon the lights of home faded into the distance and there was nothing but inky black sea as far as the eye could see.

'I think I might go out and get a bit of fresh air,' he told Jed. They were sitting in the dining cabin and he was afraid he was going to be sick.

The ferry was rolling from side to side and he staggered drunkenly as he made for the door. The cold air hit him like a slap in the face as he stumbled towards the railings. He had hoped Jed would follow him, but the door behind him remained firmly closed and as he threw up everything he had eaten that day into the churning waves beneath him, he cursed him silently. Eventually, when there was nothing left to bring up, he staggered weakly back to the cabin. It was more than obvious now that his first idea was not going to work, but hopefully there would be other chances once they got to Ireland.

The ferry docked in Dublin in the early hours of the morning and the two men wearily made their way to the nearest hotel and settled down for the rest of the night.

When Gilbert awoke the next morning, Jed's bed was already empty and, grumbling, he dressed quickly and joined him in the dining room where they ate a hasty breakfast. Jed hadn't been joking when he'd said that he didn't intend this to be a holiday.

'So, what do we do first?' Gilbert asked, as he poured himself a second cup of tea. His stomach was still not settled, and he would have liked nothing better than to return to bed.

'I'm going to see Bridie and Connor before I do anything, in case they've had any news of her,' Jed informed him shortly, standing up.

With a sigh, Gilbert put down his cup and followed him back up to their room.

Half an hour later they were striding along the cliff path and eventually Bridie and Connor's cottage came into view. Jed had written to tell them that he was coming and they welcomed him with open arms.

'And you must be Lewis,' Connor said, stretching out his hand after greeting Jed. 'We've heard not'in' but good about you, lad, to be sure.'

'I'm Gilbert, actually.'

'Oh . . . are you, now?'

Gilbert noted a change in the old man's tone and wondered what Jed had said about him – not that he cared much.

'So, is there any news?' Jed asked hopefully as Bridie ushered him to a chair and started to pour some tea.

Bridie shook her head. 'Not so much as a dickie bird. How can anyone just vanish? An' more to the point . . . why? But anyway, how long are you here for, lad? You're more than welcome to stay wit' us, so you are.'

Jed smiled. 'Thanks for the offer, Bridie, but I've booked us into a cheap hotel in the town. I'm aimin' to stay for at least four or five days. We'll just see how it goes.'

'Right y'are, lad.' She turned to Gilbert and regarded him through narrowed eyes. 'An' so you're Gilbert are you!'

He nodded. The look she was giving him made him feel she could see into his very soul, so he kept his mouth shut as the others talked of what they'd been doing since they last met.

'Well, much as I'd like to, I can't sit about,' Jed said eventually. 'So, we'll be off to start searching again. But don't worry, we'll keep you informed if we hear anything.'

'I'm coming wit' you, lad,' Connor told him, heaving himself out of his chair.

Jed shook his head and placed his hand softly on his shoulder. 'No, Connor, you stay here in the warm,' he urged. 'We're younger than you and we'll cover more ground if we're alone.'

'I suppose you're right,' Connor sighed as he sank back into his seat. 'I just pray you'll have more luck this time.'

Because of the harsh weather conditions, Jed stuck to the roads rather the cliff path on the walk back to Dublin, then they spent the day scouring the streets, stopping to ask people if they had seen Daisy and giving them a description of her. But the answer was always the same, so finally, as the light faded, they went back to the hotel hungry and tired.

The next day was much the same, and Jed's spirits sank lower and lower. The third day dawned, raining and blustery, and over breakfast Gilbert made it more than obvious that he was bored with the search.

'Perhaps we could have a day off today?' he suggested, looking at the rain as it lashed against the windows. 'It's not fit for a dog to be out in this.'

Jed scowled. 'Suit yourself, but I came here to look for me daughter an' that's what I'm goin' to do – whatever the weather.'

With a martyred sigh, Gilbert followed him upstairs to collect their hats and coats and they set off again.

It was market day and the town was bustling with people and traffic, and as two huge dray horses pulling a heavy wagon full of beer barrels came rumbling towards them at a fair old trot, Gilbert suddenly had an idea. Should anyone fall beneath the wheels of the cart, he was sure they would stand no chance of surviving. He could accidentally stumble and knock Jed in front of it as they drew level . . . He glanced up, but Jed was some way in front of him scouring the crowds for a sign of Daisy.

As the horses came closer from the opposite direction, Gilbert rushed to catch up with him. It was now or never. Suddenly he tripped and pitched forward with a cry. Jed turned abruptly and reached out to try and save him from hitting the pavement, but

Gilbert fell to the side, landing hard on the cobblestones in the road as the enormous hooves bore down on him.

This is it! he thought. *I'm going to die.* But then someone grasped his collar and in the nick of time he was yanked none too gently to one side and the horses steamed past, missing him by inches.

'Good grief!' Jed was clearly shaken as he helped Gilbert up. 'Why don't you look where you're going? You were almost a goner there!'

Gilbert was shocked but apart from a few bruises he was unhurt. It was ironic that Jed had ended up saving his life just when Gilbert had been trying to kill him.

'Are you all right?'

A small crowd had gathered and Gilbert blushed. 'Fine,' he said shortly as he brushed the mud from his coat. 'Just a bit shaken up. Perhaps we could find somewhere to get a cup of tea.'

Jed took his elbow and steered him into the nearest café where a mixture of sailors from the port and women shoppers were enjoying hot drinks.

'Sit down and I'll go and get us something,' Jed ordered.

Meek as a lamb Gilbert did as he was told. Some murderer he was turning out to be!

The search resumed as soon as Gilbert was feeling a little better but by then he was feeling downhearted and wishing he'd never agreed to the trip.

At that moment up at Brooke Farm, Daisy was making a batch of scones when Daniel appeared with a wide smile on his face and a large parcel wrapped in brown paper and tied with string in his arms.

'This is Mammy's weddin' dress. The one Daddy said you should have,' he told her as he placed it on the table.

Daisy dusted the flour from her hands and untied the string. Inside was an ivory satin gown, but as she gently lifted it and shook it out, they both gasped with dismay. The moths had been feasting on it and the skirt was covered in holes.

'Oh no.' Daniel was visibly distraught, and she ran to fetch him one of his little white tablets. 'What are you to wear for our weddin' now? This is ruined, so it is. Me mammy would be heartsore if she could see it.'

'Don't upset yourself,' Daisy urged, as she pressed him onto a seat. 'It isn't the end of the world, is it?' A thought occurred to her and she said cheerily, 'I know, I can wear that blue gown that I bought from the stall. I haven't had a chance to wear it yet and it's certainly nice enough to get wed in.'

Daniel looked slightly happier. 'I hadn't thought of that,' he admitted. 'And you did look a fair treat in it when it was altered. But I'll tell you what, I'm goin' to treat you to a new bonnet to go wit' it. I've got a little money o' me own put by, so when Daddy goes into town tomorrow you can go with him and call at the milliner's. They're bound to have something you like.'

Daisy could see how much this meant to him, so she smiled and nodded. 'Very well – if you're sure.'

'I am,' he told her, his chest swelling with pride. He'd never really had anyone but his mammy to buy anything for before. 'I just wish I could come with you to help you choose it but . . .'

'You're going nowhere until the weather improves,' Daisy told him sternly, and turning back to the ruined gown she sadly packed it away again. She had always been handy with a needle but unfortunately the dress was beyond saving.

The next morning, at Daniel's insistence, Daisy set off for Dublin with Liam and, once there, she headed for the milliner's shop. She knew she should be feeling excited at the thought of choosing something to wear on her wedding day, but instead she felt sad. Even so, once she was in the shop, she enjoyed looking around at the array of hats.

'What sort of colour are you looking for?' the kindly woman assistant asked.

'Well, my gown is blue and cream.'

'And is it for any specific occasion?'

'It's for my wedding day actually.' Daisy blushed.

The woman beamed. 'Ah, in that case we must find you something really special.'

'But not too expensive, please,' Daisy told her hastily. She didn't want to spend too much of Daniel's money.

'Try this one,' the woman urged, carrying a frothy affair of net and tulle over to her. Daisy stared at it doubtfully. It was a little too fussy for her, but she didn't want to hurt the woman's feelings when she was being so kind to her.

'Hmm, I think that one may be a little too old for you,' the woman said once Daisy had it on. Daisy stood waiting for her next choice and as she did, she glanced towards the window and her heart felt as if it was going to break as she thought of how excited she would have been if she had been marrying Lewis.

'Are you all right, dear? You've gone very pale. Would you like to sit down for a moment?' The assistant's voice brought her thoughts sharply back to the present and Daisy gratefully sank onto the chair she had pushed forward for her. 'Goodness, you look as if you've seen a ghost,' the woman went on, her voice seeming to come from a very long way away. 'Let me get you a glass of water. This happens quite often with brides trying on their hats. It's the excitement, I think.'

Ten minutes later Daisy felt well enough to continue trying on the bonnets the woman brought to her, although her heart wasn't in it. It never had been, if truth be told. Eventually she settled on a modest cream one trimmed with a single blue satin rose and a tiny veil that she thought would match her gown very well, and while the woman wrapped it her eyes strayed to the window again.

Soon she was on the way back to the stables where she had agreed to meet Liam. Eventually he appeared, swaying slightly with the effects of the tankards of ale he had downed in the tavern. It was raining again by that time and, once she was settled on the hard wooden bench seat of the cart, she hooked a sack out of the back and pulled it over her head and stayed that way until Dublin was far behind them.

As the old horse trotted along her tears mingled with the rain on her cheeks as she thought of Lewis again, but with a determined effort she pushed the thoughts away. It was no good wishing for what might have been.

Chapter Forty-One

Once again the following morning dawned rainy and grey and as Jed stood at the window of his hotel room staring down at the street below, his mood was as miserable as the weather. 'I think we may as well head for home today,' he told Gilbert.

Gilbert wasn't sorry to hear it, although he was surprised. Following his tumble, he was black and blue and ached all over. It had been a very nasty fall. 'Oh yes, why is that?'

Jed shrugged despondently. 'I think we're just goin' round and round the places we've already looked an' it ain't fair to leave Lewis doin' all the work at home for longer than he has to.'

Relieved, Gilbert nodded in agreement. 'So, what do you propose we do now?'

'I shall have to go an' see Bridie an' Connor afore we go. Perhaps while I'm gone you could go an' book us two places on this evenin's ferry? We'll not get on the earlier one now. Unless you want to come wi' me?'

'Oh no, no, you go.' He couldn't wait to get away from this place, although he dreaded to think what his mother was going to say when he walked back in with Jed. She had told him in no uncertain terms before he left that she expected Jed to meet with 'a little accident' while they were away. But it had proved much harder to achieve than he had expected . . . unless something happened on the way home of course! He had no qualms whatsoever about killing Jed. After all, he thought with no remorse, he had killed five times before – although he hadn't really meant to kill the first two.

312

The first had been the farmer's daughter, who had died the same night as Jed's young son Alfie. He had met Eunice in the woods adjacent to the quarry in Hartshill, but when she had told him she was pregnant he had tried to walk away from her. She had become hysterical and clung on to him, the silly cow, threatening to tell her father, and to quieten her down he had caught her by the throat. He hadn't meant to press as hard as he had, and everything had been made worse when he had glanced up to see Alfie's terrified face watching him. When Eunice had dropped to the floor Alfie had made a run for it, and he had shot off after the boy – he had to tell him to keep quiet about what he'd seen. It wasn't his fault that in his panic, the boy had ended up teetering on the edge of the deep quarry. Knowing he was trapped, the child had tried to turn, but somehow, he had lost his footing and all Gilbert had been able to do was watch him plummet to his death.

Then there had been Mickey Jameson. Now he had deserved to die and so had Cassie. And finally, there had been his father, an insipid little man with no backbone. He and his mother were well shot of him.

He watched dispassionately as Jed set off to say his goodbyes to his in-laws. Hopefully it would be the last time he ever saw them.

Bridie and Connor were sad to say goodbye, and even more sad that there was still no news of Daisy. 'I'm afraid we're goin' to just have to wait till she decides to get in touch wi' us,' Jed told them soberly.

'Happen you're right, lad,' Connor agreed. He hated to see Jed looking so broken. As hard as it had been for him and Bridie to see someone take his daughter's place in Jed's heart, he had hoped that Jed's new wife would bring him a measure of peace. Jed deserved that, and they knew how much he had loved Mauve. But instead, it was apparent that the poor chap had made the biggest mistake of his life. 'An' listen on, don't you trust that Gilbert.' He frowned. 'I couldn't take to him, to be sure. In fact, I wouldn't trust him as far as I could throw him!'

'Don't worry, I don't,' Jed agreed as Bridie slid yet more freshly baked soda bread onto his plate and pushed the butter dish towards him. 'You'll have me as fat as a pig, Bridie.' He grinned.

She shook her head. 'That would take some doin', to be sure. Why, you ain't as far t'rough as a clothes prop, Jed Armstrong. It's about time that wife o' yours started feedin' you properly!'

Jed chuckled. 'That'll be the day. I think Victoria could burn water. We have a woman in daily from the village to cook and clean for us.'

Bridie clucked her disapproval. 'It's a disgrace, so it is. A woman should keep her own home tickin' over an' her man wellfed. Still, I'll not interfere in your business, son.' She paused before asking in a gentler voice, 'Will we be seein' you again?'

'Of course you will. You won't get rid of me that easily.' Jed stood up and put his arms around her. 'I'll be back just as soon as I can make it. Meantime, I'll write.'

'Just see as you do now.' She and Connor saw him to the door and stood waving until he was lost to sight before turning sadly back to their fireside.

It was a dark, filthy night by the time Gilbert and Jed boarded the ferry. Gilbert wasn't looking forward to the crossing at all. He already ached from his fall, so he knew the return journey wasn't going to be pleasant. They headed for the dining cabin, which was really just a draughty wooden hut, where they purchased some lukewarm, weak tea and took a seat.

Very few people were venturing out onto the deck, and it remained that way when the ferry set off. The rain was lashing against the windows and the ship rocked alarmingly from side to side as Gilbert fought wave after wave of nausea. At one point he had no choice but to go out and vomit across the rail, but Jed didn't attempt to follow him, so once again there was no chance for Gilbert to engineer a little accident.

They arrived back in Ansley at mid-morning the following day and as Gilbert entered the kitchen and threw his carpet bag down, his mother looked up hopefully, then frowned when Jed followed seconds later.

'Why are you back so soon?' Her less than excited greeting didn't trouble Jed. He'd long since realised that Victoria had no affection for him. He knew now that he had merely been a way out of Victoria's financial mess, and he had fallen for her charms hook, line and sinker – fool that he was.

'There was no point in stayin' any longer,' he told her shortly as he dropped his own bag down beside Gilbert's. 'We were just goin' over the same old ground with not a sight of her, so we decided to come home. Where's Lewis?'

'In the forge.'

'And Rags?'

'In there with him. Unfortunately, he's as taken with that mangy mutt as you are!'

Jed nodded and left the room to go and see how Lewis was doing.

'What went wrong?' she hissed at Gilbert in a low voice so that Mrs Smith, who was cleaning in the next room, wouldn't hear her.

'Everything,' he told her miserably, before showing her some of his bruises, which had now turned a deep purple and blue. 'If it weren't for Jed hooking me out of the road when he did, it would have been me you were arranging a funeral for!'

'*Damn!*' She began to pace up and down the room, her silk skirts swishing. 'There's only one thing left for it then.' She glanced across the room to make sure that Mrs Smith was still out of the way. 'We'll have to go back to the original plan.'

'Poisoning again?'

She nodded. 'Yes, but not enough to make the doctor suspicious. You can start again this evening. Lord Harlow-Green is growing impatient.'

He shrugged. It was no skin off his nose. 'If that's what you want. Now how about a hot drink and something to eat? I've had the most awful headache ever since I had my accident.'

'I'll call Smith to get you something,' she answered. 'And there's some laudanum that the doctor gave me for women's problems in the kitchen cupboard if you need any, but don't take too much or you'll knock yourself out. It's strong stuff.'

For the rest of the day Gilbert sat huddled beside the fire. Alternately shivering and sweating, he was unable to shift his headache, which was making him feel nauseous.

'You've obviously caught a chill,' his mother told him. 'I'll get you that laudanum.'

She went into the kitchen and reaching to the back of the cupboard she extracted a small glass phial. Mrs Smith had left and Jed and Lewis hadn't come in from the forge yet, so she tipped a generous measure of the liquid into half a glass of water. Gilbert did look ill, she had to admit, so she added a little more and after giving it a good stir she carried it over to him. 'Get yourself off to bed when you've had that. You'll probably feel a lot better in the morning.'

It was a measure of just how ill he must feel when he agreed. Normally he would be getting ready to go out for the evening at this time.

'Ugh!' He pulled a face as he swigged at the medicine. 'This tastes absolutely vile!'

'Oh, don't be such a *baby*,' she scolded. She had never been the most sympathetic of women, even when the boys had been young. 'It's not supposed to taste nice; it's supposed to make you feel better, so just get it down you and get yourself off upstairs.'

'All right, all right.' He scowled as he held his nose and gulped down the rest of the water in one go, then made his way to his room.

A few moments later, Jed and Lewis came in.

'Your dinners are keeping warm in the oven,' Victoria informed them shortly from her seat by the fire. Then she picked up her embroidery and ignored them, stabbing at the material furiously. She had hoped to be a merry widow again by now, but the stupid boy had messed everything up and she wasn't in the mood for making polite conversation.

In the dead of night, Gilbert's eyes suddenly flew open and he brought his knees up to his chest as an agonising pain gripped his stomach. The sheets were damp with sweat, and he just managed to lean over the bed before he vomited so violently that he couldn't get his breath.

'M-Ma . . .' He tried to scream for his mother but all he managed was a weak croak as the pains worsened and he writhed in a tangle of twisted sheets. This was pain as he had never known it, and somehow he knew that he was going to die. Again and again, he opened his mouth to scream for help, but no sound came out.

Suddenly darkness rushed towards him and seconds later he became quite still, his hands clutching his stomach and his eyes staring sightlessly up at the ceiling, while outside an old tawny owl hooted in the tree, then, once again, all was quiet.

'Mrs Armstrong, should I give Master Gilbert a knock?' Mrs Smith queried just after lunchtime the next day. 'I'd like to clean his room.'

'What?' Victoria looked up from the love letter she was writing to Lord Harlow-Green. 'Oh yes, yes, I suppose so. He's usually up for lunch, but he wasn't feeling well last night. Go ahead.'

'Right y'are, missus.' Mrs Smith made for the stairs, muttering under her breath. She felt sorry to her heart for Jed for landing himself with this lot, although Lewis was a good lad, admittedly. But the missus and the younger son – huh! Useless, the pair of 'em! She just wanted to play the lady while Gilbert needed a good swift kick up the backside as far as she was concerned. Bone idle, he was, but then it was none of her business, so she just came in, did her job and left again.

Pausing outside Gilbert's bedroom she tapped on the door. 'Master Gilbert . . . are you awake? I'm waitin' to change the sheets on your bed an' come in to clean yer room. Could yer tell me if yer likely to be much longer?'

There was no reply so she knocked again, a little louder this time. 'Master Gilbert?'

Again, only silence, so she tentatively inched the door open a fraction. Immediately she gagged at the foul smell that rushed out to greet her and she hastily snapped it shut again. It smelled like the young devil had been sick. It wouldn't be the first time after he'd had a bellyful of ale but she'd be damned if she was goin' to clear his mess up this time.

Stomping back down the stairs she told his mother shortly, 'He'll not answer me but I opened the door a tadge an' the smell were enough to knock yer head off. Perhaps yer should go up an' check he's all right if you say he weren't well last night? I didn't feel it were my place to go in disturbin' him.'

'Oh *really*! What do I have to do to get a bit of peace around here?' Victoria hastily hid the letter in the bottom of the dresser drawer and stamped towards the stairs. Unlike Mrs Smith she didn't waste any time when she got to Gilbert's room but swung the door open ready to give him a piece of her mind, only to stop dead in her tracks at the sight that met her.

'Gilbert!' He was lying quite still, his eyes staring sightlessly and a sick feeling started in the pit of her stomach. The smell of vomit was overwhelming and she rushed to the window to open the curtains. His skin was a curious grey colour. '*GILBERT!*' her scream echoed around the house and brought Mrs Smith flying back up the stairs.

'Go and get Edward *immediately* and tell Lewis to go for the doctor . . . *now!*' Victoria barked as she shook her son's arm. It felt curiously cold and clammy.

Mrs Smith turned, almost tripping over her skirts in her haste, as Victoria shook Gilbert's arm again.

What seemed like a lifetime later, but was in fact only a matter of minutes, Jed appeared and blinked as he looked at Gilbert. He didn't need a doctor to tell him that the young man was dead. Victoria was staring down at him shaking her head and trembling as her efforts to rouse him failed. Placing his arm gently about her shoulders, Jed tried to steer her from the room.

'Come along, there's nothing to be done. The doctor will be here soon.'

Victoria turned on him like a wild cat, shrugging his arm away. 'What do you mean there's nothing to be done?' she spat. 'Of *course* there is. The doctor will help him . . . he has to . . . Gilbert is just a young man.'

Jed bowed his head. He could only imagine how she must be feeling.

319

Turning her back on him, Victoria started shaking Gilbert again, harder this time. 'Gilbert! Gilbert, wake up, do you hear me?'

Sometime later the doctor and Lewis appeared. After a glance at the still form on the bed the doctor ushered them from the room. 'Go downstairs now. I'll be there shortly.'

Jed and Lewis steered Victoria from the room between them.

'Could you make some hot, sweet tea, please, Mrs Smith? Mauve always used to say it was good for shock,' Jed asked when they came into the kitchen.

'O' course I will,' the kindly woman answered obligingly.

In a very short time, the doctor joined them grave-faced. 'I'm afraid he's gone. There was nothing I could do. It seems he's been dead for some hours. Tell me, had he been ill?'

'H-he complained of a headache last night and I gave him some of the laudanum you gave me,' Victoria told him dully.

'And he did have rather a nasty accident a few days back,' Jed chipped in, and went on to tell the doctor about Gilbert's fall in Dublin.

'Ah, that would account for all the bruises,' the doctor said thoughtfully. He was silent for a while as Mrs Smith poured them each a cup of tea. 'I think there are a few possibilities here that may have caused the death,' the doctor went on. 'It could be after such a bad fall that a blood clot formed and travelled to his heart. Alternatively, he might have had severe internal injuries that no one could have known about that caused internal bleeding. Either way, I am happy to issue the death certificate as natural causes. I'm so sorry for your loss, Mrs Armstrong. Would you like me to call into the undertaker's on my way back into the village?'

Victoria seemed to have shut herself away in a world where no one could reach her, so Jed nodded. 'Yes please, Doctor. I'd appreciate that.'

When Jed had seen the doctor out, he placed both his hands flat on the table and bowed his head in shock. He couldn't be a hypocrite and pretend that he had ever liked Gilbert, but he was also finding it difficult to accept that any young life could end so abruptly. It just seemed so wrong.

Lewis was comforting his mother as much as he was able to and so Jed strode out into the yard and took great gulps of air, Rags leaning into his leg. The dear old dog could sense when his master was upset.

A short time later the undertaker arrived. He wore a black silk top hat and brought with him a plain pine coffin to carry the body away in.

Jed and Lewis moved Victoria into the small front parlour so that she wouldn't have to watch Gilbert being carried out and then Mrs Smith went up to Gilbert's room to start cleaning.

Much later that afternoon, after Mrs Smith had left, and Jed and Lewis had gone to the church to make arrangements for the funeral, Victoria found herself alone. Her head was thumping, which was hardly surprising, so she crossed to the cupboard to take out the laudanum she had given Gilbert the night before. Taking out the glass phial, she stared at it in confusion. It was completely full. But how could that be? She had given Gilbert a very generous measure. Reaching back into the cupboard, she drew out another phial, this one half empty. She stared at it for a very long time as the terrible truth sank in. This was the arsenic that Gilbert had been drip-feeding into Jed's tea each night, and Gilbert had drunk a considerable amount of it.

She had poisoned her own son!

Chapter Forty-Two

'Earth to earth, ashes to ashes . . .' As the vicar's voice droned on, Victoria stood in her black bombazine mourning gown and her black veil at the side of the grave as if she had been turned to stone.

'Victoria . . .'

Blankly she stared to her side to look at Jed.

' . . . the earth, the vicar is offering it to you.'

Woodenly she took a handful of earth from the small box and dropped it onto the coffin. It made a dull thudding noise and then at last the service and the committal were over and the mourners began to drift away while the gravediggers stood with spades poised waiting to fill in the grave.

'Come on, love.' Despite the fact there had been no love between them for some time, Jed felt sorry for her as he gently steered her through the churchyard. It was a calm, dry day and he couldn't help but think that it should have been raining. It seemed wrong, somehow, to bury someone on such a nice day.

'You all right, lad?' Jed asked Lewis as they clambered into the carriage. They might not have seen eye to eye but Gilbert had been his brother after all.

'Yes . . . I'm all right, Jed. And thanks for organising all this. Mother certainly hasn't been in any state to.'

Jed patted his shoulder. 'I'm just sorry this had to happen,' he answered quietly.

Back at the house, Mrs Smith and a few more of the village wives had laid on a small spread for the mourners. It was a solemn and tense affair as Victoria had taken herself up to bed, but at last, everyone left, and Jed and Lewis sat silently by the fire, relieved it was all over. Hopefully now they could start trying to come to terms with what had happened.

Over the next few weeks Victoria said little and seldom left the house. Jed put it down to the fact that she was mourning Gilbert. He couldn't know that she was also coming to terms with the guilt she felt for poisoning her own son. But gradually in her mind Jed was becoming the guilty party, not her. After all, had Gilbert not gone to Ireland with him the accident would never have happened in the first place.

One day the postman arrived with a letter bearing a London postmark and she hastily hid it in the pocket of her gown before hurrying into the parlour where she could read it away from Mrs Smith's prying eyes. It could only be from one person and her heart began to beat faster with anticipation as she opened the letter. She was right, it was from Lord Harlow-Green. In the letter he expressed his sympathy for the loss of her son, but he also told her how much he was missing her and longing for the time when they could be together for always. Suddenly Victoria began to emerge from the fog of grief she had been floundering in.

Gilbert was gone and there could be no bringing him back. But David, sweet David, was still alive and wanting her. There was only Edward standing in her way, but how was she to dispose of him now that Gilbert was not there to do it for her?

There was no way she could ask Lewis to do it. He and Edward were as thick as thieves. *You will have to do it yourself*, she told herself. *After all, accidents happen all the time, don't they?* But how was the burning question.

That day she sent a message to Mrs Byron-Tate telling her that she now felt ready for a short break in London as soon as was convenient to her, and the lady in question, who was as bored with her own husband as Victoria was with Jed, was only too happy to oblige.

My dear Victoria,

I am so pleased to hear you are feeling a little better after your sad loss. And yes, I think a short break would do you the world of good. Shall we arrange it for the coming weekend? You can, of course, stay at my house the evening before we depart as usual.

Warmest regards,

Winifred x

The message was hand delivered by Mrs Byron-Tate's maid and Victoria asked her to tell her mistress to go ahead and make the necessary arrangements.

All she had to do now was inform Jed. She had no doubt he wouldn't be too happy with the idea, but it had been a long time since what he wanted had troubled her.

She told Jed and Lewis of her decision over dinner that same evening but to her surprise Jed raised no objections. In fact, she got the feeling he was quite happy about it.

'I'm sure it will do you good, my dear. Why don't you stay for a few days?'

'I might just do that, if you're quite sure you don't mind,' she simpered. She was feeling better by the minute just thinking of the time she would spend with the handsome lord. Since Gilbert's demise she hadn't dared give Jed any more arsenic and he was now looking healthy again, much to her disgust. As far as she was concerned it was he who should have died, not her son.

'I wondered if I might have my wages, please, it's Friday,' Daisy said politely.

Liam had just finished work and come into the kitchen. 'Wages? Why would I pay you now, girl? You'll be a member o' the family in a few weeks' time, so you will.' He grinned at her.

'You're quite right, but until then I am still an employee so I shall expect to be paid,' Daisy answered, stubbornly standing her ground.

Liam scowled at her as Daniel looked anxiously on. He hadn't been at all well for over a week now and Daisy was concerned for him. He'd picked up a cold, which had settled on his chest, and he'd developed a hacking cough. He didn't seem to be responding to the tonic she had fetched from the pharmacy, or to the goose fat she encouraged him to rub into his chest. And now his lips had a permanent blue tinge to them; even climbing the stairs left him breathless.

'Oh here, take it. You're a hard woman, so you are,' Liam growled as he took some coins from his pocket and flung them onto the table.

Daisy calmly collected the coins and counted them as she winked at Daniel. 'There's one and sixpence short here.'

With another growl, Liam delved into his pocket again before slamming the money down in front of her. 'Here, happy now, are you?'

'I'm only taking what I'm due,' she reminded him shortly and hurried away to fetch his meal from the oven.

A little smile hovered around Daniel's lips. He'd never known anyone who could put his daddy in his place like Daisy did. Liam had finally met his match.

It was late by the time Daisy lit her candle to make her way up the stairs, but once in her bedroom, sleep eluded her, so after a time she clambered out of bed and crossed to the window to stare down into the moonlit garden. The wedding had been booked for the first Saturday in June and the closer it came the more nervous she grew. She cared for Daniel deeply – even loved him. But it wasn't the love a wife should feel for her husband. Even so, she still fully intended to go through with the wedding. It wasn't as if she could ever have her happy ever after with the man who did hold her heart, Gilbert had seen to that, and she didn't want to break Daniel's heart.

Crossing to the dressing table she lifted the ring he had given her. She rarely wore it. It felt wrong on her finger, so she had told him that she didn't want to spoil it by wearing it all the time to do her jobs in, and he had accepted that. Now she looked in the direction of Kilmainham and wondered what her granny and grampy were doing. No doubt at this time of night they would be safely tucked up in bed with their arms about each other. She wondered if they ever thought of her or missed her as she did them. Then her thoughts moved to her daddy and Lewis, but it was no good torturing herself anymore. Very soon, Daniel and Liam would be the only family she would have.

Climbing back into bed she hugged her pillow and cried herself to sleep. Somehow, she must put the past behind her and concentrate on the future, but despite her promises to Daniel it was proving to be harder than she had thought it would be.

'I'm so glad you feel able to resume our little trips, Victoria,' Winifred told her as they sat together in her beautiful parlour in Swan Lane in Nuneaton enjoying a cup of hot chocolate before retiring to their rooms. They would be setting off for London first thing the next morning. 'I understand what a difficult time it must have been for you.'

Victoria nodded. 'Yes, it has, but life must go on. Gilbert would not have wished me to be unhappy.'

'Hmm.' Winifred became silent as she pondered how to tell her friend of the developments that had taken place since Victoria's last visit. She was fully aware of the attachment Victoria had formed to Lord Harlow-Green, although she could never work out where it might have led with Victoria still married to Edward Armstrong. 'We have been invited to a dinner party at David's tomorrow evening. Will you feel able to attend while you are still in full mourning?'

Victoria flushed. 'I don't see why not.'

There was another silence and then Winifred went on, 'There has been a new arrival to our circle of London friends. A widow by the name of Amelia Parkhurst. A very charming and attractive woman.'

'Oh?' Victoria raised an eyebrow.

'Yes, she and Lord David seem to have become very close. She's been at the last two dinner parties I have attended at his home.'

Suddenly, Victoria felt sick with jealousy. She realised then that since the letter she had received from Lord David shortly after Gilbert's death there had been no more and wondered if this widow might be the reason why. Could it be that he was getting tired of waiting for her? The very thought of losing such a good catch made her heart pound. She could hardly wait for the next day to come.

The following evening Victoria and Winifred took a cab to the lord's luxurious home. Victoria was wearing her best black gown and had taken great pains over her appearance. She would have liked to wear something a little more colourful and flamboyant, as befitted her style, but she knew it might look disrespectful to her late son. Even so, she knew she looked her best, and she was feeling confident.

Until she was introduced to Amelia Parkhurst that was, and then her spirits sank. Amelia was a very beautiful woman and younger than her by at least ten years, Victoria judged. Blonde and blue-eyed she was slight of build and her stunning silk gown in a lovely shade of blue emphasised her figure and made her look dainty and delicate.

'How do you do,' she said politely in a soft, melodic voice when David introduced them.

Jealousy surged through Victoria like poison. 'It's very nice to meet you,' she managed to say and when the woman moved away, she turned to David and gave him a charming smile.

'How are you, my dear?' he asked solicitously, although she noticed his eyes followed Mrs Parkhurst around the room.

'Better . . . now that I have seen you.'

He glanced back at her and there was no mistaking the meaning behind her words as she drew him to one side.

'I think . . . it will not be long now until my husband . . .' She took a lace handkerchief from her reticule and dabbed at her eyes. 'He is completely bedridden and doesn't even know me anymore. I think it is just a matter of time.'

She must somehow show him that she still intended them to be together.

The dinner gong sounded at that moment and offering Victoria his arm David escorted her into the dining room where she was incensed to see that he had placed Amelia on his right-hand side.

There was no doubt in her mind now. The time for thinking was over. When she got home she must find a way to get rid of Jed. Her future depended on it.

Chapter Forty-Three

May 1883

Jed had expected Victoria to return from her trip to London in a slightly happier mood, but she seemed more agitated than ever, as he commented to Lewis.

'I know,' Lewis acknowledged. 'I've noticed she seems more edgy than usual.' He had been fretting for some time about his mother's behaviour, although he hadn't spoken to Jed about it. His concerns had started the day following Gilbert's death when he had carried some household rubbish to the pile they burned at the end of each week. As he was placing the bag on the heap, something had glinted in the sunshine and, bending to examine it, he had noticed a small glass phial. It was empty but when he smelled it, it had made him gag. If he wasn't very much mistaken it had contained arsenic. But who would have used it and why had it been thrown into the rubbish?

Suddenly a picture of his dead brother's face flashed in front of him. The staring eyes, the vomit, the way he had been clutching his stomach, the yellow tinge to his lips. All the symptoms of arsenic poisoning. But who would do such a thing? Certainly not Jed. He was no murderer; Lewis would have staked his life on it. That only left his mother, but it made no sense. Why would she want to poison her own son? There were so many things that didn't add up. The bloodstained clothes belonging to Gilbert he had found in the barn, Daisy's disappearance after travelling to Ireland with Gilbert. The fact that the doctor had said Jed's illness and the way he had been slowly declining all pointed to arsenic poisoning.

There was something not right but for the life of him he couldn't put his finger on what it was.

'Do you think someone upset her while she was there?'

Jed's voice brought his thoughts sharply back to the present.

'I've no idea, but she's given Mrs Smith the day off tomorrow, which is unusual. I can't see Mother tackling the housework or the cooking. She's asked me to go into town for her tomorrow as well. She says she has some things she needs me to get for her. I offered to drive her in but she doesn't want to come.'

'That is unusual,' Jed agreed. 'She usually jumps at the chance of being anywhere near shops.'

The two men grinned at each other and got on with their work.

That evening, Victoria was like a cat on hot bricks and didn't seem able to settle to anything.

'Can't you do some embroidery or read or something. You're making me nervous,' Jed complained as she paced the floor.

She glared at him, then stamped upstairs to her room, where she stared from the window, chewing nervously on her fist. With Lewis and Mrs Smith out of the way she had decided tomorrow would be the day when Jed would have his fatal accident. She had no idea how or when it would happen but somehow, she would make sure that it did. Her thoughts turned to Lord David and her heart actually ached for him, and not just for the rosy future he could offer her. For the very first time in her life Victoria was in love and she would stop at nothing to be with the man who had stolen her heart.

There were dark circles beneath her eyes the following morning at breakfast and Jed looked mildly concerned as he asked, 'Are you feelin' all right? You look a bit peaky.'

She sipped at her tea; she couldn't face any food. 'I'm fine. I just had a bad night. I might go up and lie down a little later.' Then she handed the list she had written to Lewis. 'This is what I want you to fetch me from town,' she instructed.

He frowned as he bit into a slice of buttered toast and read through it. It consisted of some very mundane things. 'Surely you could get all these bits from the village shop to save me going into town?' he suggested.

She shook her head. 'Oh no, the embroidery silks they sell in the shop here are of inferior quality to the ones I use from the haberdashery in town.'

'All right.' Lewis thought it was a waste of time. He would have much preferred to spend his time helping Jed in the forge but seeing what a strange mood his mother was in he didn't argue. It wouldn't take him that long if he went straight there and back and didn't dally. He could be back for lunchtime.

Soon after, Jed went to begin the day's work in the forge and Lewis set off for the town. Victoria left the kitchen door wide open so she could hear what Jed was doing and, as she had thought, his first job was to get the fire going in the furnace. It was then that an idea came to her. If she waited until the fire needed stoking again, she could take him a cup of tea and then hit him from behind while he was tending to the fire. He'd be too busy shovelling coal to hear her. Once he was down, she could turn him to make it look like he had slipped and landed heavily.

Alternatively, she could put him in the furnace and let the flames consume him, but she doubted she would be able to lift him on her own. All she would have to do then is get the funeral out of the way, get the house and the business sold, and her future with Lord David would be secured before that damned Amelia Parkhurst stole him from beneath her nose!

The minutes ticked by interminably slowly as she listened to Jed banging and hammering, but at last, she heard the furnace doors

331

being opened and Jed shovelling yet more coal into it. Carrying a mug of tea in one hand and the heavy brass shovel from the hearth in the other, she set off stealthily across the yard. Rags was in his usual place lying by the door and when he saw her coming, he hastily slouched out of the way.

With her heart in her mouth, Victoria inched her way into the forge and placed the mug on a workbench. The heat was unbearable and sweat stood out on her forehead as she crept forward with murder in her heart. He had served his purpose, but he was just a thorn in her flesh now.

As she had hoped, Jed was oblivious to her presence, so raising the heavy brass shovel above her head she inched closer.

She was right behind him and about to strike with all her might when a shout from the door startled both her and Jed.

'Mother . . . *NO!*'

Her breath caught in her throat as, startled, she looked over her shoulder to see Lewis advancing on her. Before she could stop him, he had lunged forward and caught her arm, swinging her to one side and, as she made to step quickly away from him, her foot caught in the hem of her black gown and she fell heavily, banging her head on the anvil as she went down.

'My dear God . . . wh-what's goin' on 'ere?' Jed whirled about and stared down at his wife's still form.

'It was Mother . . . she was going to strike you from behind with that shovel,' Lewis told him dully. All his worst fears had been realised, which was why he hadn't gone into town but had hung about keeping a watchful eye on his mother. He'd had an idea she was up to something but in his wildest dreams he hadn't imagined she intended to murder Jed.

'I-is she dead?' Lewis choked as he stared at the blood gushing from a gash in Victoria's forehead. Her eyes were open and staring, and she was lying quite still.

Jed was visibly shaken as he dropped to his knees and felt for her pulse, but there was nothing.

Lewis swayed. 'My God . . . I've *killed* her. I'll hang for this, sure as eggs is eggs. It was me grabbing her arm that made her lose her balance and fall.'

Taking his stepson by the shoulders, Jed shook him. 'Not while there's a breath left in my bloody body you won't!' he ground out. He had known for a long time that he had just been a means to an end for Victoria – a way to get out of the financial mess her late husband her left her in. Once he had put the ring on her finger, she had never pretended to love him, but he had never thought she was capable of trying to kill him.

'Wh-what are we going to do?' Lewis asked as tears streamed down his face. He had killed his own mother, and he didn't know how he was going to be able to live with it.

'This is what we're going to do.' Jed ran his hand through his hair. 'Fetch me that mug of tea over there.'

Shaking like a leaf, Lewis did as he was told. Jed took it from him and threw it down at the side of his wife's body, then he gave Lewis the brass shovel. 'Now go an' put that back on the hearth in the kitchen. Victoria was bringin' me a cup o' tea when she slipped an' fell, crackin' her head on the anvil on the way down, right? It were an' accident pure an' simple, do you understand?'

'Y-yes.' Lewis's teeth were chattering with shock.

'Good, now I'm goin' to fetch the doctor, but whatever is said we stick to our story. It was just a tragic accident. There's no need for anyone to know what she were plannin' to do to me. We'll say that she ain't been herself since Gilbert died an' she weren't lookin' where she were goin. Now go an' put that shovel away an' I'll be back soon as I can wi' the doctor.'

Like a man in a trance, Lewis staggered away as Jed set off for the doctor.

By the time they returned Lewis was kneeling at his mother's side and the doctor stooped to examine her. 'Yes, she's gone,' he said sadly. 'I'm so sorry, Jed, and so soon after losing your stepson too.'

Jed said nothing as he stood gazing down at the dead body of his wife.

'I'll send the undertaker to fetch her,' the doctor said, patting Jed's arm. 'You've certainly been supping from the cup of sorrow lately, man.' And with a shake of his head, he quietly left.

Jed felt numb after the doctor had left. He found it hard to comprehend the calamities that had befallen him in such a short space of time. First Daisy disappeared, then Gilbert died, and now Victoria had followed him to the grave. But the only one he would truly miss was his daughter, and he knew that would go on until the day he died.

Chapter Forty-Four

Blackrock, Ireland, June 1883

'Just one more week to go, eh? An' you'll be married!' Niamh smiled at Daisy but there was no answering smile from her friend as she stared down into the tea Niamh had just handed to her. They were sitting outside the cottage watching the twins and Riley rolling about on the grass.

Niamh frowned with concern and squeezed Daisy's hand. 'You know you don't 'ave to go t'rough wit' this?' Her voice was gentle and concerned. 'A blind man on a gallopin' hoss could see that your heart ain't in it, to be sure.'

'I can't let Daniel down now,' Daisy answered miserably.

Niamh didn't agree. 'Wouldn't it be better to let him down now than to spend the rest o' your life regrettin' it? You said yourself that Daniel's health is failin', poor soul. It could be that he's got one foot in the grave already, an' what'll happen to you when he's gone? You'll be stuck wi' Liam for the rest o' your days. Is that what you really want? A life o' drudgery wit' never a kind word.' Frustrated she shook Daisy's hand up and down. 'Go an' see your granny an' grampy, I *beg* you! If they loved you as you said they did I'm sure they'll listen to your side o' the story.'

But still Daisy shook her head. 'I can't,' she said in a small voice. 'I couldn't bear it if they turned their backs on me for a second time.'

Niamh sighed. As the day of the wedding had grown closer, she had seen the bloom go out of Daisy. It was as if she had given up on any dreams she had ever had, and it broke Niamh's heart to see her friend so sad.

'Well, I can't make you, but I know one t'ing for sure, if you don't go an' see 'em afore it's too late you'll regret it for the rest o' your life, so you will.'

Daisy shrugged and soon after she pecked her friend on the cheek and set off back to the farm. No doubt Liam would have a list of jobs as long as her arm waiting for her, but she was used to that now.

Niamh watched her go with a frown on her face and slowly a plan began to form in her mind. She loved Daisy like a sister, but if what she had in mind backfired Daisy could well turn her back on her forever. She would have to give it some serious thought before she made a final decision. She would speak to Aiden about it and get his advice. Thoughts of him brought the smile back to her face. At least her life was going in the right direction and her future looked rosy. She just wanted the same for Daisy now.

The following evening, when dinner was out of the way, Niamh set off. She knew where Daisy's grandparents lived and hoped that Daisy would forgive her for what she was about to do should she ever find out. Niamh knew she would never be able to live with herself if she didn't at least try to save her dearest friend from a life of misery.

When the little cottage came into sight, Niamh's resolve wavered and she almost turned tail and ran back the way she had come, but she took a deep breath and moved on. The front garden was a blaze of colour with hollyhocks, gladioli, roses and numerous other flowers growing in profusion and Niamh could understand why Daisy had loved going there so much. She gulped and tentatively tapped at the door and seconds later it was opened by a homely looking little woman with a kind face and grey hair combed into a bun at the back of her head.

'Good evening, Mrs McLoughlin. I wondered if I might have a word wit' you . . .' Niamh licked her suddenly dry lips.

'Do I know you, lass?' the woman enquired with a puzzled frown.

Niamh shook her head. 'No . . . but I'm a friend o' your granddaughter, Daisy.'

Niamh watched the colour drain out of the woman's face as her hand flew to her mouth. 'You know our Daisy. And have you any idea where she is?'

'Yes, I do know where she is,' Niamh answered.

'Then you'd best come away in, lass. And it's right welcome you are.'

Niamh found herself in a spotlessly clean kitchen. A bunch of flowers cut from the garden stood in the centre of a scrubbed pine table, and the pretty flowered curtains were gently blowing in the warm breeze coming through the open window.

An elderly gentleman was sitting to the side of the fireplace clutching a pipe and after hearing what Niamh had said he was watching her closely.

'So? Where is she? Is she all right? We've been goin' out of our mind's wit' worry over her, so we have. An' so has her daddy.'

This did not sound like something someone who had turned their back on Daisy would say, and Niamh felt relief surge through her.

'Before I tell you where she is, I t'ink I should start at the beginning and tell you everyt'ing that's gone on,' she suggested.

Eager to hear what she had to say, Bridie and Connor joined her at the table. And so, after taking a deep breath, Niamh began to tell them everything she knew and by the time she had finished Bridie was weeping and Connor was as white as a sheet.

'Oh, me poor lass, to be treated like that by that terrible man,' Bridie sobbed as Connor put a comforting arm about her shoulder. 'I told our Jed the first time I met the chap that I wouldn't trust him as far as I could throw him, so I did. An' that lyin' wife o' his to write such a letter to poor Daisy. But tell us where she is, lass. We must put this right straight away.'

'Before I do, I've one more thing to tell you,' Niamh said. 'Daisy is set to wed Daniel Doyle next week. He's a grand lad, to be sure, but very ill and I t'ink Daisy is only marryin' him because she t'inks she has nowhere else to go an' she feels sorry for him. I don't need to tell you what his daddy, Liam, is like. He works her into the ground, so he does. An' I happen to know that Daisy loves someone else. Another one who she t'inks has washed their hands of her.'

'That other someone wouldn't happen to be Lewis Peake, would it?' Bridie questioned, and when Niamh nodded, she sighed.

'I t'ought that was the way the wind were blowin' the last time she visited. But we've no time to lose,' Bridie said worriedly. 'An' she's nothin' to fear from Victoria or Gilbert anymore cos they've both passed away, so they have. Jed wrote to tell me an' though it's wrong to speak ill o' the dead, it's good riddance to bad rubbish to the pair of 'em so far as I'm concerned. Especially after what you've just told me. But now what to do!'

She stared thoughtfully into space for a moment before saying, 'I have to go an' see her. The poor girl. All this time her t'inking we'd abandoned her – as if we ever would!'

Niamh beamed from ear to ear as relief swept through her. Perhaps there was still hope for a happy ending for Daisy after all. She'd done the right thing, and now the rest would be up to Daisy's grandparents.

'Right, well, I'd best be off,' she said as she rose from the table, and suddenly she was wrapped in Bridie's arms.

'Ah, you're a good girl, so you are,' the woman whispered into her hair. 'What time do you t'ink would be best to go to see her?'

'Well, early evening I know she's milking and Liam is still working about the farm,' Niamh told her.

Bridie nodded. 'You just leave it wit' me, lass. An' thanks again for takin' the trouble to come an' tell us what's been goin' on. It's been a livin' hell for all of us not knowin' what had become of her, I don't mind tellin' you.'

She kissed Niamh's cheek and saw her to the door and as Niamh set off for home there was a spring in her step.

Later that day Bridie and Connor set off in the trap and when they reached Brooke Farm they clambered down and tethered their old horse to the gate before entering the farmyard. There was no sign of anyone, only an old collie dog who wagged his tail as he watched them lazily from his kennel, so they approached the kitchen door and gently tapped on it.

It was opened by a pale-faced young man who looked very poorly indeed.

'You must be Daniel,' Bridie said, and when he nodded, she took a deep breath and told him, 'We need to speak to you, lad, regarding Daisy. We're her grandparents.'

Daniel looked shocked as he held the door wide for them to enter the kitchen then he ushered them to the table where they all sat down.

He looked confused. 'Daisy's grandparents? But Daisy told me you and the rest of the family had turned their backs on her.'

'Aye, that's what she was led to believe,' Bridie told him with a frown. 'But it couldn't be further from the truth, you see . . .' She went on to tell him all that Niamh had told her and by the time she had done Daniel was shaking his head in disbelief.

'Poor Daisy.' He could hardly believe what he had just heard but he didn't have time to comment for at that moment Daisy appeared, and at sight of Bridie and Connor her eyes grew as round as saucers.

'*Granny . . . Grampy . . .* But I thought—'

'I know what you t'ought, lass, that we'd turned our backs on you, but I assure you we would never do that. Come an' sit down an' let me tell you all that's gone on.' And so, while Daisy held tight to her hand, as if she feared she might vanish again, Bridie once again relayed the tale and by the time she was done Daisy was crying.

'I can't believe it! Victoria must have hated me so much.'

'She was a very wicked woman,' Bridie told her solemnly. 'But now you know the truth it's up to you what you want to do about it. Your daddy is goin' to be over the moon to discover that you're safe an' well, but your future is in your hands now.'

Daisy looked helplessly at Daniel, who had tears rolling down his face, and her heart ached for him. They were just days away from their wedding. How could she leave him?

'Daniel, I-I don't know what to do,' she muttered in a small voice.

He gently took her hand. 'There's only one t'ing you can do,' he said gently. 'You must go home, Daisy. Back to where you belong.'

'B-but our wedding!'

He smiled through his tears. 'You deserve a better life than being stuck here, so you do, wit' an invalid for a husband into the bargain.'

She squeezed his hand. 'But what about you?'

'Don't worry about me.' He gently stroked her face. 'I t'ink we're both aware that I don't have long left now an' me daddy only wanted this weddin' so he could tie you to this place as an unpaid skivvy. No, you've got your whole life ahead o' you, so you have. You must go home to your family an' your daddy. I shall be just fine, I promise.'

'But what will your daddy say?'

He shrugged. 'You just leave him to me. Now go an' get your t'ings packed an' get yourself away from here.'

'B-but . . .'

He gave her a gentle shove. 'Go on now, it'll be best if you're gone afore he comes in.'

On leaden feet Daisy went to do as she was told. She was still reeling from the shock of seeing her grandparents and hearing all they'd had to say and now suddenly she was leaving the farm and Daniel forever. Everything was happening so fast.

Minutes later she was back with her carpet bag containing her few possessions. Daniel seemed edgy and keen for them to go.

As he walked them to the door Daisy started to cry again. 'I feel so guilty leaving you like this,' she sobbed as he gently took her in his arms.

'But you mustn't. I want to t'ink of you wit' a good life ahead of you and you'd never have had that here, so go an' be happy for my sake. An', Daisy, thank you for makin' me so happy. I'll not forget you.'

'Oh, Daniel, I'm so sorry!' Daisy gently pressed the ring he had given her into his hand, and he stared down at it for a moment.

Then he gently put her from him and smiled bravely. 'You don't have to ever say sorry to me. You made me the happiest man on earth, to be sure. But you deserve better, so do this one last t'ing for me an' go an' have a good life.'

Bridie gently put her arm around her waist and leaning forward Daisy planted a last kiss on his lips before being led towards the gate where the old horse was happily cropping on the grass.

As the trap drove away, she turned to wave, but Daniel was already gone and so she looked forward again as she tried to take in the events of the last hour. Would she wake up to discover it had all been a wonderful dream? But no, she could feel the heat of her granny's arm about her on one side and the rough texture of her grampy's jacket against her arm on the other. Soon she would be back in their cosy little cottage, where she had spent so many happy times growing up. And then . . . her heart began to beat faster as she thought of her daddy . . . and Lewis. Should she write to them or just turn up back at home?

There was so much to think about but for now she would just enjoy being with her grandparents again.

Chapter Forty-Five

That evening Daisy and her grandparents sat by the fire and talked and talked. Daisy cried as she told them of the baby she had given birth to, who had never drawn breath. The innocent babe had never asked to be born, and she had grieved for her. 'I-I called her Mauve after me mammy,' she sobbed. She told them of the cruelty of the nuns at the convent and of the rows of unmarked graves at the back of it, and Bridie cried with her while her grampy sucked on his pipe and shook his head sadly.

'I dread to think what might have happened had Niamh not come to see me,' Bridie said quietly. 'Why, this time next week you'd have been married to a man you didn't love!'

'But I did love Daniel,' Daisy protested.

'Aye, you may well have done, but not the way you're supposed to love the man you marry, eh?'

Daisy lowered her head and flushed. There wasn't much got past her granny. She was a wise old bird.

'Saying that, I think there *is* someone who you do love in the right way, isn't there?'

Daisy lifted her head and shrugged. 'If you're talking about Lewis, yes, I do have feelings for him,' she admitted. 'But I have no idea if he feels the same way about me.'

Bridie chuckled. 'Well, if what your daddy told me was right, I'd say he did. He's been as worried about you as your daddy has. But sayin' that, there's only one way to find out. You must go home when you're ready an' see how the land lies. You'll know soon enough. Sayin' that, you're welcome to stay here for as long as you wish. You look like you could do wit' feedin' up, so you do. You ain't as far t'rough as a line post. That Liam Doyle must have been a right old slave driver.'

'He was a bit,' Daisy admitted. 'But it's not him I'm worried about, it's Daniel.'

Bridie bit her lip. She could have told her granddaughter that Daniel wasn't long for this world now. She had seen it in his eyes as she had seen it in others before him, and she had never been wrong yet, but not wishing to upset her she said simply, 'You an' Daniel weren't meant to be, lass. He accepts that, so try not to worry about him an' look to the future.'

Daisy spent the next two days resting and being spoilt shamelessly by her grandparents, but on the third day she told them, 'I think I'm ready to go home now.'

Bridie nodded her approval, smiling as she tried to picture how thrilled Jed and Lewis would be when they saw her.

'It's your decision, lass. As I told you, you're more than welcome to stay here for as long as you like, but I can understand you wantin' to get home.'

'I'll leave first thing in the morning,' Daisy decided. 'But on the way I want to call in and see Niamh. I have a lot to thank her for.'

'You do that, lass, an' so do we,' Bridie responded, giving her an affectionate hug. 'But I'd just love to be a fly on the wall when your daddy lays eyes on you, so I would. If it weren't for the journey bein' a bit too much for me an' your grampy, I'd come wit' you, to be sure.'

Early the next morning Daisy said her goodbyes to her granny and grampy but not before she had given her granny the lovely bonnet Daniel had bought her to wear for their wedding.

'I wouldn't feel right wearing it now,' she told her, and Bridie was delighted to accept it. She'd never owned a bonnet like it in her life.

'You just be sure to come an' see us often,' she told her as she and Connor kissed her goodbye at the door. They waved until she was out of sight and Daisy headed for Niamh's. She found her washing up the breakfast pots and at sight of her Niamh looked worried.

'I'm sorry for stickin' me nose into your business,' she said worriedly. 'Is everythin' all right?'

'Everything is perfect,' Daisy giggled as she grabbed her friend around the waist and whirled her round the kitchen. 'Granny and Grampy came to see me and I've been staying with them. But I'm on my way to get on the ferry now. I'm going home, Niamh, thanks to you.'

'Eeh, that's grand, lass.' Niamh looked relieved. 'But how did Daniel an' Liam take it?'

'I don't know about Liam, but Daniel was wonderful.' She was serious again now. 'I just hope he'll be all right.'

'He'll cope,' Niamh assured her and, smiling, she went on, 'As it happens, I have a bit o' news for you too. It's me an' Aiden – we're gettin' wed later in the year. He asked me a few days ago an' I said yes. Daddy is marryin' the widow an' movin him an' the children into the inn, an' me an' Aiden will be keepin' the cottage on here, so it's all worked out nicely.'

'Oh, that's wonderful news!' Daisy was delighted for her. She would love to have stayed there chatting all day but the clock was ticking and she didn't want to miss the ferry. But first she had a gift for Niamh. Taking the lovely gown she had altered for her wedding from her bag, she shook it out.

Niamh gasped. 'Why that's *beautiful*,' she sighed enviously.

'I'm glad you like it because I want you to have it.' Daisy thrust it into her hands. 'I bought it and altered it for my wedding to

Daniel, but I shan't ever wear it now. I had a bonnet too, but I gave that to Granny. Perhaps you could wear this for your wedding?'

Niamh's eyes lit up. 'Are you sure? It's very grand.'

Daisy nodded. 'Absolutely sure. Now, much as I hate to leave you, I must go. Time and tide wait for no man. But don't worry, I'll be back, and I'll write to you often.'

'You'd better be back for me weddin'. I want you to be me maid of honour, so I do,' Niamh told her firmly.

Daisy grinned as she gave her friend a hug. 'I'd be honoured.' And then she was off again, running across the grass as if she had wings on her feet as she headed for the ferry and home.

It was evening before the cart from Nuneaton pulled up in Ansley village and Daisy set off to walk the last leg of her journey. As she rounded the corner she saw her home ahead of her, looking exactly as she remembered. Her heart was thumping painfully as she wondered what sort of a reception she would get, but she carried on, heartened now that Granny had told her that her daddy and Lewis had never given up hope of finding her. She wondered what they would think when they learnt of Victoria and Gilbert's wicked deception.

She passed the forge, closed for the night now, and as she entered the yard a furry bundle rushed towards her with his tail wagging furiously and she dropped to her knees to hug him.

'Oh, Rags, my beautiful boy. I didn't even know if you'd still be alive.' She wept as he licked every inch of her he could reach. 'I've missed you so much.'

Ahead of her she could see that the kitchen door was open and with her heart in her mouth and old Rags limping along at the side of her she approached it and peeped inside. Her daddy was sitting at the kitchen table with a newspaper spread in front of him. He had lost some weight and his sideburns were peppered with grey but to her he looked wonderful. Lewis was sitting in a chair at the side of the fireplace reading a book, and as if sensing that someone was watching him, he glanced up and his mouth gaped open.

'Daisy!'

Her father's head snapped around and suddenly they were both running towards her and she was lost in a tangle of arms as she laughed and cried all at the same time.

'But . . . How . . . Where . . .' Jed was lost for words as he held her at arm's length and drank in the sight of her. 'We thought we'd lost you forever,' he said in a choked voice. Taking her arm he almost dragged her into the room and plonked her down at the table. 'Right, I want to know *everything* that's gone on right from the day you left here with Gilbert.'

Lewis, meanwhile, was watching her as if he could hardly believe his eyes and she felt herself blushing as she realised she would have to tell them about the rape and everything that had happened since. It was not going to be an easy tale to tell but Daisy steeled herself and, lowering her eyes, she began, leaving out nothing from the day Gilbert had raped her until the day Niamh had visited her grandparents in Ireland to tell them what had really gone on.

By the time she was done, both men were openly crying and Daisy's head was bowed with shame as she relived the rape in her mind. She was still so ashamed. How could Lewis want her after hearing what his brother had done to her?

After a time, she glanced up and the pain in her daddy's eyes tore at her heart.

He then went on to tell her what had happened to Gilbert and Victoria before ending brokenly, 'I'm so sorry for fallin' for her charms, my love! We were happy enough till she come along, so I blame meself.'

She risked a peek at Lewis but to her distress he avoided her eyes and, rising from the table, he walked away and up the stairs without a word.

Tears came again as her daddy held her close, but at least she was home and that would have to be enough.

The following morning, when Mrs Smith reported for work, she was almost as thrilled to see Daisy as Jed had been.

'Bye 'eck, luvvie.' She smiled. 'They've had faces on 'em like wet weekends these two have, ever since you went away. It's good to have you home again. But I don't suppose you'll be needin' me now?'

'We most certainly will, Mrs Smith,' Jed assured her. 'I realise now just how much Daisy had to do about the place. You've taken excellent care of us while Daisy's been away, so you two can be company for each other now and share the workload between you.'

Daisy smiled at the woman, and thought what a contrast she was to Victoria. She was probably about the same age, but unlike Victoria, Mrs Smith had never been one for following fashion. Widowed at an early age when her husband had been killed in a fall in the pit, she had done two jobs to keep a roof over her children's heads and food on the table with never a thought for herself. She was tall and slim – much the same build as Daisy's mother had been – and she had fair hair that was tied back with a bit of ribbon at the nape of her neck. Her hands were work worn and because of the drab way she dressed she looked older than she actually was, but Daisy could see that she could have been quite attractive had she taken better care of herself. She had a winning smile, and kind blue eyes, and Daisy took to her immediately and hoped that they would become friends.

The only downside to her homecoming was the way Lewis seemed to be avoiding her, but she supposed she should have expected that and kept out of his way as much as she could.

Disaster struck two weeks after Daisy's homecoming when she came downstairs early one morning to light the fire to find that Rags had passed away peacefully in his sleep.

'Oh, Rags, no!' she sobbed as she lifted his head onto her lap and her tears fell onto his fur. 'Please don't leave me.'

'He's not been well for some time. I think he was waiting for you to come back before he went,' a gentle voice behind her said, and whipping about Daisy saw Lewis standing there.

Crossing the room, he hunkered down beside her and laid a gentle arm about her shoulders. 'Come away,' he said gently. 'I'll make you a cup of tea, eh? Then I'll go and dig his grave in the orchard. He liked it there. You can help me bury him.'

'Oh, Lewis.' Sobbing, she turned to bury her head in his chest. With his heartbeat against her cheek and his arm about her shoulder, she felt as if she had come home. Even if her feelings for him weren't returned, she knew that he would always be the only man she would ever love, and if she couldn't have him, she wouldn't have anyone.

'What's to do here?' Another voice startled them and turning they saw Mrs Smith entering the kitchen to help with the day's chores.

'I-it's Rags,' Daisy told her tearfully. 'He's passed away.'

'Aw, bless him. I didn't think he'd be long,' the woman said sadly. 'But you've got to remember that you gave him a good long life. Come on, pet. Let me make you an' Lewis a good strong cup o' sweet tea, eh? It's good for shock.'

The gentle woman filled the kettle and set it on the hob to boil as Daisy sat cuddling Rags with tears streaming down her face.

Soon after Lewis left the room and returned with a sturdy box he had found in the barn. 'You have a cup of tea while I go and dig the grave,' he told her, and armed with a shovel he set off for the orchard.

Later that morning a solemn procession walked to the orchard and Lewis gently lowered Rags into his final resting place.

Even Jed's cheeks were damp and Mrs Smith gave his arm a gentle squeeze. She knew how much he and Daisy had loved the old dog and it hurt her to see him so upset.

'He'll be up in heaven now runnin' around like a young 'un again,' she told Jed softly.

He put his arm around Daisy's shoulders. 'I hope you're right, Mrs Smith.'

She smiled. 'I reckon after all this time you could all call me Peggy,' she responded.

He nodded. 'Thank you, yes I will.' And turning back to the grave again he whispered, 'Rest in peace, my loyal old friend, you'll never be forgotten.'

Lewis began to gently shovel soil over the box and soon there was nothing but a slight mound of earth to be seen and the sound of birds singing in the trees to be heard. Daisy laid a bunch of wild-flowers on the grave and, side by side, the sad procession made its way back to the kitchen.

Chapter Forty-Six

Over the following weeks Peggy Smith and Daisy grew closer and Daisy found that it was nice to have another woman about the place to chat to and share the workload with. Sometimes Daisy would invite her to stay to dinner with them. And as Peggy's family had all long since flown the nest, she was glad of the company.

'I notice that Peggy and your dad are getting on rather well,' Lewis commented to Daisy one morning when he popped back to the house.

Daisy smiled. 'I'd noticed that too, but I think he'll be cautious now after what happened with—' She stopped talking abruptly and flushed.

Lewis smiled. 'It's all right, you can say it. After what happened with my mother?' He nodded in agreement. 'I understand what you're saying but I think my mother and Peggy are, or were, two very different women.' He sighed. 'I'm afraid my mother was very vain and selfish whereas Peggy has a heart of pure gold. I actually think she and Jed would make a very nice couple but I suppose time will tell.'

Daisy nodded in agreement and for a moment their eyes locked and she felt the familiar shiver run up her spine.

'I, er . . . I suppose I'd better get on,' she said, all of a fluster. 'Was there something you wanted?' It was unusual for Lewis to come back during the day apart from to have his lunch.

'I've just got to pop out for a while, but I won't be long,' he told her.

Daisy watched him go with a sad smile. Since his kindness after Rags died, they'd at least been friendly again, and though she knew she'd have to be satisfied with that, sometimes she found it difficult to be so close to him day after day.

A couple of hours later, just as Peggy and Daisy had started to prepare the lunch, Jed came in, closely followed by a beaming Lewis.

He was carrying a large box and Daisy stared at it curiously. 'What have you got there?'

He plonked the box gently down on the floor. 'Actually, it's a present for you. I've just been to collect it. I hope you like it.'

'A present? For *me*?' Daisy looked astounded. 'But it isn't my birthday!'

Lewis shrugged. She noticed then that Peggy and her daddy were grinning too.

'Go on, open it,' they all urged, so Daisy dropped to her knees and gently lifted the lid.

'*Oh!*' She began to cry with delight as a tiny border collie puppy leapt up and began to lick her face.

'Oh,' she said again, gently lifting him from the box, laughing and crying all at the same time. 'But he's just *beautiful*.' She knew he could never take the place of Rags in her heart, but he would certainly go a long way to filling the terrible hole Rags had left in her life.

'I did check with Jed that it was all right to get him for you,' Lewis assured her. 'Farmer Bryan told me his bitch had had a litter shortly before Rags died so I went along and chose this one for you. I hope you like him.'

'I absolutely love him,' she declared, really smiling for the first time in weeks. 'But what shall we call him?'

'That's entirely up to you.' Lewis looked happy. 'How about Socks? He's got four little white feet, look, but as I said you can call him whatever you like.'

'I think Socks would be a *perfect* name for him,' Daisy answered as she rose with the puppy in one arm, and before she could stop herself, she flew across to Lewis and planted a kiss smack on his lips before blushing a deep beetroot red. 'Oh . . . I-I'm sorry, I shouldn't have done that,' she stammered self-consciously.

Peggy took Jed's elbow and gently steered him out of the room. 'Come on, lad,' she whispered. 'Let's give these two a bit o' space for a few minutes, eh?'

Once outside she gave him a wide grin. 'Ooh, those pair,' she laughed. 'Sometimes I just want to bang their daft bloody heads together. It's as plain as the nose on your face that they're potty about each other.'

'I think you could be right,' Jed agreed as they walked towards the orchard. 'And it just so happens that there's a very lovely, kind lady not so far away from me right now, that I've grown very fond of an' all.'

'You daft old thing.' Now it was Peggy's turn to blush as she gently slid her arm through his.

Meanwhile in the kitchen, Lewis and Daisy were staring at each other as they stood slightly apart.

'Actually, Daisy, I've been wanting to do that ever since you came back from Ireland,' Lewis said quietly.

She blinked in surprise. 'B-But what about what your brother did to me?' she breathed. 'I've had an illegitimate baby. I'm not pure anymore.'

Lewis scowled. 'Don't talk such poppycock! None of what happened was your fault. It was all Gilbert's. I know he was my brother, but he was bad through and through, and I was worried that you'd think I was the same.'

'But you and Gilbert are as different as chalk from cheese,' she answered. 'I knew that from the first day I met you.'

'And from the first day I met you, I knew you were the only girl for me.' He lifted the puppy from her arms and gently placed him on the ground where he began to scamper about happily sniffing his new home. 'So, tell me . . . is there any chance for me?'

'Oh, Lewis!' Tears were sparkling on her lashes. 'I felt exactly the same way about you . . . I still do, and yes there's every chance . . . if you still want me.'

He took her in his arms and as his lips pressed down on hers, the puppy sat back on his haunches and with his head to one side watched his new owners, wondering why he wasn't the centre of attention anymore. They seemed to have forgotten all about him for the moment, but, as he was fast discovering, these humans had some strange habits.

Acknowledgements

I never quite know where to begin with acknowledgements. There are so many people to thank for their help in getting this book ready for publication.

I'll start with my lovely team at Bonnier: Sarah Benton, Claire Johnson-Creek, Beth Whitelaw, Holly Milnes and far too many to mention, but you all know who you are. I'd also like to thank my copy-editor, Gillian Holmes and my proofreader, Jane Howard. Each and every one of you always goes the extra mile to make my books as good as they can be, and this one has been no exception. I'm so grateful to you all and feel very blessed to have such an amazing team behind me.

Never forgetting my brilliant agent, Sheila Crowley from Curtis Brown, who is always at the end of the phone should I need her.

My amazing readers for their continued support and encouragement.

My fur babies for keeping my feet warm and keeping me company when I am locked away typing.

And last but never least my husband for the numerous cups of tea he keeps me supplied with, and my long-suffering family, who are used to me disappearing off into my office at the drop of a hat when an idea occurs!

My sincere thanks to each and every one of you!

Rosie GOODWIN

Want to keep up to date with the latest from Rosie Goodwin?

With exclusive content from the author herself, book updates, competitions and more, the Rosie Goodwin newsletter is the place to be if you can't get enough of Britain's best-loved saga author.

To sign up, you can scan the QR code or type the link below into your browser

https://geni.us/RosieGoodwin

Hello everyone,

Well, my year started beautifully when the latest addition to our family, Albie, arrived the day after New Year's Day. He was three weeks early and tiny, but thankfully just perfect! He is absolutely gorgeous, not that I'm biased of course, and he can light up the room with his smiles.

This was followed by the release of the paperback of my book *The Lost Girl* and then came the release of *Our Fair Lily* in March. And what a wonderful response I had from you all when she hit the shelves! She spent three weeks in the top ten bestsellers and another week in the top twenty when first released, so thank you all so much for buying the book. Thank you also for your lovely reviews and messages. I'm so glad you enjoyed it. I've met some lovely people at book signings and events this year. It's always a treat to escape from the office and actually get to meet the people who read my books.

So now here is my second offering in the Flower Girls Collection, *Our Dear Daisy*. I really love the gorgeous cover my brilliant graphic designer has created for this one! And I really hope you enjoyed reading it as much as I enjoyed writing it. It doesn't seem a minute since I was writing to you about the release of *Our Fair Lily*. Time just seems to pass in the blink of an eye.

Daisy is a lovely soul and I'm afraid, as always, I didn't give her an easy time. But Daisy is made of stern stuff and rose above everything I threw at her. This book is set in Ansley, a village on the outskirts of Nuneaton and just a stone's throw from where I live, although Daisy does spend a lot of time in Ireland as well. As always, some of the places I write about are purely fictitious, such as the forge in Ansley where Daisy and her father live with Rags, their faithful little dog. As you all know I always try to slip in a pet wherever possible!

I hope you all had a lovely spring and summer. I loved pottering about the garden and enjoying trips to the coast with my family and the fur babies. But now winter is here, so back to cosy evenings in my office with my imaginary characters. I shall really look forward to hearing what you all think of Daisy and then of course we'll be thinking ahead to the publication of *Our Sweet Violet*. That will be the last of my Flower Girls Collection and then I have something a little different lined up for you! More on that to follow.

My newsletter has proved to be a wonderful success. I love being able to keep in touch with you all and let you know what I've been up to. If you haven't already please do sign up. The information is on the page ahead of this. And do also join the Memory Lane Book Club on Facebook and sign up for the newsletter there. They'll keep you up to date with what other saga authors are up to, as well as me, and there are some great competitions and lovely prizes.

So now it's back to work for me. I hope you enjoyed *Our Dear Daisy*.

Till next time.

Much love,
Rosie xx

Our Sweet Violet

Meet Violet Stroud: the third and final
Flower Girl in Rosie Goodwin's collection.
As she embarks on a new venture, can she
put the pieces of her life back together?

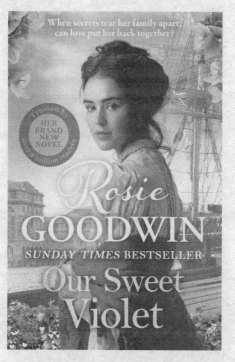

Coming soon

Prologue

Nuneaton, Early December 1888

Outside the snow was falling fast, and as the doctor joined his wife and his one-year-old son at the side of a roaring fire in their smart home in Swan Lane, he heaved a sigh of relief. As well as doing his regular morning surgery, he had been out on house calls all afternoon. Flu sweeping through the town, and sadly the old and the very young were dropping like flies, despite his best efforts to save them. It was the same every winter.

'So you're finally back.' His wife sniffed her disapproval and laid her embroidery aside. 'And I suppose you're hungry now.'

William Stroud nodded as he peeped into his son's crib. 'Starving actually. I only had time for a sandwich before I left after surgery. I haven't stopped all day.'

'Then let's hope all those that you've visited pay up,' she answered sarcastically as she rose from her seat and went to pull the rope at the side of the fire. She knew her husband was inclined to do free visits for the poorer members of the community. 'I imagine Cook would have put your dinner in the oven to keep warm, although I'm sure it will be ruined by now.'

There was a tap at the door and the maid appeared.

'Nellie, did Cook save any dinner for the doctor?'

'Yes, ma'am. Shall I lay the table again in the dining room?'

'No, no, Nellie, there'll be no need for you to go to all that trouble,' the doctor assured her. 'I can have it on a tray or in the kitchen, if you and Cook don't mind?'

'Right you are, sir. I'll go an' get it out o' the oven for you if you'd like to come through.'

He followed her out of the room. Behind him, his wife lifted her embroidery and continued with what she had been doing. William Stroud knew his wife didn't approve of him eating in the kitchen with the servants, but tonight he was too tired to care.

As he entered the kitchen Cook, who was sitting to the side of the fire in a comfy chair with a pot of tea at the side of her, smiled.

'Hello, lad, come an' take the weight off your feet,' she urged kindly. 'You look fair worn out!'

Edie Thompson had been William's father's cook before William was born and when the old doctor had passed away and his son had taken over the surgery, she had stayed on. She could still remember clearly the day William had been born and she had loved him like a son ever since. Edie was in her early fifties now and William often worried that the job might be too hard for her, but she wouldn't hear of retiring.

'I'm as fit as a fiddle,' she would tell him whenever he broached the subject and William was glad. He couldn't imagine his life without Edie in it.

Seconds later Nellie placed his dinner on the table and William's stomach rumbled with anticipation. Cook had made him one of his favourites: steak and ale pie with lashings of mashed potatoes and vegetables to go with it, and as he began to eat, he felt himself warming up.

'This is delicious, Cook,' he told her as he tucked in, and she preened with pleasure. William was always grateful, unlike that snooty wife of his.

'So, what's her ladyship doin'?' she asked caustically and William grinned.

'Now Cook, there's no need for that,' he scolded gently. 'She was embroidering I believe.'

'Huh!' Cook poured herself another cup of tea as she stared at the piles of wooden crates spaced around the edge of the room. 'I'd have thought she'd be helpin' wi' all the packin' we've still to do. It's only a month now till we move.'

'It'll get done,' William assured her. 'The nanny is seeing to all of Oliver's things up in the nursery and it looks like you've made a good start in here.'

'It's a case of havin' to! I just hope we don't all live to regret leavin' here! It's a long way away is Hull!'

'I'm sure we'll be fine once we've settled in,' William said confidently.

Nellie instantly started to cry as she dabbed at her eyes with her handkerchief. Sadly, she wouldn't be going with them. She was engaged to be married and so had chosen to stay in Nuneaton, although she hadn't managed to get another position as yet. She had enjoyed working for young Doctor Stroud and would miss him, although she couldn't say the same about his wife. Anna made no secret of the fact that she felt she had married beneath herself. She had come from one of the wealthiest families in the town and they had all been shocked when she suddenly decided to marry the young doctor. There was no doubt that with her looks and breeding she could have had her pick of any of the suitors who had pursued her, but then Nellie supposed stranger things had happened. With his thick dark hair and deep brown eyes, William was a catch after all.

She had just poured the doctor a cup of tea when an urgent knocking sounded on the front door and the cook sighed.

'Eeh, I hope that ain't somebody needin' a visit,' she said. Then turning her attention to Nellie, she asked her, 'Go an' answer that would yer, lovie.'

Nellie hurried away only to return minutes later to tell the doctor, 'There's a lady at the door demandin' to see yer, Doctor Stroud. She has a baby wi' her.'

William sighed. So much for a peaceful evening by the fire with his newspaper.

'All right, Nellie. Show her into the surgery, would you? and tell her I'll be with her presently.'

He lifted his cup and quickly drained it. 'No peace for the wicked, eh?' He gave Cook a wry grin and quietly left the room.

He saw the door to his surgery was open and he entered with a smile on his face. But it quickly died away as he found himself staring into the eyes of a young woman who was clutching a baby to her chest. She had fair hair and blue eyes with nothing but a thin shawl about her shoulders over her shabby gown to keep the cold at bay.

'S . . . Sadie!' He hastily closed the door behind him before asking, 'What brings you here?'

'I had to come,' she told him in a wobbly voice. 'I just got thrown out of my digs because I'm behind with my rent and I've nowhere to go. So . . . the long and the short of it is, you'll have to take her.'

Now William's eyes almost popped out of his head as he stared at the tiny bundle in her arms. 'What do you mean I'll have to take her?'

'She's yours,' Sadie told him quietly as she stared down at the sleeping baby, who looked to be no more than two or three weeks old. 'I never told you I'd fallen for a child because we only ever lay together the once, and I wouldn't have done if I could have kept her. But things are impossible now, so I've no choice but to leave her with you.'

'B . . . but . . .' William was clearly in shock as she stepped forward and pressed the baby into his arms.

'Her name is Violet,' Sadie told him softly. 'Take good care of her.' And then stopping only long enough to kiss the infant's forehead, she left the room and seconds later he heard the front door shut behind her.

As he stared down at the baby she woke and stared up at him from eyes that were exactly the same colour as his own.

It was then that Nellie entered the room and she too looked shocked as she asked, 'Who's this then, sir?'

'She er . . .' William didn't know how to explain her away. 'The mother has left her here with us,' he said with a catch in his voice. 'It seems that she's been turned out of her room and she has nowhere to take the child.'

'Good grief!' Nellie looked almost as shocked as he felt. 'How long for? An' what is the missus goin' to say?' Nellie couldn't imagine that Anna would want another baby. She only had eyes for her own baby son, but certainly wasn't so keen on the practical side of caring for a child, hence the nanny.

'I'll have to go and tell her what's happened now,' William answered. 'And then you'd better ask the nanny if she'll come and fetch the baby for me.'

With his heart in his mouth, he set off for the drawing room. He dreaded what he was about to do but what choice did he have? He could hardly keep the baby hidden, so better to get it over with.

Anna blinked when her eyes settled on the baby and she scowled. The nanny had already been down to take Oliver and settle him in the nursery for the night. 'Who is this?'

'A young woman who has nowhere to go has just left her with us,' he told her as calmly as he could.

'*What?*' Anna looked horrified. 'Are we a home for waifs and strays now? Why didn't she leave her at the workhouse? The brat can't stay here!'

'You know as well as I do that most babies in the workhouse don't even survive until their first birthday! Would you *really* wish that on the child?'

There was something about the infant that was tugging at his heartstrings and suddenly he knew that Sadie had been telling the truth. This was *his* child; his own flesh and blood, and no way was he about to abandon her now.

Anna marched over to him, her pretty face a mask of fury, and as she flicked the shawl aside and examined the child, she gasped, looking from the baby to her husband.

'This is *your* child, isn't it?' Her eyes were flashing.

William's shoulders sagged; he might have known he couldn't fool her. She was as sharp as a knife. 'I'm afraid she is . . . but I can explain!'

'Explain? *Huh!* How do you explain a flyblow and the fact that you've been unfaithful to me?'

'It was only ever the one time . . .' he began, but she was in no mood to listen.

'What are we going to say to people? If I can see that she's yours, don't you think everyone else will? Why, we'll be a laughingstock! Or at least *I* will! How could you do this to me?' She started to pace the floor, her satin skirts swishing.

William's anger began to rise. All Anna cared about was what people would say. 'Well, you've hardly been an angel yourself, have you?'

She rounded on him. 'And just what is *that* supposed to mean.'

The child in his arms began to whimper at the raised voices. 'I fell in love with you the very first time I laid eyes on you.' His voice was as cold as the snow softly falling outside. 'But you weren't interested in a lowly doctor. Oh no, you had set your sights higher. On a certain young son of a wealthy mill owner you were dallying with at the time if I remember correctly. Then suddenly his parents sent him abroad and you finally had time for me. In fact, you were all over me like a rash and couldn't marry me quickly enough. Until we were wed that was, and then you didn't want to know me. Within no time after Oliver was born you insisted on separate rooms, that was why I . . . Well, let's just say the night I met Sadie again I was out on a reunion with some of the chaps I went to university with. I'd had too much to drink and when I saw Sadie, a young woman who actually had time for me, one thing led to another. I'm not proud of it! Had you been a proper wife to me this would never have happened. So, what we're going to do is bring this baby and Oliver up to believe they are brother and sister. Do you understand me?'

She looked dumbstruck. 'But what will we tell people?'

'There's no need to tell them anything. We'll be gone from here in a month's time and only Cook is coming with us and I would trust her with my life. In Hull people will just assume they are both our children. Her name is Violet, by the way.'

Anna's lip curled with distaste. 'How *very* working class. Can't we at least change it?'

'No, we cannot! I think it suits her.'

She wanted to argue but she had never seen William like this before and didn't dare.

'In that case I suppose I have no say in the matter,' she said peevishly. 'But don't expect me to ever love the brat. I'm not as stupid as you!'

She flounced from the room to call the nanny. As far as she was concerned the less she saw of the child the better.

Our Fair Lily

Meet Lily Moon: miner's daughter, parlour maid, determined dreamer and the first of the Flower Girls in a brand-new Rosie Goodwin collection.

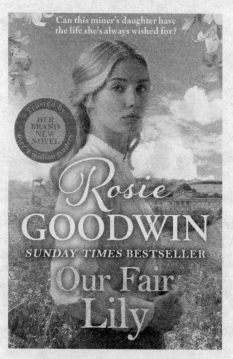

Available now

The Flower Girls

Meet Lily, Daisy
and Violet in the new
collection by Britain's
best-loved saga author,
Rosie Goodwin

The Lost Girl

Can Esme lay the ghosts to rest to save
herself and find the life she deserves?

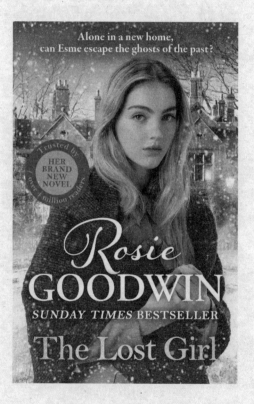

Available now

The Precious Stones Collection

Get to know Opal, Pearl, Ruby, Emerald, Amber and Saffie in Rosie's Precious Stones series.

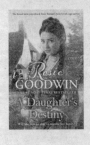  

Available now

The Days of the Week Collection

Have you read Rosie's collection of novels inspired by the 'Days of the week' Victorian rhyme?

Available now

SUBSCRIBE TODAY

There's a Take a Break magazine for everyone!

12 ISSUES PER YEAR

12 ISSUES PER YEAR

13 ISSUES PER YEAR

50 DIGITAL ISSUES PER YEAR

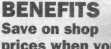

MEMORY LANE

Introducing the place for story lovers – a welcoming home for all readers who love heartwarming tales of wartime, family and romance. Join us to discuss your favourite stories with other readers, plus get book recommendations, book giveaways and behind-the-scenes writing moments from your favourite authors.

MEMORY LANE

www.MemoryLane.Club

www.facebook.com/groups/memorylanebookgroup